Amusing Visions of Heaven and Hell

A man learns that it is not what you know, but how you relate—even in the afterlife.

Prom night can be hell, but to have real demons after your soul?

A cat who knows he is a demon, but learns he can be angelic as well.

Going to Hell isn't all that bad, when it's a wise career move.

The reality of Heaven isn't exactly as this preacher envisioned.

How far would you go to save your girlfriend—would you fight a demon?

His first assignment in the afterlife is as a matchmaker for a good friend he knows won't be interested. Or he can help someone in a leper colony. Hard choice.

He sold his soul to Hell, but if he can out-trick the demon, he gets it back.

She spent centuries seducing others into sin, for her vacation she wants something a little different.

Come and enjoy a collection of whimsical stories of angels and demons who inhabit rather unusual Heavens and Hells.

HEAVEN AND HELL

Edited by:
Winifred Halsey

A Speculation Press Original

HEAVEN AND HELL

A Speculation Press Original.

Speculation Press
P.O. Box 543
DeKalb, IL 60015

ISBN: 0-9671979-8-8

Cover art by Karen Duvall

Cover design by Karen Duvall and Terry Tindill

Dedication

THIS BOOK IS DEDICATED TO MY BELOVED SISTER, PAULINE ROLHF, NEE HALSEY, FOR THE MANY YEARS OF LOVE AND SUPPORT. AND IN REMEMBRANCE OF HER STRENGTH AND COURAGE IN HER BATTLE AGAINST CANCER.

I KNOW SHE IS NOW WATCHING ME FROM HEAVEN.

Contents

The Fiber of Being

Jody Lynn Nye

Jody Lynn Nye lists her main career activity as "spoiling cats." In addition to that, she has found the time to publish 25 science-fiction and fantasy books and more than 70 short stories. She has collaborated with some of the greatest writers in the field: Anne McCaffrey, Piers Anthony and Robert Asprin. Her latest book, *Advanced Mythology* (Meisha Merlin Publishing), is the fourth in her contemporary humorous fantasy series. She lives in the northwest suburbs of Chicago with her husband and two very spoiled cats.

A cluster of men in layers of sweaters stood warming their hands over the fire roaring in the garbage can. Newspaper pages rolled across the empty parking lot near the elevated train tracks as if they were wondering where their readers had gone. Two or three groups of forlorn humanity huddled nearby. The gangs might or might not come to pester them this evening. They had nothing to steal, not even dignity.

None of the people there showed much sign of animation, except for three sitting on the bottom stair of the now-shuttered commuter train station. The muscular man with a yellow wool cap pulled down over his long black hair was flicking a knife open, closed, open, closed. The slightly more feminine-looking red-haired man clutched a saxophone that looked too shiny for the dismal scene. Between them sat a scruffy man in his late fifties with café au lait skin and ruddy-bronze fuzz on his head. He was smaller in stature than both of his companions, but where they looked casual, his eyes took in everything.

"So let me get this straight," the scruffy man said, in a low voice that didn't carry beyond the stairs. He looked dazed. "I'm *dead*."

"Yes," said the man with the knife.

"How could I have died? Nothing hurt. I didn't feel a thing."

"Do you feel anything now?" asked the redhead, curiously.

Jasper palpated his chest with his thin fingers. His spare flesh covered his thin ribs just enough so the doctor at the clinic didn't call him emaciated. Not all the time, anyhow. It came from existing on a rotten junk food diet plus the occasional bowl of peanuts and pretzels the bartenders put in front of him to help soak up the booze. He'd been too busy all his life to do anything but work. Liquor he used to dull the pain from not being able to do everything he wanted for people.

"Yeah, of course. I feel me." Jasper was firm on that.

"You were stabbed in the chest," Mick said, twirling the knife in his fingers around until the point aimed directly at Jasper's sternum.

Jasper's fingers tapped the area, but they encountered no hole, no gore. He relaxed. "You dudes are putting me on. Who put you up to it? My boss? Ella's always trying to get me to knock off the booze, but I'm not hurting anyone but me."

"Very true," Gabe said solemnly. "You died helping others, in this case, a frightened young woman. Do you remember that?"

Jasper sighed. "No. It's all fuzzy. There must have been something in my drink." He shook his head. There'd been too many drinks lately; that he remembered. Working for Children and Family Services was a hole with no bottom. No one ought to have to tell parents the simple things to do, like feed your kids, clothe your kids, and see that they went to school.

"Human beings should be more careful of drink," Mick said. "It can bring pleasure—or allow inspiration to surpass inhibition. More often it causes trouble."

Jasper looked at them with fresh suspicion. "Are you two Jehovah's Witnesses?"

"Of a sort," Mick admitted.

"You're evangelists!"

"Archangels," Gabe corrected him.

"Uh-huh, whatever. I've had plenty of your kind come to the door." Jasper crossed his arms again. He could tell they were used to better than the shabby clothes they were wearing now. He could always tell by attitude. Both guys must normally sport two thousand dollar suits and five hundred dollar shoes. Why else would they be slumming in a neighborhood like this? Rich people sometimes liked to pretend they were poor because they didn't have to do it all the time.

He remembered the faces of the two men surrounded by blurry light as they helped him up off the barroom floor and hustled him out of the bar. 'Much less traumatic,' was how they'd put it. They helped him to a place with a lot of light, but his eyes wouldn't focus. He could tell from a quick check of his pockets that his wallet was missing. In fact, his pockets were empty to the seams. Whoever had rolled him had taken everything, including his apartment key. The guys had assured him that everything would be fine. They told him to call them Mick and Gabe, short versions of the names he botched when he tried to pronounce them.

"Your glass contained cheap beer: not the brand you paid for, but nothing more harmful than that. Your forgetfulness is normal. It takes time to remember so soon after death."

"You keep saying that!" Jasper cried. "Stop saying that I'm dead. I'm right here."

"Wait," Gabe said, shushing them both with eager hands. "Here they come again."

Into the silence of the night broke a scream like a whirlwind advancing. Jasper cringed. He knew the sound of motorcycles. Had to be the Colombian Pharaohs. This was their turf. He'd counseled a lot of hurtin' kids who'd wandered into the wrong place by accident wearing the wrong colors and been rolled on by the Pharaohs.

Sure enough, five oversized, overstroked, overchromed bikes zoomed into the midst of swirling paper. Two of them came to a screeching halt close enough to the burning trash barrel to bowl over the men standing by it. Jasper stared in disbelief. He'd seen this before, all of it, more than once. He knew what was going to happen next, every single thing.

The gangbangers swung off their bikes, in no hurry. Their leader, a big Hispanic kid with wiry black whiskers growing down the sides of his pudgy face and hair stuck up with mousse. He walked up to the nearest geezer who was trying to get up, a faded black man of seventy or more. Waiting until the man was on his feet, he knocked him over with a backhand slap. The other bangers followed suit, swatting the old dudes down like flies. As their victims tried to rise, they pushed them down again. And again. He wanted to jump off the step but Mick held his arm. Finally, one old brother, a little taller than the rest, managed to get to his feet out of range of his tormentor. By the flare of his nostrils Jasper could tell he was blazing mad.

"Now, you folks hold on there!" he roared. His voice was hoarse with age, but there was power behind it. "You've got no business coming here harassing people who ain't never done nothin' to you. Get on your bikes and ride away!" He punctuated his words with a firm finger in the direction of the shining bikes.

"Shut up, old man," the leader said easily, striding over to confront him, standing several inches taller than his victim. He backhanded him into a pile of boxes and turned away, laughing. Jasper was furious. He didn't think it could happen the same way it had before.

But it did. The old guy rose from the boxes with a discarded fence post in his hand. With two strides, which must have surprised him as much as it did the gangbangers, he took a two-handed swing. It connected with the skull of the gang leader, who dropped like a rock. Screaming like the devil possessed him, the old man flew at the other bangers, whapping them with the length of wood. They were so surprised they just stood there for a while, until one of them felt blood dripping down into his eyes. The punk's brows drew down and he snicked a knife out of his pocket. Jasper was sure the old guy would miss it and shouted a warning. The old guy whirled, batting the knife far away, out of the pool of light. He advanced on the punk, who backed away.

"Now, you get out of here!" he bellowed. He straddled the gang leader, pointed the fence post at him. "You move it out of here before I beat this dumb sucker's brains out!"

If he had any, Jasper thought, derisively. What mama ever raised her boy to become a thug who drove a $35,000 motorcycle to harass old folks who didn't have a dime? To his amazement, and to the old man's as well, the gangbangers slunk over to their bikes. Keeping an eye on him they roared off into the darkness. The old man waited a moment, then flung his weapon away from him. He went back to standing with his friends at the fire. They were so far downtrodden that none of them did much more than give him an appreciative, embarrassed look, to which he paid little attention. Jasper was proud of the old man's accomplishment, too, but his admiration was nothing to compare with Mick and Gabe, who were whooping with delight.

"Marvelous!" Mick chortled.

"So beautiful in his rage, was he not?" Gabe demanded, pounding Mick on the back. "He could be you!"

"I'd be honored to wear his aspect," Mick said. Jasper thought the two of them must have learned to talk out of some high-class book. "Do you see there, Jasper, my friend? Behold a future angel. On the day he is called to the Most High we shall sing him into the ranks with joy."

Jasper shook off Mick's hand, disgusted. They were ruining the old guy's beautiful moment of triumph with the crap they talked. When he'd met the two...a little while ago, he wasn't sure how long...almost the first thing out of their mouths was that they were angels. He knew better. Angels had fancy nightshirts, wings and haloes, and magical powers, not patched blue jeans and saxophones. Okay, he thought he'd watched the same scene, moment for moment, just a little while ago. He was having a hallucination, that was it. He'd heard of déjà vu.

"Let's see it one more time," Gabe urged. Jasper relaxed. All right, the joke was over. They couldn't induce déjà vu. Gabe raised a hand. Suddenly the night was still once more, the homeless men clustered around their fire, the gangbanger was gone from where he had fallen. The same piece of newspaper rolled close to Jasper's feet...

"No!" Jasper cried. "Stop it!"

The two angels looked at him. "Why?"

Jasper sprang to his feet, getting in between them and the scene, stopping himself from seeing it. He couldn't believe it, didn't want to believe it, but he had to. It was all happening again. Again! "You can't do this to these people. Jacking them around, making them get up and...and *perform* for you!"

Mick's beautiful eyes were gentle. "Time is not linear, Jasper. I have told you this before. Gabe has told you the same. You must get away from that mindset. It will no longer serve you."

Jasper was adamant. "All I know is what I see," he said furiously. He had no choice now but to accept everything his companions had told him. He couldn't deny that they seemed to know things without anyone telling them. And they had replayed time. But why would God bother with a poor mixed-up man like him? They must be angels, as they claimed, or maybe aliens or super-powerful magicians, but for sure no one had ever taught them morals. "*What's the matter with you?*"

Gabe looked up at Jasper. "Why are you feeling sorry for these people? I distinctly remember you calling them 'scumbags' before."

"Well...that doesn't mean I want 'em to dance around like puppets! What about human dignity?"

Both men looked at Jasper without comprehension. "What?" asked Mick, blankly.

"It's wrong!" Jasper exploded.

"Oh!" Gabe nodded. He patted the stair next to him, but Jasper folded his arms, refusing to move. "Jasper, we are not 'jacking' these humans. *We* are reliving the moment over and over again, not they. It only happened once, but it happens forever. We merely move to the beginning of the sequence. We can see it as many times as we like." He gestured towards the circle of lamplight. Involuntarily, Jasper looked around. The big black man was rubbing his hands together over the licking flames. Any moment now the gangbangers would come back, he knew it. "They're not aware of us. They're occupied in their own thoughts, now, here. And then, because their perception is not eternal, they will move on to the next tick of time."

Jasper didn't get the fancy jargon. "Well, it looks like you're yo-yoing them."

Gabe smiled. "Another interesting term. You have a most colorful manner of speaking, my friend. We only wish to enjoy this action over again, as you have seen reruns of movies. The actors have only performed once, haven't they? It is the same."

"But why this?" Jasper asked. "You have a bunch of poor dudes being harassed by a street gang. That's not funny, but you laugh every time." He looked at them accusingly. "How come you didn't get up off your pretty behinds and help him?"

Mick raised his fingers and made a tweaking motion in the air. The sound of the action now taking place under the street lamps stopped abruptly. "Orrin Danvers does not need us. This is a matter for his conscience, for the strength of his conviction. He had to do something, and he did it, effectively. Those men had been provoked many, many times by the gang. Among them only Orrin Danvers can still be roused. He was moved to action because he felt the wrongness of that final attack in the very fiber of his being."

Jasper nodded. "I felt it, too." He eyed them with suspicion, sure he'd caught them out now. "If I'm dead how come I'm still feeling things?"

"It's part of being human," said Gabe, a dimple appearing in his cheek. "The very fiber of your being—did you ever wonder where the phrase came from?"

"Ella's always after me to eat more fiber. She says it's in vegetables. I eat potato chips and corn chips!"

"Not that kind of fiber," Mick said, with a grin that crinkled his eyes.

Jasper wasn't queer, but he could see where women and a bunch of guys he knew could fall into those long-lashed, dark-blue eyes of Mick's and keep sinking even if he used that switchblade of his on 'em. He'd seen plenty of pretty-faced abusers who traded their looks for absolute obedience from their victims. Still, Jasper's instincts told him Mick was good through and through—a strong goodness, like a laser beam. Through all the years he'd worked for DCFS, Jasper had never been led astray by his instincts,.

"It's what makes living beings different than celestials," Gabriel said. "You are born into an existence rich with texture, filaments reaching out in every direction. Even after you die, you still retain memory of having had it."

"But I've watched you! You touch everything."

"It's not the same. We touch it. We know it, but we are unconnected to it. It's how we serve God with our observation, not with our bodies as humans do."

"You make being corporeal sound low," Jasper growled.

"Far from it," Mick assured him. "It's earthly, true, but that does not lessen its importance. Why else would God have given substance—fiber, if you will—to you, his most precious creation?

"Those who know understand know the body is a teacher. Listen within yourself. Your body has a memory. Every time you cut yourself you relive what happened each time the same thing occurred, and when it will in times to come."

"*That* sucks," Jasper said.

Mick laughed.

"You do not retain only pain, but the thoughts and feelings of those times, too. You learn from them, or you don't. That's your source of wisdom, greater than what we possess."

"And yours?"

"We were never corporeal. We are as the Most High made us."

"Well, so are we, uh, humans," Jasper said.

"He gave you free will. Because you're mortal, but that doesn't give you permission to commit sins. Free will makes you capable of committing sins, but your higher nature should step in."

"What if people don't...um...use their wisdom?"

Michael smiled, lending his face a terrible, dangerous beauty. "If they are only foolish, and not evil, they remain blessed souls, and are blessed with the peace of the Most High. If they are both good and wise they may gain the greater responsibility of angels. An awareness of Earthly temptations is necessary to make a difference to others."

"Uh-huh," Jasper said, sitting down beside Gabe. "Are there marginal souls, ones who made a little bit of difference, but not enough?"

Gabriel smiled. "Those are our favorites," he said. "They are the ones who get a second chance, under our personal scrutiny, to prove themselves. Like you."

Jasper felt a chill. He glanced over at the beefy Hispanic kid, now stretched out on the pavement. "Could I end up going to hell?"

"Absolutely not," Mick said. "Your options are not between good and evil, but between rest and action. You will either spend eternity at peace, in the light of God's love, or assisting other souls. That is a more exacting mission."

"If I chose eternity at peace, would I be able to visit Earth?" Jasper asked hopefully.

"No," Gabe said. "Your work there would be done. You would attain your reward in heaven."

Never to see Chicago again? To sit on his behind for all eternity, what, playing harps? Number one sounded like eternal boredom.

That wouldn't be heaven to him. It'd be hell. "I like number two," he said firmly to the beaming angels. "What do I have to do to sign up?"

Mick's smile increased in brilliance until Jasper was surrounded by whiteness.

When his vision cleared they were no longer sitting under the El tracks. He spun around, trying to see landmarks.

There were no landmarks, unless you counted clouds. Above him stretched a high ceiling of heartbreakingly beautiful blue, around him a sculptural, monochrome landscape of rolling, floating, heaving waves of white. Looking down he spotted variations in color: a patch of green trees, a brown horse, a flock of blue birds, but everything was overwhelmed by the predominance of pearlescent white.

At first Jasper thought his companions had abandoned him. Then, he realized the blinding, multicolored pillars of light beside him were talking.

"...made the transition well, for the first time," said the taller beacon. "Welcome home, Jasper." When his vision adapted, he recognized Mick's high-cheekboned face in amongst all the glory. The tattered clothes were a memory. In their place Mick wore white draperies from neck to feet. White was too feeble a name for the gleaming hue, but it was the only word Jasper could think of. Sprouting from Mick's back were feathered wings ten feet wide. In his hand the switchblade was now a blue-white sword with a golden hilt. Light split when it touched the edge. Gabe, too, was utterly transformed. His red hair swirled around his head like fire, and the saxophone had become a long, skinny trumpet.

"Wow," was all Jasper could say. Mick grasped Jasper's arm and easily lifted him off his feet. The two of them floated along with Gabe flying ahead, his huge wings spread, his trumpet to his lips. The sound was the most beautiful thing he'd ever heard.

There was so much to absorb. Figures on the cloud-surface glanced up to see them as they passed. Jasper had never seen so many happy, content, good-looking people of every race and age, all clad in pastels with wings sprouting out of their backs. Jasper felt totally out of place. His bronze, freckly skin, the product of a mixed-race background, and dark clothing seemed too stark against all the muted colors.

Cloud piled on cloud like whipped cream mountains. They flew upward toward the peak from which rays of light whiter than the clouds issued.

"Where are we going?" Jasper asked, staring at them. "Are we going to see...You Know Who?"

"Do you wish to?" Mick asked. "Then you shall."

"No! I mean, so long as my status is shaky…I'd rather not face Him until I'm sure…what I'll be doing."

Mick smiled. "Then we shall stop at the home office instead."

He and Gabe didn't need words to communicate. At the same moment they banked their gorgeous wings to zoom down to the surface.

"Why does heaven need an office at all?" Jasper asked.

"Forms are so important to the Most High's Earthly creations. He wishes them to be comfortable even in the afterlife." Gabe stretched out a hand to catch Jasper as he started to slide through the springy surface. Jasper fought for footing. "You must concentrate on staying up," he added. "There is no fiber here for you to connect with. This is not a place, but a state of mind. It makes it easier for some of our recording angels to cope with their clients if they have a specific place in their mind. They were only human, you know." He grinned, showing Jasper he was letting him in on the joke.

Jasper clung to the proffered camaraderie. This place felt so amazingly right. He wanted desperately to be a part of what was going on here. He'd been so frustrated on Earth. Here he could really make a difference, he knew it. If they would let him try.

The place where they had *looked* like an office. In spite of the pearly wisps swirling around in the air and poufy white stuff for furniture and internal walls, this was where things got done. Blessed souls and angels of several ranks (Mick told him how to tell the difference by the type of wings) came and went, smiling at one another, conferring on matters too deep for him to comprehend. Jasper could feel respect and, yes, love between them all. If only the bureaucracy on Earth could have worked this well. Here things actually got done!

An archangel, by the multicolored aura around him, settled to the surface and greeted them.

"Micha-El, Gabri-El," he said, with a smile. He turned to Jasper and bowed. "I am Rapha-El."

Well, this his chance to stand up. Jasper ignored the pinging of his nerves and strode – bounded, really – to face the newcomer. "Are you the dude I'm supposed to talk to? These two guys here say that I'm hanging in between two kinds of afterlife. Now, I've got no choice but to believe what they say, so I've got to tell you that while I'm honored to get up here, I don't want to sit on my tail for all of eternity just doing nothing."

"Why, what would you have us do?" Rapha-El asked.

"Let me prove myself," Jasper said.

"You have no need to do so," the archangel said. "You are welcome to stay here. You served good during your life. You would be comfortable."

"I'd get bored!" Jasper exploded, then immediately regretted his outburst. Everyone stared at him. "I want to be able to go home once in a while."

"This is home," Rapha-El said, gesturing around at them.

"I mean my real home, where I feel comfortable!"

"I beg your pardon," said a small voice behind him. He jumped aside to allow a small angel in glasses to pass. She smiled timidly at him and the archangels as she went by. "Dr. Asimov needs more paper."

"Of course," Rapha-El said, gesturing her toward a supply cabinet. The angel fished through it and flitted shyly away, a box held to her chest.

Jasper did not expect to see supply cabinets in heaven. Nor glasses, either, when he thought about it. Wouldn't everyone who went to heaven suddenly have perfect bodies? A quick glance around at the others and down at his own skinny form told him that wasn't so. And why should it? he thought defiantly. He wasn't anyone perfect. He was himself.

The tension of the moment had been broken. All the other angels went on about their business, leaving Jasper and the towering archangels alone.

"What does it matter to you to be able to see Earth again?" Rapha-El asked. They didn't move, but the 'home office' seemed to float away from under their feet. "Your time there is finished."

"I'll miss it," Jasper said, desperately. "I want to see ball games at Wrigley Field. I want to smell fresh dirt in a garden. I want to see commuters on the train doing the crossword. Ordinary stuff. Doesn't anyone else ever say that to you?"

"Not often. They are happy here."

And everyone did seem to be. Jasper knew all the hymns they sang in church that told when people got to heaven they'd be reunited with their loved ones in the light of God's love. Old people with young faces sat in pairs, looking deep into one another's eyes. Parents cuddled babies. Children with glowing cheeks romped together on the ultimate playground with no fear of harm as a gentle-faced old man with thinning black hair and green eyes made them little toys out of cloud-stuff.

Not only humans enjoyed the reunion. He saw more than one boy soaring across the blue sky with a dog galloping beside him. Men and women alike sat in the midst of clusters of cats. A narrow-headed Siamese with slightly crossed eyes came to swipe his cheek against Jasper's leg before returning to the company of a white-haired man surrounded by five more Siamese cats.

It was so wonderful Jasper wanted to stay, but that would ruin his chances forever of getting more responsibility and more freedom. He knew part of his dilemma was pure contrariness. When he got back to Earth, he knew he'd want to go right back to heaven, too. If he got angel's wings, he'd be able to come and go between both places, a privilege he would give anything to get.

"Well, I wouldn't be happy," he said resolutely. "I know I've messed things up, especially myself. But I've got to have some wisdom or I wouldn't be on the fence, now would I?"

"Very true," said Rapha-El. "What do you suggest?"

"Test me. I'll show you how much help I can be." Jasper felt as though he was applying for a job.

"Are you sure you are ready to take on the responsibilities of an angel?"

"Yes!"

Rapha-El nodded. "Then so it shall be. I advise you to observe your companions first before you take on an assignment of your own."

Jasper dusted his hands together. "Whatever you say, Rapha. Let's just get this show on the road, huh? I've got me some wings to earn!"

As swiftly as he had ascended to heaven, Jasper was back on Earth.

It was autumn wherever they had landed. Sunlight greeted them through the leaves of a big tree turning a golden-hued orange. Mick and Gabe stood together before it with their arms raised and broke into song.

"Wow, what was that?" Jasper asked, when they had finished.

"Our paean to the tree. We celebrate God's creation of its beauty."

"That's fantastic!" This being an angel stuff sure had its up sides. Pretty music, good scenery. Heaven was nice, but there was nothing like being back on good old Earth. He tried humming the tune. He'd had a decent baritone. It just sounded different when they sang.

Ten steps beyond the maple was a big oak heavy with acorns. Its leaves had gone a warm russet tone. Jasper gave it an appreciative glance and kept walking, but the angels stopped and repeated their song. They did it again at the next tree, and the next tree, and the next.

"Hey, hey, hey!" he protested, as they were about to serenade a pale gold ash tree. "Do you have to do that every time we see a pretty tree?"

Mick looked at him in surprise. "Yes."

Jasper was crestfallen. "Oh. Do *I?*"

The black-haired angel gave him that beautiful smile. "No. This is part of our responsibility as archangels."

"Are you going to do that for every tree in this forest," Jasper asked, "before we get around to the mission?"

"That is correct."

Jake sighed and resigned himself to be patient. The tree song was great the first time, even the 1,000th, but he couldn't help but get tired of it. And when they saw a rainbow overhead, *well*, that was an opera! They also serenaded noon, passing showers, birds in flight, sunset and sunrise.

"Don't you get tired of singing the same thing over and over again?" he asked them as at length they finished with the last tree, a puny little thing with only a few orange leaves clinging to it. To his relief they emerged into a meadow. Not another tree for miles.

Gabe raised a carroty eyebrow. "We don't sing the same thing. That is this tree's song. Can't you hear the differences?"

Jasper was beginning to think that being an angel was just as boring as being a blessed soul. "No. How many trees was that?"

"Only the Most High's bookkeeping angel knows that. God sees every sparrow and knows every tree," Mike reminded him.

"Man, what a boring job!" Jasper didn't want that one, that was for sure. "I prefer field work, myself."

Micha-El drew his sword and pointed. "Here come the people we must help."

Jasper squinted across the field in the mid-morning light. Thirty or forty people hurried toward them. At first he thought they must be extras in a movie, because of the baggy clothes and headcloths they were wearing, but no actor would let himself get as for-real dirty as these people were. He must be in the Middle Ages. These folks looked scared. A cloud of dust in the distance showed him what they must be running away from.

Michael brought his sword up over his head in two hands, and brought it down in a single stroke. From where his blade touched, a ravine shot out across the field, widening and deepening until Jasper could no longer see the bottom. Brandishing the sword in one hand, he seemed to burst into white fire.

The running mob saw the light and began to hurry towards it. Gabe, also in his finest robes, beckoned to them from a narrow bridge that now spanned the chasm. The crowd stopped, cowering, not knowing what to do. A trumpet call from behind spurred them forward. Gabe turned to walk across the bridge. At last the leader of the little crowd got up his courage and followed. The rest of the group came after him. The bridge looked as fragile as spiderweb, but it didn't even sway.

A band of armored horsemen came riding up, shouting and pointing spears after the fleeing refugees just clearing the far end of the bridge. Jasper was irresistibly reminded of the motorcycle gang. Michael watched with impassive eyes as the horsemen rode right past him onto the bridge. He waited until they were halfway out, then brought his sword down on the span. It shivered and cracked, dumping the horsemen into the chasm. Their echoing cries died away. The ravine closed, leaving not so much as a furrow to show where it had been. Michael's aegis dimmed, and he came to join Gabriel and Jasper, who stood agape. The postulant swallowed a few times.

"I can't do that," he said. "I won't…I *won't* do that."

Michael laid a kindly hand on his shoulder. "No one will ask you to. Most of our tasks are simpler. Let us show you."

To Jasper's relief, the archangels led him on a round of missions throughout time. They restored a drowning child to an African woman wearing a leopard skin. They reconciled an Imperial Japanese family at the deathbed of their patriarch. In fact, they did all the mushy things that he'd ever seen in the movies or read about in Readers Digest. By then he'd been with the angels for months, or maybe years. He wondered, for the first time, what had become of his body, and decided he didn't really want to know. He liked hanging out with Mick and Gabe. If you paid no attention to the funky way they talked, they were okay dudes.

"So," he asked one day, "when do I get my wings?"

"You have them," Mick said. "At present they are postulant's wings. If at any time you wish to return to heaven and take your rightful place as a blessed soul, you are welcome, and none shall question your right to them.

"No, no, I want the real thing," Jasper said. "So long as I can hold on to what makes me the man I am. My fiber, if that's really where I keep my memories. You sure you've got none of your own?"

"No fiber, no memory," Gabe told him. "We know what God wants us to know."

"But you've got personalities of your own. Mick's touchy, and you're sort of sentimental. You both got a funny sense of humor."

"That is not proof," Michael said. "Those might merely reflect the difference in our functions. I defend. Gabriel summons."

Jasper tilted his head. "Yeah, and maybe you've got personalities because you learned something on your own."

"None of our depth is ours. It comes directly from God. We are his servants and his creatures. We do not learn as you do."

"*Could* you learn?"

The angels looked at one another. "We don't know. If the Most High wishes us to, we will."

"I think you'd like it. I just hope I never lose it."

"It limits you," Mick warned. "If you wish to experience the pure joy of the celestial spheres you must let go of the trappings of corporeal existence. Be free."

Jasper shrugged. "I dunno if I want to. Dunno if I can handle that much freedom." He grinned sheepishly. "I'm beginning to have sympathy for Lucifer."

Gabe led a classroom of children out of a burning school. Mick stood watch over a drunk passed out in the middle of a muddy street as horses galloped all around him. Gabe appeared briefly to a black-and-white-clad Puritan in jail who was in danger of losing his faith. Mick and Gabe stood on both sides of a British football arena during a close game to prevent riots from breaking out. Jasper watched them take steps to protect, guide and comfort.

"It looks easy," Jasper said, after Mick turned away an arrow that would have plunged into the back of an Iroquois warrior. "I think I can do it.

Gabe raised an eyebrow. "Do you think so? Are you ready?"

"Yeah," Jasper said, confidently. "I've been watching. You just do the right thing at the right time."

"I see," Gabe said, with a glance at Mick. "Then the next assignment shall be yours."

To Jasper's dismay an angel's job wasn't as easy as they had made it look. He tried to protect a girl from being stoned, but failed to take into account that the punishment was taking place at the bottom of a wall. When he had scared off the mob and turned around to his client, he found her nursing a fractured skull from a rock dropped on her from above.

At his next job he scared a woman kneeling at a prie-deux asking for divine guidance into dropping her clay lamp. Flames shot along the spilled oil and caught on the draperies and hangings on the walls of the wattle-and-daub house. It burned down. It took intervention by both Gabe and Mick to protect her large family long enough for them to escape. Jasper was mortified.

"I'll get the next one right, I swear," he vowed. The angels did not chide him, but swept him through time again.

He completely screwed up his assignment. Two boys running away from a velvet-clad noble on horseback proved to have been thieves who had robbed the lord of his purse. Jasper felt like kicking himself for not getting all the facts before he made the miracle of a vanishing bridge for them and dumped the old dude in the lake.

"You are trying too hard," Gabe said, kindly. "Perhaps you are becoming disoriented from the time shift. We will make it shorter."

They arrived in plenty of time for Jasper to take a good look-see around. His subject was a guardsman walking sentry duty on a torchlit river walk before a door cut into a high stone wall. No question about it: he was one of the good guys. Jasper admired the outfit: pants tucked into big boots that folded over at the knee, a flowing white shirt under a close-fitting coat, which in turn was under an ornamental cape that covered the man front and back. The hat was the most special thing: black felt with a big old ostrich plume curling around one side. Jasper could tell he was proud of himself and his job by the way he strode up and back, smoothing his little beard and curly moustache with one gloved hand.

A couple of men in rough, dirty clothing started sneaking through the gardens toward the door. Jasper, his senses angel-enhanced, saw them with no problem. He tapped his client on the shoulder. Surprised, the guard spun around. He glimpsed movement.

"Halt!" he cried. From under his voluminous cape he produced two pistols. "Halt in the name of the King!"

One of the men made for the door. The guard discharged the gun. The report on the quiet night air sounded like a bomb exploding. The man fell down. His companion bared his teeth and rushed at the guard with a knife. The guard shot his other pistol, but missed the target in the dimness.

"To me, King's Guards! To me!"

But no other guards came. Instead, more peasants swarmed out of the dark, wielding rakes and other makeshift weapons. The guard whipped out a sword and started laying about him, dealing with one peasant after another. Jasper got right into the heart of the action, standing back to back with his client, flinging enemies away with force that astonished even him. No one would stab him in the back while he was there to help.

"An angel protects him!" wailed one of the adversaries, running away. Others fled at his words.

"It is no angel!" a harsh voice shouted, triumphantly. "See!"

Jasper felt a weight slump against him. With growing horror, he turned just in time to catch the guard as the man fell, blood dark on his snowy white collar. His throat had been slashed. Jasper did not even care that the peasants had breached the door in the wall and were pouring through into the garden beyond by the dozen. He knelt over his fallen charge, and wept. The archangels appeared at his side, their eyes grave.

"I thought he'd be able to fight them off like the old man in Chicago did," Jasper said miserably, cradling the dead man.

"You could not know," Gabe said, gravely. "These were more vicious and determined. They feel their lives depend upon their actions. That is different."

Jasper clutched his head. "I should have shielded him instead of throwing the attackers away one at a time. I missed one. How can I be forgiven for that? Let me go back in time and save him!"

"You can't do that," Mick said. "It is as it is, and it will never be any different no matter how often you pass through that segment of time."

"How can you be so patient?" Jasper yelled. "I killed a man! Nothing I've done has been right. Nothing!"

"Are you sorry for his death?" Gabriel asked, his voice gentle. "For we are with him, as we have been since the moment of his peril."

"Wish I'd known that," Jasper said miserably. "No, I'm glad I didn't. It would have made me more careless than I was, and that was bad enough!"

"You did know in your heart that we had our hand over him," Michael assured him. He gave Jasper that smile of his. "But you kept going, as you have throughout all of your missions. As you did in your job on Earth. We admire that in you."

"Why don't you just let me go and screw up, and I'll report back when I think I've made good?"

"We're here to guide and protect you," Michael said, "but we must also protect the other children of nature. What you wield here in the unseen is powerful."

Jasper was taken aback. "Sorry. I didn't think about that. I didn't think I could hurt anyone but myself. Until now. I'd rather not put anyone else in danger, or be a burden to anybody."

"We are touched by your willingness to take all pain onto yourself, but it is not necessary."

Jasper thrust his palm into the angel's chest in a vain effort to shove him aside. "You're wasting all this time on me." Mick was unmoved, literally and figuratively.

"We have all the time in the world. It is not linear, remember?"

"Yeah, I forgot," Jasper said bitterly. "How many times you gonna watch that, huh?"

"There is no enjoyment in this," Michael assured him. "The truth is that he was fated to die. We might review it to see where it is *we* failed."

"Yeah, and how can *you* fail? You're perfect!"

"No, we are not perfect. We are only angels. Only God is perfect. God never gives you more than you are capable of handling."

Jasper stalked away down the stony path. "I wish I could believe that."

Mick and Gabe caught up with him effortlessly. Mick spun him to look square in his eyes. "Jasper. We never lie. The Most High will give you as many chances as you need. Only you can say when you are giving up."

Jasper thought of Wrigley Field. "I'm never giving up. Never!"

Jasper was beginning to hate himself. It wasn't good enough for him that the archangels said he had all of time to prove himself. If his job was to help people he wanted to do it before he forgot what life was like. He saw how complacent the other souls were getting in heaven. He wanted to get up on a soapbox—all right, a tall cloud—and shout out that there was more down there to be done. Back on earth, in his own time, kids were at risk. Women and minorities were still getting treated like dirt. People all over the world couldn't figure out who they were, and could use a hand finding out. Angel power could do all that, and more. But he had to accept that he was a little different. On his mind all the time was the threat—all right, so Mick hadn't made it a threat—that he would be relegated to that complacency if he couldn't pull this off.

The recording angel with glasses was really nice. He felt like a fool accepting another assignment from her since he'd blown every one of his last missions, but she never gave him a single sign of disapproval.

"You should do well," she said, placing a little chunk of cloud in his hand. "Your subject comes from a time and place similar to your own." Jasper glanced down at the image of a pale-skinned woman with short hair waving around her face. She looked harried. He saw blue sky behind her, but no landmarks.

"I will look forward to seeing you when you return," the angel said. Jasper knew she meant it. Resolutely, he turned away. He had to keep hold of that fiber the archangel dudes told him about, or he'd start believing everything everybody said.

He put up his palm and blew the wisp off it. Where it floated was where he was going. Jasper kicked off the cloud to follow.

Before he'd even managed to make it out of the 'home office,' Gabe and Mick were beside him, their glorious wings outspread, making their own sunlight.

"You are ready?" Gabe asked, his sapphire blue eyes dancing.

Jasper sighed. "What are you guys doing here?"

"It's our duty to accompany you," Mick said.

"You're not dressed for this assignment," Jasper said. "Aw, heck..." As he spoke, their aegises shrank and dimmed. Mick's golden halo became his yellow woolly hat. Gabriel's trumpet bent and deformed into a saxophone. Their robes became clothes: Mick in a leather coat and jeans, and Gabe in a suit with narrow lapels. Jasper was sorry to see the transformation, both for the loss of beauty and the fact that they were coming with him. He couldn't stand to fail in front of them. "I'd rather go alone."

"Too late," Gabe said cheerfully. "We are there."

The wisp circled around their heads, then dissipated. Jasper found himself standing on a rough path surrounded by trees and plants. Looked like a forest preserve. In fact, it looked like Fox Bluff, where he'd gone to picnics with his family every year since he was a tad. The sky was overcast, lending a gloomy grayness to the scene.

The sound of sobbing made him spin around. The other angels were gone from sight in a flash. Jasper followed the pathetic sound a little farther along. A woman with pale skin and short hair sat rocking back and forth on a bluff above a rapidly-moving river. She clutched something to her chest. To Jasper's horror he realized it was a gun. Her finger was on the trigger. He edged toward her. With every bob she dislodged small stones and sand that fell away to the rushing water. Suddenly, he realized what she was going to do: kill herself and let her body drop off the steep path.

"Hey, ma'am, you'd better get back," he said. She didn't turn around. She was talking to herself in a very low voice. Suddenly, the gun went off, the bullet ripping through the leaves above her, and she began to cry. He was afraid she would try again, but he couldn't get her attention. He was missing that little detail that made it possible to communicate. He studied her more closely, using all his experience as a counselor.

She was looking at something else, something below her. Probably the water. If she got too fascinated with it, too into the zen of the moment, she could raise the gun to her head and pull the trigger while her fears were distracted. Her hand went up.

Quick as thought, Jasper went back to the first moment he'd seen her, then again, running the moment back in forth in time like a tape. Like a tape...it had only happened once, he reminded himself. He skipped forward and saw the woman getting up and laughing. So...he must have done right, right? He wanted to think that way. He could not fail again. She needed to hear him. But how?

Jasper thought he must be missing something. Gabe's movie analogy from that first night came back to him, pounding at his mind. That was it! Just because he and the archangels had watched the scene under the El tracks from the same angle didn't mean *he* would have to see it that way every time, right?

He'd never really liked heights, but since he'd been all the way to heaven it seemed silly to get nervous about a sixty-foot drop. Jasper went back to the moment he'd first seen his client, then kicked off and got right out in the air. He came up level with her eyes and got in her face, right in her face, willing her to see him, not the gun in her hands.

"Hey, lady," he said. "Put that away. Someone could get hurt. You wouldn't want that, would you?"

She jumped, and the gun went off. "Who are you?" she whispered, staring at the man hovering before her. Jasper knew how it had to look. He kept his voice low and calm.

"Just someone who wants to help you."

Her head bowed lower and she cuddle the gun closer.

"No one wants to help us."

Us? Jasper looked around. He didn't see the kids at first, but he saw three small, frightened faces staring at them. Three little children huddled against a tree-trunk, trying not to look down. She'd brought her kids up here. To watch her die? The thought chilled him. He had to get her talking.

"Hey, it can't be that bad," he said, trying to sound casual for a guy standing in mid-air. "You get overwhelmed. It's natural. We take too much on our own backs. You get to feeling like no one else is there to help. You're wrong. You know, there are people back home looking all over for you."

"No one cares," the woman said, miserably.

Jasper glanced over his shoulder. Running through the event before he knew the sun was just about to break out. Suddenly a beam of light hit the water behind him. The gleam came up behind his head like the glory around an archangel. He knew from first-hand experience how impressive *that* was. Her mouth dropped open, and the hand holding the gun fell to her lap. With a mental thank you to "Touched by an Angel", he continued talking. "*We* care. You can't end like this. Your children don't deserve it. You don't deserve it."

"Sure I do! I'm no good. I got no job, no money. It's so *hard* to make it. I can't afford to go to school and get the skills I need..."

Jasper let her pour out her troubles, his heart going out to her. He had heard all of this before, so many times from so many people, always under the worst and most hopeless conditions. He couldn't make it all better for her, but this time he knew he could help.

He almost laughed. He had been so afraid of this mission, having to do the angelic hocus-pocus that he never wondered what the archangels were really looking for in an angel. Suddenly he knew. He had to be himself, and what he was was someone who listened and found solutions. He wasn't Mr. Derring-Do, or Mr. Vision in the Night. He was Mr. Good Advice, no more and no less. As long as he could hold on to that, he could help people.

"Look, ma'am, It sounds like you've been getting bulldozed, when you ought to be getting assistance from half a dozen agencies. Those are your rights. What you need to do is go to DCFS and ask for Pat Nehrsteiner. She is a fine person. She will act as the coordinator for your case. Here's the number." He felt in his pockets, and laughed at the absurdity. "Can you write it down? I don't have any cards."

The woman looked at him oddly. "You're a funny kind of angel. You talk just like a person."

"That's all I am," he said. "I am a person and you are a person and I want to help you. Can I?"

"Oh, yes, yes!" Relieved, the woman put out her hand to him and stood up. To Jasper's alarm, she slipped on the crumbling bank. The gun flew out of her hand. Her feet overshot the path, and she plummeted downward. Jasper reached for her, but her flailing limbs knocked his hands away. The children screamed with terror. The eldest reached out to help his mother. He, too, fell off the bluff. Jasper was mortified, seeing them plunging toward the river. He glanced around for the archangels and realized he was on his own.

Well, they might not be there, but Jasper grasped their techniques. He willed himself to shoot ahead in the sequence of time and dropped so that he was below the woman as she fell. He appeared just in time to catch her in his arms. He ran up the air to the top of the cliff, put her safely on the path with her other two children, then sprang backwards in time to rescue her son.

Time overlapped so that the woman's feet were just touching the ground when he returned with the boy. The family threw their arms around one another. Jasper glanced back, then realized he couldn't see the other images of himself existing at the same time as his present self. Probably a good idea, he reasoned. Jasper marveled at how he'd been able to slipstream so well, being here, there and everywhere all at once, like he'd always been doing it. He wanted to try another jump into the past to see how the rescues looked, but the woman grabbed hold of his wrist and held it hard, sobbing.

"Thank you, thank you, thank you! I didn't know angels could touch people!"

"I didn't either," Jasper said, uncomfortably. He pulled away, but his fingers left a glow on her skin. She touched it. It faded quickly, but she seemed transformed because of it. Her eyes were full of awe. Jasper rubbed his face in exasperation. "Ah, c'mon, lady, I'm just a caseworker."

"You are an angel," the woman said, touching his cheek. All of a sudden he knew her name and everything about her. Her name was Torry Mulhare. Her three children had two fathers between them. She'd never been married. Her mother and aunt lived with her. She was the sole support of the family. He was all the more grateful she had lived.

He watched her cuddle her children, giving each a hard hug. All of them were crying and promising to behave better, but she just kept kissing them. The last thing she did before she took them up the stony path was throw the gun into the river. The archangels appeared beside him as soon as she had gone. Both were nodding, their eyes eloquent. Jasper shot them a wry look.

"You run through that one more than once?"

"We needed to see every detail," Gabe said. "It was worth watching."

"It is a moment we will enjoy seeing over and over again for eternity," Mick said, with that beautiful smile. "You understood her so well. We were impressed."

Jasper turned to them, his fists clenched. "My clients are going to be human, right?"

"Yes," said Gabe. "Or animal, or plant, or mineral, or pure energy."

"Well, I think it'll be all the better for all of 'em if I hold onto the fiber part of me. I can relate better to 'em if I keep my experiences. Right?" They were nodding again. "You knew I was going to say that, didn't you?" He looked at them accusingly. "You knew all along I would make it."

"The Most High knew it from the moment of your conception," Mick said. "The only one who needed to be convinced of your advocacy and passion is you, and you had to convince yourself."

Jasper was embarrassed. "You don't go through this with all your candidates, do you." It wasn't a question. Again the archangels nodded.

"As we said at the beginning, you are one of the rare ones," Gabe said. "We learned from you, and perhaps will continue to learn from you throughout time." He paused. "You're one of the reasons we sometimes regret never having had human fiber. Those flaws you wish to retain are a divine creation in themselves. You're an example of why mankind is the Most High's favorite creation."

"Not you?" Jasper was surprised. "Not angels?"

Mick shook his head, the radiant joy of his face dimmed a little. "No. Because given all your flaws, or perhaps because of them, you can ascend to a divinity higher than angels. You are not made good or evil. You choose goodness."

Embarrassed by the admiration in their eyes Jasper didn't know where to look.

"Ri-ight," he said. "Hey, I've got an idea," he said. "Let's go back to last autumn and sing to a tree. You guys sing good. I bet we can get some absolutely *classic* doo-wop going."

"Whatever you wish," Gabe said, hefting his saxophone. He shot a humorous look at Mick. "We cannot *wait* to hear how you use your skills to relate to forests."

Prom Night

Shalanna Collins

Shalanna Collins is the pen name of a lifelong writer from Dallas, Texas. A graduate of Southern Methodist University with degrees in computer science and mathematics, she is also an accomplished pianist and avid trivia player. Her first novel, *Dulcinea: or Wizardry A-Flute,* was the first runner-up in the 1996 Warner Aspect First Novel Contest.

The demon Asperioth felt himself being conjured just as he was finishing up a complex three-day working. Since the tug first came when he had his hands full, he couldn't even try a countermeasure. The working was too strong, anyway; someone out there must have his Name. He rose up into the air tail-first, cursing and dropping the components for the last step of his spell as he was sucked into the vortex between the demons' realm and that of the mortals.

The feeling was like being pulled butt-first through a knothole. A too-small knothole.

He materialized in a forest clearing bathed in the light of the full moon. Someone must know a little about what they were doing. His hooves crunched on pine needles; the scent turned his stomach. Looking down, he saw he stood in the center of a salt-encrusted pentagram inscribed in a double circle engraved in the soft dirt. Apparently, someone knew quite a bit.

He blinked. As his infravision adjusted to the harsh light, he could make out a petite figure. A young human female stood before him with black-draped arms upraised, her toetips barely tangent to the edge of the magickal figure.

Her voice squeaked forth with a whiny nasal accent. "Asperioth, I command thee!"

She'd heard his Name somewhere, or read it in a book, he supposed. Well, that made things tougher for him: once they knew your Name, you couldn't resist the conjuring when you were called. That was part of the reason he'd been pulled so suddenly. And unless you could fool them, you were compelled to obey. Within reason.

"What do you want from me, O woman?" Asperioth couldn't quite remember the language, the exact phrasing that he was supposed to use. It had been so long since he'd had his Name called by a mortal. "I have little time to spend here. Tell me your desire."

"I want more power." Her eyes gleamed in the moonlight. "More power at my command without all these material components and . . . rituals." Her lips parted, revealing slightly pointed canines at the edges of her smile, and she glanced over her shoulder. Asperioth followed her gaze to a naked human male, almost as young as she, panting on a woolen blanket behind her. The youth lay unnaturally twisted and still, as though stunned from a working. It was a sophisticated method of raising power; she was no newcomer to the Craft, nor apparently to the rules of diabolical magick.

"I could give you more power in the same way this one has given it." Asperioth beckoned, hoping he wasn't leering too obviously. "Come hither into the center of my pentacle, and I shall grant your request."

She grimaced. "I don't want to bear a demon child! Babies ruin your figure." Her nose wrinkled, and she shook her head. "Anyway, I've never heard of anybody going into the pentacle with the demon."

Asperioth winced. "Please -- we prefer the more correct term, 'antiangel.'"

"Whatever."

Asperioth spread his arms wide, then pulled them in a bit as a shower of tiny blue sparks shot from the edge of the pentacle's central pentagon, in which he stood. "I will do you no harm and plant no seed. You will find I can give you great pleasure as I increase your power."

She gave him a hard look. "Don't mess with me. You can give me power at my command just with a word. I want that word of power."

Well, it had been worth a try. "All right. But within the confines of this figure, I feel cramped and uneasy. When I am made to be so, I cannot think." The pentagram seemed claustrophobically small; it was squeezing his potbelly and his rear pillows. "Rub out a line so I can come forth, and I will grant you a word which will allow you to command power in an instant."

"Forget it." She glared at him. "You're not coming out here, and I'm not coming in there. Do I look stupid? You stand right there and think fast. Just give me the word."

All right, he would give her a word. But first he had to know what it was worth to her. "What is the payment you are willing to give for each use of this word?"

She scowled, pushing her wild dark hair back behind one ear. "What are you talking about?"

"I mean there is a cost for each use of the word. The power does not come from the sound of the word alone. It must be paid for by the sacrifice of some mortal component."

"Such as what?"

He paused for dramatic effect. "Your pet... the use of your right arm... your singing voice ..."

The figure on the blanket stirred, rubbed his forehead, and groaned. "Go with the voice. That wouldn't be much of a loss."

She whirled on him. "Quiet, Brian!" Turning quickly back to Asperioth, she said, "Those things are not negotiable. They're too personal. Isn't there something else?"

The demon cocked an eyebrow. "Something else?"

"Yeah. I mean, somebody else. How about somebody else's soul?"

"Bindi!" came an offended cry from the blanket.

"I don't mean you, stuperino." She growled it out of the corner of her mouth. "No, I mean like... somebody I don't care about. Like the kids at school." Her teeth sparkled as she licked her red lips. "Yeah, like that. How about the kids at school?"

"That could be satisfactory, except..." Asperioth looked at her with new respect. She was almost as free from the burden of compassion as he was. "It cannot be without their knowledge. I do not mean that they need to know what is to happen, though of course that condition brings you even more power. You will have to have their loyalty, and at the moment of sacrifice you must command their complete attention. Only those whose attention is focused on you for the amount of time your complete working requires will be taken in exchange when you speak the word. You must have their full attention and do the majority of your working before them, and then speak the word at the height of their concentration."

After a pause, she nodded. "That'll work, I guess. So I have to get their attention, like in the hall or something."

"Yes." Because he respected her ruthlessness and her brazenness in demanding such things so confidently of a power like himself, he gave her a gift, told her one of the catches. "But if the focused attention is interrupted, such as by someone coming along who manages to disrupt or dispel the crowd, the working will be wasted and the spell lost."

She looked pained. "So, like, I have to do it when there are no distractions, like some teacher coming along, or a hall monitor. And that means the pizza place is out, too; those waitresses don't care what kind of scene you're making, they refill the tea glasses. Could even call the manager." She narrowed her eyes. "You're saying I should do it when they're together in a group, they need to be looking at me, and kind of like in tune with me, and without interruptions."

"Correct."

"Yeah, like... like at a dance. Like at the dance. What if I do my ritual when they're all looking at me, the queen of the prom?"

"If the situation meets the requirements I have set forth, it will be acceptable. Perform your working and raising of power in the normal way, and then when their attention is at its height, speak the word of power and the spell will be done with the additional power." She was growing tedious, as did any mortal when musing upon the uses of the powers they'd demanded. His own abandoned spell would be ruined, unrecoverable, if she kept him here much longer. He could feel the steam of anger rising out of both ears. He decided to use the menacing appearance of that phenomenon to his advantage. "I have explained sufficiently. Therefore, it is courteous to release me now."

The girl gave a half-smile. "Hold on to your shorts. You haven't even given me the word yet. You do think I'm stupid, don't you? Well, for your information, I'm smart. I'm thinking there might be more catches to this thing that I need to know about."

He'd already told her more than he had to. "Do not anger me, mortal woman. Use the same courtesy you would use to a fellow magician, or better. You forget what I am and what you are."

"Sorry. Jeez -- "

He clapped his hands over his ears before her invocation of Light could do any damage. "Please! No need for that kind of talk. I have your word of power." After waiting a suitably solemn moment, he pronounced a word in the magickal tongue. Guttural and hissing all at once, it would be a challenge to her.

"Can't you give me an easier one?" She squinted.

"The words are the words." He sent a hostile light out of his eyes to convince her. "They cannot be other than what they are."

"All right, all right. Say it again clearly so I can get it, and you can go."

He pronounced it again for her, slowly, to be fair, because she had proven herself admirably wicked. "Use it wisely. Remember the price."

She smiled and raised her arms. "I release thee, Asperioth, and return thee to thy proper realm. Depart now, and may there ever be peace between me and thee. So mote it be."

He felt himself slipping back into his own realm. "Oh, yeah, and thanks," he heard her calling as he clattered back onto the floor of his own workroom.

"Mortals today," he muttered, picking himself up and dusting off his legs, which were covered with dried cinders from the floor. "No respect, no respect at all."

* * *

I wasn't trying to steal a magickal grimoire from my sister's bedroom. Who'd think she had one? I thought I had her diary!

It was the morning of my senior prom. Ellie and I sneaked it out from under Sharron's mattress on impulse, Ellie tugging at my arm and saying, "Fred, we really shouldn't; it's none of our business, and she's going to hate me."

"She won't hate you. She'd never suspect you—she'd know it was all my idea. Anyway, she'll never know." Okay, we're awful, snoops or worse, but I was afraid Sharron was making it with the musician she'd been dating, that loser scum, and I was going to haul him down for it. Or haul her over for a VD exam, or the Pill if she didn't already have it. I just wanted to know, dammit. I probably wouldn't do anything.

"Fred, you know she'll know. Sisters just know when their brothers have been messing around with their diaries and things."

I ran my hand through my hair. "I don't care. I need to find out about that creep and what's going on." I had to see if my little sister was being taken advantage of; she was only sixteen going on a jaded thirty-nine, and since our parents had careers that took all their attention, I felt I should keep abreast of her exploits. Call me old-fashioned or anal-retentive as you will, but as the older brother, I thought it was my moral obligation. Besides, I kind of liked playing the man of the house. My girlfriend Ellie would keep my findings in perspective.

"Okay." Ellie's short chocolate-milk-color hair had flopped into her face, and as she pushed it back, I could see she was pinker than usual. She giggled. "I'm going to feel terrible about this later, but I love reading people's journals, especially people who aren't really writers. Plus, I'm up for some excitement. But not too much—so let's get out of her room."

The diary was digest-sized, with a cover of embossed leather. The raised design attracted my fingers, and I caressed it absent-mindedly without registering what I was doing; it was a rich chocolate shade, or maybe more of a sueded bronze—no, it looked coppery now. The thing seemed to change colors under my hand. It colored darker and lighter, like a huge mood ring, at each touch.

I adjusted my glasses. It must be a trick of the light; we'd stepped into the stairwell, where the sun shone through Mom's newest stained glass window. Sure, that was the explanation. The book was unnaturally light for its size; perhaps it had been hollowed out, a hiding place for drugs? I dreaded finding anything like that. I hesitated a moment, but Ellie giggled again and pulled me by the hand as she trotted up the stairs.

We headed up to the third floor. Sometimes it was really cool to live in a restored Queen Anne on the corner of Dixie and Melrose in downtown Renner, Texas. This whole floor was our library and computer room, lined with bookshelves and comfy chairs. Sharron never came up here; her current interests didn't include reading or staying home.

Side by side, we plopped into Mom's cushy loveseat. After a moment, Ellie crawled into my lap. I pulled out my Swiss Army knife, prepared to fiddle with the diary's awesome-looking lock, but the cover popped open as my blade neared it. The book flipped to the first page.

Instead of my sister's crabbed handwriting, we saw a gorgeous spread of pastel portraits. Me, Mom, Dad, and Sharron herself, all pictured in realistic detail, with our names inscribed below our images in silver script, and some funny marks I'd never seen before emblazoned all around us. The marks had an odd glow to them, reminding me of an aquarium lighted from within.

Ellie gasped. "Your sister's an artist?"

"Not that I knew about."

At the bottom of the page I noticed a glitter-embossed arrow. No, it was a jumble of letters squashed close together. After a moment of study, I could make it out as a sentence in that balloony Peter Max font found on 1960s-era black light posters. It read, "Turn the page."

Ellie shifted uncomfortably. "That arrow just appeared. It wasn't there when you first opened the book."

"Sure it was." I turned the page to reveal a two-page layout of full-color comic book panels, drawn like the old Archie comics, but with all of us, my classmates and friends, as the characters.

Ellie screeched when she recognized herself. "My butt isn't that big! Is it?" Without waiting for an answer, she grasped the book and began running her hand over the pages, her voice full of wonder as her finger landed on each image in turn. "And that's Donnie, and that's Jason, and that's Ethan, and there's John. And Tiffany, and Steffanie, and Alyxzandra, and..."

I interrupted her litany. "Uh-huh, kinda looks like our graduating class." These were fairly good likenesses, in fact. "I had no idea my sister could draw flies." In fact, I hadn't seen her lift a pen for months, even to do her homework.

The weight on my knees grew heavier. "You gain ten pounds or something?" I asked Ellie. She didn't even make an exasperated noise at me; it was as though she hadn't heard. She stared at the page. It was full of color and detail; it was real eye candy.

After a moment, Ellie hit me on the knee. "No, I haven't. Can't you read? Pay attention. This is the story of our prom."

"Hmm." Possibly it was meant to be that. It was a story about a dance, with several panels showing typical prom activities. Lovely tale, up until the middle of the second page, where an entire panel was devoted to a huge dragon covered in glimmering scarlet scales. At least I thought it was a dragon, but with the face of a lion, feathery blue wings, and long white horns jutting from the top of its head. The beast broke through the roof and materialized in the party's midst, bringing in a dreadful stormcloud to replace the crepe paper-streamered ceiling. The weird part was that it wasn't a static drawing; it all seemed to be happening as I watched.

"I had no idea she admired us this much." Or at all. I cleared my throat. "She's not being very creative. It looks to be your typical comic—excuse me, graphic novel."

Strange, though; the dragon wasn't inked, but shimmered in copper and red metallics, a kind of dried-on powder. Could this have been done with a computer and color inkjet printer? I scrubbed at a corner of one frame with my fingertip, licked it and rubbed again, but no ink came off. The page had the texture of a printed comic book. Where had it come from? "Do you think this was done in pencils, or what?"

"I don't know, you goon. I'm no artist. I'm following the story." Ellie clawed at the bottom edge of the page. "I can't get hold of it."

She couldn't turn the page, but when I reached for it, the corner fairly leapt between my finger and thumb. The pictures were blurry, not quite finished, when the page first flattened out, but in a moment colors came into them and brightened, black outlines inking on as we watched. It was as if the scene were being completed because we were reading on. Of course, that had to be part of the illusion. What illusion?

"This could be done on the computer, but..." I still clung to the rational world, figuring out how the paper might be specially coated to let colors appear when body heat touched it, like slow glass or some other science fictional discovery. Frankly, it worked like a laptop's LCD screen. A movie on paper?

"Hush." Ellie put her hand over my mouth. "Basically, here we are dancing wilder and wilder, and then people are turning blue and crashing to the ground. Then we're getting sucked into this huge tornado sort of thing, which the dragon is doing with its breath. Then in this panel, demons swarm in and jerk out the people's souls." She squinted. "The pictures kind of flicker and change as I look at them."

"The light in here plays tricks. The new sheer curtains blowing around or something." I squinted, but I didn't think it was our eyes.

She slipped her hand back over my mouth. "I'm serious, Fred." She looked at me, fear beginning to glimmer behind her eyes. "It's very realistic, isn't it?"

Actually, what she wasn't saying was what we could both see: the figures were moving and the scenery shifting just like the graphics on a Java-scripted animated Web site, acting out the disaster. I knew the pictures weren't moving, but some part of my brain insisted they were. I kissed Ellie's palm, and she took away her hand.

"Now can I answer without you slapping your hand over my mouth?" I meant to tease her, but my voice quavered like a little old man's. I cleared my throat, shaking my head to clear it too. "This is really disturbing stuff. And it couldn't be Sharron's own work. I wonder who drew this? Probably that weirdo she's dating. Perverted of him to still be fixated on high school when he dropped out over a year ago."

Ellie shuddered and huddled close. "Freddy, this thing is weird. It's scaring me."

I couldn't accept what I had seen. "The drawings didn't move. We only imagined it." But the pictures had acted out a story, and one I didn't like. Now they lay still, as though awaiting my next move. I turned the final page, and saw the conclusion of the tale: the roof of the ballroom caved in, gore and splayed limbs sticking up out of the gaudy wreckage of the decorations, and a cloud that looked like a clump of protoplasm rising out of the chaos and being sucked in by the dragon. It was ridiculous, yet chilling. "A typical comic-book ending, see?" But my voice held no conviction.

Ellie shivered. "That's supposed to be what's going to happen tonight, isn't it?" She pulled back from me a bit. "In somebody's twisted mind."

"Of course not." We stared at each other.

Finally Ellie said, "Is your sister in therapy? Because if she isn't, there's no shame in it. I mean, I think she needs to be."

"Babe, I don't know what to think. I can't figure out where this comes from. I knew she wasn't really into school these days... but..."

I tried to turn the page back, but it made me wait this time, a long moment. I finally got hold of it and flipped back.

The comic was gone. All we saw was calligraphy, writing that I at first could not even make out to be English words. "What the hell?"

Then I recognized a few words. "Party of the first part," "Aspirant agrees to commit the destiny of one (1) human spirit (soul) to the Magus Prime for each magicker authorized to act as a mortal channel..." What the hell?

"It's a contract," Ellie said, wonder in her tone. As we watched, a dotted line formed across the bottom of the page. I was holding a pen. Where had that come from?

Sign here, the words forming beneath it read. Ellie reached for the pen, slowly, as if she were in a dream. I held it away. "I don't think this is a good idea."

"Goddammit, I knew it would be you getting into my stuff." Sharron's voice, screeching out from the top of the staircase behind us, startled Ellie off my lap onto the carpet. I slammed the book shut. "Careful with that! You're going to get someone killed."

"With this?" I tried the wide-eyed innocent tactic, flapping my wrist back and forth with the book like a ninny.

Sharron wasn't just angry, she was red as her hennaed hair. "What the hell are you doing with that?"

I thought the offensive tack was the most promising. "I want to know where you got this thing. It looks like a prototype for a new screenless computer or something. It must be worth a lot of cash."

She lunged for it, but I was still taller and stronger. I held it up over my head away from her while she flailed at me ineffectually. "Give that here! You don't know what you're messing with."

I blinked. "You make a salient point. What, exactly, is this?"

"None of your damn business." Her eyes narrowed.

"How did you know I had it? You were nowhere in the house, yet you rushed right up here."

"How do the pictures move?" Ellie glanced guiltily at me.

"Give. Me. That. Book." Sharron's blue eyes were ice.

"I need to know. Just tell me what it is, and I'll hand it over and never bother it again. Hacker's honor." She knew that oath meant business.

Sharron darkened to mahogany. "I suppose, if you've seen as much as I suspect you have, from what she's just said, you deserve to know more. It'll serve you right. You won't tell anyone, because they'd just put you on antipsychotics." She laughed a sort of dead chuckle.

"Right." Ellie nodded, her bobbed hair flipping around her ears. Ellie is beautiful, with coffee eyes, café au lait hair, and compatibly tan skin, but she's kind of puny at only five feet and a hundred pounds. I wished she'd keep quiet, because although at five-seven and 185 pounds I was a match for my sister, who is charitably called "chunky" and "large-framed," Ellie wasn't. And Sharron looked like she'd like to deck one of us.

Instead, she kind of sagged into the chair across from us. "All right." Sharron sighed, flipping her cascade of auburn braids up over the chair back, making them seem to stand on end. "Short version. I have become a sorceress, working with Rasoul"—her musician buddy—"to close many majickal gateways that various demons have prepared for invading this world. We're in a crisis right now, and that grimoire is one of our spirit guides who is under a curse and has been incarnated in the book. It gives us advice and is invaluable to our work. I can explain more if you want to come to Gathering, but I never thought you'd want to hear it. You've never been very religious." She crossed her arms. "Anyway, now you know."

"Oh. Well, sure. That's logical as hell." I snorted to let her know she wasn't snowing me at all. Ellie looked totally stone-faced, but I knew her little Catholic-schoolgirl mind was clacking away, enumerating the names of the demons and their domains, and thinking how demonic invasions were a perfectly believable thing as the millennium approached. To me, on the night of our senior prom, the very thought of binding up a demon, let alone believing in one..." Come on, Shar. You can't think I'm going to buy that line of crap."

"See?" Sharron spread her palms wide. "I knew there was no use telling you. That's the reason I never brought you in on it, although Rasoul thought you would be an asset." That surprised me. "Of course, I was right. You're no use in situations like this."

Feeling guilty about Rasoul's implicit compliment, I glared at my sister. "Come off it. What's the real story?"

"It's all true. And now hand me the book; you promised." I had promised to hand it over, after all, if she explained. And she had explained after her fashion. I was a man of my word, so I silently handed the heavy thing over. By now it seemed a brick.

Sharron inspected it as though I were a well-known counterfeiter. "Stay away from my stuff, especially this. Computers are your bailiwick, and technology destroys magick. Until you get a lot more spiritual, you don't want to delve into it. I'm serious." She got up and stalked down the stairs, undoubtedly to return to the heart of her coven.

"That had to be the truth." Ellie climbed back up on the loveseat, eyes sparkling. I just looked at her. "We have to find out more about this. Let's follow her. I always wondered where witches hung out."

"Witches? Come on." I tried to keep my tone breezy. "Aren't you forgetting something, Ell?" She looked blank, and this time it was me sighing. "The prom, babe. We've farted around and wasted the morning. Don't you need to go frizz up your hair and paint on your dress and do all that stuff to get glammy?"

Ellie frowned and looked away. "I don't even really want to go. I'm all out of the mood. Besides, aren't you even the least bit curious? I'm freaked out by this whole deal. Sharron's blown my mind into a contemplative state, not suitable for partying." She patted my knee. "Let's just stay cuddled up here and smooch."

I reached for her. "While I have no objection to that, it wouldn't be fair to you to miss your senior prom." I didn't kiss her; I made her wait. "Remember, you wanted our photo taken in front of the Caribbean backdrop, and you wanted to be so gorgeous it made Bindi Festwaul look like Richard Nixon in drag."

"I don't care any more." She shuddered. "I can't stop thinking about that comic or whatever it was. It spooked me."

"Forget it, Ell. Sharron must've been playing with us. She's gotta be down there laughing now." As I said this, I almost believed it.

Her gaze was level. "But what about the book, and how the pictures changed?"

I tapped the back of her hand softly. "That thing's from a stage magicians' shop. That musician friend of hers must've gotten it for her to freak me out. She knew I had looked in her diary before, and this time she was ready for me."

"Fred, I know what I saw."

"Well, it wasn't real." And now it seemed it couldn't possibly be, as the sunbeam stretched to signal afternoon, streaming in across our knees, and lit up the orange cat lying on the windowsill. The morning now seemed like a too-imaginative daydream. I was sure there was something strange about the book, but I preferred to forget it, leave my sister to dabble in the occult or whatever, just don't involve me in it.

Let me become an investment banker and get my Lotus to drive, my villa on the French Riviera, my wardrobe of five-thousand-dollar suits, but leave me out of all weirdness. "It was an elaborate and well-planned practical joke. It's April, after all, and she must have planned for me to find it on Fools' Day." I gave Ellie my best crooked grin, which usually won her over to all my logic or illogic.

I must've looked impish and convincing. Or she wanted to believe. "Well, if you're sure." Ellie still looked skeptical. "I kind of can't remember exactly what I saw in the book," she finally admitted.

"Me, neither." I had to lie. I was sure I remembered perfectly, but I also remembered that Ellie'd been in kind of a trance when the book had tried to entice her to sign her soul away to the Magus Prime in exchange for being a majicker, whatever that entailed.

"I guess we let our imaginations carry us away. But I still don't want to go to the prom. It's shallow and superficial and silly, and I'm not popular, and you're a computer nerd. What were we thinking?"

"Um, silly as it sounds, we have fun at dances." This was unlikely but true. "And what about all the money I laid out for the evening? The tickets are nonrefundable."

I'd appealed to her pocketbook, Ellie's second dearest possession next to her Bible and rosary. She finally smiled. "The only reason I'm going is to keep that Edwina Winifred from saying I couldn't come because my family's too poor for me to get a dress." She pecked me on the cheek and scrambled down. "Pick me up on time, now. Our reservations at Jimanny's are for 7:30, and they'd be glad to give them away." I assured her I would be uncharacteristically early.

I had time to play on the computer for a while, because it wasn't going to take me that long to get ready. But the computer wouldn't cooperate; it said it had to run the disk scanner, that it hadn't been shut down properly last time, that it had found and removed two new viruses, and finally that it thought one of the disk drives had lost some important operating system files. I powered down to punish it and decided to fix it all later. Instead, I went downstairs to mess around in the kitchen and watch game shows on the satellite TV. I consumed several sandwiches and an entire pound cake before it was time to beautify myself for my mystical, magical Senior Prom.

The rented jacket was perfect, but I couldn't find my tie. Jerking open the drawers in the downstairs bathroom's linen closet, I pawed through them; suddenly, the grimoire bounced out into my hands. Sharron'd changed hidey-holes, but she hadn't chosen well. It was as though the book had wanted me to find it.

I glanced around and kicked the door closed, opening the book before I realized I was going to do it. Calligraphic script scrolled beautifully out before my eyes. It took me a moment to "see" the words, like those optical illusions where you are supposed to see a vase instead of the facing profiles. But I was getting the hang of reading it. It read: "Take me with you. You will need me when the trouble begins."

"Huh?" I couldn't help answering aloud. "What trouble?" When it was silent on that count, I brought up the more important issue. "Why do you choose me to speak to? I'm president of the Renner High Skeptics. I don't even believe in conditional probability."

The book paused, then scrolled out words in gold script. "I like you. Your name is made of the runes thorn, and ghee, and fay, and norn. Very auspicious."

"Fred? Are you still in there? I gotta get on the toilet!" My sister was never tactful about bodily functions.

I closed the book. "Coming out right now." I might look at it later, try to figure out its tricky secret. It had to be a computer somehow, something that musician had gotten at a pawn shop or stolen, didn't know its value. I was thin and the jacket's inner pocket was deep. I shoved it in atop my wallet.

One last check in the mirror; I straightened the bow tie. Looking good. I tossed my hair back and shrugged once for the casual effect. Yeah, all right; I took a deep breath and grabbed my keys.

At Ellie's house, her dad clapped me on the shoulder and suggested alternative Marines-type hairstyles, as always; her mom snapped a dozen photos with one of those disposable flash cameras so all I could see for a moment was spots. I patted down my jacket, the book warm within the pocket. It seemed to radiate contentment and the feeling that all would be well. Her three younger sisters hung, moony, over the stair railing as we left.

Ellie's prom dress was short, stretchy, and black, with a sweetheart neckline and a very flattering, rump-hugging cut. She wore black fishnets over white tights. Her hair shone, curled softly under and held back with a glittery headband and barrettes. She grabbed my hand and skipped to the car, apparently completely recovered from her earlier frame of mind. "Fred! Come on, I'm ready to party!"

The mood of the evening was casual and fun, with nothing to remind us of the crazy pseudo-prophecy. Even the total tab for dinner at the fancy French restaurant wasn't that daunting. Well, the total was $66.66; I pointedly ignored that.

The theme of the prom was "Essence of Deepest Africa." Instead of crepe paper and puffy cotton clouds, as the comic had predicted, the ceiling was hung with Spanish moss. The place was decorated with African art and sculpture; I almost knocked over a totem pole as I ducked a jungle branch coming in. All around us were those braided-trunk fig trees with white twinkle lights strung all up and down them, looking cheerful. I let out a breath I hadn't realized I was holding. "Some politically correct fiend made all these masks?"

"Guess the art department had a project going." Ellie ran her hand admiringly across a piece of sculpture. I found the masks all over the place--and one in particular—disconcerting, vaguely threatening. I shook off the feeling that the carvings, with their jeweled eyes, were watching me closely.

Further inside, the ballroom was dark but glimmery: light flowed down from tiny bulbs sparkling way up in the ceiling, with only a few along the baseboards to guide our steps. Brown batik-y tablecloths and flickering scented candles were on the tables, and all manner of exotic woodcarvings were ubiquitous. Our name cards were held in the reluctant hands of squat, angry-looking sculptures. The closest I could come to identifying the smell of the place was that it was like applewood smoke.

A DJ was already spinning tunes, so after we sampled the various multicolored punches—none of them spiked—we merged into the crowd of dancers. We were good, finding we could anticipate one another's moves. Over the dance floor there was a huge skylight, and beneath that an indoor pond, an extension of the hotel's large pool outdoors that was connected by a twisting river. The surface of the water reflected stars, candles, and floating magnolias. From the windows onto the terrace, the moonlight streamed in, full and creamy and luminous.

On the wall nearby hung the largest of the artworks, a huge mask that I couldn't stop sneaking looks at. Its face was elongated, oblong, with a pointy long nose and a squarish chin wrapped around with silver wire; but unlike the other masks, its eyes were closed, and it had sage green paint on its eyelids. It wore a tall, stylized crown topped with a pair of long, inwardly curved horns. It was presumably a representation of an African queen. Its expression was what I could only call demure, but patient.

Between songs we separated to admire the splendor. "Wow." Ellie spread her arms. "Feel the energy."

I decided to yank her chain. "Sure, why not? Everybody's got hotel rooms for having sex after, except good Catholic girls like you."

Ellie squeezed my hand. "You said it. But we're going to be glad we waited."

I couldn't help sighing. Well, I tried.

The music faded, and someone tapped on a mike. On the stage, the student council and prom committee were assembling. Tapping the mike was the president of the prom committee, Edwina Winifred.

Popular despite her thick glasses and flyaway ginger-cat bobbed hair, Edwina was one of the socialites that didn't treat the out-crowd badly, but on the other hand we weren't best buddies, either. She was so thin I called her "stick woman." She cleared her throat, and we all came to attention. Her big watery eyes blinked behind their fashionable specs. "Good evening. Let me welcome you to Renner High School's Senior Prom in Deepest Africa, where a magical evening awaits us. Our class this year has been—"

The whine of feedback drowned out the rest of her sentence. "Let Miss High and Mighty's part be over soon so we can get back to having fun," Ellie whispered in my ear.

The sparkling chandeliers brightened a bit. As I nuzzled Ellie's neck and got repeatedly slapped away, Edwina long-windedly thanked everyone who had helped plan and who'd stayed up all night decorating, to dutiful applause. "Tonight has a certain mythic power. All our energy is focused now on our future, but tonight is a night we will never forget, shining in our memories for its glamour, honors, and excitement. And it's all embodied in our king and queen of the dance. Now for what we've all been dying to see: the king and queen of this year's prom!"

The class had voted by secret ballot last week—I hadn't, but presumably those who cared had--but everyone knew who it would be: Bindi Festwaul and her boyfriend George Renfield, head cheerleader and quarterback. Duh. In Texas, who else?

Sure enough, the applause started and those two came up from the back of the stage, beaming their superiority complexes just the way real royalty does. Bleah.

Into my ear, Ellie whispered, "Which opera plays when Bindi's rodent-like falsies get pricked by George's frat pin? Deflate-her maus!"

I groaned. "*Die Fliedermaus*," you know, "*Trinke, Liebchen, trinke schnell, trinken macht die Augen hel*l," and all that. Only an opera buff like me would even get that one.

"Eeeeee!" shrieked Bindi into the microphone. Privately I called her Miss Thing. "This is such an honor! I can't believe it! I'm so happy! Thank you all!"

Miss Thing's dress was a shimmery sequined creation she'd been melted into, but instead of Jezebel red, it was a muddy army green. The effect was that of thousands of tiny dragon scales, except she was so skinny that on her the suggestion was more like that of a snake, one before the Fall when serpents still had limbs. She looked pallid under her typically heavy makeup. A streak of pure white ran from forehead to nape through her cropped raven hair, reminiscent of a skunk; I didn't know what the motive had been for the new dye job, but it went along with her whorish turn-out. George was vacant as ever, a square and lumpy blonde with a buzzcut, bony shoulders, and knuckle-dragger arms. A lizard for Miss Snakey Thing.

Miss High and Mighty returned to stage center carrying a tiara, put it on Miss Thing, and handed her the flowers. I briefly fantasized we would have a rerun of the climactic scene from the movie "Carrie," but it was not to be. The royal pair paraded themselves around the stage as people shrieked and applauded.

The DJ cued a slow song by a rapper who was sappily bemoaning the lack of romance, but it had that definite street-jungle beat. A pink spotlight fell on our faux royalty, and they began a slow dance. We all followed suit as the chandeliers dimmed again. The spotlight followed them offstage and into the center of the crowd. Seemingly, only candlelight led our footsteps.

Ellie rested her head on my shoulder and sighed into my ear. Her shoes had higher heels than I'd realized. She smelled heavenly, a combination of gardenias, sweat, and sex—don't ask me how, but that's what it was. I breathed it in deeply and tried not to stagger. We tottered around in what I imagined was a sort of waltz, trying not to bump into the other couples. We were all packed in there like brushes in a car wash. About then I became aware of a faint murmur, an odd chant that wasn't on the CD, and I knew it wasn't Ellie.

It was coming from Miss Thing. Singing along with the songs was usually totally frowned upon by the in-crowd, who laughed at and tortured the drama students. What was up? We were close enough for me to catch a few of her mutterings, and they made absolutely no sense. She sounded like "Chunga wunga moomba chumba, junga wunga boomba chunga."

All of a sudden she seemed to notice my stare, and she locked gazes with me. I continued shuffling my feet next to Ellie's, but I felt rooted to the floor. Those were not Bindi's own grey eyes; there was something horrifying in her gaze, more than just her usual nastiness and contempt for nerds like me. As she kept up her chant, I couldn't tear away my stare. Looking at her eyes was like looking down a manhole into the abyss, at the pure unadulterated evil of a woman possessed. Had George Renfield finally cracked and slipped her some weird new drug?

The music was faster now, and all the couples separated. Maybe there had been something in that punch, or the DJ had been drinking, because the music was getting weird. It swirled around us, changing keys, full of chromatic runs, first going into the lowest frequencies I could stand, then throbbing into a techno version of a drum circle, except with high-pitched wailing. A red light strobed, picking out each couple in turn. The dance floor became one big animal, a hive, an anthill of synchronized, syncopated movement.

The chaperones melted into the corners. Shadowy, darkening, the room even smelled weird, the applewood smoke odor replaced by the faint stench of an overheated barbecue grill as the music pulsed faster and faster. I jerked as the doors to the outside swung closed with a pop, making me feel the air had been sucked out of the room the way it was rumored you could do if you slammed all the doors of a car at once. The air tasted singed, grew thicker. I started to ask Ellie if her asthma was acting up, because I felt I could hardly draw a breath, but I saw her eyes were glazed over, cloudy, as were everyone else's nearby. My instincts said to lie low, let no one know that I wasn't hypnotized—if that was what was happening. I deliberately slowed my breathing, barely holding down a panic attack.

The masks on the walls came alive, smiling. No, grimacing. The statuary seemed to be moving, the topiaries from the tables becoming Shetland sheepdogs circling us, hemming us in. In our center, Bindi quivered, vibrating all over with the force of the chant. She was encircled by a swirling fog. No: demons swirled in the very air around her. I didn't believe in them, but what else could they be? Forms swarmed in the fog, patterned light that suggested grimacing faces, glowing hooves, bodies checkered red and black. This had to be an optical illusion. Yeah, that was what it was: Bindi was putting on a show for us. No wonder the tickets had cost a mint. That girl didn't settle for being the center of attention; she had to be the biggest exhibitionist in the place.

I felt the shift in the mood of the room. The music pulsed, the circular beat throbbing over us, washing everyone with a frenzied wave of desire. The room grew warmer, even more airless and close —no, unbearably humid and hot. It made me claustrophobic. I tried to bolt, then merely to stand still, but I could not. My arms and legs moved on their own, without my thinking about them. I couldn't resist dancing.

We all took our places around the Queen of the Prom. Spontaneously we formed a circle around Bindi as she chanted and yowled like a cat in heat, the song bewitching us with its charms, even though I couldn't understand a word of it. Her hands rose ecstatically, and her skin grew dusky. She broke into a shimmy, her skin crawling. I did a double take and realized it wasn't her skin crawling—it was the serpents.

Bindi was draped with living serpents, hissing and undulating as they snaked across up and down her arms and the length of her torso. She had shed Renfield in favor of a large, sinuous reptilian partner. I noticed that I was no longer dancing with Ellie. My new partner was a slithery-looking albino woman with red irises for eyes and pointed dragon teeth, moth-eaten cottonball hair in clumps, and a drippy pointed nose. Her long crooked arms kept reaching for me as she stomped her extremely bowed legs in their odd boots with long, twisted wire laces. An incubus, or was it a succubus?

Ellie was next to me, dancing with a similarly appointed creature. I couldn't turn away or change partners; I was somehow linked to this creature, as if it were buying me from a store and I was obligated to stand for inspection and consumption. Its eyes glimmered as my head swiveled back towards it.

Okay, I would resign as president of the Skeptics Club. Atheists eventually dig foxholes, and I had to acknowledge there was no other explanation for this, no way these weirdoes could have gotten in here. This was a supernatural event.

Everyone's dancing had gone beyond the "*Dirty Dancing*" style and become quite indecent. I felt foreign tendrils at the edge of my consciousness as my minion scrutinized me. Perhaps these beings were feeding on the sexual energy of all the dancers. They meant to work us into a frenzy and then kill us, kind of like what I saw metaphorically in the book.

The book! It must be the reason I still had my wits. I slipped my hand inside my jacket during a particularly contorted dance move, on the pretext of an itch. My fingers closed around the blessed tome. It was warm to my touch.

I eased the book out just as the maniacal laughter started, coming from Bindi and each of our demons. They knew we were trapped. What they apparently didn't know is that I wasn't under the spell. I opened the book and saw wriggling runes that suddenly resolved into words:

"It's about time. Quickly, read me. Aloud."

"By circle, crescent, and star..." I felt completely ridiculous, but no one seemed to hear me, so I continued, louder. "By circle, crescent, and star," I read, pointing to each ikon on the page in turn, like a child deciphering his first primary reader, "show me what powers here there are."

A swirling vortex formed around us, obscuring the trappings of the ballroom. We were at the eye of a storm, a hurricane sans rain. The wind teased those at the edges, lifting skirts and shawls and mussing hair.

"The winds are being called to accomplish the next step. Act swiftly," urged a baritone voice next to my ear. I looked around, but saw no one. Again, the voice: "Read now."

I licked my lips. No sound issued forth when I opened my mouth. Laryngitis or magickal strangulation?

I looked back down at the book. "Issue the challenge now," continued the spidery writing, "unless you desire all the mortals in this room to have their souls devoured by the chimayos." Following this, there were several lines written all in capitals, and I knew these comprised my spell.

"Hear me, O judges, the keepers of the hidden powers. Hear me in this, the most secret of appointed hours." I spoke in a loud voice, aiming my words at Bindi.

"What? Who's that?" She peered over the still-glowing footlights. "I command thee, be still."

Everybody was staring. I opened my mouth and found it cotton-dry. I struggled to form words. Now I knew what writers meant by a "red miasma," because the color itself surrounded me. It's tough to explain. But as the redness tried to overcome me, I knew I was having an effect. The letters squiggled on the page as I read aloud, and I could hardly make out the words, sensing the book's excitement as well as my own impending panic.

"By the power of the sea, the fire, the leaf, and the rock, I call for fairness. Justice is being mocked. By the spirits of the air, the wing, the claw, and the moon, I challenge the authority of this spell of doom."

Demons swirled around me in the red fog. I struggled to keep my voice from cracking; it was an effort to speak.

All at once the mask I'd noticed earlier materialized as a six-foot-tall face in the air before me, a spirit made solid. My heart tom-tommed, but I managed to keep a grip on my book. The lady mask's expression was no longer demure as it met my gaze.

Its lips formed words. "Who dares challenge the chimoyas summoned here tonight for the feasting on mortal spirits?"

"I do." I couldn't believe I was saying it. I tried to read the next lines forming on the page, but my voice seized up and I couldn't get enough air. Words wouldn't form in my mouth. Help. Oh shit, what do I do now?

"Dammit, Fred. I can't believe this." Behind me, my sister's voice.

I couldn't take my eyes off the demonic image, but a stupid question popped out of my mouth. "Sharron, how did you get here?"

"I'm not here, you ass. Well, I am, but I'm not there physically yet." Lights flashed around me as Sharron's voice spoke urgently into my ear, although I couldn't see her anywhere. "I was at a gathering when I felt power going out of the book. Naturally, we heard this magickal ruckus for miles." Her voice took on a tone of scolding. "It's a wonder your meddling hasn't killed you yet. When I realized what must have happened, I started scrying to find you. And now I see you are in it butt-deep."

"Sorry."

Her image appeared then between me and the face, thin as through water, and wavering. "I'm projected through the astral plane. I can't get there quick enough physically, so I can't send power to help you, but only give advice."

Apparently, she was powerful enough that the mask had paused, as though she had her turn in a formal debate. Sharron was in full witches-from-Macbeth regalia. I reached for her arm, but my hand shot through her. "Can we fight them off if we all link arms and pray, believing that right will triumph?"

Her image stabilized. "All that New Age stuff about joining hands and concentrating, clapping for Tinker Bell—well, it's like a Chihuahua repelling a Caterpillar; not the insect, but the earth mover. Use the book."

"What's going on, Sissie?"

"It's fairly obvious. That queen of yours has promised the African spirits your life-force in exchange for her institution as a devil's mage."

"I always knew she was a b--a witch...."

Sharron's virtual lip curled. "I wouldn't do it, myself. Think of the rule of three, the karma returning later to blast her three times as bad. But it's up to her." She shrugged. "She'll have hell to pay, pardon the pun." Her image lifted one eyebrow. "I'll read that to you if you're having trouble."

Movement down on the page caught my eye. The letters were now in a big primary-school chalkboard font, red and glowing. "Hurry, idiot!"

Sharron chanted with me the invocation from the book. "Spirits of the land, sea, and air, hear me out: this is not fair. These mortals have given no consent, for sacrifice is not their bent. Your agreement now we must contest. She had no authority, thus these mortals should still be free. Before you take them, we must ask of thee: give us a test, see who's the best."

The mask's motherly voice answered. "Our powers are well matched." It--she--mask stared at me. "Unlikely as it seems, we must honor your challenge. Yet you are not one of us, nor is the mortal woman yet." He meant Bindi, furious nearby, all fists and clenched teeth. "So the battle must be decided using a metaphor that our two mortals can comprehend."

The room dissolved away. We were alone, Bindi and I, standing on a grassy field. So we would choose avatars and fight with teeth to the death, then. But white lines painted themselves every few yards along the grass, and I realized where we were. A football field.

Bindi's excitement sounded in her voice. "Home team advantage. Go, Scouts!"

"No." I couldn't play it this way. "That wouldn't be a fair trial. I don't even watch pro games on the squawkbox. Let's have something fairer."

The mask's voice reached me, and I heard its eyebrows ratcheting up a notch. "You are bold to ask. Speak forth."

"Endgame." I gestured. The playing field blurred, morphed underfoot, becoming a life-size chessboard complete with living chessmen at the ready.

"No!" shrieked Miss Thing. "A board game, all right, but not one so hard. I can't do this one."

Obligingly the field beneath our feet changed, and now we were standing in the Secret Square. The mask hung in the dark sky over us, clouds scudding around its evil bulk.

"Tic-Tac-Toe? Oh, piddly-poop!" I heard Ellie yell from a corner of my imagination.

"Not so straightforward as it may appear," said the devil mask. "You must win each cell."

"Just like Tick-Quack-Dough and Hollyweird Squares!" said Miss Thing, satisfaction in her voice.

The mask put a spotlight on me, then quickly swapped it to her. "For your mark. Which square?"

She had the sense to choose the middle square of the grid. I was toast. Although I knew that the prayers of a sinner could go unheard, and figured that since I had dug this hole when I stole the witch-book I probably didn't deserve angelic help, I started praying: Please, if you can forgive whatever I've done to separate myself from prayer, from You, please hear me and save us, save us all. But I didn't know whether my prayer could go though. I was, after all, in the midst of the sin of speaking to devils.

"Riddle me this." The demon smiled. "A tiny tree, despite its size, can dig and dig for a yummy prize. What is it?"

"Um... wait... what?" Bindi fumffered and waffled. A blank look, then anger. And foot-stomping.

The mask's tone darkened. "You must answer swiftly."

Bindi squinched up her face and stared upward. "A willow tree? Like, the roots toward the water?"

The spotlight extinguished itself, and one came on to highlight me. Over Bindi's shouts of, "I meant a little, bitty one!" came the question to me:

"Which square?"

"The same one, the middle."

"Good choice." It was mocking me, I could tell from the way its eye sockets flickered in amusement. "The same riddle."

My brain was a dry beach, the tide way out there, no ideas, not even an empty shell on the sand. Suddenly my sister's voice came to me. "I have the link again now. We're with you, Fred. You're an A student in English. Think about those old riddles in the Greek myths. But modernized a bit. We know you can do it, Fred." Her voice ebbed away, and I took a deep, prayerful breath.

The answer washed up on my mental shore. "A toothpick!"

The mask slowly formed a grin. An "X" appeared where I stood, in the middle gridhole.

"It's not fair!" Bindi yelped.

"Must we always be fair?" The voice was amused. The red smoky light swirled around us, and the demonic spotlight coalesced around Bindi again. "Choose me wise and play me well, or you may find yourself in..." The voice trailed off into what I had to think of as demonic laughter.

"Grandstanding," came Ellie's voice in my ear from far away, reminding me that somewhere back in the reality that I loved stood

Ellie and the others I meant to save. I wished this were some wacky kind of delusion. Could there have been LSD in the punch? But I had to use Ockham's Razor, think of Descartes' argument for trusting my senses, play it as if it were real... for as far as I could know, it was.

Bindi whined. "I need the top middle."

"Your riddle. Dry me, crumble me, boil me, I cool. Now what's in your cup alongside your gruel?"

She bit her lip. "What's gruel? No, wait; it's like oatmeal, so you must mean orange juice!"

The demon face turned to me as her spotlight faded and mine came up. "For that same square. Your answer?"

I closed my eyes. Which saint was the patron of fools? Hey. Anybody up there! Please, it's not for myself, but for all of these people. Send me a clue! I opened my eyes to face the demon. Like an answer to prayer, the word formed on my lips. "Tea!"

I could hear the applause in my head. The mask looked irritated. My "X" appeared top and center.

Bindi stomped both feet. "I summoned you; this just isn't fair."

"I do not answer to any mortal." The face shot her a withering look, eyes flashing. She cringed a bit, and I almost felt sorry for her. Almost. "Your square?"

She blocked me at center bottom. "Make it not weird."

"All right, then. A modern item you are very fond of." It chuckled. Bindi looked at me as though she'd like to melt me.

"Bubble, double, toil and trouble. Before I lose one more bubble, drink me down, on the double!"

She looked around wildly. "Is that Shakespeare? You know I flunked English. What bubbles? It has to be a witch's potion!"

The light faded around her and brightened around me. This one was tough. There could be so many correct answers: soda, beer, champagne—that one could be good, since it was invented by a monk. But I chose the one I thought would be Bindi's favorite. "A carbonated soft drink, like a Coke." My voice came out a hoarse whisper, but it reverberated through the room and the crowd as if I had shouted it. The mask closed its eyes and thunder rolled over our heads as the lights dimmed. In the demonic light I stood, unsure. Would they kill us anyway? Was there honor among demons?

"That is an answer that fits." The demon's voice was quiet, seductive. "It is not the one I sought. But by the rules, I cannot say you are incorrect." After a moment it spoke again. "We will test you with one last question. If you answer correctly, you will win the square."

I took a deep breath, almost choking on the odor of brimstone. Again I prayed silently. It couldn't hurt. My sister's voice sounded in my ear. "You can do it." Ellie's reached me, faintly: "I love you." It gave me new strength.

The demon's jeweled eyesockets sparked. "Light as a feather, though nothing's in it, but the strongest of you can hold it but for a minute. What is it?"

My mind was blank. Feathers, emptiness, barbells. I thought of technology defeating magic, but it didn't help. Time crawled past in slow motion. What was empty, light, unholdable...? Love, your temper, a child's awe, an angel, what?

The voice boomed forth, filling my ears. "We must have your answer immediately."

I sucked in a breath. Suddenly I knew I had the answer. "A breath of air!"

My third X appeared in the lower middle, and then a glowing crimson line shot through my row of X's. I had won.

Cheering noises brought my head up. On the ceiling, I saw a balcony full of people cheering. They were all my dead relatives, even Grandpa, and a teacher I used to love. "Gram!" My hands went up involuntarily, but they smiled and I started to recede, the field whooshing through time and space.

The gameboard segued away at our feet and left us standing back at the prom ballroom. We were back in the circle of mortals. From the stage, Bindi's eyes flashed at me. "You've crossed the wrong witch, Fred Harper!" Oy vey, I whispered to myself.

The demon voice addressed me again. "We bow to your victory, then--for now. Because it amuses us to, and because we have seldom seen your like. Few have the courage to do something as foolish." The lights dimmed, then brightened. "You have, however, enjoyed an unfair advantage. We will, if it amuses us, return when you have no such assistance."

Oy vey twice.

Then it threw me a spitball. "Yet now there is one more thing that you must do, and that is to make your payment to the powers you called upon. We shall be watching your solution." It faded away with a chuckle.

Our fellow revelers were still frozen in place as the mask withdrew, became simply a wall hanging. The wind had died, and the flickering candlelight revealed only a group of kids standing in a ballroom. Everyone seemed stunned. They blinked, gazed around with dazed expressions. How much had they seen, and what did they remember?

"What?" I looked back down at the book I still clenched. "What was that supposed to mean? How do I get everyone back to normal?"

My sister's image brightened in front of me; she stood, hands on hips, looking irritable, like a catfight-weary Elvira with dreadlocks.

"You heard him. Now you have to pay for the power you called upon, the power you volunteered to channel. Just like filling up the Camaro at the gas station."

"Even though it chose me?" This entity had, after all, sought me out.

She gave a short laugh. "It's only fair. You wanted to do what it suggested. And now you must restore the balance. After all, you never signed the contract it offered to begin with. It basically took you on good faith, the same as your gasoline credit card does. I suggest you fulfill whatever it asks of you."

I looked down at the writing in the book. When its meaning registered, I tried to close the book, but my hands wouldn't work. The entity—I realized I didn't even have a name to match to it—had reworked the contract that we'd seen this morning, except this time it had a name filled in beneath the dotted line.

It wanted Ellie.

Ellie was suddenly able to move. She rushed to my side and stared at the page. Then she looked up, unsure where to address her question. "You want me to pledge to become a ... sorceress?" Ellie's coffee eyes sparkled as I winced.

"No!" I knew she shouldn't do this. This was my fault, and I should be the one to pay. "Take me."

"You cannot become a witch." The writing didn't even hesitate this time.

"Why not?" I felt kind of insulted. "I was good enough to read the defense incantation."

"You do not truly trust the unseen." That was an understatement. "She has the spirituality we want. Unless you sacrifice your skepticism, you cannot sign." I thought I had done that tonight, but I wouldn't argue.

"I want to sign!" she cried, dismay written on her features. "But... I'll have to ask my priest."

The chandeliers dimmed, then rebrightened. I imagined that the book's entity, had I been able to see him or her, would have winced.

"You don't have time for consultations." Sharron sounded tired. "Just sign or don't sign. It's up to you. It's Fred who's got to give them what they want."

Ellie looked at me, then down at the book. A pen materialized in her hand. Before I could react, she scribbled something.

The contract glowed purple, and the writing erased itself as a sparkle of light raced all along the ink. To replace it, new writing scrolled out. "You will be contacted upon the next full moon. Until then, prepare yourself." The book squirmed in my hands, wanting to close. I obliged it, feeling hollow-chested. How had I let this happen? I should have been able to protect her. Taking her punished me more than taking me would have.

But Ellie's eyes shone with excitement. "Of course Father Geddes will never let me. But don't worry, Freddy—I didn't sign my right name."

"Oh, God," Sharron said. "Please don't tell me you pulled something like that. They know who you really are, you know."

I groaned. But whatever she'd done seemed to have worked, because gradually everyone started blinking, moving around, normalizing. A murmur started, and turned into a buzz of excited chatter. The DJ cued up an oldie, and everyone except Bindi resumed dancing, even though most looked somewhat bewildered. The spell had been dispelled, everyone's karma or whatever restored. Or did they even remember anything?

So I could be contacted again at any time by...whatever that was. The evil stuff. Great. I supposed it was up to the good entity to make the next contact, as well. I also supposed I would have to adjust to coping with two witches.

I shook my head. "Bad enough that I find out this morning my sister is this thing, but now you, too?"

"I know." Ellie looked sheepish. "But, wow, I'm flattered they wanted me. I'm kind of curious to see what happens next."

"Oh, God," said Sharron's voice as her image faded away. "You naïve little fool. I only hope they don't..." We didn't hear the end of her sentence. I was kind of glad.

Now people were flowing over, coming up to me, trying to congratulate me. George, down from the stage, punched me on the upper arm. "Wow. What a show!"

"Huh?"

"You and Ellie were the last people I'd have guessed that Bindi would choose to do that routine with her. But what a show! Man, you all had me convinced I was hypnotized there for a while." He shook his head. "Everybody's going to be talking about that little skit for a long time to come."

"Okay." I coped as well as I could as people continued to come by. Apparently, one or both entities had allowed them to experience the event as a little show put on for their benefit, with the use of slides or lasers or whatever kind of computer they imagined could do that, and everyone but Ellie and I was convinced we'd been hired as part of the entertainment. As the congratulations slowed down, I pulled Ellie aside and hugged her close. "Let's go home."

Sharron, in the flesh, confronted us at the door. "I told you, keep your hands off my stuff!"

"So you made it here. Only slightly rumpled, I see."

She threw me a look of disgust. "Getting here astrally and now physically wasn't a simple thing. But give me the book now, before you attract any more unwanted supernatural attention."

I flourished the book. "Here! Keep it happy and far away from me."

She snatched it away, and it disappeared into the folds of her black robe. Looking down at herself, she scowled. "Goddammit, I forgot about this outfit. I gotta get out of here before somebody notices me."

I got Ellie into the car without further ado.

"Aren't you glad we came to the prom after all?" Ellie's eyes were dreamy as she sighed, laying her head against my shoulder. She actually seemed to be energized by the evening's events.

"No." We looked at each other, and I sighed. "I love you, Elspeth Exia Valentine, but I can only hope that the next time you're up for some excitement... I'm not with you."

The Department of Prayers and Petitions

Stuart Barrow

Stuart has a PhD in Chemistry, and a strong desire to never again set foot in a laboratory. He is currently working for the Australian Public Service, which he finds rather agreeable, all things considered. This is his first published short story and he's feeling rather chuffed about it.

At the final interview, the Angel looked at me over its glasses. I'd never thought of Angels as having glasses. Or paunches. And the tie was a complete surprise.

"We'd like to offer you the job," it said. "We feel that our department would make good use of your abilities."

"Oh," I said. "Oh." I looked up at its face. I'd been expecting to be told I wasn't what they were looking for. "You, uh, know that I'm not exactly religious?"

"Yes," it said. "Nevertheless."

"And, uh, I was given to understand that one had to be, well, good. In a strict Catholic sense."

"We..." It paused. "At the present moment, we feel that our department does not require goodness so much as efficiency."

"Well, I—I don't know that...I mean, my last position..."

"Mr. Smith."

"Jones."

"Mr. Jones. We are offering you a unique opportunity. I have looked at your resume, and believe that, under our present circumstances, you represent everything we are looking for in an employee."

"Oh. Um, great. So, I'd be, what, an Angel?"

"You'd be an Associate Intercession Request Processing Officer, Class II."

"An..."

"Yes, Mr. Jones, you'd be an Angel. You'd be the Angel Jones."

I signed. I mean, their retirement plan alone was unbelievable.

* * * *

Nobody knows of the Angel Jones, of course. I was working under someone who I figured was the patron saint of minor bureaucratic flunkies, St. Worthington.

"Please," he said on my first day in the office, "Call me George." Everyone calls him St. Worthington, but I suspect he'd rather be St. George. Nobody ever prays to St. Worthington, even if he is a full IRPO.

The training officer was a cherub. At least, he was a short fat naked guy with wings—I hoped he was a cherub. Most of the training class just tried not to look at him. He showed us around the Office—Department of Prayer Receipts, the Filing Department, the Intercessions Department—and introduced us to some of the first-name saints. No-one big, you know, just a couple of the minor historical saints who weren't too busy, but they were the first people we'd met who had actually been ordained rather than just hired. We went past St. Jude's office. The Angel Saunders, who'd been hired as an associate intercession request processor (Class I) in Jude's office paled visibly at the sight of the ceiling-high piles of case-files. "Are all those Jude's?" she asked the cherub.

"No," he said, "Those are just yours."

The Angel Cruz showed me around our section, taught me the ropes.

"We handle assessments on prayers to the saints. Basically, people aren't always up on their mythology, and they'll pray to St. George when they want Theodore, or St. Christopher when they want Stephen, or anyone, when they just want someone to talk to. Those usually go to Dymphna, but there are exceptions. Jude's a special case—they've got specialist officers who decide when something really is a hopeless case. We don't handle 'OK, God, prove you exist and I'll believe in you' prayers anymore—send them down to storage. Anything else addressed to the Big Guys has probably been misfiled—put it in the refiling pile with a red sticker on it. The Big Boss is a bit of a micromanager, likes to look at everything himself. One regular case in ten goes to him for checking." He pointed to another pile.

"That'd have to be a lot of cases," I said.

"Well, he *is* God," said Cruz.

I had a look at the case on top the refiling pile once: "deargodohgodI'mgoingtodiehelpmeplease..." There's a ten month backlog on prayers.

* * * *

It took me a while to get my head around the heavenly hierarchy. Essentially, the way I figure it, you're hired as an Angel, and then you get promoted to Archangel, who seems to be an Angel in charge of other Angels. After that it gets complicated, with cherubs and dominions and thrones and seraphs—obviously there's an order to it, but it's pretty hard to work out. The higher guys have more wings and bigger haloes, except for the cherubs, who are short fat naked people with dinky wings. Gender is pretty much optional for the higher ranks. Well, except for the cherubs.

Cruz came into my cubicle one day. "Prayer for you, Jones." I was stunned, but it turned out to be from my sister, wishing me well in my new job. I'd been there almost a year. "Mum's still a bit confused about the whole thing. I told her you weren't dead but had gone to a better place, and she went off about goldfish and stuff. You know what she's like. By the way, I know it's a lot to ask, but I've applied for a job at the Department of Health—can you do anything to help?" I wasn't authorized to perform intercessions myself, so I passed the prayer on to St. Worthington. Made his day. My sister, ten months in the Department of Health, was promoted twice in the next six weeks. I made Class I before any of the other Class IIs in my induction. It's not what you know, I suppose.

The next time I saw the recruiting Angel was at my performance appraisal. It had lost the tie and the glasses, but not the paunch. It asked me how I was settling in. "Have you considered Guardian duty?" it asked me. I'd met my first Guardians only recently, while I was having a drink with Cruz one evening at the *Peaceful Rest*. Scary little guys, they earnestly want what's best for you. It freaked me out.

"Not really, sir," I said.

"Your performance has been quite good, I see."

I didn't say anything. I'd seen Worthington's statistics, and I was on just the other side of average. It asked me a few other questions, whether I felt I was maximizing my potential and if Heaven could help in any way to do so, how I was enjoying my work, and so forth.

"Do you have any questions about the process?" it asked. It brushed its wings out of its eyes. I hadn't noticed how many pairs it actually had at the interview.

"No, sir."

"Any questions about Heaven in general?"

"No, sir."

It signed the form. "Thank you, Smith. That will be all." I didn't correct it. It had signed the form for the Angel Jones.

Saunders and I were selected for an exchange to the Chinese Afterlife, as a goodwill exercise or something. I'm hazy on their background, but they pretty much invented the whole celestial bureaucracy thing. Their postage service was unbelievably efficient —I suppose with ancestor worship it has to be. My sister's prayers reached me almost as soon as she sent them (usually Christmas and my birthday). Of course, I still had to forward them to St. Worthington for intercession, so it's not like she got a timeliness advantage, but, you know, it was nice. Saunders and I were broke the whole time we were there (next time I'll tell my sister to burn some money for us) but it was fun. I dread to think about the poor Chinese guy who had my job for two months, though. Not to mention Saunders'.

I got to know Saunders pretty well after that. She told me that they mostly hired devout Catholics and dedicated bureaucrats in our office—most other denominations' prayers go straight through to the Big Boss, but it seems to depend on the tenets of the sect. I'd imagine that Catholics have a head for hierarchies that would be an advantage there. I told Saunders that I wasn't really a Catholic or a bureaucrat, and she said she knew because she'd looked at my personnel record before China. She said she thought I did pretty well, though.

Cruz told me he was thinking about applying for Guardian duty. He was evasive as to why, but I narrowed it down to one of two reasons: a desire to do more earthly good than he could as an administrative Angel, or a desire for the Angel Desmeine, a Guardian he'd met once at the *Rest*.

Worthington invited me into his office one day. The recruiting Angel was there.

"Jones, um, I believe the Principality has, um, an offer for you." He looked nervous.

"Sir?" I asked.

The Angel checked his clipboard quizzically, then looked up and said, "Jones, we'd like to offer you a development opportunity." St.

Worthington flinched slightly. "We've been very impressed with your work, and we'd like to offer you a position in one of the offsite offices."

"Oh. Oh, I see."

"You, uh, don't have to take it," said Worthington. "It's purely voluntary."

"Of course," said the recruiting Angel. "Of course."

I told them I'd need to think about it.

Saunders wasn't impressed. Well, if she was impressed, she sublimated it into sarcasm.

"You're not seriously considering it," she said.

"Well, I was." I had been. You can't stay an administrative Angel for eternity, I figured.

"You do know what they're offering."

"I, uh… it's a promotion, I suppose."

"Jones, you're an idiot."

I said, "Hey!" but it was perfunctory. She had a point. I had no idea what she was talking about, and I wasn't really clear on what the duties of the new position were.

"Think about this, Jones. You've got Heaven. It's where God lives and works. How many offsite offices do you think we have?"

"Well… there'd be one on Earth, wouldn't there?"

"Yes, Jones, that's why we have Guardians. And you, Jones, are not a Guardian."

"There's messengers."

"Yes. And are you a messenger?"

"So, it's, what, Baptist Heaven? Anglican Heaven? Do they have Angels?"

"Still onsite, Jones. You're probably not metaphysically fit, anyway."

"So, if we're not talking about Earth, and it's still offsite, it can't be…Oh…"

I tried to sound Worthington out about the whole thing, but he became rather difficult to chase down. He wouldn't meet my eye when I finally did get hold of him, and I decided not to bother. Most of the other Angels in the office started avoiding me. I mean, it was supposed to be voluntary, but they were acting like I'd already grown horns or something.

Cruz was fairly good about it, though. He still talked to me at the *Rest*, anyway.

"They're just like us, really, aren't they?" he said one night, after a few pints.

"Just like me, anyway," I replied.

"I mean, it's all part of the same stuff, isn't it? You've got us, you need them. There'd be no point us being here if it wasn't for them being there."

"Are you going to get philosophical? I don't think I can handle that right now."

"Have another drink, then."

"I mean, why bother hiring me in the first place, if you're planning on sending me there all along? It doesn't make any sense."

"You want to know what doesn't make sense?"

"Giving you more beer? You *are* getting philosophical."

"Apart from that. You've never wondered how the Hell God gets behind on the paperwork? Our whole damned job doesn't make any sense."

"Cruz, you really should watch your language." I forced a smile. "For Heaven's sake."

I think it was Saunders that decided me, in the end. She decided to go Earthside. I thought she meant Guardian duty, but she didn't.

"I'm going to try for sainthood," she told me. "There really isn't much scope here for promotion—it's not like there's going to be any vacancies on the Seraphim council or anything. Whereas I can go back home, perform a few miracles, die, get beatified, bang, instant career. And it's not like I'm low on faith anymore."

"You know, a while ago the thought of death as a vital career move might have been unsettling."

"It's not so different from what you're doing."

"I haven't decided to do it, yet."

"You have. And I've decided to do this."

"But why? You're doing a pretty important job. I couldn't do it. They need you here."

"Jones, we don't get prayers until ten months after they're prayed, at least, and that's if we get them at all. Did you know that they estimate that something like 24% of prayers go completely unanswered? And in our section..." She shuddered. "I really don't want to talk about it. But you can't just stamp something and refile it and expect that to make everything better."

I didn't know what to say. "And you're really sure about this? You think you'll be better off in the real world?"

"Yes, Jones. I really think I will."

"I mean, it's a pretty nasty world, especially after being here for so long. You'll be completely on your own! I suppose you could always pray, but..." I shrugged helplessly.

"I'll plan ahead. I have thought about this, Jones."

"I can try and look out for you, if you want. I think I'll have intercession privileges in the new position."

She smiled, then. "Probably not exactly what I need, Jones, but I appreciate the offer. You're not bad. Not all bad, anyway."

"Saunders, do you know why they offered me this position?"

"I think so. It makes a certain kind of sense. I mean, they cause enough problems down there without us appointing people who are actually *evil.* And obviously they can't be trusted to do their own recruiting, there'd be all sorts of problems with that. So, you're a nice enough guy, but you're on the books as being, you know, a bit of a sinner, so it's not like we're appointing the Archangel Gabriel or anything."

"So it was pretty much fated from the start."

"I don't really know our position on fate, but, yeah, pretty much."

"So why did you try and talk me out of it?"

"I...think you're better than that, Jones. I really do."

So, Saunders resigned, and I decided to go with what I'd been hired for. I felt that if I wasn't actually going to be doing any good anyway, at least I'd be doing something necessary in the grand scheme of things. I made sure my sister's prayers would be forwarded to Worthington, and wished Cruz luck with the Guardian thing, hung up my halo and swapped my wings over.

You could say my career went to Hell, but I think it could have been worse.

The Eternal Reward

Tom Dullemond

Tom Dullemond was born in Holland, but now lives in Brisbane, Australia with his lovely wife Clare. He has sold fiction to the '*AustrAlien Absurdities*' anthology and the '*Hastur Pussycat! Kill! Kill!*' *anthology*. Tom can be found roaming the internet at www.asmoday.com. He is probably not going to heaven.

Blessed be, I sighed, and it was my last. My deathbed was a prison from which I rose with relief and an almost feverish anticipation. I lifted slowly, carefully, from my mortal remains, and turned to hang facedown in the air of the hospital room. The ever-present pain trickled from me into the body below me. Around me my friends and family prayed with all their hearts. I could feel their breath against my ephemeral skin, buoying me upwards, their prayers charging the air. They did not see me die, so devout were they in their worship; faces clenched, fists clenched, jaws clenched.

I was glad to go, under the circumstances. I did not care to glance down at my body as I hovered above it—I knew what I would see, since I'd been seeing it in the shaving mirror for months now: old, papery skin; a feeble framework of a man, like a sagging papier-maché mannequin hanging off its chicken-wire skeleton. I was not that old, in years, but my body was ancient. I died peacefully, and I did not even hear my death rattle as I floated above.

I heard nothing.

I slowly rolled in the air, until I faced the off-white plastered ceiling. A tiny crack ran from one corner of the small room to the other, and I tracked it with my uncannily clear vision as I rose on prayer, like a ship's sail catching the wind. I could feel myself billowing in the metaphysical breeze.

Daring a glance behind, still charged with the rapture of my death, I saw only white mist. It did not deter me, for after all there was no point in returning, and in amazement I ran a hand through my hair—only to find I *had* hair. Gone were my grey wisps. In a rapturous frenzy I ran my hands over my face, and found it just as I remembered before my illness. I was in my mid-thirties again; I had shed ten years as easily as I had shed my mortal form. I praised the Lord in my heart, closing my eyes in thanks, and found I was wearing my finest Sunday suit—charcoal with matching tie—and a crisply starched white shirt.

The mists suddenly parted and I was left standing in a vast opulent hall. The ceiling was a flamboyant fresco of cherubic angels and richly clad Renaissance hedonists some thirty feet above. Uncountable gold-trimmed pillars of purest alabaster reached from an immaculate marble floor to support this vast heaven of art.

It was a little too Catholic, as far as I was concerned, but who was I to complain about the Lord's choice of décor? I stood in the centre of the hall, lost, but I was not afraid.

Presently the sound of heels on marble came floating on the air. I turned until I spotted a young man in a double breasted jacket in the distance, barely visible for the pillars that stretched out into the distant brightness. He was walking directly towards me, head down as he made some notations on a small notepad. I stared at this perfectly mundane image—a young businessman on his way home after work—and tried to reconcile it with the rococo architecture through which he walked. I muttered a prayer to calm my heart.

He must have been fifty yards away when he looked up from his notes, still walking, and said, "John E. Murray? Pastor?" His voice was as clear as if he'd been standing right next to me. Astounded, I nodded, and he saw that slight movement across all that distance.

He continued to move towards me at his unhurried pace, and asked, "What's the 'E' stand for, then?" He had one of those smarmy English accents, and I stood straighter as he approached, refusing to answer until he was a decent distance away from me.

"Ezekiel," I said tightly. Some of the rapture was fading from my extremities, and I began to wonder if the Good Lord was testing me before my final ascension.

"Right-o. Small filing error. No probs. Follow me." He'd only just reached me, and without stopping continued right past. Surprised, and a little offended, I turned and eventually followed. The Englishman finished writing something and tucked the notebook away inside his jacket.

"Always good to see a man o' God," he said over his shoulder, by way of making light conversation. "Where you from, then?"

I blinked, confused by the steady progression of pillars on either side of me, the unending ceilings of art, as if every man who had ever lived was painted there, staring at me. "Where are we going?" I didn't think my place of origin was of any great importance here.

"Well, you've earned your eternal reward, right?"

I nodded dubiously.

"So what's your pleasure?"

I stopped nodding. "What do you mean, precisely?"

"What's your pleasure? What do you like to do? What do you *want* to do? You've got an awful lot o' time to fill." He laughed, and reached inside his jacket with one hand, pulling out a battered packet of cigarettes. He mumbled something, but I was so shocked at the sight of the vile tobacco that I missed it. When I realised he was offering me one I nearly choked.

He eventually shrugged and put the packet away. "Don't blame you—never did get the hang of them m'self. The name's Daniel, by the way." He may have held out his hand but I ignored him, eyes closed, begging the Lord for strength. This Daniel was clearly some devil in disguise, trying to tempt me, and I would have none of it. What a thoroughly unpleasant individual.

After that uncomfortable encounter Daniel kept his mouth shut. We walked through the interminable architecture for what must have been ages, until suddenly I spotted a change in the distance—the pillars and artwork ceased there, and instead a vast blue open sky stretched out over the endless marble tiles.

And now I saw other people in the distance, through the forest of pillars, all heading for this open space. Most of them had a 'guide' like Daniel here. I prepared myself in case he tried something.

No preparations were sufficient to shield me from the sight that met my eyes when I stepped onto the plain, however. My jaw dropped and I gasped. Daniel kept walking, but I was lost and had to stop.

Ahead of me on this open plain of marble stood the largest city I had ever seen, cast beneath a black shadow like a stain over the bright plain around it. It dwarfed the interminable skyline of New York, that monstrous den of filth I'd had the displeasure of visiting once in my youth, and pulsed with a fierce corrupt life. It was a vast concrete, steel and glass expanse, lit garishly by myriad electric and neon lights. Skyscrapers clawed at the night sky, reflecting the red, yellow and green lights of a bustling metropolis. I noticed that a lot of the people I'd seen had abandoned their guides and were running with joy towards the city.

Daniel was talking to me.

"Excuse me?" I asked carefully. I didn't want to upset him, really. If he was a sinner—or worse, a devil—I did not need to hate him. Either way the Lord had already condemned him, and so I should feel only pity in my heart.

"That's the City o' God," Daniel said proudly, and pulled out the packet of cigarettes again. I didn't know why—he hadn't lit one before. He started patting his chest and pants pockets until he'd convinced himself he could not find what he was looking for. "Goddamn cigarettes. You got a light? No, o'course not. Fuckin' hell."

I was still reeling from the jab of his casual blasphemy when he delivered his uppercut of a profanity and sent me reeling. I stared, horrified, at this madman.

"What's wrong?" he asked, and he looked genuinely concerned. "You all right?"

"I..." I wanted to tell him that I *could* forgive him, that there was hope for him even now, when it seemed too late. Perhaps he usually wandered through the pillars, always in sight of this black City of God, never quite reaching it. I glanced at the sprawling city and was not wholly convinced of its Godliness.

"What's up with you? Nervous?"

"I can forgive you, Daniel, for your profanities. The Lord loves you very very much; he loves all his children. If you come with me, I can—"

"Hey hey hey! Stoppit right there, pal."

I stopped, more in surprise than anything else.

"Don't deny Him, Daniel. If you embrace Jesus in—"

"Listen Pastor, I'm a bloody Catholic Priest, all right? Or I was. I spent my whole life telling people what you're trying to tell me. I'm bloody sixty-five. I'm only doing this chaperoning gig on the side, for a bit of a change."

A Catholic. That explained it. I was surprised he wasn't burning in Hell.

Daniel read my face and frowned. "Now don't get all high and mighty with me. I'm *clean*. Otherwise I wouldn't be here, you idiot. Otherwise *you* wouldn't be here." That seemed to be enough explanation from him. "Now let's get cracking, OK? It's Tuesday, and there's an orgy on in Matthias' Hall tonight—I don't want to miss it. You're welcome, if you feel up to it." He began to chuckle at some personal joke, but stopped when I did not join in his mirth. In fact, while he seemed sinfully keen to continue, I did not take as much as a step towards this 'City of God' where it clung to the horizon like a foul wart. Around us, in the distance, another trickle of new arrivals burst from the pillars and the high-ceilinged art to rush in joy towards its spires and lights.

"There are a lot of people going to your City," I observed, trying to erase the last few seconds of conversation from my mind.

"That's nothing, really. You should see the truckloads being delivered to Hell. It don't stop."

"I think you're a devil sent to corrupt me," I said frankly. I was dead, after all. Daniel just stared at me.

Then he burst into laughter. "I'm a devil? A-haaa ha!" He coughed once, a sharp bark, then cleared his throat. "I've been called a lot of things, but that's a first. A fucking devil, ha ha! Well, it doesn't matter anyway. You're here now, you're saved. Doesn't matter what the hell I am. You going to join us in that orgy or what? If you're not ready for sex, I know a guy who does a great buffet. There's all the food you can eat here, and more. All part o' the deal."

I was praying so hard that I didn't even notice the way he peppered his words with casual filth. A Catholic priest indeed! I caught his last words and leapt on them. "A 'deal'? A devilish pact, I fear. What's your part of this bargain?"

"I've done my bit," he said. "I spent my life practising what I preached, not coveting anyone's ass, that kind of thing. Now I'm here. I used to run a hostel for the poor before I died."

I was having trouble understanding what he was trying to tell me. It was difficult enough to accept that this blaspheming man had been a priest, but that he also expected me to believe that he'd spent his life doing charitable works...? And here he was inviting me into an...an *orgy*? He was certainly a devil, and I did not really wish to continue my conversation with him.

With this in mind, I said, "I cannot believe that a pious man, even a Catholic, would be suffered to stoop to such acts of debauchery here. You are a liar, sir—one more sin to add to your litany."

Daniel was shaking his head. "Hello—this is the eternal reward, mate. Reward. You understand that part? Now come on to the City. If you have any questions someone'll be able to answer them there."

I steeled myself but followed. It was clear that this lost soul had led me straight to the edge of the Pit, the eternally shadowed City far ahead of us. I had faith in the Lord's wisdom, though, which is why I let him guide me there. I was certain that somehow my presence here was fated, that I was sent to encounter Daniel that I might bring his soul to Salvation.

* * * *

Soon enough I realised this so-called City of God was beyond belief.

I'd grown ever more apprehensive as Daniel led me closer to its boundaries and we came under its dark shadow. It was noticeably cooler there, like a fine summer evening back home, except that I could hear the wailing of thousands of lost souls—wailing? It sounded more like *cheering*. I did my best to ignore the hundreds of other recently departed, most of whom headed ecstatically to their damnation. Daniel, too, seemed buoyed by the proximity of the City. Was all of Hell celebrating Damnation? I held on to the strength of my faith, but I did not believe for a moment that I would be able to save them *all*.

The marble floor turned to bitumen here, and then we were on a road, a wide freeway. There were no cars (thank the Lord for small mercies), just hundreds of souls, wearing a bewildering array of garments of all colours.

Something incredibly bright and incredibly beautiful appeared on a balcony overlooking the freeway, a balcony on perhaps the fifth floor of a huge hotel. It looked like a man, but he was flawless, perfect. Daniel followed my gaze and laughed with glee. He began to point out the brightness to some of the other souls, and shortly everyone was cheering and pointing. The bright man did not react, but simply watched. I began to have an inkling of what—or rather who—that figure was, but Daniel grabbed my hand and said, cheerfully, "See. That's proof enough—that's an angel, right there, in the flesh, so to speak. They're really quite nice, when you get to know 'em."

I did not dissuade him of his delusion. That had been an angel, certainly—the brightest angel of them all, Lucifer; their Lord and Master here in the Pit. I wondered how these poor souls could not see it. We thankfully passed beneath His foul gaze—could he smell me, one of the Saved, amidst all this sin? Our large group of newly departed souls began to mingle with a huge crowd of revellers. I saw new souls hug old ones in recognition; I saw lines of cheering faces throw confetti over crowds of strangers. To my relief, I recognised no one.

"We just have to finish the paperwork," Daniel said, as he grabbed me again. He began to lead me towards a vast row of booths stretched across the road. They looked like tollbooths. What was the toll here? One's immortal soul? Rows of newly arrived people stretched from the booths, trickling through on the other side to be swept up in the vast crowd of revellers. I saw bottles passed from celebrant to celebrant and looked away—only to catch a young couple *fornicating* in the shadows of an alley! I slowly tore myself away from the incredible spectacle, because Daniel was prodding me towards one of the booths. I moved several steps forward in the line, then looked over my shoulder for the couple, but the crowd blocked my view. Sinners!

Shortly we stood at the booth. Daniel produced his notepad and handed a piece of paper to the bored lady inside. She glanced at it. "Ezekiel," Daniel said at her questioning glance.

She nodded and typed something on a keyboard, reading text off a monitor. I wondered what she would say—it was unlikely that they would have my name on file here in the Pit.

"431st street," she said, mechanically, and handed me a key. "Apartment 72a."

I stared. Daniel grabbed my sleeve *again*, and dragged me past the booth. A hundred thousand sinners cheered my entrance into Hell.

* * * *

"How long have you been here?" I asked my guide as we boarded the train in a dingy subterranean station. Unable to resist an attempt at Salvation, or at the very least clarification, I added, "And don't you find it somewhat strange that the City of God is in permanent darkness?"

"Fifty years," Daniel responded immediately, though I thought he might have been only half-interested in my conversation. A coquettish young lady at the other end of the carriage was eyeing him, and he made no attempts to ignore her. Presently he answered my second question with, "If you want sunshine, you just got to go out of the City for a picnic, or something. There's plenty of forest out there. In the City it's not always night, you know, just mostly. It's so we don't ruin any parties. There's *always* a party on somewhere."

"You are a poor deluded sinner, trapped in Hell." It was the nicest thing I could say.

"And you're right here with me, you lucky sod. Now as much as I like you, and all, once we get to your apartment I'm out of 'ere, right? I have places to go, you know."

I could not respond to that at all—I was only here to try to save him. Otherwise I would have left this city right now and...what precisely? I felt a thin prickle of dread. How would I find Heaven in that infinite hall? I could only hope that when whatever trial I was faced with had ended, that someone saintlier than Daniel would lead me there.

I couldn't let it end there, though, not while I had another quarter hour train ride ahead of me. "Why are you not concerned for your eternal soul, Daniel? Surely you don't want to spend eternity among the Damned?"

He broke contact with the young lady, and frowned angrily at me. Obviously I had hit a sore point. "Are you going to get it through your fuckin' head that *this is not Hell!* Why the hell would you be in Hell? Obviously you must have been following the rules pretty closely, or I wouldn't have been sent to get you!"

His argument was circular—he was trying to convince me that we were not in Hell because I would not have arrived here if it were. Although that was flattering, I have never been a prideful man and would not accept his mad logic.

"I think I am here to save you, Daniel, or at least to try."

"Why would I want to be any more saved than I already am? This place is great. The people are friendly and exciting; you can do anything—and anyone—you like. There's music, dance, food, women. If this is Hell—shit."

"If this is *Heaven*," I countered, ignoring his language, "then where are the churches?"

He looked at me very strangely. The rattle of the train tracks filled the silence.

"Well?"

Daniel stared at me. "What the hell do we need churches in *Heaven* for? You want to talk to God? Pick up the bloody phone! It might take you a couple of years to get through, but the hold music's pretty good and we have plenty o' time." He laughed.

I was not laughing. This poor soul was lost indeed—he *liked* it in this place. He was damned and wanted to *stay* damned. It was incredible. I prayed for guidance, but I did not know if the Lord could hear me here.

The train slowed at my stop, and Daniel threw me my apartment keys.

"Now off you go and get settled. When you're feeling a bit less grumpy you can come and look me up—I'm in the register. See ya!"

I stepped out onto the platform, alone. The roar of the train faded into the distance and I looked at the key in my hand. A small red plastic tag had the apartment's address printed on it in dot matrix characters. I sighed and began to climb the stairs. I should have known that it would not be easy to carry the Damned out of the Pit once they were in.

The streets here were by no means as crowded as those near the entrance to the city, but there was still a sizeable mob of shoppers, garishly lit by bright neon advertising as they marched from shop to café to restaurant. Someone was singing a song in the distance. The streets were clean.

I shook my head and found a street directory. 461st street was just around the corner, and praying against all hope I made my way through the crowds and into a long street of apartment blocks. Lights blazed happily through countless living room windows. I could see movement behind a couple of them but did not look too closely as I passed, remembering my earlier glimpse of that dirty couple.

Apartment 72a was small, clean, and pleasant. For a brief moment I was confused—this tidy establishment was not the kind of place I expected to see in Hell, but then again nothing I had seen so far since leaving the mists that had brought me here had been what I expected. Several small books had been arranged on a single neat bed. I regretted not having a Bible with me—I always found it comforting in these moments.

The thickest of the books said:

John. E. Murray
GUIDE TO HEAVEN
(721st Ed.)

in large gold print on a brown vinyl cover.

That was the point where everything stopped for me. *Everyone* here thought this was Heaven. I supposed that without anyone like myself to remind them of their sins, they wouldn't know any differently, especially if the literature itself encouraged their delusion.

Slowly I opened the self-styled 'Guide to Heaven'. There was a map of the city, with large sections highlighted and marked with numbers for later reference, I supposed. Flicking through the book I saw map after map, interspersed with occasional colour photos and short passages of text. I read one at random. "*Gargouille's Early French Cuisine* is one of the oldest and best established restaurants on the Strip," it gushed. "*Gargouille's* has recently undergone a change of management, but this reviewer vouches that for sheer elegance and gastronomic ecstasy with an old-style European bent, it—" I snapped the guide shut in disbelief and dropped it back on the bed. A small folder lay beside it, and when I opened it I was faced with a telephone directory. "Emergency Numbers" the heading exclaimed in bright yellow.

The top number was 0-777, and the descriptive text was 'The Trinity (expect minor delays)'.

The other numbers listed the disciples, the apostles, and a handful of important martyrs. At the bottom a separate line read, "Dial 0 for general enquiries". I reached for the telephone and dialled '0'.

Five seconds later a recorded voice was bleating in my ear.

"For problems with accommodation, please press '1'. For public transport inquiries, please press '2'. For—" I waited for the menu option that would let me speak to an operator and angrily stabbed the button.

Five seconds later another recorded voice—a man's voice this time—told me that I was 302nd in line, and that my call was appreciated. If I could just wait, an operator would be with me shortly. Vivaldi's 'Il Pastor Fido' began to play in the background and I hung up. I *liked* 'Il Pastor Fido.'

I began to shake uncontrollably. If this was Heaven, as everything seemed to indicate, it was a foul, corrupt Heaven.

I picked up the 'Guide to Heaven' and flicked through it again. I closed my eyes when I spotted a section headed 'Red Light District' and flicked instead to the index. Somewhere there must be a...I found a section titled 'Administration'.

On the relevant page I found a small number, printed almost as an afterthought. It said, 'Complaints'.

I got through immediately, which was a relief. A rather surprised young woman's voice said, "You wish to *what*?"

"This is 'Complaints', isn't it?"

"Y...yes."

"I wish to speak to someone in charge. I am very unhappy with this city. I fear that the Lord Jesus—" and I swallowed here at my imminent blasphemy, "I fear He is not aware of the foul pit His glorious City has become."

"You...?" The lady put the phone down and I could hear some frantic scrabbling. Something knocked the receiver and I heard muffled voices. Then the phone was picked up again and an infinitely warm, smooth as liquid bronze voice asked me, "How can I help you, Sir?"

I could not tell whether the speaker was male or female. I could only think of the bright angel I'd seen on my arrival, and thoughts of the black betrayer Lucifer flickered through my thoughts. No, I was beginning to accept that this was not Hell—rather, this was a Heaven cast adrift from all morality. Was this the task the Good Lord had given me? Did He wish for one of His flock to bring this corruption to the attention of lesser authorities? The Lord always lets us choose our destinies.

"Hello?" the liquid voice asked again.

"Yes," I began, trying to control my shaking. "I wish to complain about the amoral behaviour of the citizens. They are fornicating; they are dancing; they are glutting themselves with rich foods and wine. This disgusting licentiousness must cease at once if we are to find Salvation!"

"Sir," the angel said, carefully. "Sir, you're in Heaven now. You don't need to find Salvation, because, uhm, well, you've already found it." He laughed pleasantly. "Do you understand?" He was talking to me like I was mentally ill-equipped to handle the concept.

I could not respond immediately—what was he trying to say?

"What are you trying to say? Are you trying to defend the fornicators? Fornicators are on a train ride straight to Hell!" I was screaming into the handset now.

"Ah, Sir, that's true Sir, but you're in Heaven now." The golden voice sounded more confused than annoyed.

"I know I'm in Heaven. That's not the problem. The problem is *Heaven.*"

"I see, Sir. Could you tell me your address? I'll send the Inspector of Complaints over right away to help you."

I blurted out the address before I realised he was just trying to palm me off. "Now wait here young man!" I screamed, completely forgetting who—or what—I was talking to. The angel politely hung up on me and I was left holding a dead telephone.

There was a knock at the door.

Tentatively I hung up the phone and walked to the door. I fiddled with the spy hole and had to shut my eyes at the incredible blaze of light that shone through. Half-blind and filled with trepidation I unbolted the door and pulled it open. A middle-aged man in a long trench coat and a grey Stetson hat stood in the hallway. He was smoking a cigar and stubbed it out on his palm when he saw me.

"John Ezekiel Murray?" he asked, and stepped into my room before I had the opportunity to respond. He looked at the 'Guide' where I had left it on the bed and smiled.

"That's me," I finally said. I smoothed my suit self-consciously.

"I hear you have a problem with the arrangements?"

I took it he was referring to Heaven Itself.

"Absolutely! The Lord condemns this foul iniquity. Everywhere I look I see worldly temptation."

"Well, uhm, what did you expect, John? You're in Heaven—it's generally regarded as a nice place to go when you die."

"N...nice!?" I blurted.

"Look, what exactly is your complaint? I must say we only get a certain sort of complaint here usually, and they're not exactly common."

"My complaint is that the City of God is nothing more than a filthy Pit of Iniquity!" All my frustration was coming out at once. I was not here to save anyone. This miserable place was all the Heaven there was. "I told that angel on the phone that this place is fallen to Corruption!"

"A Pit, hm? I can assure you the people in the Pit aren't having nearly as much fun as we are up here. That's the way it works."

"But...but they're *fornicating*! I saw two of them on the street just today!"

"Good for them. I've always been amazed at how people can screw away their short lives on earth—they're obviously forgetting that fifty years of deprivation is nothing compared to an eternity of indulgence."

I couldn't believe this Inspector. I couldn't believe any of this.

The man was checking something off a list he'd produced. "It's all right," he said, not looking up, "I thought this would be the problem: it usually is. Let me see... You were a preacher, weren't you?"

"Yes."

"I think I know a place where you'll feel right at home—a lot of religious people like yourself go there and it's a ways out of town, but it's also more your cup of tea, so to speak. Bear in mind, though, that if you hand in your keys we can't let you back in. Space is at a premium, you know." He wasn't patronising me—the man was very polite and obviously cared about my complaint. The Lord only knew why complaints were not more common—I would have thought there would have been more men of God here in my position. I briefly thought back to Daniel the Catholic priest and shook my head.

"That's quite all right. I have no desire to stay here." I thought of something. "How long have you been here, if you don't mind my asking?"

He'd popped the unlit cigar back in his mouth and began chewing on it. "Since about 4000 B.C. my friend," he sighed, then laughed heartily. "A hell of a long time!"

* * * *

The morning finally dawned, as Daniel had told me on the train that it would. I'd been reading through the 'Guide' and saw that it would only be light for about four hours. Then the shadows would return and the city would begin to party again. I shook my head in disgust, but I was relieved that I at least would be spared these sins: the Inspector was arranging a car to take me to a more acceptable place. He was due to meet me in a few minutes. I pocketed the 'Guide' and went downstairs to wait.

The sky above the city was deepest cobalt blue, with not a cloud in sight. A few cars passed me, and several scantily clad young ladies waved at me before bursting into embarrassed giggles and disappearing into one of the cafés. I shook my head resignedly.

A long black limousine pulled up at the curb. A couple of people watched as the Inspector opened the door and waved me in. Carefully I stepped inside. It was a shamefully luxurious vehicle, with full leather interior and a pleasantly fragrant odour. I closed the door and the Inspector yelled for the chauffeur to go. He handed me a small rectangular package and I looked down—it was a Bible.

"Thank you!" I exclaimed, joyously. "Praise the Lord!"

He smiled and nodded, producing another cigar and popping it between his teeth. Out of politeness he did not light it and I offered a prayer of thanks.

"You're welcome," he said.

The ride was pleasant, and we passed through endless shopping districts and streets exclaiming the virtues of countless dance clubs and other dubious establishments. The Inspector opened a small sliding door and pulled out a miniature bottle of chilled champagne. With a practised twist he uncorked it and poured himself a glass. He did not offer me one, but I would have refused—alcohol is the Devil's drink, after all. I briefly wondered whether it still mattered, now that I was dead—what would it do to me, one of the Saved? The Devil couldn't come up and claim me, or he would have claimed all of the populace of the City by now. I shuddered and derailed my train of thought. This would not do at all! I clutched my new Bible to me and waited to see where we were headed.

After about half an hour the limousine had to slow as we approached the outskirts of the city, where the ubiquitous crowd of well-wishers continued to welcome the newly arrived. We crept carefully through the crowd, then accelerated when we hit the main freeway. Shortly we were out on the open marble plains, and drove in a slow curve around the city. The sky was brightly lit and the land was featureless in all directions, save for the exquisite marble tiles that reflected the deep blue sky.

My heart lightened as we left the City behind us. I began to have an inkling of where we were going, but I buried my sudden overwhelming sense of joy for fear of being disappointed.

An hour later, and with the Inspector nursing the last of his champagne, the marble gave way to clean, healthy meadows. The limousine continued its journey on a well-packed dirt road.

Shortly I saw my first church and could barely contain myself. There were people, too, working on the land. Some of them straightened and stared at us as we drove past. I was right—this was a second place, for those souls who had earned their eternal reward and did not wish to tarnish their immortal souls with the corruption of the City. The Good Lord had provided after all.

We passed five more churches before a small village appeared on the horizon, and I noticed we were headed directly for it. The

Inspector put away the empty bottle of champagne and his empty glass as we pulled up outside an old wooden church.

"This'll be your church, John," the Inspector said. He opened his door and stepped out. A small crowd of people watched as I did likewise, clutching my Bible. The people looked tired, hungry, and lean—good farmers one and all, working this land beneath the cold blue sky. I was filled with elation and turned to the Inspector. The people were watching him, too, though no one said a word.

The Inspector and I walked carefully into the church. Inside, it was pleasantly bleak—I'd been worried, from the opulence that had first greeted me on my arrival in Heaven, that this might be a Catholic church. Instead, it was properly white-washed, and several austere but functional pews lined the inside.

"When do I begin?" I gushed. I had not been this ecstatic since that first loss of pain, my first tentative drifting into the afterlife.

"Well, these folks haven't had a decent preacher for a long time."

"They look like fine men and women."

"Well, they don't spend their time, uhm, fornicating and dancing, and all—they did enough of that kind of stuff on Earth." As he spoke people began to file into the church, filling the pews hesitantly from the back. I watched them joyously, and thought, just for a moment, that I recognised one of them. I had an aunt who died many years ago—was that her? She'd been a smoker and drinker, though, come to think of it. I didn't see her again and figured it had been a figment of my imagination.

"I'm pleased to see you like it," said the Inspector. "Any one of these people will help you with a room once you're done here, but I'm warning you, they'll expect a lengthy sermon."

"I have all of eternity," I smiled at him, allowing myself a laugh. There was a reciprocal twinkle in his eyes, and he shook my hand. The grip was strong, warm, and dry.

"I might drop by once in a while," he promised, and I waved him goodbye. Then I strode up to the pulpit and faced the faithful.

The congregation looked up at me, misery and hunger in their eyes. There were hundreds of them, maybe even thousands. It was a miracle the building could hold them all. One of them began to wail; the long, mournful keening you might hear from a puppy that's lost its mother.

I turned to Genesis, for this was a new beginning and should be celebrated as such. The gathered watched me find my place and assemble my thoughts, and then I looked up at them, ready to begin. I could see the fear of Damnation etched into their faces.

I was in Heaven.

Vampire's Friend

Jacqueline Lichtenberg

Jacqueline Lichtenberg is the creator of the Sime~Gen Universe and primary author of the Bantam Paperback *Star Trek Lives*! She is a well published SF and vampire author and reviewer. She is co-owner of the popular internet domain, simegen.com.

David Silberman locked the door of his dry cleaning shop, and pulled it to behind him. The sun was going down—not his favorite time of day anymore. But today, the eve of Yom Kippur, was the worst.

He moved out to the edge of the strip mall's parking lot and paused, staring down the side street toward the Orthodox shul.

There were still many cars in the lot of the strip mall and the street was full of traffic. The goyim didn't know there was anything special going on in the world of Magic.

David had never been very religious, not even by Reform standards, until he'd seen a Vampire invoke a pagan god's assistance—and get it.

He'd had another object lesson when that same Vampire had saved his life from a demon's attack by tearing down the doorpost of his room and thrusting it into his arms, kosher Mezuzah against his heart.

He'd often wondered if the Mezuzah would have saved him if it hadn't been so perfectly kosher. But most of all, he wondered if he'd really been saved. He'd participated in a revenge-murder, and had a pagan serial killer for a friend. He'd gotten involved in idolatry, not just regular magic. He'd never respected those who called themselves pious Jews but isolated themselves from other Jews and from everyone else. He'd just never had anything much to do with G-d. *So why is my conscience bothering me?*

He just didn't want the supernatural in his life anymore. He wanted to forget the Vampire and just walk away from it all. But he couldn't. The Link was permanent, maybe Eternal. So he'd spent the last few months surfing the 'net for information, and every time had ended up at the website of this local shul reading something the Rabbi there had written.

As dusk gathered over the city, he felt the Vampire wakening in his mind, a growing buzz of not-quite awareness. The mental Link between them could only be closed, not vanquished. Lately, it made him feel…unfit.

He started down the side-street toward his house, walking on the side opposite the shul, still not sure what he would do. Before he'd left he shop, he'd emptied his pockets and put on shoes that had no leather in them. He wore a hat. He could go into the shul, even though he hadn't bought a ticket to the High Holy Day services. *I could just stand in the back.*

It had been a year since he'd separated from Malory Avnel, or Arnaud Lemieux as he called himself in New Jersey. All year, the Vampire had scrupulously avoided stirring the mental link between them. He owned and operated a Motel 6 on I-80, leaving David to his Fairlawn dry cleaning shop and studying for his stock trading certification and his spiritual nail chewing.

A morally upright, completely ethical, totally honorable Vampire who kills at least two humans a month calls me his friend. Worse yet, I call him friend—most of the time.

He paused across from the shul. It had been a brick church, circa 1900 that had burned down. Only the foundation had been left when the Orthodox shul had bought the land.

Some people were arriving, parking their cars in the lot behind the shul where they would stay until after dark tomorrow. The women were dressed in various colors, many of them wearing white, the married ones with their heads covered. The men wore business suits, white yarmulkes, and kittels—the belted white smock they would be buried in. No black hats and curls hanging beside their ears, but some men wore their prayer shawls while some carried theirs. The prayer shawls were white wool with black stripes—not a silk one; not a single blue striped one anywhere. Everyone wore sneakers and carried Machzorim—the prayer books that contained the day's special prayers. *I couldn't possibly fit in among them. I wouldn't know how to pray.*

"G'mar Chatima Tova. Come on, you'll miss Kol Nidre if you stand out here!"

David started, stifling a gasp. It was an older man with a fringe of white beard and a jolly paunch. A hand touched his elbow, urging him on across the street. "The Rabbi's drasha you can afford to miss, but not Kol Nidre when Yussel's davening."

"Yussel's davening?" He couldn't remember what davening meant.

The man held open the door for David urging him inside. "He doesn't just sing, he really prays, and the Gates of Heaven open."

Davening means praying.

They came to the inner door to the sanctuary on the men's side, a stream of men shuffling in before them. David hung back. "I don't have a seat."

"No problem. My son is home with his week old son and his wife. They're both sick, so you can have his seat. It's a mitzvah to miss shul, even on Yom Kippur to care for the sick. We'll take turns staying home tomorrow, so you'll still have a seat all day. Manny Rubenstein," he announced, holding out his hand.

"David Silberman." He shook the firm, dry hand.

In a twinkling, the old man had procured a prayer shawl and machzor from a cabinet and installed David in the chair next to his own on the aisle near the door. While he exchanged greetings in Hebrew with everyone around him, David arranged the shawl as everyone else had theirs and looked at the black book in his hands. The printing had worn off the binding. Inside, it had English on one side and Hebrew on the other. He turned to Kol Nidre.

So far his hands weren't burning—G-d wasn't rejecting him. He sat in a room full of ordinary people, facing three steps up to a stage with a beautiful cabinet, hung with a white drape, the Aron Kodesh, no doubt full of Torah Scrolls. An electric Eternal Flame hung over a lectern on the floor level facing the cabinet. On the stage, in front of the cabinet, another lectern faced the audience. Behind him a raised dais held the reader's lectern where men were gathering to begin the service. On the side wall a Memorial Plaque had a lamp lit beside every name carved there. All pretty standard for a synagogue. But behind him, beyond a filigreed symbolic barrier sat the women and children, divided from the men. Everyone chatted as if this were just another ordinary day.

Then, a man opened the Aron Kodesh exposing the ornately dressed Torah Scrolls to view and everyone stood up, silence falling. David stood. The silence became palpable. The silence tensed. The door in his mind beyond which the Vampire lurked slammed shut, leaking not a whisper of Malory's presence. *He's uncomfortable with the Torah.* The silence thickened. The silence thrummed.

A baritone voice inserted itself without disturbing the blanket of silence and proclaimed melodiously, "Kol" paused, and enunciated, "Nidre"—drawing the word out until it echoed back from the ends of Time—"Ve-esarey"—parting the fabric of reality,—"Vshvuei"—sculpting the silence—"Vaharamei"—reaching to the beginnings of Time—"Vekonamei"—the Torah Scrolls glowed, as if floating beyond the Gates of Reality.

On the second of the three repetitions of the entire prayer, David lost track of the words, carried on the sound of the voice that dripped tears of dread sincerity and earnest entreaty. The man wasn't singing. He was representing the whole of the people of Israel before the Throne, as would the High Priest of the Temple.

On the third escalating repetition, David felt the Gates opening, felt the cold heat of Divine Attention, knew that attention was on him. A peculiar fear gripped him, a thing he'd never felt before during any of Malory's brushes with the supernatural.

And suddenly, he was standing in an ordinary room full of people, hiss of air conditioning dominating, lit with ordinary lighting. Then with an eruption of quiet shuffling and coughing they sat down, kids whining, and the sound of traffic passing outside with thumping stereos.

I don't belong here.

As the Rabbi rose to take the lectern on the stage facing the congregation, David put the prayer shawl and machzor on his seat, thanked the old man, and bolted for the door.

I am not going to try that again. I'll find a Reform shul if I ever feel the urge again. But I really, really don't want the supernatural in my life!

Outside, the street still bustled with Monday evening traffic. Three kids were playing basketball in a driveway. An airplane droned overhead. The sky was darkening, but you still couldn't quite see stars through the haze. No hint of the supernatural. No hint of time being visible, palpable, open to his senses from beginning to end.

Hands in his pockets, shoulders hunched, eyes on the sidewalk before him, he started toward home. He rounded a curve in the street, momentarily finding himself alone in the quiet residential neighborhood. Trees rustled, leaves crunched under his feet. A pigeon whirred to a stop, perching on a branch. It's dropping spattered audibly on the concrete beside his foot, missing his shoe.

Automatically, he looked up to Heaven, mouthing, "Thank You!"

Something streaked across the indigo sky leaving a rainbow froth behind, pointing to the space between two houses across the street. The rainbow froth evaporated without a trace, but David knew just where the something had come to rest—next to his own house.

No. It was a decision surfacing from somewhere below his belt.

He crossed the street diagonally, cut across his own small lawn, and took the stairs to the porch two at a time. *No.* He fetched the key from the potted Holly, opened the door, and put the key back. *No.* The whole neighborhood was unnaturally silent. The stars were visible. It was now truly Yom Kippur. And his shoes were clean of bird dropping.

He went in his front door, touched his fingers to the mezuzah and kissed them, closed the door, locked it, and went through the living room to the kitchen. His fingers where he'd touched the mezuzah tingled pleasantly. That had never happened before. *OK, You win.*

He went out the side door to look in the alley beside his house —the house Malory had paid for, in full, probably with money taken from the criminals he drank to death.

Buried in the thick ivy between the garbage can and the air conditioner was a lozenge shaped zone of scintillating color. *Force Fields. It's an Alien from* Star Trek.

He stepped back inside, closed the door and leaned against it. The subliminal whisper in his mind that was the link to Malory was still silent. The Vampire wasn't giving him this hallucination.

Although a fan of science fiction, an avid viewer of all kinds of fantasy TV, David had considered he had a good grip on "reality" until he'd met Malory.

Star Trek *is not real. Whatever is out there—is real.*

He took a spare blanket from the linen closet and went back outside. In the full dark, the glowing bundle lit the alley. The people in the adjacent house were away at shul, though they'd left the lights on.

He crept around the garbage can and waded into the ivy. Nerving himself up to it, he touched the glowing bundle. His hand jumped back of its own accord and the colors flashed and swirled where he'd touched. But nothing else happened.

He threw the blanket over the colored light and rolled the limp, flexible thing into the blanket. It didn't seem very heavy, and wasn't even as tall as he was. He heaved it into a fireman's carry and made for the back door. When part of the blanket touched the mezuzah, the light filtering through the blanket flashed white, then subsided leaving David's body tingling pleasantly, as his fingers had. *Whatever this is, it's not very evil.*

It was heavier than he'd thought. By the time he reached the guest room, his knees were sagging. He dropped the bundle onto the double bed and unrolled it.

Seen against the dark blanket, the glowing oblong seemed to have some structure, three pairs of calyx-like segments folded up around it, meeting in a zigzag line down the center.

He wasn't about to pry the segments apart. It was either an alien from another planet sans starship, or it was supernatural. It had taken a good fall, and it was hurt. He knew what he had to do, but he thought about it very hard first. He really didn't want to.

He waited. He raised one hand to the ceiling and waved it suggestively, "Nu?" No response. OK, you win.

He picked up the phone, dialing from old habit—a habit unused for more than a year. The Vampire's answering machine said, "Leave a message."

"Malory? Pick up would you? This is David, and I've got a problem."

"Arnaud here. I doubt it's one I can help you with. I've been staying out of your way tonight."

The door in his mind trembled but stayed leak-proof. "Thank you. I do appreciate your effort. But I think you need to get over here. I've got something to show you—explaining just won't work."

"You're inviting me into your house?"

David heard the eyebrow rise to the never-receding hairline. "Into my house, yes. Hurry."

The pause lengthened. "Half an hour. I'll bring the car."

"Fine, but hurry. Oh, and Mal, just in case it matters, please forgive me for any wrong I've done you this year. I sincerely apologize, and I'll do whatever it takes to make it up to you."

There was a long silence. "You are forgiven and you owe me nothing."

Forty minutes later, the Vampire rang the bell. Arnaud wore a dark silk suit with a conservative tie against a perfect burgundy shirt with a white collar. His shoes were polished to a fine gloss. He strode into the living room and headed straight for the guest bedroom without even glancing around. He had, after all, seen the place through David's eyes for a year.

The alien was still motionless on David's guest bed, wrapped in glowing swirls of color.

"Mal . . ."

"Arnaud," Malory corrected, absently as he circled the bed studying the oblong.

David told him everything, starting with the bird, the streak of color and working back to the otherworldly experience in the Orthodox Shul. "I'm not Orthodox. I don't know why I went there."

"It wouldn't have mattered where you went. It would have happened to you anywhere. I told you, you can't hide from the Potencies." Malory reached out and touched the alien.

It flashed, and Malory's hand sizzled and jerked away. Suddenly there was a human-shaped image sitting up on the bed, shrouded in gossamer color, but definitely there.

Two amethyst eyes appeared in the head, though the features remained blurred as if by a veil, and two arms with proper joints and hands appeared. The zone of colored-shimmer extended now behind the being and the knees appeared, though the feet were shrouded in moving mists. The trunk seemed androgynous, the skin a pearly white.

The eyes swept the room. The suggestion of a wide mouth, high cheekbones, aquiline nose, all in a pale face gave the impression of alarm, perhaps bewilderment—confusion not fear.

Rubbing his scorched fingers, Malory spoke. "I know you?"

The being centered on Malory, assessed what he was, and scrambled back to plaster itself to the headboard. Before finishing the move, it relaxed, more of its face showing. "Oh, it's you!"

David blurted inanely, "You speak English! Ma ... Arnaud, does every demon in the universe know you?"

"Of course I speak English, how else could I deliver messages? Where's the demon, Meshobab?"

"There's a demon named Meshobab involved in this?" asked David, alarmed.

Malory said, "Sometimes they call me Meshobab. David, this Messenger is often called Bozez—or that's what some people call him because he shines so brightly. He's not a demon; he's one of the Messengers your God sends to Earth, usually with good news. Is your message for us?"

Bozez seemed to take a breath to answer, then froze, inspected the room, peered at David, and frowned. "I don't know. I can't remember." And now there was panic in Bozez's voice.

Malory was so stunned, he forgot to breathe. David filled the sudden silence with the most inane remark he had ever uttered. "Well, you took a nasty fall. You'll remember soon."

Malory eyed David, and charitably ignored him. "Other than that, how do you feel?" He stood back, inviting the Messenger to stand.

Slowly the glowing layers of colored gossamer that almost resembled a person hitched to the side of the big bed and stood.

Once unfolded, the being appeared to have wings extending behind it, and the glowing nimbus around it seemed to concentrate over its head.

And then David realized what he was looking at. The prophet Isaiah had described the Seraphim, and David had memorized the passage from a recorded reading by Theodore Bikel. "In the year that King Uzziah died, I saw the Lord sitting upon a throne, high and lifted up, and His train filled the temple.

"Above it stood the Seraphim: each one had six wings; with twain he covered his face, and with twain he covered his feet, and with twain he did fly.

"And one cried unto another, and said, Holy holy, holy, is the Lord of hosts: the whole earth is full of His glory."

"You're a Seraph!" accused David.

"Oh, no nothing so glorious." Bozez fluttered nervously, but politely aware he was nearly filling the room, was careful not to knock the bedside lamp over. "I'm just a messenger." He looked worried. "But why am I here?"

Malory described the streak David had seen in the almost-night sky.

"I don't remember that."

"What is the last thing you do remember?" asked David.

"I was on my way down Jacob's Ladder." The being paced, wrapping his wings tightly about himself again. He muttered in what sounded like several languages. Malory listened intently, and David watched Malory.

Finally, Bozez turned to Malory and said, "Either I slipped on something, or the Ladder broke under me just as the Gate opened. Is this Enemy action? Is that why you're here?"

"I don't see how my god could be involved. Even my god can't break the Ladder. But... cause you to slip? The demon Xlrud could do that, I think..."

Bozez considered that. "No, probably not without the Lord's help..." He whipped around to stare at David. "Where did you say you were at dusk?"

Mouth dry, David just stared. *I am not responsible for an Angel falling to Earth! No! I didn't do this!*

Malory repeated what David had told him of the experience during Kol Nidre.

David objected, "But the Gates don't keep Eastern Daylight Saving's Time. It's sundown at different moments in different parts of the world!"

Bozez heaved a sigh. There was no other way to describe the body-language message his not-quite body seemed to project. "I thought you had learned that from Xlrud. Time is a property of the Matter/Energy Interface. It doesn't exist above the Material plane because—" He broke into a grin that spread from eyes and mouth to infuse his aura with a myriad bright, scintillating sparks until he was a blinding white.

Malory shaded his eyes and retreated toward the door. "I can't take much of that, you know, Bozez!" To David he added, "See why he's called Bozez?"

The Angel reined in his brilliance, folding in upon himself again. "Sorry. But I remember!"

"Your mission?" asked David.

"No, just how Xlrud used you to try to get Meshobab away from The Lord and you foiled him beautifully." Deflated, he added, "But

I've no idea what I was supposed to do now." The Angel sounded even more worried.

"My mother always said," started David. They turned to look at him politely. "Um, well, when you forget something, you should retrace your steps and you'll remember."

"Worth a try," allowed Malory. "Go on back up and see if you can find where you fell from. Maybe you'll remember. In any event, you can find out why you fell."

"I'm sure the Message had something to do with David and Time. You're probably right. I'll never remember as long as I'm embedded in Time. The Message may have something to do with why I fell. I'll be right back."

The gossamer wings of colored nothing unfolded and filled the room with shimmering blur. David was certain that the other two pair of wings also unfolded and whirred but he was too busy shuddering in awe to observe carefully. The whirring vibration produced by those wings apparently hit a note that resonated with the human nervous system.

Somewhere during this, he felt his body come apart into whirling sparkles, and coalesce again. And so did Bozez. Malory though, was no longer in the room.

"Did it work?" asked David.

"Would I be here if it did?"

"You said you'd be right back."

"Not that right-back. Meshobab! You can come back now." Bozez went to the door and opened it, moving out into the corridor. "Meshobab? I didn't mean to get so bright, really I'm sorry to distress you..."

They found the vampire in the living room seated in David's reading chair, unsurprised at Bozez's failure to climb The Ladder. "Something is wrong. The Gate is open. The Ladder is still there. Why can't you climb it?"

"I don't know. I can't get a grip. It's like there's a piece missing."

David said, "You're probably still stunned from the...impact of landing." *He is not a fallen Angel!* "It'll be better in the morning."

"I don't think so," said Malory. "That God of yours is up to something. Jacob's Ladder can't break. It is reality. His Messengers don't lose their memories. Xlrud might be playing some game here, but it wouldn't be working without Divine complicity. The Message is in this Situation somewhere. It's up to us to figure it out. And I think we only have until sundown tomorrow when the Gate closes."

That was the first sensible thing David had heard all evening. "I didn't mention," said David. They turned to him. "The old man—he said that missing the Service to care for the sick was a mitzvah. Do you think Bozez is sick?"

Malory considered the Angel. "No. He can't die."

"But he's in distress...he's lost, cut off."

"Scared," admitted Bozez with an air of shame. "Nothing like this has ever happened before."

"So our job is to get him back where he belongs," said David. "And we have to do that before the Gate closes."

"How?" asked Bozez. "You can't climb."

"We could summon Xlrud..." started Malory.

"Oh, no!" objected David. "No way can we control that demon. Besides, summoning, trapping and forcing a demon to do our will doesn't seem like a very Yom Kippur thing to do."

"That's it!" Malory got to his feet and began to pace. "We've been handed a problem and it's a test. We have to solve the problem within the rules."

"A game?" asked David, offended. "This is the most solemn holiday of the year!"

"A challenge. A lesson. A test," said Malory. "And it's not my god who's behind it this time. All this is beyond him. I can't even guess what this is really about."

David ran his fingers through his hair and shrugged. "Me, neither." Other than what Malory had taught him, David knew nothing much about magic, and most of the fiction he imbibed wasn't very educational.

Bozez said, "I think David is right. I think I have to go back up to find out what it's about. And I can't."

"You need a boost," said David. "We need some kind of magic that can catapult you over the broken rung in the Ladder."

"The Ladder can't be broken," insisted Malory and Bozez in chorus.

"Well, the illusion of it being broken then. From our point of view, for us at this moment in Time, it is broken. Maybe everyone else out there praying up a storm is getting Messengers to bring them Enlightenment, but our Messenger has amnesia. It's up to us to help the Messenger, not the Messenger to help us. So what kind of magic can boost an Angel into Heaven?"

They exchanged blank looks. Malory, Master of so many Magical Systems he couldn't even count them all just shook his head.

David paced the three steps across the living room and back again. He'd never paid attention in Sunday School. He'd memorized his bar mitzvah portion by rote, and actually had no idea what the words of the Torah actually said. All he knew about Judaism, he'd learned on the 'net over the last few months.

And suddenly he was back in the shul with Yussel's voice shaping the Silence into pure emotion, the image of the elaborately dressed Torah Scrolls floating in a haze of light, as if the inside of the Aron Kodesh was in another dimension. Over the Aron was inscribed the words sung in every Synagogue when the Torah was taken out to be read. Etz Haim, Hii.

"There's another way into Heaven!" said David. "There's Jacob's Ladder. And there's the Tree of Life. The Torah is the Tree of Life."

Bozez blinked skeptically. Malory said, "They're really the same thing."

"But not exactly the same. A real Torah Scroll—not a printed book, but the real hand-written on lambskin, actual Torah—the actual words given to Moses—they have the power, the kind of Magic needed for this."

"I think he's got something," allowed Bozez cautiously. "It would be like climbing a different face of the Mountain. It's the same Mountain, but the terrain is different. There could be a glacier on one side while the other is clear. But we don't have a Torah Scroll. I can recite the whole thing from memory but memorized recitation doesn't penetrate to the Material plane the way the written document would."

"This night of all nights, every Torah Scroll in existence will be in use," said Malory. "The custom, as I recall—and I think it's still practiced—is for the men to learn Torah all night."

"I'll bet in Reform Temples they don't," said David, not actually sure.

"It wouldn't work unless the Scroll is perfect," offered Bozez. "Magically perfect."

Malory said, "There's that shul just down the street that David went to this evening."

"There'll surely be people there all night," said David. The kind of people in that congregation would surely observe such ancient custom—at least some of them would.

"Good," grinned Malory. "Then we won't have to break in."

David envisioned a Vampire, an Angel and a lapsed Jew breaking into an Orthodox shul in the depths of the night on Yom Kippur. Malory could pull it off. He could turn to mist and sift into any building, and he was an expert on alarms. This is insane. But he couldn't help grinning at the image in his mind.

"I can get us in," said Malory. "I can make anyone there think we're members of the congregation. The cabinet where they keep the Torah Scrolls is probably a decorated fireproof bank vault the way it is in most shuls these days. Tonight it'll be open so we don't have to crack the safe."

"I don't know their customs," warned David.

"I can blend in," said Bozez, "at least when I remember not to blaze up too brightly."

"If we blunder, I'll be sure no one notices," assured Malory. "We'll just drift in, find a perfect Scroll, and Bozez will be on his way."

* * * *

Five hours later, David was wondering how he could have thought it would be that simple.

The shul's front door had been unlocked, and they had just walked in ahead of Malory. But from there on it had gotten complicated.

Malory had winced and trembled at passing the mezuzah on the door, lagging behind them.

David had whispered to Bozez, "He's been telling me the truth, hasn't he? That he has eternal life because The Lord God of Abraham, the Creator of the Universe, Blessed him to offset the curse of a pagan god?"

Bozez regarded David meditatively. Then he allowed, "That's a good enough way to explain it. He's not Evil; he's just a victim. Don't blame the victim for the crimes of the victimizer. In fact, it's rarely a good idea to blame at all."

Behind them, Malory mastered his aversion and slid through the portal, hugging the left-hand doorpost, away from the mezuzah.

Then, in the lobby, he stopped, staring intently at the sanctuary.

Over a year ago, during their encounter with Xlrud, Malory had explained that his aversion to Judeo-Christian power was caused by his own god's curse clashing with the Blessing of the Eternal that he carried. The psychic noise did him no harm, but he suffered miserably—even debilitatingly. Now, he couldn't keep the effect from leaking through to David.

"There are six men in the building," Malory reported with his Vampire senses. "Four in there, and two upstairs. I think six—no seven Torah Scrolls. Four in there, and the rest are upstairs."

One man emerged from the main Sanctuary on his way to the Men's Room and greeted them casually. "Nachman is learning upstairs, and the Rabbi is down here. I'll be right back."

They decided to join the Rabbi in the Sanctuary. A space had been cleared among the chairs and a long table had been set up. The table was covered in large, leather bound books, gold lettering on the covers, some open, some stacked.

As they came in, the Rabbi and a group of men were on the stage next to the Aron Kodesh, which stood wide open. The Rabbi, a young, energetic, clean-shaven man in shirtsleeves, was holding forth. Every once in a while David recognized an English word.

All the Torah Scrolls in the Aron had been moved to one side, and the back wall of the Aron was open. The light in the Aron dimly illuminated a large space beyond the back wall, almost another room, lined with shelves, stacked with books. There was even a Torah Scroll.

"So," concluded the Rabbi, "we'll have to get that latch repaired after Yom Tov. Meanwhile, be very careful not to place a Scroll against the back of the Aron, it shouldn't fall open during davening. Chaim, remember not to let the time-lock engage after Ma'ariv tomorrow, and I'll have Irv get at it before Shacharis."

They carefully closed the back wall and rearranged the Scrolls so they rested against the side walls of the Aron. The one in the center was propped on a stand so it didn't lean against the back wall, and they closed the Aron, pulling the curtain across the door.

Then the Rabbi turned, saw them and greeted them heartily, inviting them to sit with him at the table. Everyone made room for them. David had no idea what they saw, he just grinned and nodded affably and pretended he knew what he was doing. The Rabbi began lecturing again in a mixture of languages.

Malory said, in a normal tone, "They will see and hear only three members of the congregation sitting here and listening intently even if we move about. And I was right, they didn't lock the Aron Kodesh, just closed it. Bozez, come see if you can find a Scroll that will work."

"Wait—he's missing the point..."

"Bozez, you're not going to sit here and teach the Rabbi are you?" asked David, unsure why he was appalled at the idea.

"Well, but The Rambam... no, I guess that wouldn't be a good idea until I find out what my mission is." He rose to go with Malory.

"M-Arnaud, wouldn't it have been easier to make us invisible?"

"Not in here with all this noise," answered Malory. "It's too hard to concentrate." Scrolls and even the books produced a discordant, psychic shrieking David could feel despite Malory's efforts to shield him.

"David, sit there and pretend we're beside you to keep my illusion going. Give us time to see if there's a Scroll here we can use."

Malory and Bozez went to the Aron and opened it. No one noticed. The Angel reached out to touch the Scrolls, and the whole Aron burst into a superheated blaze of white that surrounded Malory and Bozez and started to billow out to fill the room. Nobody at the table noticed. They were involved in an argument.

It had seemed like an eternity before the two closed the Aron and came back to the table, defeated. Malory collapsed into his chair, and if David hadn't known better, he'd have said the Vampire was sweating.

Bozez said, "They're all very good, but none of them is perfect."

"We'll have to try upstairs, then. David, do you know where the stairs are?"

"I saw a broad, carpeted stairway in the lobby."

"Good." He paused, glaring hard at the men around the table. "Now they won't remember we were ever here. Let's go."

Following signs, they found the upstairs hall, which normally were used, for children's classes and larger celebrations. For the High Holy Days, it was rigged out as a second shul with portable lecterns and a small, beautifully draped, Aron Kodesh on a small stage.

At the door, Malory stopped them. "It's not so bad up here. I think I can get these men to join the ones downstairs. Just a moment."

By the time he'd finished, and the two men had passed them on their way to join the Rabbi, the Vampire was shaking with the effort. This is worse for him than he's letting on.

But now they had the large auditorium to themselves. And their luck held. The less ornate, plain wood Aron wasn't locked. And one of the Scrolls was perfect—or perfect enough to suit Bozez. He blazed up so brilliantly that Malory complained again, retreating, and Bozez apologized profusely.

They took the jangling silver crown off the top spokes, pulled the long cover up, unfastened and unwrapped the binding strap, and put the scroll on the Reader's Desk to unroll it. "There, now see if you can use the words to Ascend," said David, casting his gaze upward and sending a fervent entreaty to Heaven.

Bozez passed his hand over the words, glancing apologetically at Malory, and then unfurled all his wings and filled the room with light, motion and color. But after a few moments, he shrank and wrapped himself up again. "Almost, but I can't get into it to climb—if that makes any sense."

"I have an idea," said Malory. "You're going to need to traverse the entire Scroll, from the Beginning Word to the very End. It's the whole thing—holistically—that is The Tree. The little excerpt you're looking at now is only a twig—it won't hold your weight." He began to move chairs. "Here, let's make a clear space to unroll the whole thing."

David looked at the diagonal length of the room, then at the Scroll. "It'll never fit."

"Well, let's see if enough of it will. Maybe it's like a plane runway. If he can get going, he'll take off before reaching the end."

They created an open strip of carpet from corner to corner of the room, carefully picking up bits of detritus, children's toys, and whatnot to make a clean strip for the Torah. The Vampire's waning strength was apparent in his every move. He was in a hurry to get this done, knowing his strength wouldn't hold out against the forces in this building.

Bozez strove to keep his dazzling light down to levels Malory could stand, but as each page of the Torah Scroll was revealed, he got brighter and brighter. Finally, they had most of the Scroll exposed, laid out diagonally across the room. At last, Malory said, "OK, try it now."

Reverent, enraptured, and humbled, the Angel stepped onto the first words of the Torah Scroll, wings unfurling to fill the room again. *Here we have all these elaborate rituals for reverently handling a Scroll,"* thought David, *and he goes and walks on it!*

Bozez took a step, and then all David saw was a gossamer rainbow streak flashing along the length of the Scroll, and then his eyes just gave out from the brilliance.

When it was gone, the fluorescent lighting in the room seemed like total darkness.

He blinked his way back to Reality and yelled, "We did it! M-Arnaud, we did it!"

There was no answer.

"Mal?" He looked around. The Vampire wasn't in the room. He looked behind the stacks of chairs they'd made, behind the lecterns, and then saw the door was slightly ajar.

He found Malory in the hallway, fallen face down, as if he'd been fleeing the room when he passed out. Kneeling beside the Vampire, David found him as dead as his daytime coma ever made him. He hadn't turned to ash, which was a good sign. But it was still a long time until morning. He shouldn't be in his coma yet.

He wasted several minutes poking and prodding, pleading with Malory to wake up. He even tried opening the door inside his mind to let Malory talk to him mentally, as he had sometimes done during the day. Nothing.

Without Malory to control what the men were seeing, how could he get them out of the building? They'd walked down the street from the house, but David knew he'd never be able to carry the Vampire home, even if the street was wholly deserted which it wasn't.

He thought about going to get his car, but where could he hide the Vampire while he was gone? And there was the mess they'd made of this room. If people found it like that, they'd have the police here looking for a vandal.

And it would be daylight soon. He couldn't take Malory out in the sunlight.

He dragged the limp body back into the room and set about rolling up the Torah Scroll—normally a two-man job. He knew he'd never get it set to the correct page—he couldn't read a word of it—and he didn't even try to get it rolled up snug and tight enough. It was a big struggle to get the binding wrapped around it and fastened, and then with nobody to hold it upright, it was hard to get the covering in place because the spokes weren't close enough together and the Crown and Pointer wouldn't fit right either.

He'd just have to leave it that way, hoping they'd think some children had messed with it.

Rearranging the furniture by himself took more than three times as long as it had taken the three of them to move everything. He could barely budge the lectern by himself, and the rows of chairs had to be set up straight.

All that while, Malory lay dead, not breathing, heart not beating. David worked against the clock, but still by the time the room was presentable, it was close to dawn. He couldn't get Malory out of the building now before people began arriving.

And he had to get Malory out of sight and store him where no sunlight—or children, would get at him until nightfall. Soon the building would be full of bored children and even more bored babysitting teens—

Usually, when badly hurt, the Vampire would recover with sunset. Maybe not this time, though.

He opened the door to the hallway and peered out. Voices rose from the lobby—the small group of men who had learned all night discussing going home to freshen up before the day's services. "No, we shouldn't lock up. Tully will be here in a few minutes." A toilet flushed. A door opened, and the voices faded. The door closed, echoing through the empty building.

A few minutes. How long is that?

He had one chance, and he knew Malory would never thank him for saving his life this way. But the one dark place the children would not go was the cabinet behind the Aron Kodesh where they stored the books that were so damaged they couldn't be used anymore. The psychic "noise" that so disturbed the Vampire would be greatest there. He'd have daymares from it, but it wouldn't actually harm him. But it would make him helpless.

He's just stunned from Bozez's light. He'll recover, and everything will be fine. If we can get away with this, he...and I... won't have to move again.

The Vampire was much taller than David. In one corner of the room, there was a dolly used to move the folding chairs. How he'd get it down the stairs, David had no idea.

How did they get it up here? Where were the chairs normally stored?

He unloaded the rest of the chairs from the dolly, pulled and heaved the limp body onto it, and jockeyed it out the doors. The dolly about filled the hallway, and it was too wide for the stairs. He raced up and down the hall, past school rooms, and finally found an elevator in a corner.

As he reached for the button to summon it, the doors opened. He propped them open with his tush as he sidled the dolly into it. He ended up on the wrong side from the control buttons, and as he was maneuvering over the dolly to reach them, the doors closed and the elevator descended to the only other floor in the building. Then he remembered. The Orthodox wouldn't push elevator buttons on the Sabbath or Holidays, so they had the elevator rigged to run automatically all day.

It opened at the back of the caterer's kitchen right across from a huge closet full of folding chairs and what looked like a collapsed party-tent. He was tempted to store the body there. But the doors were open. Someone might want more chairs, and then what? Maybe rolled in the tent? But it was trussed up neatly, and no doubt was huge and heavy. And he didn't have much time.

He made for the Sanctuary, battering the swinging doors open with the bumper on the front of the dolly because he couldn't stop it in time. The dolly wouldn't go more than a yard into the room, there were so many chairs in the way.

Racing the clock, he ran up to the Aron, pulled the curtain, opened the doors—lofted a hearty prayer of thanks that the doors were unlocked,—carefully and reverently moved the central Torah Scroll, pushed open the broken door in the back, ran back to heave and drag the comatose Vampire up onto the stage, pushed the flopping body through into the dark cubby, where it fell in an awkward pile, replaced everything, closed up, and ran back to the dolly which was propping the door open.

"Oh, you didn't have to do that! It is my job, after all."

Aware of beads of sweat rolling down face and body, David looked up to see a wiry old man in black with fringes hanging out from under his jacket and a very large white yarmulka on his head smiling at him.

The shock paralyzed David.

"Here, let's get this back upstairs," offered the old man, pulling the dolly out of the doorway.

David went with it. "Uh, um, well, I didn't finish in there yet. I thought I'd be done before you got here."

"That's very nice of you—uh—I don't recall your name."

"David Silberman. I own Silberman's Dry Cleaning. I'm not a member here, but ..."

"You wanted to do a special mitzvah for us. Our gratitude will be with you."

The old man insisted on helping replace the dolly, then pulled David into continuing his routine of picking up and straightening the covers on the lecterns, checking and arranging, returning books to their proper places, sorting the chairs according to the names on them by the chart on the wall, all the while reciting the rules about what they could and could not do on Yom Kippur to make the shul ready for the crowd. He wouldn't even knock down a cobweb.

All David could think of was the Vampire behind the Aron Kodesh. Malory's subliminal pain leaked through the portal in David's mind and he was beginning to regret this decision. There were nearly fourteen hours of this to endure. Even if he went home, he'd still feel it. But he couldn't go. He had to watch. He couldn't leave Malory alone here, rendered helpless by daylight and the excruciating psychic noise. But, if that rear door fell open, what could he do to prevent anyone from discovering the Vampire?

I should have hidden him in the shrubs and gone to get my car. No, I'd never have made it. Heaving a dead body out of the shrubbery in front of a shul at the crack of dawn on a weekday on a busy street—no. On Holidays, the police patrolled the synagogues with special attention, particularly at night. He knew he'd have been caught. Irrational as it was, he knew it.

Eventually, the old man noticed him stopping to stare at the Aron Kodesh. "It is beautiful isn't it? It was made by one of our members, an artist. The Sisterhood made the drape for us, every stitch by hand. Wouldn't think anyone did hand embroidery these days, would you?"

"Uh, not like that. It's magnificent." It really was, but that wasn't the focus of David's attention at the moment.

"Young man like you . . . not married, are you? Ah, didn't think so, well, I'll talk to my wife about that after Yontef. People will be here in a few minutes. Let's check upstairs."

OK so it's not so different from a Reform Temple. They climbed the stairs together, David aching in every joint, moving as slowly as the old man. He pushed into the upstairs auditorium ahead of David and stopped. "Did you do this?"

"Uh, no," lied David. "Is something wrong?"

"No, it's just that the chairs are all straight. Let's get the table put away and check the Seforim."

They folded up and stored the table, stacked the chairs, and collected the stray books, putting them back in the shelves.

While they worked, people began to sift into the room, the noise from downstairs growing every time the door swung open.

As they went back down, the old man offered him another seat he knew would be vacant, but David explained he'd already been invited by Manny Rubenstein to share his son's seat.

"That's just like Manny. Terrible thing about his grandson. If you need anything, just let me know. I'll see you after Neela."

Neela?

Then Manny arrived and collected David as if he belonged to his family, settling him with all the books he'd need. "Missed you for Ma'ariv last night. Glad to see you this morning. Yussel will be davening Musaf."

"That's wonderful," agreed David clueless.

There ensued five hours of ever growing, frustrated bewilderment. He never stood, sat, bowed, pounded his chest, or sang out an Amen on cue. Every so often, Manny or his son who replaced him periodically, would peer at the prayer book David held and flip some of his pages backward or forward for him, then point to the Hebrew text. After a while, they gave up and just swapped books with him, giving him the correct page.

The congregation sang four-part harmony as if they'd rehearsed for weeks, but only the men's voices could be heard. There were long songs, responsive readings, and at odd moments, while the Reader was chanting, the congregation would burst into song for a sentence or two, then fall silent. And all of it in Hebrew. There was no way to follow it in English, but everything seemed to be repeated and repeated again.

After an hour or so he gave up and just watched the clock, trying not to concentrate on the growing headache from Malory's pain. And he prayed. *Let Malory—Meshobab—recover! And let us get away with this. Just think how upset everyone here would be to discover a Vampire in the Aron Kodesh on Yom Kippur. We can't have that, can we? And I'd really like to know why Bozez fell off The Ladder, and if he's all right now. Ok, it's idle curiosity. I don't really need to know, but I'd like to. I took a liking to that Angel.* And he kept arguing as best he could while the congregation prayed unintelligibly.

At breakfast time, he got hungry but when his stomach realized it wasn't going to get fed, it shut down until lunch.

The Rabbi spoke for about half an hour and David almost understood his point. "The Hebrew word for "sin" is "Chet." The prayer "Al Chet" is a comprehensive list of sins for which we ask G-d's forgiveness. The word "Chet" also means to "miss." When one misses a target, this too is "Chet." Teshuva—repentance—is not only for sins which one may have committed, it also encompasses failure to fulfill whatever potential G-d gave us. That too is called "Chet" and requires amending our ways."

There was a lot of his potential he hadn't lived up to. He'd been taking the coward's way out for the last year, just because he was uncomfortable with having Malory in his mind, and Malory's supernatural friends—and enemies—in his life.

Right after the Rabbi's talk, Yussel took the podium and once more, for David, the Gates opened.

As the feeling of G-d's attention on him intensified, the pain from Malory's distress receded. He even forgot to be embarrassed when everyone around him dropped to their knees and put their foreheads on paper towels they had spread on the floor. They did it several times, and the final time he actually managed to go with them.

While he was curled on the floor, with Yussel crying out a Blessing in tones of raw entreaty, David suddenly knew he was guilty, and G-d loved him anyway. Tears erupted from somewhere deep within and wracked him with sobs.

As they stood up and rearranged their prayer shawls, people passed tissue boxes around and many noses needed blowing.

It was after two p.m., right after the men of Cohen ancestry had trooped up onto the stage in front of the Aron to recite the Priestly blessing when Bozez appeared again.

It was the first time all day that Malory's hiding place was out of David's sight behind a wall of bodies, and it made him nervous. If that broken door in the back wall of the Aron should fall open, the body would be discovered. The sun was streaming into the windows, lighting the whole area.

The Cohenim hitched their prayer shawls up over their heads while facing the Aron. The Reader called, "Cohenim!" and they turned to face the congregation, arms raised under their shawls, hands spread but invisible to the people. Most of the men around him had raised their prayer shawls or buried their eyes behind their books, or turned their backs. But David didn't copy them. He couldn't take his eyes off the Aron with so many people up there.

As the Cohenim repeated the words the Reader sang, in slow, solemn, precise tones, drawing out each word with melodic chanting in between, David felt a strange warmth and saw light swirling and gathering around and above the group of men. In the midst of the brightness, the compact form of Bozez appeared, glowing in shades of white, and unfolding rainbow wings until David could see his face well enough to recognize him.

The Angel's voice rose out of the men's chorus, blending the voices into a supernal harmony. The sound resonated in David's bone marrow, turning his flesh to gossamer light.

As the final word, Shalom, Peace, filled the room, Bozez swept his wings around himself, turned toward the Aron and held his hands up in the position of the Priestly Blessing. David knew it was for Malory. Then the overly bright Angel glowing even more intensely, flicked out of sight. A moment later, he was back. He looked David right in the eye, and formed words in his mind. "Oh, my Message before was that you should learn to enjoy the humor of the Situation. It'll make life around Meshobab much easier. Thanks for the lift!" A flash, and he was gone again.

The Cohenim shuffled and rearranged themselves completely oblivious to the Messenger, then the congregation was singing again. A number of people were wiping their eyes with tissues, but nobody had noticed the Angel.

They took a break then, many people going home for the interval, but the Rabbi gathering a group to learn more about the customs of Yom Kippur. David didn't dare leave except for a few moments to go to the Men's Room.

And an hour or so later, everyone came back again for the afternoon service. It seemed to David that they did everything all over again.

The next time they repeated "Al Chet" it turned him inside out. He could think of an instance where he'd committed each and every sin listed and somehow he understood what he had done wrong, and why it was wrong, and he truly was horrified at his own stupidity. He deeply regretted he couldn't make amends if he lived a hundred lifetimes.

Then he remembered what Bozez had said about Time, about Malory being immortal, about what it would be like to look at human life from an immortal perspective.

We take our sins too seriously—that's why we keep doing the same thing over and over. We don't deal with the current Situation. We react to memories of similar Situations in the past and fail to live in the present—and we miss the point. It's not that we take ourselves too seriously, it's that by reacting to new Situations as if they were in fact the old Situations that they resemble, we fail to live up to our potential. My current Situation is that I have the Supernatural in my life. I can't get rid of the Vampire without getting rid of G-d.

While he was still dwelling on how stunned he was by this revelation, and how much simpler it would make his life if he could manage to remember that insight after all this was over, someone blew the shofar.

It wasn't a recording, and it wasn't a pipe organ faking it. It was an actual, real, once-part-of-a-living-animal ram's horn someone blew their own breath into. He'd never heard anything like it before. It was a soul-shattering sound.

Each individual peal vibrated all the way through his flesh, sizzled through his brain, turned his eyes to jelly, and made him need to scream with fear, ecstasy, elation and humility all at once.

When the sound stopped, the Gate was closed. He knew it, all the way through to the center of beingness. He was no longer a focus of Divine Attention.

And with that, Malory's distress grabbed his whole mind and heart.

But a new Reader took a place at lectern near him and everyone kept right on praying. According to the prayer book, they were doing the Evening Service. It was several pages long, but they raced through it all at blinding speed which was just as well since Malory was awake and hurting worse than ever. The Vampire was helpless and scared, and just short of panic.

Hang on, Mal, I'm coming to get you out of there. It'll be all right. Bozez came back.

He felt the vampire's pained astonishment at his use of the Link. He was weak, and confused, but replied, "Take your time."

And then people were leaving. He had to thank the Rubensteins, and give his phone number to the old man who wanted to find him a wife.

The social amenities were very brief since it was a mitzvah not to delay breaking fast. And David managed to contrive to hide himself behind the open door of the book cabinet in the sanctuary as the old man was closing up. Shortly, the building fell into utter silence except for the cars starting outside, and people calling happy greetings.

When he was certain everyone was gone, he came out of hiding. All the lights were off except for the Eternal Flame, which could hardly be called a light.

By feel, he groped and stumbled his way up to the Aron. As he had guessed, the time-lock was not engaged, as the Rabbi had instructed, which meant that someone would be along soon to fix the latch. He turned on the little light inside the Aron, moved the Scroll and opened the back panel.

He found the Vampire sitting Indian fashion among the worn out books, the old Torah Scroll cradled in his arms, his head tucked down because of a low shelf, suit rumpled, tie askew, wearing a pained expression. "Dare I ask what happened?"

An Angel took a pratfall to teach me to have a sense of humor! Something inside David gave way and he burst into divinely inspired laughter.

A Plum Assignment

Sharon L. Nelson

Sharon L. Nelson is a librarian who lives in a small Midwestern town with her husband and two very spoiled cats. Her story *Passing Through* won the 1999 ISFic short story contest, and an excerpt from her novel *All the Wealth of the Indies* was a semi-finalist in the 2001 Heart of Denver Romance Writers "Molly" competition.

"What you ask is impossible. It simply cannot be done." Q. Ashton Randall, the former Viscount Wolverton frowned sharply at the placid surface of the marble-edged pool at his feet. To his immense irritation, the pool did not reflect back his chiseled, classically handsome features. Instead, all he could see was the image of a plump young woman seated in an armchair, bent closely over a book. From the little he could see of her, the woman's hair was a mass of uncontrollable curls. Her skin appeared pale and splotchy, and her gold-rimmed spectacles were perched on a nose that reminded him more of a turnip than an organ of olfaction.

"I'm afraid you don't have much choice in the matter, my dear chap," his companion said cheerily. Ashton turned to glare at him. With his sparkling white wings and silver robe Graham looked as if he had just stepped off the top of the Queen's Christmas tree, a golden-haired, blue-eyed, porcelain-faced parody of an angel if he ever saw one.

The difficulty was that Graham was not a parody of an angel. He was a real one. To make matters worse, he had just been assigned to Ashton as his superior here "Upstairs," as it was quaintly termed.

"I'll be quite pleased to provide any assistance you require, of course," Graham added with an encouraging smile. Ashton noted that Graham had perfect teeth. But after all, everyone here did.

For the thousandth time Ashton mentally kicked himself for diving in front of the carriage at Pall Mall. His long record of previous debaucheries had clearly marked him for an alternative destination in the afterlife, and he suspected that the occupants of

"Downstairs" were far more to his taste than this bland, simpering bunch. But rules were rules, especially here; his last, and only, good deed had canceled out a lifetime of bad behavior, and that was that. He was assigned to the celestial realm for all eternity.

Stuck with Graham until the end of time.

Ashton rolled his eyes. "I've already told you. I know Benny's taste in women. And that—woman—does not remotely begin to meet his standards."

Graham opened the scroll in his hand, pursing his rosy Cupid's lips as he re-read its contents. "The assignment is quite clear. Lucy Spencer, only niece and ward of Leticia Spencer, is to meet Benjamin St. Leger, twelfth Duke of Woodmarle, on the night of the Duke's annual ball. They are to become lovers."

"Lovers?" Ashton felt his eyebrows crawling into his hairline. "Benny wouldn't let a woman who looked like that into his scullery, let alone his bed."

"Nevertheless, that is what is to happen." Graham tidily rolled up the scroll and peered into the pool again. "I'm sure she has a great deal of hidden potential."

"It's very thoroughly hidden, if you ask me. And I've never been greatly fond of hide-and-seek."

"But you were always fond of women," Graham said brightly, quickly unrolling the scroll again. "It says right here—"

Ashton ignored him. He'd been fond of women, all right—strong, handsome women with a gleam in their eye and a taste for whisky and mischief, not some mousy bookworm with peepers too weak to see across the room. And his best friend Benny had been even more exacting about his bedmates than Ashton had ever been. Even if Benny did, by some miracle, manage to lose his head over the girl, she looked to be so prissy that she'd not let him glimpse so much as an ankle until she had him firmly and eternally bound in holy wedlock.

That brought to mind another complication. He turned to Graham. "Doesn't encouraging them to become lovers rather smack of immorality?"

Graham gave him a beatific smile. "We have a little saying here that the Lord works in mysterious ways. But it is not as scandalous as it sounds. If all goes well—and we are fairly certain that it shall—the Duke should marry Lucy very soon after they, ah, prove their affections to each other." He bent closer to Ashton. "I'm not privy to the highest levels of the administration, of course, but rumor has it this is quite the plum assignment, not something we normally hand out to first-timers. Lucy's granddaughter will be an important philanthropist and humanitarian, helping millions of mortals yet unborn through her political and financial support of important medical research. That is why this assignment is so very important."

"A grandchild, is it? I'm to do all of this for a sprout that won't exist for likely another forty years?" Ashton frowned." What do they need us for if they have everything planned out to the tenth generation?"

"Oh, we're very much needed," Graham replied. "The Master only works in possibilities. There are certain outcomes He would prefer over others, of course. That is where our role lies, to gently shape circumstances so events will head in the preferred direction. But each mortal is always free to say 'yes' or 'no' to their destiny. Take your case, for example."

"I'd rather you not."

"But yours is a textbook case, Quigley."

Ashton winced. "Must you use that name?"

Graham blinked at him, his pale blue eyes round as two moons. "It is your given name. Why shouldn't I use it?"

"Because I detest it. Why can't you call me Ashton instead? Everyone else does—er, did."

Graham peered at the scroll again. "It says here that Ashton was your father's favorite spaniel's name. You took it over after the dog Passed On."

"And I preferred it infinitely to mine," Ashton said, scowling at him.

"But it's not your real name, Quigley. So calling you that would not be being entirely truthful, would it?" Graham chirped. "Getting back to your situation—as I was saying, you could have stood by and let that little girl be crushed to death instead of leaping in front of the carriage. No one pushed you. In the end, it was completely your choice. Was it not?"

Ashton recalled the wide-eyed look of terror on the little girl's face as the massive coach-and-four had barreled down the street directly at her. He had never been one for sentiment, let alone bravery, yet he found himself unable to stand by and let the disaster unfold in front of him. "I suppose you are right," Ashton finally grumbled.

Graham beamed at him again. "There, you see? So, getting back to business—your job is to guide and influence, but in the end each of your charges will make up his or her own mind as to their fate. It is possible that despite your most earnest efforts, Lucy may refuse the Duke."

Ashton glanced down into the pool again. The young woman had now assumed a most undignified posture, sprawled horizontally across an overstuffed armchair in the library with her legs dangling over one arm. He considered that it was far more likely that the Duke would refuse Lucy than the other way around.

"Say, I have an idea!" he suddenly said to Graham. "I used to be quite chummy with Benny. Why don't you assign me to him instead of Lucy? I'm sure I could persuade him as to her, ah, charms."

"Sorry, dear chap, but that assignment's already been given out."

"Can't I ask him to swap?"

"Oh, no, you couldn't possibly," Graham said with a flutter of hands and wings. "He was a Knight Templar when he was alive, and is quite well respected here. Plus he has several hundred years' seniority on me, let alone you."

So much for having a superior with backbone. "All right," Ashton said. "You're the one who said I had free will when I was alive. Does that apply now? What happens if I refuse this so-called 'plum' assignment?"

Graham tapped the side of his nose and bent his head towards Ashton. "Just on the Q.T., Quigley, it's terribly bad form not to accept an assignment, especially one's first. I do have a fallback assignment, but I was hoping not to have to bring it up."

"Bring it up anyway."

Graham withdrew another scroll from his voluminous sleeve and unrolled it. "Should you refuse this assignment—or fail to complete it satisfactorily—you are to be assigned to an elderly gentleman in a leper colony in Benares. He's already lost his nose and a foot, you see, and he's probably going to drop a finger or two soon. He needs some company and cheering up. Might be quite the extended tour of duty, though. I understand he comes from a very long-lived family."

Ashton shuddered and looked in to the pool again. Lucy had now molded herself into the chair in such a way that she looked more like a sack of potatoes wrapped in a dress than a human being. But compared to an old man who was rapidly shedding body parts, she was an absolute succubus.

"All right," Ashton sighed. "I'll take on Lucy."

* * * *

Ashton stood behind the thick damask drapes in Lucy's study, preparing to make himself visible. He'd practiced the technique with

Graham several times, but there was a bit of a trick to it. It reminded him of riding one of those new-fangled bicycles, where one had to pedal and steer and keep one's balance all at the same time.

Ashton concentrated on the instructions Graham had given him. He began to feel himself coalescing, his body gaining substance until he could feel the scratchy linen lining of the drapery pressed up against his newly-formed nose, which promptly wrinkled in distaste. Whoever the Spencer's housekeeper was she needed a stern talking to; the draperies were unconscionably musty and coated with—

"Ahhhhhh-CHOO!"

"Who's there?" came a female voice from beyond the curtain.

Ashton snuffled, enraged. One of the things he had learned shortly after his arrival Upstairs was that his angel's body denied him the pleasure of a glass of wine, or a fine meal, or a woman; yet, it could apparently sneeze. *What a grand design.* He squared his shoulders and stepped out from behind the curtain.

The room was shabbier than he had expected from seeing it in the pool. The edges of the carved walnut desk in the center of the room were chipped and worn, and the upholstery on the chairs and the spines of the many books on the shelves were faded with age and use. Lucy, too, was unfortunately not improved by viewing her in the flesh. At this close range her thick brows and freckles were far more alarming than he had anticipated. Her pale, puffy face was certainly nothing to write home about either, especially when it had a ferocious frown on it, as it did now.

"Who are you?" she asked.

Ashton stated his name, then froze, horrified, for the word that emerged from his lips was not "Ashton," or even "Randall," but "Quigley," his hated, dreaded, real name. He tried it twice more, with the same results: "Quigley, Quigley."

Her frown deepened. "Very well, your name is Quigley! Who are you, and why are you standing in my library?"

Ashton didn't answer her, distraught over the discrepancy between what he thought he was saying and what was coming out of his mouth. Had his altered condition also made it impossible for him to tell an untruth? The image of his stolid Aunt Bertha in Sussex suddenly came to his mind. She'd make a good test case.

"My aunt is a hippopotamus," Ashton said.

Lucy crossed her arms over her chest, still frowning. "I'm delighted to hear your aunt is a very nice person. But what does that have to do with why you are in my house dressed in that ridiculous costume?"

Ashton felt his wings droop. "Nothing, I suppose." Well, might as well get on with it. He raised his wings and squared his shoulders to match. "I am here, Lucy Spencer, to tell you that you have been called to a Higher Purpose."

"Yes, I know."

Ashton blinked. "You do?"

"Yes. I've been called to be a physician. One of the first women physicians admitted to the Royal Free Hospital. And you are impeding the process of my becoming one. Now go away, I have a great deal of studying to do." She picked up a thick leather-bound volume and began flipping through its pages.

Ashton fumed. So that was how he was to be treated, like a rag-and-bone man? He'd never had any female treat him so dismissively in his entire life, and he was not about to start Eternity by breaking his run of successes. He formed his lips into his most charming smile.

"Miss Spencer, I am not sure you understand the nature of my mission."

"I'm not sure I've any need to," she replied without looking up. "Good day."

"Miss Spencer—"

She glared at him over the tops of her spectacles. "Sir. If you do not take it upon yourself to leave under your own power this instant I shall be forced to ring for my coachman. He was a prizefighter in his day, and I'm sure he'd have no trouble with the likes of you."

"Wouldn't he?" Ashton spread out his wings to full width, and slowly raised himself until he hovered three feet above the library floor. "I don't think he's ever dealt with the likes of me."

Lucy glanced up at him again, apparently unimpressed. "The swami Uncle Randolph had to dinner last year not only raised himself in the air like that, but he shot fire out of his nose at the same time. I was quite taken in by him until I found out it was all done with wires and a bit of whisky. Now, I don't know how you got your apparatus into my study, but I must insist you dismantle it and leave immediately."

"There aren't any wires," Ashton said through clenched teeth. "Go ahead and take a look."

"Will it make you leave any sooner?"

"It might."

"Very well then." She removed her spectacles and laid them on the open book, then stalked over to Ashton, looking him up and down. She knelt and waved her hands beneath his feet. "I must admit, it's quite a clever system. The next time I'm in need of entertainment for a party I'll be sure to call upon you. Do you have a card?"

"NO!" Ashton thundered.

Lucy clapped her hands to her ears. "Ouch! That hurt!"

Ashton let himself float back down to the floor with a sigh. What had he been thinking? Despite Lucy's lumpish form she was a woman, and a woman was best persuaded by gentle handling, not pyrotechnics.

He adopted his very best conciliatory tone, the one he had used when Lady Celia had caught him in a most indelicate situation with a French chorus girl. "My apologies, Miss Spencer. I'm still getting used to...a number of things. I didn't realize I was able to project with such volume. And I sincerely apologize for interrupting your studies, for they are obviously important to you. If you could give me just a few moments to explain my situation I would be eternally grateful." *Quite literally.*

Lucy rubbed her left ear, grimacing. "Look, I don't know what it is you want with me, but if you don't leave in thirty seconds I'm ringing for Brady." She stretched her right hand towards a needlepoint bellpull.

Well, thirty seconds was better than none. "Miss Spencer," he began, "why did you decide to become a physician?"

Her head cocked to one side, like an inquisitive bird's. She hadn't been expecting that one. "To help people, of course."

"What if I told you that by going along with the plan I am about to present, you could help thousands—perhaps millions—of people? Certainly far more people than you would ever be able to help as a physician. Would you hear me out then?"

She looked at him suspiciously. "I suppose."

"Good. Kindly stop strangling that bellstrap, then, and please take a seat."

Lucy lowered herself into a nearby armchair without taking her eyes off him. Ashton groaned inwardly as he heard the chair creak under her weight.

"Very well," she said. "You have my full attention."

Ashton gave her a formal nod. "Thank you. To recap, Miss Spencer: I have been charged by a, er, Higher Power to bring about certain actions which are to result in the betterment of mankind, and in which you play an important role. Unfortunately I am not at liberty to divulge the exact nature of these occurrences, except for one: which is that I am to ensure that you attend the Duke of Woodmarle's ball six weeks hence."

Lucy hooted with laughter. "You're here to invite me to a ball? Oh, dear, dear me! I must be further out of touch with Society than

I realized. I had no idea invitations were now being delivered these days by unemployed actors wrapped up in bedsheets." She looked Ashton up and down, nodding. "I grant you it is a terribly clever idea. Quite original. But I hope this Duke fellow is paying you well—those wings must have cost a fortune to let."

Ashton counted to ten—twice—before answering in his iciest, dressing-down-the-servants tone. "Miss Spencer. The wings are not 'let'—I own them, in the most intimate manner you could possibly imagine. In addition, I am not, and never have been, an actor. But I am—well, I am an angel, and I have a job to do—a job which you are making exceedingly difficult, by the way."

Lucy rolled her eyes. "Oh, for Heaven's sake! What sort of idiot do you take me to be? Do you honestly expect me to believe you're an angel?"

"Yes. I do."

"Quigley, I am a woman of science. Angels do not exist."

"And I am here to tell you—entirely reluctantly, I may add—that they do." He extended his hand towards Lucy. "Here. Touch my hand."

She jerked away from him, cramming herself, stiff-backed, into the chair. "I'll do nothing of the sort."

"Then allow me." Ashton reached out and grasped the tips of Lucy's plump fingers.

She shuddered. "Let go! Your hands are as cold as ice!"

"As the lady commands," Ashton said with a nod. He allowed the hand holding Lucy's to slowly dematerialize until her unsupported hand dropped back to her lap.

When he looked at her face again her skin had gone dead white beneath her freckles. "H-how did you do that?"

"It's rather complicated to explain. I'm still learning the finer points of it myself. But be assured, Miss Spencer, it is no parlor trick."

She looked up at him. "Angels don't exist," she repeated shakily.

"Once upon a time I shared that same belief, Miss Spencer. But I have been most earnestly proven in error. Now—may we return to the business at hand? In six weeks you are to appear at the Duke of Woodmarle's ball. He will see you there. And...he will fall in love with you."

A brilliant red flush overtook the pallor of Lucy's skin. "Don't be ridiculous. A man like that would have nothing to do with me."

"In six weeks, I can make it so he will." He paused; the words had come out exactly as he had thought them. *It's not a lie, then,* he considered. *Does that mean I can actually do it?*

Lucy shook her head and turned her face from him. "Well, now I truly don't believe you. And even if I did, I...I have absolutely no interest in attending the Duke of Marble's ball."

"Woodmarle," Ashton corrected. "His name is Benjamin St. Leger, twelfth Duke of Woodmarle. One of the oldest families in the country. And, I might add, the key to your future."

Her color was still high. "Even if I was interested in your silly scheme—and I most assuredly am not—I'm far too busy at the moment. I must keep up with my studies or I'll never pass my exams at the end of Term."

"That's no difficulty," Ashton said brightly. "You don't need to study at all. I'll just nip the answers for you."

"You most certainly will not!" Lucy leaped to her feet and faced him, her eyes ablaze with fury. "If I am to set an example for other young women in medicine, I absolutely must achieve my success honestly. Besides, what sort of an angel are you, offering to steal things and encouraging me to cheat? I have never heard such a despicable thing in my life! Really!"

Ashton looked at Lucy and, far deep within him, felt a sudden and unexpected glimmer of hope. With her eyes flashing, her skin flushed and her chin held high, she was almost...pretty. Well, passable, at any rate. The raw material was still undeniably rough, but there was a spark of something there with which he could work with.

"Lucy, you are absolutely right," he said, returning to his conciliatory tone. "I should never have suggested such a thing to such a fine, upright young woman as yourself. I am simply not used to dealing with mortals of your sterling moral character." He inwardly sighed with relief as the last phrase passed through his lips unaltered. "All I am trying to do is to help you to help mankind. What I propose may sound outlandish, but it is no joke. You will have whatever assistance I am allowed to provide through the entire process. Believe me, the outcome of this assignment is as important to me as it is to you."

The passion had faded from her eyes, and she looked pale and lumpish again. She wriggled back into the chair and folded her plump hands in her lap, frowning again, then suddenly looked up at him.

"You say that my meeting this Duke will help a great many people?"

"I have it on highest authority."

She nodded gravely. "Very well. Tell me what it is you want me to do."

* * * *

Ashton nodded with approval as Lucy walked across her study with her heavy leather tome—but this time it was balanced on her head, not in her hands.

"Good," he said. "Much better than last week. Remember not to roll your shoulders forward."

Lucy nodded, causing the book to tip backwards. She quickly reached up to steady it with her hands and resumed her stately pace across the library floor. She turned carefully at the far bookcase and began gliding back towards him.

"Quigley? May I ask you something?"

"Within limits."

"Yes, yes. You've gone over that quite thoroughly. I know I can't ask about the future." She bit her lip, hesitating. "But can you tell me...what the Duke is like?"

Ashton stepped to one side as much to allow himself a few moments' thought as to allow Lucy to finish traversing the full length of the floor. "Benny? He's about my height, blonde hair, blue eyes; considered rather dashing by the ladies, all in all. I think you'll like him."

Lucy frowned. "No, that's not what I meant. What is he like? What does he like to do?"

A number of things that are best not described to sheltered young ladies. "Er...he likes horse racing. And the theatre." *Actually, the actresses at the theatre, but I'm not about to mention that either.* "Cards at the club, riding to the hunt. The usual things young men like."

"Oh." She had stopped in mid-stride. "Is he a kind man?"

"Kind? I suppose so." Ashton had spent most of his time in Benny's company in a near-constant state of intoxication, so it was difficult for him to be sure. But Benny had never been a mean drunk; on the contrary, he had constantly been buying rounds for the house in the dingy little pubs in which they had gone slumming. He had treated his mistresses well, and his dogs and horses too. That counted as kindness, didn't it?

Lucy nodded, this time carefully enough to not disturb the book perched on her head. "I'm pleased to hear that. Perhaps...it won't be so bad, then. Maybe I'll even enjoy it."

Ashton had an alarming series of thoughts about what "it" might be. "What do you mean?" he asked cautiously.

"The ball. If the Duke is kind to me at the ball, I might actually enjoy it. I always hated balls. I love to dance, but I was so rarely asked because...well, you know." She paused in front of the walnut pier mirror that stood between two of the library's windows. "Look at me."

"You underestimate yourself, Lucy. Especially now." He had to admit she had made remarkable progress in only one month. Ashton had steered her towards the better shops to improve her wardrobe, and encouraged her to eat a bit less clotted cream on her scones at tea. He passed on to her tidbits of women's grooming he had observed from overnight "guests" from his past, and schooled her in posture and deportment as he was doing now. Little things, perhaps, but they had added up to make a difference.

He stepped behind Lucy as she stood in front of the mirror. Only Lucy appeared on its surface, for, as with the reflecting pool Upstairs, he could not see his own face. "You've come along remarkably well, Lucy. I'm quite proud of your progress."

She smiled prettily, as he had taught her to do. "Thank you, Quigley."

He winced, thankful she couldn't see him in the mirror. The only thing he disliked about Lucy's transformation was the necessary refinement of her personality. A woman's role was to please a man, not irritate him, he told her: she couldn't very well go about scowling at men and contradicting them. When he had told her that, she had scowled at him and contradicted him. She eventually acquiesced when he reminded her of the importance of their mission, but there were times when he missed her former prickliness.

A small, feminine frown creased her forehead. "I hope all this work will be worth it. It's been very difficult to do all of these things, and to study, too."

"I don't think you'll have anything to worry about there." Ashton had followed Lucy to lectures and on rounds, and sneaked a peek at the supervising physicians' notebooks. The comments about her had been entirely favorable—save for a few remarks about her "unfeminine forthrightness," and those had lessened as of late. "But if you're concerned I can still nip the exam for you," he added helpfully.

She smiled. "That won't be necessary. However, thank you for your kind offer."

Ashton smiled in return at her politeness, despite the griping sensation where his stomach used to be. A pliant, pleasant Lucy just didn't seem right to him somehow. But that was the type of woman Benny had always liked best, and his job was to make Lucy acceptable to him.

He stepped out from behind her and squared his wings. "Now then," he said. "Time to work on your curtsey again."

* * * *

Ashton hovered next to Lucy as she stepped out of her carriage and presented her invitation to the bewigged footman at the door. As she entered the house he allowed himself a small moment of triumph. Lucy's dress was as magnificent as he had hoped it would be, the emerald satin glowing in the lamplight of the Duke's hallway. Her body filled it perfectly, now pleasantly rounded in all the right places instead of lumpish and unsightly. A heavy application of face powder had acceptably dimmed her freckles, and her hair had been tamed into an attractive upsweep accented by a single fresh white orchid that Ashton had filched from a neighbor's conservatory.

True, Ashton admitted to himself, she'd never be able to compete with the polished Court beauties that were Benny's favorite fodder. With the worst of her dowdiness stripped away, though, perhaps the Duke would be interested enough to take a second look—and then hopefully a third and fourth.

Ashton held his nonexistent breath as Lucy entered the ballroom to be announced. It was a notorious breach of etiquette for her to attend the ball unescorted, but Lucy had refused to drag any males of her acquaintance into what she had taken to calling "this hare-brained plot of yours." But he reasoned that her coming alone could be another factor that might draw Benny's attention to her, and so he had let the matter stand.

Slipping ahead of Lucy, he entered the ballroom. The sight of it brought a sharp pang to his heart. Among the swirling dancers and strolling couples he recognized dozens of friends and acquaintances, and it shook him deeply to see them move past him without a glance. This had been his world, not so long ago. All that had changed now.

"Where is he?" Lucy whispered anxiously, bringing him back to the present.

"Straight ahead of you."

Lucy squinted, frowning. "I can't see him. I told you I should have worn my spectacles."

"At a ball? Out of the question. And stop frowning. You'll disturb your make-up." He touched Lucy lightly under the arm. "Now, let's see how we fare. Watch your step on the stairs."

Benny, as was his habit, was in the very center of the room where he could be sure to garner the most attention. A portly white-haired man was speaking earnestly to the young Duke, but Benny appeared not to be listening to him and was staring off into space in the direction of the entrance to the ballroom. Ashton nodded. *Perfect*. Benny couldn't help but see Lucy as she descended down the stairs.

"Miss Lucy Spencer."

Ashton hovered just above the stairs at Lucy's side as she descended the slick marble steps into the ballroom. She wobbled a bit on the third step, and Ashton mentally kicked himself for not insisting she practice wearing those shoes with their delicate little heels. But she made it down all six steps safely; good. He turned back towards Benny to gauge his reaction.

Benny's bright blue eyes flicked a glance in the staircase's direction. Then he turned towards the portly man, gave him a grin and a hearty slap on the back, and turned towards the card room.

Ashton stood, slack-jawed, in the middle of the ballroom as Lucy continued on past him. Benny hadn't even looked. Once. He'd given Lucy no more of his attention than a spot on the wall. No, Ashton corrected himself, Benny'd pay attention to a spot on the wall; he'd order one of the servants wash it off immediately. Lucy, on the other hand, hadn't even crossed his consciousness.

Lucy paused in the middle of the floor, staring with a puzzled frown at the spot where Benny had been standing. *Oh, bad move*, Ashton thought. People were now stopping and staring at Lucy, who, despite her quite acceptable appearance, was still scandalously unescorted. Ashton slipped to her side. "Let's cross to the far side of the room, shall we?" he prompted.

Lucy moved elegantly, head high, to stand beneath one of the innumerable potted palms ringing the ballroom. "What went wrong?" she said in a low voice.

"I'm not exactly sure." He gave Lucy and encouraging smile, then remembered she couldn't see it. "Stay here, enjoy yourself, and I'll go see what can be done."

To Ashton's immense distress Benny decided to secrete himself in the male-only preserve of his card room for several leisurely hands of piquet. By the time he emerged, reeking of cigar smoke, a middle-aged fellow with thinning red hair had swept Lucy into a quadrille. Ashton let her finish the dance and the one following, thankful that Lucy was at least able to enjoy herself for a few moments. But when the dance ended and Lucy's partner excused himself, Ashton realized Benny had disappeared from the ballroom again. Ashton sighed in exasperation. He had never realized that Benny was so blasted peripatetic at his parties.

He finally tracked down Benny entering his billiard room. He quickly returned to Lucy's side in the ballroom. She was downing a cup of punch and enviously watching the dancers again.

"Do you play billiards?" Ashton whispered.

She jumped, sloshing the punch down the front of her dress. "I wish you wouldn't come up on me when you're invisible," she rasped. "Now look what I've done." She looked down unhappily at the spreading dark circle on her bodice.

"Well I can't very well appear wings-and-all in the midst of this mob, can I? Do you play billiards or not?"

"A little."

Ashton fumed. He detested when women indulged in this sort of prevarication. "Do you mean 'a little' as in 'you can barely hold a cue,' or 'a little' as in 'you can beat any man in the room, but you're far too modest to admit it'?"

"The former, I'm afraid," she murmured.

Ashton sighed. "Well, I suppose you don't actually have to play. All he has to do is notice you, and the billiard room is certainly smaller than this one so we'll have a better chance."

"But what about the dress?"

This was a dilemma. Benny liked a well-dressed woman; but on the other hand, by the time Lucy had found a water closet and repaired the damage done by the punch, they might lose their best chance of cornering the Duke. "We'll chance it the way it is," Ashton grumbled. "Now march."

Lucy scowled at his tone of command, but followed him to the doors leading into the Duke's opulent billiard room. The green-shaded lights hung low over the table, leaving the rest of the room barely illuminated. The room was not only dark, it was crowded, the table surrounded three layers deep by onlookers.

"I can't go in there," Lucy muttered, peering over the elaborately coifed head of a woman standing in the doorway. "It's packed."

"Shove your way in, then."

"Honestly, Quigley, you can be so rude at times."

The woman at the doorway turned, looking Lucy up and down. A disdainful smile appeared on her lips as she caught sight of Lucy's chest. "In need of a bit of tidying up, aren't we?"

Lucy blushed furiously crimson. "No, thank you. I'm fine just the way I am." She squeezed in past the woman, giving her a none-too-gentle jab to her corseted ribs as she passed.

Ashton was not quite sure what happened next, but the woman at the door shifted her posture in a most unseemly way and suddenly Lucy lurched forward. Her hands instinctively stretched out to break her fall, shoving the man in front of her square on the back. The man fell forward as well, jostling the arm of the current player. Ashton watched in horror as the cue in the player's hands jammed down into the surface of the billiard table, putting an enormous tear into the green cloth surface.

"What ho, Barkeley!" Benny's merrily intoxicated voice boomed from the far side of the room. "No more billiards for you tonight! I guess I win by default, then!" With a wave the Duke squeezed out the back entrance of the room and down the corridor back to the ballroom.

Ashton turned to watch Lucy being helped to her feet by a pair of gentlemen. Her face was brilliant red, and she was apologizing profusely to the man who had torn the billiard table with his cue. Behind her, a number of the guests were shaking their heads disapprovingly at Lucy, including the woman at the doorway, who snickered as she left the room.

Ashton left Lucy in search of a W.C. and went off to look for Benny. He had returned to the ballroom, where he was standing beneath one of the giant potted palms and grinning like an idiot at a pretty young Marchioness that Ashton vaguely remembered as being recently widowed. Ashton felt a knot where his stomach should have been. The doe-eyed brunette was exactly Benny's type, and by the way she was batting her eyelashes at him the attraction was mutual.

Ashton had not tried speaking to any mortal save Lucy. Could he plant a whispered word in Benny's ear—or better yet, a sharp kick in the shins—to divert his attention away from the woman? There was only one way to find out. He slipped around knots of flirting couples and jewel-encrusted matriarchs, making his way towards the Duke.

"You are Quigley, *ja*?" said a deep, rumbling voice behind him.

Ashton spun around, his nose at mid-Adam's apple to a massive form in a silver-gray robe. "Yes. What of it?"

"I am Wilhelm. I am assigned to the Duke."

Ashton took a step back and looked the former knight up and down. Despite the fluffy white wings at his shoulders, Ashton had no difficulty imagining a barrel helm set atop that heavy, square-jawed face—not to mention a broadsword in those meaty hands. He swallowed quickly. No wonder Graham had been intimidated.

"Delighted to meet you, Wilhelm," Ashton said. He glanced over at Benny, who was chortling over something the Marchioness had said. "Would you mind telling me how long you're going to wait before you ensure that our friend the Duke makes his advance on dear Lucy?"

"There is no reason yet to interfere," Wilhelm rumbled. "Things must take their course."

"'Take their course'? He hasn't even looked at her yet!"

Wilhelm's lip curled ever so slightly. "You must learn patience. It is a problem with you newcomers, *ja*? There is yet time. The Duke's ball lasts until dawn."

Ashton glanced at the Duke again. Benny had just chucked the Marchioness under the chin, causing her to blush most handsomely. "I have no doubt that the Duke will be dancing until dawn tonight—but not with Lucy, and not in a vertical position, if you catch my drift."

Wilhelm's heavy brows drew together. "Very well. I will do a favor for you. But just this once." The knight moved to Benny's side and bent to whisper something in his ear just as a passing couple blocked Ashton's view. A few moments later there was a loud shriek and a sharp clapping sound. Ashton peered around the couple to see Benny holding the side of his face and the Marchioness stomping off through the crowd, her expression oozing indignation.

"There," Wilhelm said, returning to Ashton's side. "I've done my part. The rest is up to you."

Ashton turned around to locate Lucy once more, but the emerald gown had utterly disappeared from the sea of guests. He finally spied a spot of tousled reddish-brown underneath another one of the innumerable potted palms. A large damp spot remained where she had daubed at the punch stain on her bodice.

He glided over to Lucy. "Now's our chance," he whispered to her. "Hurry, before Benny finds himself ensnared again!"

Lucy frowned, peering through the fronds of the palm. "I don't see him. Where's he gone to now?"

"Across the room, under the window. He's standing to the right of the man with the blue sash. Now go!" He materialized one arm enough to give Lucy a little shove.

Lucy stepped out from under the palm, and promptly collided with a passing footman bearing a tray of champagne flutes. Ashton watched in horror as the glasses somersaulted in mid-air, showering Lucy and the footman with their contents before landing on the polished marble floor in a crescendo of shattering crystal.

"Oh, blast," Ashton heard himself say. The word he had thought of was far, far worse than 'blast.'

* * * *

Lucy stood on the sidewalk outside of the Duke's mansion, waiting for her carriage to come 'round. Ashton had pleaded with her to stay a while longer, for the ball would last for hours yet. But Lucy had been adamant. She was not about to risk another humiliating episode in an attempt to meet the Duke, and told Ashton so in no uncertain terms.

There were a number of other early-departing guests on the walk as well, but they had all crowded together so as to leave a circle of space around Lucy, where she stood all alone in her ruined finery. As he stood at her side, Ashton caught the glimpse of a hidden smile or the sound of a muffled snicker here and there throughout the crowd.

"I hope you're satisfied," Lucy said. Her voice sounded as if a cord was wrapped around her throat.

"Hush, Lucy. Not here."

"Why? So they won't think I'm mad because I'm talking to myself? I've already made such a fool of myself, I don't see how I could possibly do myself any greater damage."

Ashton looked at Lucy's face. Her eyes were red-rimmed and beginning to look puffy. Women's tears had always been his undoing. An apology...yes, that was a good start. It had always helped his case whenever he had admitted to being in the wrong—especially when it was the truth.

"Lucy, I'm terribly sorry about what happened," he said quickly. "It's entirely my fault, all of it."

She gave him a dismissive shake of her head. "It's my fault for going along with it. I should have known better. All my life I thought I knew who I was and what I wanted to do. But you...." Her lower lip quivered for a moment. "You made me want something I thought I could never have. You made me believe I could be like other women, wear fine gowns and dance at a ball and attract the attentions of a man like the Duke. You made me believe it with all my heart, Quigley. I trusted you."

Ashton bowed his head, unable to bear the look of hurt and betrayal in Lucy's eyes. He had tried to make her something she was not, and in the end all he had done was crush her spirit, the best and truest part of her. How could what he had done possibly be in the service of a greater good? He'd have some very choice words to say to Graham when he returned. If Graham didn't like it, he could stuff it up his arse. There had been rebellious angels in Heaven before; perhaps it was time for another one.

Still, that would not salvage Lucy's damaged pride and reputation. "Lucy," he said, "I'll make this up to you. I don't know how, or when. But I promise you I will, if it takes me the rest of Eternity."

She shook her head again. "It's all right, Quigley. In a way you may have done me a great service. From now on I'll keep my mind on my work and never be tempted by such vanities again." Her carriage arrived and she entered it, her tousled head high and her back straight. Ashton thought of joining her in the carriage then changed his mind. There was nothing he could do or say tonight that would help her. But help her he would, somehow.

Lucy's carriage door had just swung closed and the driver was on the way up to his box when he heard hoarse shouting in the distance and the sound of someone running. The elegantly dressed crowd in front of the Duke's began to murmur and shuffle nervously, like overbred horses on a tether. A moment later Ashton heard the shout of "Fire! Fire!" drawing closer.

Lucy's head popped out of the carriage window. "Fire? Where?"

A young man broke through the crowd, his workman's Saturday best suit torn and smudged with soot. "At the vaudeville, Mum," he panted. "The Prince George."

"That's nearly a mile from here!"

"I know, Mum. But we've gotten little help from the toffs we've passed on the way." His jaw clenched for a moment as he glanced at the aristocrats surrounding him. "The firemen are there, but there's many hurt and no one t' tend to 'em."

Lucy swung open the coach door. "Get in." As the man clambered into the seat across from her she pounded furiously on the coach ceiling. "Brady! The Prince George! Now! And Quigley, get in here this moment!"

Quigley, startled, slipped into the coach as it lurched into motion, thankful he was not in corporeal form; otherwise he would have left a limb or two on the Duke's sidewalk when Lucy had slammed closed the carriage door.

Lucy looked around the carriage, frowning. "Where are you, Quigley? I hate talking to you when I don't know where you are."

"Be you speakin' to me, Mum?" the soot-stained young man said.

"No, to someone else. He's invisible." The young man's eyes grew round as saucers. Lucy frowned at him. "Don't goggle so. Do you want our help or not?"

The young man nodded, a barely perceptible shake of the head.

"I'm to your left," Quigley interjected. "Do you want to see me?"

"No. This is no time for parlor tricks," Lucy said sharply. You said before you wanted to help me, to make up for all you did. Did you truly mean it?"

He nodded, then remembered she couldn't see him. "Yes."

"Good. What I need you to do is go back to the Duke's house and round up every carriage and spare pair of hands you can. Get them to the Prince George. If you do that, I will consider our debt settled. Do you agree?"

"Yes."

"Good." She bent forward towards the young man. "Let me see your hand. It looks as if it's bleeding."

Ashton gathered himself up and hurtled out the carriage, soaring upwards into the star-pocked night sky. As he rose he saw a dull red glow and a pillar of billowing gray smoke some distance away. Lucy was heading there, into danger, and for a moment he wanted to follow her to see her safe. She had asked him to perform another duty, however, and he had promised to do so. He swung about in mid-air and flew back to the Duke's mansion.

Benny was out on his doorstep now, a frown upon his face. "Pity about the fire," an elegantly dressed young toff said to the Duke.

"Yes, it is," said the young woman beside him. "What a terrible shame. I imagine it will be in all the papers tomorrow."

Ashton's non-existent stomach burned with anger and embarrassment that when he was alive he'd likely have done the same thing, tut-tutting about such tragedies but making no move to actually help. He had to do better for Lucy, but how? In the shadows he caught a glimpse of a massive gray figure and moved towards it.

"Wilhelm!" he hissed. "I need your help!"

"What now?" the knight asked.

"I have to talk to Benny and all these people. I have to convince them to go help at the fire at the Prince George, and I don't know how to do it."

"Is that all?" Wilhelm shook his head. "*Ach*, that Graham, he teaches you nothing. Whisper in their ear what you want them to say."

Ashton frowned. "What *I* want *them* to say?"

"*Ja*. If you wanted the Duke to say something to everyone, what would you want him to say? He will then say it."

"That's what you did with the Marchioness, isn't it?"

"*Ja*." Wilhelm raised a warning hand. "But don't you ask me what I told him to say to her. It was not a very nice thing."

"Doubtless it wasn't." Ashton slipped in to stand beside Benny, forming the words in his mind, then bent quickly to whisper in the Duke's ear.

The Duke suddenly straightened and his expression became stern. For a moment he stood immobile, and Ashton feared he had done something terribly wrong to his old friend. It certainly would not have been the first time today he had made a mistake, after all.

"My friends," Benjamin St. Leger announced, "I think we must do more than feel sorry for these people. I think we must come to their aid."

"I agree!" a man shouted.

"Yes, we should help them!" a young woman in a pale mauve dress cried out. Other shouts of agreement soon rang out, and out of the corner of his eye Ashton saw a large gray figure moving among the crowd, whispering here and there. Some of the speakers looked perplexed by what they had just said, but as everyone seemed to be in agreement they were all soon calling for their carriages and demanding to be taken to the Prince George.

Ashton flew upwards again, streaking back to the scene of the fire. The narrow street outside of the Prince George was crammed with people passing buckets as a few hand-pumps manned by firemen spat water at the cherry-red flames now licking out of every window of the theatre. Ashton looked around frantically for Lucy amidst the screaming, milling crowd and finally located her across the street from the theatre.

"No, don't put him there!" she said to a pair of men bearing a badly burned elderly man in their arms. She stepped over to the burned man, shaking her head. "He's too far gone to help, poor fellow. We must concentrate our efforts on those that can be saved." She turned to a young woman sitting on the curb, peering at her face. "Yes, it will blister, and I'm sorry, but it may scar. But I assure you, you'll be all right. If you're not too hurt, can you help me with that boy over there?" She walked the young woman over to two men who were holding down a shrieking young man as a third man cut through the sleeve of his jacket with a pair of heavy shears.

Ashton watched as Lucy knelt by the young man's side. His eyes were glassy, wild with fear and hurt, his breath coming in short, harsh gasps. "Easy, now," Lucy said. "Let me have a look." She lifted the man's arm, turning it slightly, her hands avoiding the charred and bleeding areas as she carefully assayed the damage. Ashton was amazed that Lucy's plump, stubby fingers could move with such grace and tenderness. The man was breathing easier now, a bit of color returning to his pale face, seemingly calmed by Lucy's touch alone.

"I know this is very painful," Lucy said to the man. Her voice was gentle and soothing, utterly unlike the voice with which she had barked out commands only moments before. "But the pain is a good sign. It means the nerves were not destroyed. You need to get clean water on this arm, though, as cold as possible. These good people will help you with that." She looked up at the group of onlookers gathered around her. "You will see to him, won't you?" Though her voice remained quiet, there was no doubt as to the tone of authority in it.

She rose from her knees, addressing the larger crowd still bringing out the wounded. "Please, everyone! Those who are less hurt attend to those who need more help! We'll have carriages soon to bring them to hospital!" She quickly turned to a sobbing young woman bearing a child, assessing both their injuries and giving them a kind smile before sending them on to one of the makeshift medical stations she had organized.

Ashton watched, astounded, as Lucy moved through the crowds, diagnosing, directing, comforting. She was fierce in her orders when she needed to be, but always gentle whenever dealing with a patient. She looked a wreck: her hair had tumbled down into a tangled mass of curls and her face and hands were smeared with soot and blood. But there was an inner light within her that transcended her appearance, and each person she spoke to looked upon her with thankfulness bordering on adoration. Ashton swallowed. Here was a true angel doing heroic service; by comparison, everything he had done counted for truly less than nothing.

Lucy turned from her latest patient stepped out into the street, staring back towards the Duke's mansion. "Damn you, Quigley, where are you?" she muttered.

"Here," Ashton said.

She turned towards his voice. "Are they coming?"

"Yes. Very soon." He looked up to see Benny's phaeton thundering down the street, driven by the Duke himself with the Duke's coachman seated next to him, hanging on for dear life. Ashton turned back to Lucy but she had already moved on, directing a group of men to help load the severely injured into the arriving carriages.

Benny stood up in his phaeton, watching Lucy for several long minutes, his mouth agape.

"By God," Ashton heard Benny mutter. "What a woman!"

Ashton felt his invisible wings droop until they touched the ground. Benny was utterly appalled by her. He could well imagine what Benny must be thinking of Lucy's ruined appearance and dictatorial manner. There was no hope for her now.

Lucy suddenly turned to face the Duke's coach. "You there!"

"Me?" Benny said.

"Yes, you. And the man next to you, too." Lucy's words cracked out like a whip. "You're both strong young fellows. Get down from there and carry the wounded!"

Ashton froze, waiting for Benny to snap at her high-handedness. One did not address a twelfth-generation Duke like an errant chimney sweep.

Instead, Benny jumped down from the driver's seat with a grin. "Yes, Miss!"

"Wait!" she said. "Are you loud as well as strong?"

Benny blinked at her. "Loud?"

"Yes. Can you bellow?"

The young Duke grinned even more broadly. "Like a stuck bull, if need be."

"Then come with me. My voice is tiring, and I need someone to shout out my directions. Can you help me with that?"

"Most certainly, Miss."

Lucy pointed down the street. "We must get that line of carriages organized. It's starting to look like Bartholomew Fair."

Benny nodded. "It'll be my pleasure, Miss."

Oh, and it will be, Ashton thought as he watched Benny and Lucy dash down the street together to order the carriages into some semblance of a line. He'd seen the look in Benny's eyes as he'd looked Lucy up and down. He'd seen it many times before, but never with such intensity. Whatever the Duke had seen in Lucy, he had liked it. Immensely.

Ashton watched as the pair moved through the site of the disaster during the rest of the night, Benny bellowing out Lucy's instructions and sometimes adding a colorful directive of his own. Despite the seriousness of the situation he saw they were often smiling as they worked, and at one point he saw Benny take Lucy's hand into his own and give it a reassuring squeeze.

Wilhelm arrived some time later and briefly instructed Ashton in what needed to be done to ease the passing of those who were dying. Ashton at first quailed from the work, but then thought of Lucy's immense bravery and compassion. He certainly could do no less than she. He was grateful to discover that his recent experience in Crossing Over was helpful, and with a few words he was able to ease the fear and bewilderment of those who were breathing their last.

So immersed was he in his work that he barely noticed the final extinguishing of the fire and the coming of the dawn. He had just murmured the last words of welcome to an elderly woman when he looked up to see an exhausted Lucy being gently handed into the phaeton by Benny. A few moments later the Duke gathered up the reins and drove his carriage back in the direction of his London house.

* * * *

"Astoundingly good work," Graham said. "Everyone is very pleased with you, Quigley, very pleased."

"I don't see why," Ashton said, staring down into the reflecting pool at an image of Lucy and Benny, beaming at each other at their wedding breakfast. "I technically failed the assignment, you know. My instructions were to have Lucy and Benny meet at the ball."

"I don't believe so, dear chap." Graham pulled out his scroll again. "They were to meet the night of the ball. You arranged it all quite perfectly. And, I might add, saved a number of lives in the process. We didn't anticipate Lucy arriving at the fire until much later, if at all. Free will, you know."

"The night of the ball?" Ashton said. "They didn't have to meet *at* the ball, just the night of the ball?"

Graham consulted the scroll. "That was the assignment."

Ashton felt his jaw drop. "I could have just arranged for them to meet at the fire? Lucy never needed to attend the ball at all?"

"Apparently so, dear chap. Why are you so out of sorts about such a minor detail?"

Ashton pressed his forehead into his hand. Six weeks of coaching Lucy for nothing. Six weeks of hanging about the hospital, following her every move, watching every morsel that entered her mouth. Six weeks of canvassing dress shops and scouting neighbor's conservatories for nothing. But truly, had it all been for nothing? He'd not have gotten to know Lucy so well otherwise, to be able to look beyond her spectacles and turnip nose and see the spirit and compassion within her. And that, he decided, would have been a great pity.

"Never mind, Graham. It doesn't really matter."

"Glad to hear it!" Graham said. "Ready for your next assignment?"

Ashton felt his jaw twitch. "The leper colony in Benares?"

"Oh, no, no, no," Graham said. "It's been decided that since you seem to have a knack for these sort of things, there's another matchmaking exercise we're going to send you on." He pulled a scroll from his sleeve, scanning it quickly. "It doesn't look as if I've all the details yet, as it won't happen for a number of years Earth time. But it involves a young woman in a convent and a nobleman, somewhere in Austria I believe...."

Ragnarok Can Wait

Susan Sizemore

Susan has written over 20 books and a dozen short stories in the last ten years. This is her third angel story, although none of her angels have been traditionally angelic. Her only explanation for this particular angel story is that she lives in Minnesota.

"There's been a mistake?" Peter Jordan's voice was quite calm, his expression as blandly polite as ever. His hands were folded serenely on top of his desk. No outward demeanor reflected any of the inner alarms the word *mistake* set off in his soul. Miss Hagaarsdottir's fierce frown and looming presence did not intimidate Jordan. That word, *mistake*, did. "What sort of mistake?" Jordan continued in the mildest possible tone.

Mild or not, he was aware that all eyes in the office were on him and the tall woman before his desk. Alert silence and stillness hung in the air like the last held breath before the Apocalypse.

"Really!" Jordan announced. Leaning so that he could peer past Miss Hagaarsdottir, he waved a hand at his assistants and sent them scurrying back to work. All but Miss Ise, who continued to watch from the desk opposite his with her usual bodhisattva-like calm.

Hagaarsdottir reclaimed Jordan's attention by banging her fist on the desk. Then she propped her spear against the edge of his desk and placed a PDA before him. She tapped the tiny data screen with one blood-encrusted fingernail.

"I see last night's Wild Hunt went well," Jordan said, noticing her hand.

"It did. You should have come."

"You know how I feel about that sort of thing."

"We will make a man of you yet, Peter. I have told you that I would go to the Gregorian chanting concert with you if you would indulge in outdoor activities with me."

"Are you asking me for a date?" A flicker of hope lit in Jordan's soul that her mission here was not quite so dire as her words indicated.

Hagaarsdottir smiled at him, then shook her heavy blonde braids and returned to business. "This needs your personal attention."

Jordan gestured toward the arched main door of the Front Office. "There's so many people to see here, and—"

"There are always so many people to see." She banged the butt of her spear on the floor. "My part of the infinite land may not have as many incoming residents as the more modern sections, but those who come home to us can be—impressive."

"And trouble makers?" he guessed. The thought of anyone causing trouble *here* was chilling.

"You need to see him for yourself, Peter." She reached over the desk and yanked Jordan to his feet, without any regard for his dignity, or supervisory position. "Come with me."

None of his staff dared to crack so much as a faint smile when Hagaarsdottir dragged him out through the pearl and gold filigree arch, though Jordan did catch a glimpse of amusement cross Miss Ise's serene expression as he and the valkyrie passed her by. When they were beyond the arch, Jordan hesitated for another instant to glance reassuringly at the double row of clients waiting patiently in line for he and his staff to make them welcome, comfortable and happy in their new homes. Most of the newcomers were trying not to stare nervously, or in downright terror, at the impressive sight of the frowning, well-armed, six foot seven inch Asgardian Incoming Liaison marching before him.

Her snort of amusement at their reactions was not lost on Jordan. "Seeing you might lead some of them to think they've ended up in the wrong place," Jordan whispered to her armor-clad back.

"Somebody's ended up in the wrong place," Hagaarsdottir said darkly. The look she gave him over her shoulder was equally dark. Thunder rumbled overhead to match her mood, and the howling of direwolves could be heard within the thunder.

Several of the new people discovered that it was impossible for the dead to faint, though they certainly tried to at Hagaarsdottir's expression. Concerned seraphim began to move among the crowd, offering consolation, and to take lunch orders to distract the newcomers from the current situation.

For the sake of not traumatizing any more incoming souls, Jordan decided to use up a minor one of his monthly budget for miracles, and transported himself and the Valkyrie away from the watching crowd. They reappeared within an instant, on a stormy hillside high above a fjord filled with crashing waves of molten lava. Ravens and gulls circled overhead, black birds and white crying out raucously over the distant sounds of storm and battle. The bloody gates of the fortress of Valhalla in the Norse afterlife realm of Asgard loomed on the other side of the fjord. Huge black wolves prowled before the mighty gates, dwarfed to the size of small dogs by distance and the size of the fortress of the old gods. Beyond the mighty fortress a dark forest and jagged, snow-capped mountains loomed beneath the swirling storm clouds. Lightning cracked across the sky, and thunder boomed.

It was all very ominous and eerie, very Wagnerian, but not particularly homey. Jordan ignored the scenery and turned his attention to the small screen of the personal digital assistant Hagaarsdottir had passed to him earlier.

"Is this about an incoming?" he asked as he peered at the tiny print on the screen. He made very little sense of the information at first glance. "I didn't think you'd had any incoming since the incident involving that Miami motorcycle gang back during Hurricane Andrew."

"Them." Hagaarsdottir sniffed in disapproval. From her it sounded more like a snarl, but Jordan knew it was a ladylike sniff.

"They died saving the lives of others or they wouldn't have arrived here," he reminded the Valkyrie.

"The gods have to take what they get these days," she answered. "The bikers fit in well enough, but frankly—" She cut herself off, and pointed at the data on the PDA. "It's Mr. Jansen. He has to be reassigned immediately, Peter. His presence is far too disruptive."

Jordan scanned the statistics on one Randall Jensen and his place in the afterlife. "Ethnically correct."

"Ya."

"Raised Lutheran, I see." Jordan glanced at Hagaarsdottir. "He must have converted to the Old Religion if you ended up with him."

She frowned ominously, and clutched her spear tensely. "Really?"

He read on. "There's no conversion date here from Christian to the Norse pantheon."

"He believes in Vikings."

Jordan didn't believe it was the icy northern wind that caused the chill to run up his back.

The Valkyrie shook her head, swaying her heavy gold braids. "I don't think believing in Vikings should be enough. *You* have to tell them it's a mistake."

He looked at her suspiciously. "Them?"

"He's changing everything," she complained. She began to cry. "It's a mistake. You have to put everything back the way it must be."

Jordan reached up and patted Hagaarsdottir's armored shoulder. "There, there."

"I don't like change. Not here."

"Even heaven changes." At an accelerated rate lately, he added to himself. "Even in the Muslim Paradise." There was trouble in several paradises, if truth be told, and around here it always was. For example, the Druids and Hindus had been having a huge influx of new believers. It had been necessary to assign more reincarnation advisors, mostly from an under-qualified pool of Victorian Spiritualists, since most of the New Agers with sufficient qualifications hadn't gotten around to exiting their current existence yet. This had caused complaints from the Buddhists, who claimed that the celestial bureaucracy was caving in to a popular fad and far too many souls were returning to the Wheel of Suffering than should be, which made more work for *them* back on earth.

Jordan always preached to his staff that it was the wonderful diversity of belief systems that made the afterlife so stimulating to manage, but sometimes... He didn't try to comfort Hagaarsdottir with a sermon about the inevitability of change, not when the Asgardian Liaison was concerned about a glitch in her own world-view. She was a Daughter of Odin, firmly set in her own ways. She was happy to keep her spear sharp, collect the souls of worthy warriors from among mortal-kind, and wait for the Last Battle that would bring about the death of gods and worlds.

Jordan didn't personally believe that Ragnarok would be the ultimate end of the universe, not anymore than he believed in Armageddon, or the Dance of Shiva, or that the universe would expand from the Big Bang until it reversed itself and fell back into nothingness or the universe would keep on expanding until everything was so thinly spread out that it became nothing. All beliefs were perfectly correct for those who believed in them, but he liked to keep an open mind. Keeping an open mind was how he'd gotten his job, since he found all beliefs equally fascinating. Plus, Jordan had been told by the Supreme One that he was the only person in all the varieties of Heaven that everyone seemed to be able to get along with.

Jordan went back to studying Mr. Jansen's case. "I see he was a high school physical education teacher from Bemidji, Minnesota; married, father of two teenage boys. Cause of death was a heart attack on Sunday afternoon two weeks ago while watching television." He lifted his gaze to Hagaarsdottir. "I see he went directly to Valhalla instead of passing through the main office. You are the Asgardian Liaison, and it's taken you two weeks to discover an error of some sort?"

"No."

"No?"

"I told him immediately that he was in the wrong place, but he wouldn't listen." She gestured with her spear toward the gates of Valhalla. "I thought that it would work out in a few days. You know how disoriented new arrivals who don't go through the orientation process can be."

"I do, indeed. Going straight to heaven or hell can be a traumatic experience. The ones with fanatical surety of their place in the afterlife generally experience a period of disorientation when they land exactly where they thought they were going."

She nodded. "Frequently they don't belong where they end up at all."

"Liaisons such as yourself are there to counsel such people," he added.

Hagaarsdottir drew herself up in offense at his mild statement. "I know my job, Peter."

"Of course you do," he soothed—though he wondered how a problem could exist if she'd done her job correctly. Since he neither wanted to hurt her feelings, nor become intimately acquainted with the sharp end of her spear, he refrained from voicing any criticism of the Valkyrie. "Go on," he urged. "You were explaining about Mr. Jansen."

"I discovered the error immediately," she explained. "I attempted to counsel Mr. Jensen. He wouldn't listen. Then *they* wouldn't listen."

"They?"

"Them." She waved toward the great, grim fortress of the Norse gods once more. "Oh, bother!" She banged her spear hard on the rocky ground. Overhead, circling ravens cried out in alarm at her shout. Jordan squeaked in alarm when she grabbed him by the wrist. "See for yourself!" she declared, and yanked him forward.

The next moment they were standing before the gates of Valhalla. Frankly, the place looked a bit tacky. The great stone walls showed signs of cracking, and moss grew in many places. The direwolves' spiked iron collars were covered in rust. Weeds sprouted up between the steps leading to the great gates. The timber of the gates themselves was worn and gray, and sagged a bit on their hinges. Jordan knew there'd been problems in several of the old paradises. He recalled a report of the great world tree, Yggdrasil having come down with Dutch Elm Disease, that the holy raven population was dropping off, the dragon Fafnir being seen by a vet for a bad case of scale mange. Even the beer wasn't as good as it used to be. Valhalla, like Hell and the Elysian Fields, and a thousand other afterlife alternatives, just wasn't getting much business these days.

Consequently, things were getting a bit tacky in the older, less popular, belief systems. The deities and demons of these places had not proved any help in keeping entropy from settling in, as they had trouble focusing on the idea that the were personified parts of a Universal Godhead rather than God of the only religion that actually mattered. Besides, gods tended to protect turf and territory, and were terrible at compromising. Neo Pagans, Joseph Campbell and television evangelists brought a trickle of business to these out of the way afterlifes, but Jordan was concerned that soon all the souls dwelling in the ancient heavens and hells would have to be relocated. *And where am I going to put several thousand refugee baby sacrificing followers of Moloch?* Jordan worried, tapping the screen of Hagaarsdottir's PDA while he thought. Perhaps he could consult Mr. Hitchcock about finding space in the new, special effects laden hell. The Molochians might lend a certain—

"Your thoughts are an infinity away, Peter," Hagaarsdottir complained. She wagged a finger under his nose, while snatching her data device from him with her other hand. "Focus."

"I was wondering about—"

"Someone else's problem but mine," she accused.

"Yes," he had to admit, since lying was not an option here. He focused on the trouble in Valhalla. "You haven't actually told me what's wrong with Mr. Jansen."

"He won't leave."

How could that be a problem? "An after death conversion? Congratulations. They're rare, but—"

"It isn't that," the Valkyrie cut him off. "We tried to make him leave-at first. He wouldn't go. Even after Thor threw his hammer at him. Jansen just laughed, and said he wasn't intimidated by a comic book hero. He offered the god a lite beer." Her bottom lip trembled, and she sniffed again. "And Thor took it. I don't know what the world is coming to." A tear rolled down her fair cheek. "Lite beer in Valhalla." She swiped at the tear with a thick gold braid.

"Don't cry, dear," Jordan sympathized. "You'll rust."

This time he took her hand, and led her up the blood-stained stairs. A pair of tall sentries confronted them at the gates. Jordan peered at the fair-haired, bushy-bearded guards curiously. There was something odd... He couldn't recall Vikings warriors having a penchant for wearing purple uniforms—or any uniforms at all, for that matter. "Didn't their helmets used to have wings?" he asked Hagaarsdottir.

"Times change," one of the sentries answered.

"You see," Hagaarsdottir said, and led Jordan passed the guards.

This was odd, Jordan admitted, but kept his expression bland and his senses alert as the gates opened for he and Hagaarsdottir to enter the great hall of the most sacred place in the Asgardian afterlife.

He immediately sensed something different in the air, and considering the place always smelled of half-cured animal pelts, burned meat, stale ale, blood, and unwashed bodies, sensing something different wasn't easy. He sniffed delicately, but knew that wouldn't do. He girded his courage, stood still, closed his eyes, and forced himself to take a deep breath. There *was* something new, something...

"This place smells like a gym locker room," Jordan announced. He opened his eyes and peered carefully around the smoke filled feasting hall of Valhalla.

Hagaarsdottir shrugged her shoulders diffidently, and sighed. "I know."

The place was usually a mess, since it was in constant use by thousands of deserving barbarian warriors continually feasting, wenching, guzzling ale, gorging meat roasted over the huge round hearths that lined the center of the great hall. When they weren't roistering, the Norse warriors merrily hacked each other to bits, and the defeated rose to pound their killers on the back, and go on to the next joyfully joined battle. Such were the rewards of the reverent while they waited the coming battle where they would face the frost giants and other forces of evil in a conflict that would bring about the end of the world. There'd been an addition of chopped Harleys, tattoos and modern fire power to this ancient mix since the bikers moved in to Asgard. But all in all, the motor cycle gang fitted into the general scheme of chaotic mayhem and underlying sense of doom that had been the essence of Valhalla for many thousands of years.

Today was different.

It took Jordan a while to pinpoint what the new and disturbing essence that permeated the place was as he and the Valkyrie picked their way slowly beyond the main doors of the feasting hall. It gradually dawned on Jordan that besides the smell of sour sweat, there was an air of purpose about the place. There wasn't a horned helm, battle axe or roast oxen in sight, Jordan finally noticed. Squinting through the smoke thrown out by the row of great hearths, Jordan eventually made out a sea of purple and gold. It took quite a while for the details of the vision to sink in, longer for him to make even the slightest sense of them. All the while Hagaarsdottir remained at his side, looking more despondent by the second. Occasionally she dabbed her eyes with her braids. There *were* Vikings everywhere, thousands of grunting, sweating, scarred, hard-muscled warriors, faces red with effort, eyes aglow with fanatical determination. They were wearing purple and gold uniforms, and they were doing push-ups in the cleared space of the feasting hall. They all looked fiercely determined and inspired.

Jordan looked around the edges of this bizarre scene, his mouth open in shock. He eventually focused on a glint of gold in a distant shadowed corner. He made out a group of forlorn Valkyries. They looked like they were holding bundles of...was that glitter from tinsel? Pom Poms. They were holding pom poms, weren't they?

Hagaarsdottir wandered toward her war-sisters. Jordan heard shouting, and cast a brief, suspicious glance toward a tall, thin, red-haired man standing before Odin's finest and shouting orders at the barbarian horde. Then he hurried to catch up to Hagaarsdottir.

"What's going on here?" he asked as they joined the other warrior maidens. The valkyries, he noted, were also dressed in purple and gold, but the costumes were far more revealing then their usual attire of chain mail and plate armor. Goodness, but there was a lot to reveal. Jordan wasn't sure if he should avert his eyes, or if a certain amount of appreciation for natural attributes was a healthy, wholesome thing. Jordan was not a being who like having ambiguous reactions—especially since part of his reaction included a passing vision of how Hagarrsdottir would look in one of the skimpy outfits. This was hardly professional, so he kept his gaze above chest level of the tall valkyries, cleared his throat, and said again, "What is going on?"

The warrior maidens ignored him and concentrated on Hagaarsdottir.

"Do we have to dress like this?"

"I don't want to be a cheerleader," another complained. "I want to play."

"You'd certainly make a better quarterback than Balder, Brunhilde."

"Hodur could do better, and he's blind," said another. "Balder'd look better shaking his—golden curls—on the sidelines than I would."

"Besides, he's dead. I don't think a dead god should be allowed to play, even if Odin did give him and Loki dispensation."

"Only because he wants to use the direwolf as a mascot."

"I don't understand what Odin's doing at all," Hagaarsdottir said, turning to Jordan. "You have to make him stop before the world doesn't end!"

Jordan hastily recalled his knowledge of Asgardian cosmology. He recalled that Loki, the god of mischief had tricked the blind god Hodur into killing the beloved god Balder. The other Norse gods had not been able to ransom Balder back from the underworld, and Loki's punishment for his crime was to be chained to a rock where his vitals were continually gnawed by a huge wolf. Neither Balder nor Loki were supposed to be freed until the end of the world. Jordan believed that the entrails gnawing wolf was then scheduled to eat the sun as its part in the great cataclysmic battle of Ragnarok that would end the world.

He gathered from the valkyries' comments that the traditional scenario for the ultimate destruction of the world was off schedule and out of kilter. Caused by the Minnesotan intruder in Valhalla? His suspicion that Hagaarsdottir was somehow overreacting to a simple situation was suddenly put to rest.

"Take me to him," he said, and the next instant he and Hagaarsdottir were standing before Coach Jansen. He tugged on the coach's sweatshirt sleeve. "Sir?"

Jansen cast a distracted glance at Jordan, then spoke to Hagaarsdottir. "Not you, again. Listen, miss, I've told you, women don't play football, not in any school where I coach."

"You are not in school," Jordan pointed out.

"A tall girl like you ought to try out for the basketball squad." He waved a hand toward the warriors running drills. "I've got a lot of work to do before Saturday's game. So, why don't you—"

"Sir!" Jordan said, spouting impressive wings and a fiery sword. "Listen to the messenger of the Creator!" *Fanatics*, he thought with a weary inward sigh as Jansen's pale blue eyes finally focused on him. Jordan allowed the wings and sword to vanish now that he had the coach's attention. "Mr. Jansen," he said, in his usual mild way, "I believe you believe in Vikings. The Minnesota Vikings, to be precise."

"Finest team to ever take the field!" Jansen answered. "Go, Vikes!"

"As you say, sir." Jordan gestured toward the warriors. "Purple uniforms do not make these vikings Vikings. There has been a mistake. You do not belong here."

"These are my people!" Jansen proclaimed. "I came from this stock. Look at 'em," he added proudly. "Endurance, strength, determination, fearless fighters! When I'm through with 'em—"

"You don't seem to understand," Jordan cut in. "*You* don't belong *here*. We already have a Football Heaven." It was fairly new, and consisted mostly of couches, television sets and endless supplies of junk food and beer, but it did exist. "I'm sure you'll be quite happy—"

"Watching endless games on the tube? I'm a coach, boy! I build winning teams."

"Sir, these are the residents of Valhalla, not a high school athletic team."

"Don't you think I know that?" The coach narrowed his eyes at Jordan. "Do I look like an idiot to you?"

"No, of course not, sir. However, you seem to be unaware that you are disrupting a cosmology that has a fixed belief in universal events. These warriors died bravely in battle and were brought to the fortress of Valhalla here in Asgard to celebrate their victories until such time as their god Odin calls upon them to uphold good versus evil in the final battle that will end the world."

"Ragnarok," Jansen answered, and spat. "Load of bullshit. It's a quitter's philosophy. We don't have quitters on my team."

"But, sir—"

"I couldn't believe what this bunch of misfits was doing when I got here."

"I understand your shock, sir. Your twenty-first century sensibilities must have been shocked at the violence, barbarity and crudeness of—"

"What I found was a bunch of aimless slackers," Jansen informed him. "These are my people, my ancestors."

"Oh, dear."

"I couldn't believe these were the same Vikings who'd conquered Europe, founded Russia, settled Iceland, discovered America—"

"Wrote the sagas," Jordan added helpfully. "Established trade routes and cities. Viking history isn't all pillaging and adventure, you know."

"Of course I know!" Jansen exploded. He shook Jordan's shoulder, then pointed at the artificially green grass and the multitude of men in purple jerseys. "That's why I stayed. That's why I realized this place needed me. There was no purpose here, no spirit, just acceptance of a foregone fate. When I walked in here there was nothing but debauchery, boredom and waiting for Ragnarok. You call that heaven?"

"Well, no," Jordan agreed. "But I don't call anywhere heaven."

Jansen frowned at him. "We have to work on you, boy."

Jordan slipped out of the coach's grasp. "A large part of my job is accomplished by not believing. I'm supposed to make sure that believers get where they belong. In your case—"

"I'm staying right here."

Jordan spread his arms out toward the mob. "But why?"

"Purpose," Jansen answered emphatically. "Inspiration. Team work. Like I explained to Odin and Thor, their boys need to develop a real competitive edge if they expect to beat those frost giants come the big one."

Jordan cleared his throat, then explained. "They aren't supposed to beat anybody. It's supposed to be mutual annihilation."

"Who says?"

"Don't you know your own mythology?"

"That's just how it is," Hagaarsdottir said. "It was good enough for Asgard until you came along."

"Why?" Jansen demanded.

"What do you mean, 'why'?" For the first time in years Jordan felt himself going red with annoyance and frustration. "That's just the way the Asgardian belief system—"

"It's un-American."

"Of course it's un-American! What's being un-American got to do with it?"

"I don't buy it."

"You don't have to!"

Jansen pointed to his players. There was a lusty roar from thousands of throats in response. "Neither do they," Jansen went on. "Not anymore. I don't coach a losing team."

Jordan closed his eyes. He counted to ten, then opened them again. "Mr. Jansen."

"Coach."

"Coach Jansen. Football is not the Norse national sport, berserking is the Norse national sport."

"Got a lot in common, too," Jansen answered with a smug grin. "Wait until you see my front four thousand up against Notre Dame."

"Notre Dame?"

Jansen stroked his chin thoughtfully. "Of course I don't like taking pros up against a college team, but since they've had about a half century to practice—"

Jansen planned to take the multitude of Valhalla up against players from a different heaven? Where had this idea come from? "Does Coach Rockne know about this proposed game?" And why hadn't Hagaarsdottir explained Odin's compliance with all this? Because she didn't want to spend the rest of eternity shaking pom poms? Jordan didn't blame her. Valkyries probably made lousy football widows as well.

"Odin's negotiating with Rockne right now," Jansen said. "You see, having the Vikings fighting each other all the time was what got them stale in the first place. You need competition if you're going to win."

"Yes. I see your point there."

"Peter!" Hagaarsdottir protested.

"I said I see his point, I didn't say I agree with him."

"You will," she predicted glumly. "Everyone always does."

"Our players need some fresh blood," Jensen went on. "Figuratively speaking," he hastened to assure Jordan. "I don't stand for any of my players breaking any rules."

"Or other players' heads?" Jordan asked hopefully.

Jansen laughed. "Between our boys and the Irish we figure we can fill a stadium for the most spectacular Super Sunday of all."

"Yes. Yes, I can see why you might think that." It probably would be popular. Football had fans even in afterlife centers not wholly dedicated to the worship of the game.

"Peter..."

"Chances for ecumenical get togethers are limited since jihads, crusades and pogroms are frowned upon by upper management."

"Knew you'd come around." Jansen clapped him on the back.

Jordan couldn't fault the plan on any theological grounds. Not if Odin was going to change the groundrules about Ragnarok. Hanging around on the world tree waiting for the end must have gotten boring for the old god, and the chance for a little excitement might bring in some new followers for the moribund religion. But Jordan really did wish the proper forms had been filed for this sudden change of heart. Reformations were supposed to go through channels just like everything else.

Jordan sighed. "I've got paperwork to do on all this, you know."

Jansen's hand landed on his shoulder again. "Your office is already on top of it. Miss Ise told me we wouldn't have to worry about a thing. She's taking care of the necessary forms. Hasn't mentioned it to you, eh?"

"She doesn't like to disturb me with—"

"Bet you don't know about the office football pool, either." Jansen chuckled. "The boss is usually the last to know."

Jordan looked from Coach Jansen to Hagaarsdottir. "There's nothing I can do here. I'll be going now."

Jansen gave a dismissive nod and turned to consult a waiting member of his coaching staff. Jordan recognized the assistant coach as the war god, Thor, holding a clipboard and wearing a billed cap on top of his winged war-helm. The sight was enough to make Jordan dust his hands of the entire subject. He turned and walked away

"But, Peter," Hagaarsdottir said, catching up to him. "What do I do now?"

He paused, and then slowly smiled at the voluptuous Valkyrie. "Why don't you and I stop for a drink at the Benedictine abbey? Then we can discuss starting a women's basketball league."

Hagaarsdottir considered his suggestions for a moment. Then she laughed, threw down her spear, and put her arm through his. "You know, Peter, I think you are right. I don't really know what basketball is—but you can be our first coach."

VACATION

Jennifer Dunne

According to her parents, Jennifer Dunne has always been an angel (they were fond of quoting "There was a little girl, who had a little curl..."), which no doubt explains her lifelong fascination for how the "other half" lives. Her books include *Raven's Heart* (SF romance), *Dark Salvation* (vampire romance), and *Shadow Prince* (fantasy).

Saffron exited the limousine in stages, first just the tip of a black stiletto heel peeking beneath the open door, then a shapely ankle, followed by an impossibly long leg, stretching slowly from within the dark interior of the limousine until her shoe settled firmly on the cobblestone drive. Her pale white hand, the long red nails glistening in the sunlight as if they'd been freshly dipped in blood, extended languorously through the doorway.

Three bellhops rushed to help her from the car.

Her fingers closed around the nearest of the outstretched hands, tingling as she made the connection. His name was Albert. He lived alone, and dreamed at night of a beautiful, dark-haired woman who would kiss and caress him, and devour him slowly with her ripe berry lips.

Saffron allowed Albert to draw her out of the car. He gasped and blinked, confronted with his secret image of desire made flesh. His fingers tightened on her hand. With a few soft words, Saffron could make him abandon his position, forgetting everyone and everything of importance to him in an endless spiral of craving until there was nothing left of him, and his soul belonged to her master.

She licked her berry bright lips, tossed back her long, flowing black hair, and pulled her fingers from his grasp. She was on vacation.

* * * *

As she approached the front desk, the manager elbowed one of the clerks aside and leaned forward onto the gleaming marble counter. “Checking in, Miss?”

She reached into her tightly laced leather bustier and withdrew a credit card from its resting place between her breasts. The manager’s eyes widened, and he held the thin rectangle of plastic with near reverence.

“The name is Cubis.” She gave it a foreign pronunciation: Coo-bee. “Saffron Cubis.”

He keyed the data into the computer, which promptly displayed her reservation. Saffron breathed a sigh of relief. She’d been promised a vacation, a reward for her excellent service, but she hadn’t really believed it was possible. Her master’s penchant for practical jokes was well known.

“Welcome to The Slice of Heaven Resort and Spa. We’ve reserved a deluxe pool side suite for you. You will be staying with us for seven days?”

“One can accomplish much in seven days,” she said, admiring her master’s sense of humor.

The manager nodded, oblivious to the joke. “We have a number of package deals to make your stay more enjoyable. How many daily spa treatments would you prefer?”

“None.”

“None?” The manager’s eyebrows lifted. “Don’t you wish to indulge in the spa’s restful atmosphere, to relax and let your cares drift away?”

“You mean, recline in pampered luxury, not lifting a finger, as your trained staff cater to my every need?”

“Exactly!” He smiled broadly, fingers poised over the keyboard to accept her order.

Indignation swelled her fragile bustier. “Sloth is a sin! I plan to be busy on my vacation. Very, very busy.”

* * * *

Alone in her suite a short time later, Saffron studied the scrap of paper lying on the table. Faith, justice, prudence, hope, temperance, fortitude, and charity. She planned to experience all seven virtues before her vacation was over.

She glanced at the second list. Pride, anger, avarice, gluttony, lust, envy and sloth. Those were the reminders of her work, and she was equally determined to avoid them. Much as she loved her job, this was her first vacation in seven hundred years, and she wanted to take full advantage of the chance to do something different.

So far, she'd successfully avoided sloth. Lust had been harder. Dressed as she was in the tight bustier, miniskirt and stiletto heels, she'd been hit on by every man from the front desk to her suite. And some of them had been extremely enticing.

No, the only way she'd survive the week without giving in to her nature was to remove temptation. She'd have to transform herself so that she was plain and unappealing.

Normally, she could alter her appearance whenever she wished. But her master had limited her power to the initial transformation, and the transformation that would take her home. For the length of her stay here, she was to all intents and purposes human. She would have to transform herself using strictly mortal methods.

Saffron tapped one crimson nail against her full lips. She had no idea how one went about becoming unappealing. Perhaps if she took her centuries of experience at appealing to men's baser instincts and simply reversed everything, that would suffice.

In most cases, men created her image with long hair, dressed in exotic, revealing garments. So she'd find ordinary, modest clothing and get her hair cut.

She glanced at the list of virtues. Modesty was not on the list. Damn. Well, she'd do it anyway.

A guide to all of the resort's many services sat on the desk, and she quickly flipped through it. She found what she was looking for on page eight. The resort contained a shopping complex, complete with a beauty salon and three women's fashion boutiques. Surely she'd be able to find what she was looking for there.

An odd sensation trembled in her chest. Puzzled, Saffron wondered if the body created to meet Albert's fantasies contained some strange flaw. But the sensation did not feel unpleasant. In fact, it was rather nice, in a way completely unrelated to sex. She had no frame of reference for it. The nearest description she could think of was that her breath felt lighter than air.

Gradually, the sensation dissipated. Still no closer to an answer as to what had caused it, she dismissed the phenomenon from her thoughts. Instead, she concentrated on what clothing she would need to purchase.

Jeans and sneakers, first of all. She could blend into a crowd if she wore jeans and sneakers.

The strange sensation returned, even stronger. Saffron placed her fingertips lightly against her chest, hoping to feel some external source.

The tingle increased. Eyes widening, Saffron repeated her last thought. Hope. She was feeling hope.

Throwing her arms wide, she danced about the suite in gleeful abandon. Her plan was going to work. She was finally going to experience the fabled virtues.

* * * *

Saffron's eyes widened as she stepped into the first boutique. So many clothes! In so many colors and textures!

She ran her fingers over a sky blue denim shirt, embroidered with the resort's logo in gold. It was as soft and supple as sable or mink. And much less ostentatious.

She plucked the shirt off the rack, then made her way down the aisle, snatching up every other garment that caught her eye. By the time she reached the sales clerk, Saffron could barely see over the pile of clothing in her arms.

"Would you like to try those on?" the woman asked.

"Yes." Saffron wasn't entirely certain, but it seemed the safest answer.

The clerk opened a tiny closet door, and gestured Saffron inside. She frowned, wondering if it was some sort of trick. Then she saw the mirrors, plush carpeting, and tiny couch within. The elegant room was disguised as a closet to fool the undeserving.

Back on familiar ground, Saffron swept inside, only slightly disturbed when the clerk closed the door behind her. When nothing in the room transformed, she settled onto the couch to explore her acquisitions.

She shimmied out of her miniskirt and kicked off her heels. Grabbing the closest pair of jeans, she pulled them on, and looked in the mirror. The jeans fell off, pooling around her ankles.

Saffron frowned. Perhaps the conditions of her vacation were like the conditions of her work. She would not be allowed to wear anything other than what her target fantasized for her. But that didn't seem right.

She pulled the jeans up again, this time holding them against her waist. They were an extremely poor cut, bagging around her legs and bunching up at her waist. It was no wonder they'd fallen off.

Letting the jeans fall to the floor, Saffron reached for another pair. True, she'd be unappealing in those. But she'd also be unable to walk.

The second pair were better, but still poorly tailored. That a store which obviously catered to wealthy buyers of quality should carry such shoddy products mystified her. But now at least she understood why the clerk expected her to sample the garments before purchasing them. Most of them weren't worth buying.

The third pair slid over her legs like a second skin, the soft, brushed cotton hugging her curves like a lover's caress. Saffron danced lightly around the cramped room, bending and swaying. The jeans followed her every move. These, she would buy.

She dug through the pile on the couch, pulling out another pair that looked like the ones she wore. Just holding them in front of her, however, she could see that they would be as baggy on her as the first pair.

Confused, she examined them more closely. That's when she discovered the tiny piece of cloth sewn inside, describing the garment. She quickly shucked off the pair she was wearing. That had a description, too.

She compared the two tags. They were identical, except for a boldly printed number. The pair of jeans she liked had a number 10. The other pair had a number 16.

Checking the two discarded pairs on the floor, she found that they both bore similar tags. One was labeled 16, and one was labeled 12.

Pleased that she had figured out the code on her own, Saffron located three additional pairs of jeans numbered 10. They looked nothing alike, being a deep green, black, and brilliant peacock blue, with different arrangements of buttons, snaps and zippers. But they were all 10's, and they were all wonderful.

Next, she turned her attention to the shirts. Rather than waste her time, she searched for the tiny tags, and only picked up the ones labeled 10. That left her with a pile of eleven shirts in various colors, styles, and designs.

She unlaced her bustier and let it drop to the floor. Stretching as well as she could beneath the low ceiling, she breathed deeply, enjoying the sensation of her ribs moving in and out with each breath.

Turning back to the pile of clothing, she pulled a soft, butter yellow T-shirt over her head. A brilliant pink daisy, glittering with diamond dust, wrapped its petals around her breasts. She wasn't sure what Grrrl Power was, but it sounded appropriate for a demon.

She quickly disrobed and pulled on the next shirt, the long-sleeved denim top that had first caught her attention. Perfection. As were the other nine.

After changing back into the peacock blue jeans and the Grrrl Power T-shirt, Saffron folded the rest of her finds into a neat pile, and placed her miniskirt and bustier on top. She considered leaving them behind. After all, she wouldn't be needing them again. But she suspected that might be a sign of laziness, and she refused to succumb to sloth.

One hand on the door knob, she hesitated, considering the other sins. What about avarice? She was only going to be here for seven days. Did she really need eleven shirts?

She nibbled her lower lip. How many times did people change clothes during the day? She didn't know. She suspected it had something to do with their activities, but since her activities were usually confined to a single room, and called for getting out of her clothing as quickly as possible, she was at a loss.

Grabbing four of the shirts at random, Saffron yanked them out of her pile and tossed them onto the garments littering the floor. She would buy seven. If she needed more, she could always buy them later.

The warm glow tingled in her chest again. Saffron smiled, then laughed out loud. Another virtue. This time, it was prudence. Two in one day! This was easier than she'd thought.

* * * *

After charging her new clothes to her room and arranging for them to be delivered, Saffron's next stop was the beauty salon. The receptionist took her name, room number, and request for a hair cut, then rang a small bell on her desk. A stylist, a young woman with classically perfect makeup, manicure, and softly waving brown hair, came out to introduce Saffron to the salon.

"Would you like deep conditioning, hot oil treatment, or nutrient mud treatment?"

Saffron glanced at the receptionist. She thought she'd been quite clear about what she wanted, but the stylist hadn't spoken to the receptionist. It seemed an inefficient way to run things.

"I want a hair cut."

The stylist smiled, and led Saffron to the back of the salon where a row of leather-upholstered chairs reclined before marble sinks. "Yes. But do you want your hair strengthened or improved prior to cutting it?"

"Why would I want you to do anything to it if it was only going to be cut off?"

The stylist's eyes widened, although she didn't raise her eyebrows, no doubt trying to prevent wrinkles. It made her look like a fish.

"But your hair is so beautiful. I assumed you wanted a trim."

"It will grow back." In seven days, when she took a new assignment, she'd have an entirely new body, no doubt once again with long, flowing hair. "I want it cut short."

"Such a drastic change!" The stylist shook her head. "Is there a man?"

Saffron laughed. For the first time in seven hundred years, no man governed her behavior. It was also the first time a human blamed anyone but her for her actions. Her master would appreciate the irony.

"This is just for me."

"Perhaps you would like to use the computer imaging system to preview your style before we do anything drastic?"

Saffron waved a hand, dismissing the idea. She wasn't about to admit that she was looking for a style that would be unappealing.

"Whatever you choose is fine. Nothing too trendy or chic, though. I want it to be simple and ordinary."

The stylist sighed. "If you're sure?"

"I'm sure."

"Then take a seat, and I'll shampoo your hair."

Saffron settled into one of the comfortable leather chairs, and the stylist piled her hair into the sink behind her. Then the woman guided her head backward, until her neck rested on the curved rim.

Warm water sluiced through her hair. "Is this too hot?"

"It's much hotter where I come from. This will be fine."

Saffron closed her eyes and enjoyed the feeling of being pampered as the woman vigorously lathered and rinsed her hair. Perhaps she'd make time to have a few of the spa treatments after all. At the rate she was achieving the virtues, she'd be done well before seven days. If she indulged herself after that, it wouldn't be slothful, merely a reward for having reached her goal.

The scent of fresh apples filled her nostrils as the stylist massaged a fragrant cream into her scalp.

"Just a light, leave-in conditioner," she explained. "To make it easier to cut and style."

She squeezed Saffron's hair, wringing out the water, then wrapped it up in a thick towel like a turban. Saffron smiled, recalling the last job on which she'd worn a turban. It had an ostrich feather. She'd found some very creative uses for that feather.

She pinched her thigh, hard. The sharp pain distracted her, but it had been a near thing. No, she wouldn't allow the spa to pamper her, even if she experienced all of the virtues on her first day. Pampering left too much time to think, and thinking would lead her right back to those seven sins she was trying to avoid.

Saffron followed the stylist to a new chair in front of a wall of mirrors in the main room of the salon. Two other stylists were busy with clients, the rapid snips of their scissors making a chorus like the chirping of birds.

Saffron's stylist ushered her into another comfortably padded chair. After wrapping a striking gold and black cape around her neck, the stylist released Saffron's turban.

With surprising speed, the transformation was complete. When the stylist finished with the scissors, she combed gel through Saffron's hair, then used an array of brushes with one hand while holding a dryer in the other. The final result could have graced any fashion runway in the world. A sleek bob hugged the curves of Saffron's head, while curling wisps teased her forehead and beckoned from behind her ears. It was a style that begged a man's hand to stroke it, and completely counter to Saffron's desire for plain, ordinary hair.

The stylist faced Saffron's chair away from the wall mirror, and held a hand mirror in front of her face, so that she could get the full effect of her new hairstyle.

"What do you think?"

"It's short, all right. I was hoping for something plainer, though."

"Oh, this is a very simple style! I used the curling brush and styling gel, but you don't have to. You can just wash it and go in the mornings."

"Can I see it like that?"

The stylist grimaced, so upset that she forgot to worry about wrinkles. But she dutifully picked up a spray bottle and wet Saffron's hair, then dried it with a towel.

Her bangs hung into her eyes, and she had an all-over rumpled look. She was still beautiful. Albert's fantasies had seen to that. But at least her hair and clothes no longer called attention to that fact.

"Perfect!"

The stylist removed Saffron's cape with a snap. When Saffron rose, the stylist escorted her back out to the receptionist's desk. Once there, the stylist bent and whispered to the receptionist, then turned and disappeared back into the depths of the salon without a word. Apparently she was too incensed over Saffron's lack of styling gel to say any more.

The receptionist pressed some keys on her computer. Somewhere beneath the desk a printer hummed, then the receptionist placed the printout inside a burgundy leather folder and handed it to Saffron.

"If you wish to charge this to your room, all of the information is already provided. You just need to add a gratuity and sign it."

Saffron opened the folder, and saw a neatly itemized bill totaling eighty-five dollars inside. Enough men had taken her out to dinner over the years that she understood about gratuities. The stylist would expect seventeen dollars.

Anticipating a pleasant tingle of virtue, Saffron made the gratuity twenty dollars. She felt nothing.

Surmising that the increase hadn't been large enough to be considered charity, she quickly changed it to thirty-four dollars, doubling the expected gratuity. Still nothing.

The receptionist held her hand out for the signed bill, preventing Saffron from experimenting further. She closed the folder and handed it back to the woman, then breezed out of the salon.

She didn't care where she was headed. She was much more interested in finding out why her attempt to experience a virtue had failed.

* * * *

Unable to find an explanation for her failure to experience charity, Saffron decided the only thing she could do was continue her efforts. The next morning, she set out to hike up a nearby hill in the resort's nature preserve.

Glancing at her map when she entered the preserve, she decided to bear left and take the most challenging route to the top. She wanted no question about whether or not she was displaying fortitude to finish this hike.

The beginning of the climb went smoothly. She admired dew-spangled spider webs cloaking bushes in veils of gray. Rabbits, squirrels, and other small, furry creatures that bolted too quickly for her to identify were nibbling at one last meal in the shadows before returning to their homes and hiding for the day. From invisible perches in the trees, soft bird song called out the beginning of the day. It had rained during the night, and the earth smelled thick and loamy. She stopped once and breathed deeply. Succubi were sensual creatures, and the sights, sounds and smells brought her deep pleasure.

All too soon, the path turned to hard stone broken by knotty roots. The birds fell silent, the animals disappeared, and the morning mist transformed into oppressive humidity. Saffron's legs ached, and her lungs labored to draw oxygen from the heavy air. She rubbed her arm against her forehead, wiping away the sweat that dripped into her eyes and burned. Her body had obviously not been imagined with this kind of exertion in mind.

A neatly carved sign announced that she was halfway to the top of the trail. Saffron groaned. Everything hurt. Her new sneakers rubbed her feet. Her pretty red and white shirt clung to her back and sides, completely soaked with sweat, and was striped with green and brown stains from where she'd pushed through branches that hung over the path. Similar stripes marred her jeans. Red welts scored her arms, where she'd learned a valuable lesson about the flexibility of birch branches. And she didn't even want to think about what her hair looked like.

It would be easy to turn around and go back. Well, not easy exactly, since it would still be at least another two hours' hike to retrace her steps. But it would be easier than continuing upward.

She paused, leaning against the sign, to rest her aching leg muscles. Before they had a chance to stiffen up, she pushed away from the sign, and started uphill. She was going to experience the virtue of fortitude if it killed her.

Another hour into the climb, she thought it might. Saffron struggled over a boulder, the latest she'd traversed in the trail that was now more rock than trees. She collapsed on top of the boulder, panting for breath. Closing her eyes, she waited for death, and her master's gloating return to tell her she'd failed.

Gradually, her breathing returned to normal. She wasn't going to die. Contemplating the hike remaining, Saffron almost wished she would. But then she'd never have the chance to experience the other five virtues. No, she had to continue trying, even if she ultimately failed to succeed.

The tingle of virtue shook her whole body. And with it came a source of energy she'd never felt before. She would make it to the top of this hill.

Sliding off her rock, Saffron began the slow, careful process of putting one foot in front of the other and dragging herself up the path. The rush of new energy explained something she'd long wondered about. She'd had only three failures in her long and successful career, the highest conversion rate of any of the demons she worked with. But those three failures had troubled her. Unlike most men's resistance, which she easily wore down, the more those three resisted, the stronger their resistance had been. Now she understood. Their virtue had fueled their efforts. Paradoxically, the more she enticed them, the stronger she made their defense against her enticements.

She understood that, now. But what she still didn't understand was why it had taken so long for her to experience the virtue of fortitude. She'd been slogging up this hill all morning, and her determination had never invoked the virtue. Yet, when she'd all but given up on the effort, that's when she felt it.

Going over the moment again and again in her memory as she climbed, Saffron realized that at the moment when she felt the tingle, she hadn't been thinking about the hike at all. That seemed to be the key.

She stopped in the middle of the trail, one foot braced against the rocks before her and one hand wrapped around a sapling to pull her up to the next level. The fortitude hadn't been for climbing the hill at all. It had been for continuing her efforts to experience the virtues.

Her excitement building, she ran through her memory of the other two virtues she'd experienced. Both had caught her by surprise, as she tried to plan her course of action. Just like this virtue had.

Saffron thought she'd figured it out. The virtue wasn't in the action. That's why her efforts at charity hadn't paid off, and why she'd been climbing for hours with no reward of fortitude. The virtue came at the moment when she decided upon a specific action, and brought the strength to follow through on that decision.

Now she knew what she'd done wrong. But her new understanding made it clear that she'd been overly optimistic about her ability to experience all seven virtues. It wasn't enough just to do good things. She had to actually be a good person, and she wasn't sure she knew how.

* * * *

The rest of her hike passed in a blur of exhaustion, but somehow she made her way up to the top of the hill, and dragged herself in to the tiny observation center. The attendant immediately rushed over with a bottle of water, and helped Saffron to a chair. Soon, an air-conditioned minivan was whisking her away to the comfort of the hotel.

A long, hot shower later, Saffron felt sufficiently restored to get dressed and go out in search of food. Her stiletto heels made an odd contrast with her jeans and peasant shirt, but she couldn't bear to put the grubby, sweaty sneakers on her clean feet.

The maitre de at the gourmet restaurant informed her that there would be a half-hour wait before she could get a table. More interested in the speed with which food arrived than in its quality, Saffron went into the resort's bar.

Couples clustered at the tiny tables. A few men congregated in chairs fanning out around a large screen television showing men in uniforms running into each other. Saffron had never been interested in sports, but enough of the men she'd seduced had been passionate fans that she could at least recognize the game as football.

She sank onto a bar stool and asked for a menu. She chose the largest, juiciest hamburger on the list.

"And to drink?" the bartender asked.

Saffron flipped the menu over and scanned the available drinks. In addition to common cocktails, beer and wine, the health-conscious resort offered a variety of non-alchoholic drinks and blended fruit specialties.

"The Southern Sunshine."

He nodded, and proceeded to throw slices of fruit, orange juice, and ice into a blender. He poured the frothy, foamy concoction into a tall glass, added a wedge of pineapple and a straw, and placed it before her.

The sweet fruit drink satisfied her immediate craving for food, and she turned in her seat to watch the other patrons of the bar. A five-piece band was setting up in the corner, near the minuscule scrap of dance floor. She wondered what kind of music they'd be playing, and if she could convince any of the men watching television that they'd rather dance.

Saffron laughed softly. Of course she could. She could have them fighting each other for the honor of escorting her onto the dance floor if she wished. The question was not could she, but should she?

A man walked into the bar. He left the stool beside Saffron's left open, and claimed the next one.

"Beer," he ordered, pointing to the Sam Adams tap handle. "I spent the last hour of my ride dreaming of an ice cold, foaming draft. And the biggest burger you serve."

His short brown hair was still damp, and Saffron detected a light hint of the resort's sandalwood soap. No matter how badly he'd wanted that beer, he'd taken the time to shower first.

She smiled. "I know the feeling. I spent all day hiking."

The man took a long swig from the glass mug set in front of him, then put it back down on the bar with a satisfied sigh. "Perfect."

He turned toward her with a grin, a fleck of foam dotting his upper lip. "Pardon my atrocious manners. My name's Lucas."

"Saffron."

They chatted amiably about their experiences so far at the resort, although both fell silent when their meals arrived. Saffron devoured her burger, licking her fingers and using the thick slabs of fried potato to soak up any juices she'd missed. She finished her drink, using a spoon to scoop out the bits of fruit that remained at the bottom of the glass.

Her immediate hunger had been met, but she didn't feel satisfied. She wanted more. Saffron's skin tingled in a decidedly nonvirtuous way, and she suspected her hunger had more to do with the man beside her than the plate in front of her.

He pushed his own empty plate aside, and devoted himself to draining his beer. She watched him swallow, marveling at how warm the bar had become.

"Another drink?" the bartender asked.

She didn't want another fruit drink. A crisp glass of white wine would be perfect. Saffron opened her mouth to order, then thought better of it. The last thing she needed at the moment was to lower her inhibitions.

"Mineral water, please."

A pleasant tingle reminded her that she'd just practiced temperance. She didn't care.

The band finished setting up, and launched into their first tune, a spicy mambo. Lucas waved off a second beer, and turned to her.

"Would you like to dance?"

His smile was devastating. Saffron gulped half of her mineral water in a desperate attempt to cool off. It didn't help.

"I would love to dance."

The two of them took to the dance floor. With the rhythm of the mambo pounding through her, Saffron flowed through the dance. She and Lucas advanced and retreated, swayed from side to side, and circled each other in perfect harmony. She'd never had a dance partner that matched her own grace and exuberance so well.

She lost count of the number of songs the band played, but when the music finally stopped, the patrons at the tables around the dance floor burst into spontaneous applause.

Saffron blushed, a reaction so unfamiliar that she lifted a hand to feel the heat in her cheeks. She wasn't embarrassed at her dancing, although there was a reason some wag had compared the mambo to vertical sex. No, what had taken her completely by surprise was that she'd forgotten the people were there.

She was trying her best to stay away from lust, but it was hard with Lucas right there, holding her hand, and glowing with a thin sheen of sweat. His palm burned against her back, and she felt the pounding of his pulse beneath her fingertips where they once again rested beside his neck.

Breaking away from him, she hurried back to the bar. "I need another drink."

The bartender had a glass of mineral water poured and waiting for her by the time she arrived. She drained it in a single long swallow.

"You know, after that long hike today, so much dancing has really tired me out," she said. "I think I'd better call it a night."

"Can I escort you to your room?" Lucas flashed another of those devastating smiles. "I wouldn't want you to fall asleep in the hallway halfway there."

A part of Saffron admired his technique. Nothing objectionable in his request, a legitimate explanation, and no pressure to accept his offer. If she refused, she'd feel churlish and petty. But if she accepted, they both knew what she'd be agreeing to. She wanted to say yes. But she couldn't. She'd sworn off lust for the week.

"Just to the door," she finally answered.

"Fair enough." He signed for both bar tabs with an illegible flourish, then tucked her arm in his and escorted her out of the bar.

They walked slowly, postponing the inevitable, but they eventually reached her door. She unlocked it and pushed it open, then hesitated in the doorway. Lucas glanced over her shoulder at the parlor beyond.

"Nice suite. Spacious."

His unspoken comment hung on the air between them. There'd be plenty of room of two.

Saffron chose to ignore the implication. "Thank you for the dance. Maybe I'll see you tomorrow?"

He nodded, and stepped away from the door. "I'll be here all week."

Escaping into the safety of her suite, she closed and locked the door. That had been close. Too close.

She started pacing, wishing she had the wings and tail of her natural form to bleed off some of the energy rippling through her. She'd experienced more than half of the virtues. And there was no real reason to avoid the sins. So what if they were part of her work? She loved her job. She should indulge her true nature, and have mad, passionate sex with Lucas for the rest of her time here.

But then what would happen? Her master's rules regarding the men she seduced as part of her job were quite clear. After they'd had sex with her, they must be given the opportunity to renounce her. None ever had, but she knew of coworkers whose assignments had repented of their indiscretions. All of the men she'd slept with, however, had chosen to renounce their former lives, giving up everything in the vain attempt to recapture her. That they never did was just one of the sufferings her master inflicted upon them after their deaths.

She couldn't do that to Lucas. She couldn't make him pay for her weakness.

The tingle of another virtue lightened her heart. So that was justice. The warm glow convinced her that she was on the right track.

She pulled open the curtains and looked out upon a steaming hot tub. If she stayed, even if she tried to hide herself, she was certain to see Lucas again. The resort just wasn't big enough to avoid him. And she wouldn't lie to herself. If she saw him again, she'd sleep with him.

But if she left now, he'd be safe. He might be angry that she'd left without saying a word, but he'd get over it. Eventually, he'd forget her. And Hell would have no claim on him. He'd find his reward in Heaven.

She almost missed the mild tingle of another virtue. Faith. She laughed at the irony. Working as she did, it required no faith to believe in the damnation of souls, but that a man might be virtuous enough to find paradise required belief in something she'd never seen.

Six out of the seven virtues. Not bad, even if she'd hoped to experience all of them. It would have to do.

Closing the blinds so that no one would accidentally see her transform, she invoked the magic that would end her vacation.

"I am Saffron Ula Cubis. I call upon the powers of Hell to restore me to my rightful form."

Her wings unfurled with a great snap, ripping her shirt into pieces. The scraps of fabric fluttered to the floor. The back seam of her jeans burst as her tail tore through the thin denim.

Time to go home. She would gladly give up her five remaining days as a mortal so that Lucas could have an eternity free from suffering.

As she faded out of existence, the warm glow of Charity enfolded her.

* * * *

Saffron knelt on the black marble floor in front of her master's desk. She heard the shift of fabric against leather as he leaned back in his tall chair.

"Home so soon?"

"Yes, master. If you don't mind."

"Not at all. I have another assignment for you."

Not Lucas. She could seduce anyone but Lucas. "Whatever you will."

"Your target is the husband in a husband and wife talk show team. I want them both, so I'm assigning you a partner."

Saffron dared to look up. She'd never worked with an incubus before.

Her master snapped his fingers, and the air behind Saffron gusted over her with a sulfurous cloud. And the slightest hint of sandalwood.

“He’s also returned early from a vacation. I believe you’ll work well together.”

Saffron turned, reminding herself of her master’s propensity for cruel pranks. The incubus stood proudly, muscled legs wide apart and wings half spread. He looked totally unfamiliar, until he smiled. The smile still devastated her.

“Lucas!”

“You didn’t think a little thing like going to Hell would keep me from seeing you again, did you?” he asked. Pulling her to her feet, he nestled her beneath his wing.

She could hardly believe her good fortune. Her master had rewarded her with something far greater than a mere vacation. Lucas was already a denizen of Hell, so nothing they did could cause him pain—only extreme pleasure, for centuries to come.

She fit her body against his, reveling in his warmth, and turned to face their master. “What’s our assignment?”

The Morality Clause

H. David Blalock

H. David Blalock says the short story is his favorite art form. He has been writing for print and the internet for about 25 years, trying to perfect his version. This is his latest attempt.

Ashteroth glowered at Gaillard and huffed, generating a small smoke ring that wafted to the ceiling of the corner executive suite. Gaillard frowned. The demon had appeared in the form of a horned devil. Spikes sprouted from nearly everywhere, and it had planted itself in his executive chair. That piece of furniture had been made especially for him at considerable expense. The demon shifted in his seat, making the expensive leather squeak and tear. Within a few moments, the suite began to reek of sulphur. Gaillard suspected it would take weeks to get the stench out of the carpet.

"Mr. Gaillard, when you signed the contract five years ago, you should have read it thoroughly," Ashteroth said. "I know you were under a lot of stress at the time -"

"I was standing on the rail of a bridge, getting ready to jump," Gaillard reminded him.

"Quite. But you must admit things have been much better since."

Gaillard had to nod in agreement. "True."

"So, we have met our part of the bargain?"

"Yes."

"Then we have to require you live up to your part."

Gaillard paced back and forth. He pulled a Cuban cigar from the inner pocket of his Armani jacket and paused to light it. As an afterthought, he looked at Ashteroth. "You don't mind if I smoke?"

"I do continually."

Gaillard resumed his pacing and pondered his situation. "Let me see if I understand. You are here to foreclose on my contract because I haven't been keeping up with the paperwork?"

"Well," Ashteroth hummed, "not paperwork exactly. Reports. As it clearly says in Section 22, subparagraph B(3)(g): `Regular reports on the degradation of the subject soul shall be made'. Now, I think a case could be made that the definition of the word `regular' could be stretched to as far as annually, but you haven't made a single report in five years."

"You make this sound like some kind of government program."

"Who do you think writes their program proposals and designs their forms?"

Gaillard stopped and stared at the demon. "You?"

Ashteroth waved one three-fingered, hairy paw. "Not me personally. Although there was that form I did for the IRS back in '53." A far away look came to his eyes and the vertical slit pupils dilated as he considered times gone by. "Some of my best work, really. A masterpiece of obfuscation. Generated hundreds of audits." He snapped back to the present. "I work mostly in personal contracts such as your own nowadays. We have an entire bank of lesser demons who inspire bureaucracy. It is, after all, a hell of a business. But let's get back to the matter at hand, shall we?"

Gaillard began pacing again and puffed hard on the Cuban.

"Now, I am willing to allow a waiver on the past five years' non-conformance and cease foreclosure on one condition," Ashteroth said.

"And that is?"

"You immediately begin adhering to the requirements of the morality clause."

Gaillard stumbled a little. "Morality clause?"

"Yes. As of today we will require that—"

"*Morality* clause? A contract with the devil has a *morality* clause?"

Ashteroth huffed again. As the smoke ring rose he shifted, the horns on his back tearing again into the chair. "Of course. That's what it's all about, isn't it? Your continuing degradation, lack of moral fiber, downward spiral of conscience, et cetera."

The glimmer of an idea began to shine in Gaillard's mind. "If I do not adhere to this morality clause, then what?"

"Then the contract is broken and foreclosure is immediate," Ashteroth said, as if it should be patently obvious.

"I see."

"Good. Now, the contract requires you to break at least one commandment a week for the remainder of your natural life," Ashteroth began.

"Wait just a moment," Gaillard interjected. "How can I stretch ten commandments into a lifetime?"

Another smoke ring rose to the ceiling and a new tear appeared in the chair. "Mister Gaillard, get out your Bible. There are hundreds of commandments in the first six books, more than enough to keep you busy for a very long time."

"Oh."

"I think we are being more than generous here. I will personally be back in one year to take your report. Or to foreclose. Do you understand?"

"Um, of course. May I ask for one thing?"

"Why, of course, Mister Gaillard. What more can I do for you?"

"May I have a hard copy of the contract for reference? I wouldn't want to miss out on any other requirements, you understand."

Ashteroth waved his paw and a heavy volume appeared on the desk before him, a good six inches thick and bound in a suspicious material. "There you are. Only too happy to oblige."

"I appreciate that."

"Anything else you need?"

"I don't think so."

"Then I bid you good day, sir."

There was a huge smoke ring, a loud pop, and a parting three-foot gash in the chair. Gaillard took a moment to mourn the loss of his favorite executive seat, then turned his attention to the idea.

Three hundred and sixty five days later, Ashteroth appeared in Gaillard's office. Gaillard had had the foresight to have only cheap furniture in the room. Almost immediately after the demon's arrival, the furniture began to reek of warm plastic.

"Mister Gaillard, how good to see you," Ashteroth smirked. "Are you ready with your report? I sincerely hope you are."

"I am."

Ashteroth's smirk became a full-faced grin. It was not a pretty sight. "Very well, Mister Gaillard. Proceed. I hope you realize how important this report is." The demon flexed his taloned fingers and loomed over the man menacingly.

"You wrote that contract, didn't you? It is a masterpiece of convolution and legal cul-de-sac," Gaillard said hurriedly.

The devil swelled a little at the flattery. "It's the result of nearly three hundred years of experience. I pride myself in it."

"And well you should," Gaillard stroked. "In fact, I wanted to ask you about a particular piece of the contract, if we have a moment."

Ashteroth tilted his head a little and eyed Gaillard suspiciously.

"If you recall, we briefly discussed the morality clause?"

"Yes -"

"And you reminded me that I was required to meet its stipulations on penalty of default?"

Ashteroth grumbled something incoherent.

"Now, the contract states I must break one commandment each week for the rest of my natural life," Gaillard continued. "It does not, however, stipulate which commandment, nor does it prevent me from breaking the same commandment multiple times."

"Uh," Ashteroth grunted, lifting a finger and starting to say something.

Gaillard cut him off. "Now, you told me I could use any of the commandments in the first six books of the Bible. You recall that?"

"Yes—"

"Then I have chosen Deuteronomy 23:21."

A low rumble began and Gaillard realized it was coming from his guest. It rattled the windows and trembled in the floor. He did his best to ignore it as he went on.

"If you recall, this verse states: `When thou shalt vow a vow unto the Lord thy God, thou shalt not slack to pay it: for the Lord thy God will surely require it of thee; and it would be a sin in thee.'"

The rumbling grew deeper and louder. Gaillard could see the demon's form shaking now. He gulped and pushed ahead.

"For every day of this last year, I have stated aloud that I do not intend to honor the contract I have signed with the devil. This meets the requirements of the contract and the morality clause, as it is a violation of a commandment and a sin. However, if I continue to do this for the rest of my life, which I fully intend to do, then I am not bound by the contract, I am only living in sin, which is forgivable by confession of sins."

The floor began to ripple now and pictures fell from the walls. Plaster rained from the ceiling as he went on.

"You gave me the idea yourself. Morality is flexible only in an atmosphere bereft of regulation. Your definition of morality gave me the ability to meet the contract while at the same time realizing there was a way out. I am using the letter of the contract to cancel my obligation to the contract."

Gaillard made his way to the door of the suite, carefully watching the seething demon that boiled in the middle of the room. Everything loose in the apartment had begun to swirl around Ashteroth as he listened to the report. Gaillard knew that the demon was required to hear the report in full and could not act until it was complete.

"I have gone each day for the last year to a priest and confessed my sin. Each day I have received absolution. I expect the priest will soon tire of my continued sinning, but according to the Bible, God will not. I know you will be watching me and returning each year for your report, but don't expect to receive anything much different from what you hear today." He opened the door and stepped into it, dodging a falling piece of plaster. "However, if you wish to avoid further fruitless meetings, I will be happy to release your master from his side of the contract. You might be losing a soul, but look at it this way, you will be saving millions each year."

"Gaillard!" the demon howled.

The door shut quickly. Ashteroth stopped his pyrotechnics and glared at the door.

“I hate lawyers,” he said.

There was a large smoke ring, a loud pop, and Gaillard’s apartment stank for a year.

Demon Puss

Terri Beckett

A self-confessed cat-addict, Terri Beckett has been living in the Caribbean for the past four years, and has only recently returned home to Wales. With her cats, of course. D.C. is not intended to resemble any particular cat, but rather a variety of black cats (let them remain nameless!) of the author's acquaintance.

Although he was a demon, his mother was an angel. He knew that she must have been, for the mere thought of her soft fur, her gentle reassuring murmur, the feel of her rough tongue cleaning him, and the taste of her warm sweet milk made him close his eyes and flex his paws and purr. Which is not truly demonic behaviour, but then, he did have some angelic blood. Most of him, however, had to be demon. Presumably from his father, of whom he had no memory at all. Of his own demonic self, he had no doubt, for did not his human, Miranda, say within a very few days of bringing him to her lair, "Kitten, you must be a demon!"

That was after he failed to jump cleanly on to the top shelf of the cabinet, his hind paws dislodging a highly-prized ormulu clock (which disgorged its innards irreparably over the floor) on his precipitous way down. Following that, he had stalked, caught, and eaten a bird (for demons relish the taste of salty hot fresh blood and the crunch of bones) but then he had thrown up on the best rug, probably because of an instinct to eat grass for dessert.

So, his people-given name became D.C., for Demon Cat, and he lived up to that as fully as he knew how. As he grew from a scrawny kit to a full-grown cat, his fur thickened and sleeked to a true ebony, his eyes gleaming green, his teeth white and sharp. Oh, he was a handsome beast, and he knew it well, for often Miranda would take him in her arms and sigh over his beauty. "If I could only find a man as beautiful, as faithful, as good as you, my darling D.C...." And he would purr, and flex his paws, and remember the wonderful scent of his mother, the angel.

It is not only angels who can grant wishes.

There was a man in her life, one George, and he and D.C. cordially disliked each other. George had to hide it, however, lest he incur her wrath, for she made it plain that the cat was her beloved. But secretly, he hated the cat, and would try to kick it when it came too close — and once, when she asked him to take the animal for its shots at the doctor, he opened the door of his car and thrust it out onto the highway. He pretended that the cat had escaped, of course, and was most apologetic—until D.C. arrived back on her doorstep, crying (most piteously!) to be let in. He was unharmed, being protected by his demon-luck, but had made sure to dishevel his fur and roll in mud. How she cried with delight when the cat sprang into her arms! George kept up the pretence and made much of it and exclaimed at its fortunate survival, but D.C.—D.C. wore his ears just so, and slitted his eyes so, and stared at him, so that George knew that the cat knew, and he was discomfited.

To begin with, George was not allergic to cats—but D.C. worked a magic, and shed on him all he could, leaving sleek black hair and scent on his clothing. Soon George could not be in the same room with D.C. without wheezing and sneezing. D.C. used his demon-powers with subtlety and cunning, and when it seemed to him that things were moving too slowly for his liking, he hastened things along by using George's shoe instead of the litterbox.

George was gone soon after. History. Miranda wept a little into D.C.'s satiny fur, and was soothed by his purring. Two more males were equally swiftly dispatched. Miranda began to wonder if she was destined to be single forever—but Miranda, of course, did not know of her Demon-Cat's powers, and how, in a thoroughly undemonic way (but we must remember that his mother was an angel) he longed for her happiness. How could he not? He loved her, as much as his demon-heart would allow, for the kitten-self deep within him was reminded of his mother, and how she had loved so him tenderly and completely.

In the nights, as Miranda slept, D.C. would stalk the apartment, weaving a magical web with each soft paw-pad, singing a silent chant as ancient as Eden. He would sit at the patio window and watch the moon, drawing that eldritch light with his eyes, savouring the dark. And each morning, he would be at Miranda's side when she woke, stretching as if he had slept as deeply as she. They would breakfast together before she left for work at the local library, and when she had gone D.C. would curl up on her bed and smell her scents and dream of the perfect mate for his Miranda.

He would, naturally, have to be devilishly handsome. He would have a sense of humour. He would share her interests. He would respect D.C.'s part in her life. He would make her happy.

Those criteria established, D.C. set himself to work his magic.

Even demons have their limitations.

The first of his Summonings was suitably handsome, it was true, but had as much sense of humour as an avocado. Which is to say, hardly any. He was also incredibly vain, spending hours about his grooming, and while Miranda was indeed happy for a little while, D.C. knew that this could not last.

He was right. At least this time, Miranda did not cry.

The second attempt was good-looking, and was able to make her laugh. Alas, he devoted all his spare time to football, and there is only so much of that game that a girl can be expected to take. Long before the NFL playoffs, he too was finished. Played off.

It was the night of All-Hallows, that most magical of times, when the doorbell rang. Miranda, with D.C. riding her shoulder, went to answer it, and was confronted by a quartet of monsters. "Trick or Treat!" they howled, "Trick or Treat!" In all his young life, D.C. had never encountered anything so terrifying. With a yowl of his own, he launched himself from Miranda's shoulder, fleeing into the night. But they were everywhere, monsters of every variety, chanting and wailing, and D.C. forgot his powers and let his feline instincts guide him. Ears flattened, fur bushed, he ran as fast as his paws could carry him, down the path and over the gate, across the sidewalk, into the road—

Brakes squealed. Something huge with glowing eyes loomed out of the night with horrifying speed. D.C. felt a terrible force strike him on the shoulder, flinging him aside as if he were no more than a featherweight. He hit the road hard, and knew nothing more...

He woke to hear Miranda crying, which was a sound he could not abide. Opening his eyes, he tried to lift his head, to reassure her, but everything hurt, and he could not help a little whimper of pain.

"I don't think he's hurt bad," said a voice he did not know. "But we should take him to the veterinarian to be sure."

This was not good. D.C. abominated the veterinarian, who stuck him with needles and performed other obscenities but seemed immune to demonic cursing. But he needed help, so he did not struggle when Miranda wrapped him tenderly in a big towel and cradled him in her arms all the way to the doctor's office.

"...nothing broken, but he's bruised and shaken up. Keep him quiet for a day or two, and bring him back if he's not better by then."

Miranda hand-fed him that night, with slivers of tuna, and he lapped water from her fingers. He did feel much better the next day, though very stiff, and spent much of the time sleeping. He woke to hear that same voice he had heard following the monster-attack.

"...just wanted to know that he's okay. I'm just so damned sorry..."

D.C. looked up into a kind face, with eyes as green as his own, and hair as black. The voice was deep and mellow—the hands that touched him were gentle but strong. "How're you doing, Big Guy?"

D.C. squinted his eyes and purred, sensing that this was no mere pretence—this male liked cats, knew and respected them. This male might well be fit mate for his Miranda...He had brought flowers (for Miranda) and chopped chicken-breast (for D.C.) She had invited him in, and brought him to visit the invalid, and D.C. found his appetite much stimulated by the taste of the succulent chicken. He managed to eat it all, staggering to use his litterbox afterwards, and then falling asleep again, lulled by the sound of their voices.

By the time he was completely well again, the new male was a constant visitor. Miranda and he would go out together in the evenings, and there was a new glow of happiness about her that D.C. found delightful. She spent more time with him, petting and grooming him, telling him of her days and of her dates with her new beau. "...and you like him, too, don't you, puss? He thinks you're a splendid animal—he says he grew up with cats, and he's never seen one handsomer."

Well, this was a given. D.C. purred and squinted his eyes at her, expressing his pleasure. She leaned down to kiss his head, and whispered in his ear: "You know, I think he might just be The One..."

D.C. purred harder, kneading his paws against her. Yes, and if it was so, then he, D.C. the Demon Cat, had been the instrument of their meeting!

"...and we share the same initial, too. If I believed in coincidence... Miranda and Michael. Michael and Miranda..."

It took all D.C.'s control not to leap to his feet. Michael! This could not be! Michael! D.C. had Summoned this male himself, it could not be that somehow he had Called the Warrior Angel, the Adversary! But when he thought it through, it seemed that he should have known. The signs were all there. The kindness, the gentleness—it all fitted. What could he do? Demon though he was, he knew he was a minor demon, and he could not hope to defeat the Archangel—or at least, not in direct conflict. He would need to use his utmost cunning. In short, he would cheat.

He was careful not to show his enmity. Let the Adversary see him as merely a housecat, a harmless pet, not recognising the demon-self that lurked in his soul. He was carefully polite, even affectionate, deigning to accept the toys that Michael brought to 'amuse' him, even adopting the frisky and playful attitude that had first enraptured Miranda. But how he longed to sink his teeth into that gentle hand! To rip and tear with fang and claw! Instead he would curl beside them as they sat together, rolling to expose his soft underbelly, purring when they stroked him. Michael was particularly good at stroking—the sensation of the big hands smoothing his spine-fur rhythmically over and over was—well, just short of heavenly. And the chin-rub was ecstasy. A cat could not ask for better! It would be so easy to capitulate, to just—give in, and accept that he had met his match.

This was weakness, and demonically he scorned it. He must work hard to prevail, but prevail he would, whatever it took.

He began with the allergy-spell he had worked on George. It should have been easier, for Michael never tried to avoid him, and indeed held him as closely as Miranda, burying his face in D.C.'s fur. Shedding on him had no effect whatsoever. He seemed immune to cat allergens. D.C. did not want to resort to the shoe-trick unless he absolutely had to—against his better judgement, he found he liked Michael too much—so he ate grass with dedication until his belly rumbled. Then, as Miranda and Michael sat at dinner, D.C. leapt to the top of the bookcase. He stretched his neck, hunkered low, raised his spine fur and coughed a warning cough.

"Haaargh—-hargggh—-haaarrrGHHH!"

It was a masterpiece of dramatic proportions. D.C. stared wide-eyed as the result of his compulsive ingestion of grass arched out and splattered on the carpet. He was fastidious in all his habits, and this disgusted even himself. It did not disgust Michael.

"Hairball trouble, Big Guy?" he commented sympathetically.

"He's not done that since he was a kitten, and ate a bird!" Miranda said, concerned. "Do you think he's sick?"

"Hardly. Cats are smart, and if there's something upsetting their digestion, they get rid of it. Bet he's eaten a whole load of grass —yes, I thought so..."

D.C. swivelled his ears into the 'horn' position, narrowed his eyes, and stared down at his enemy as demonically as he knew how.

"From his expression, it looks like he's still got indigestion, though. He better not have any of this chicken until his stomach settles down."

D.C. hissed in annoyance. The chicken smelled wonderful, and with his stomach emptied, he was hungry. But now he would be denied his treat!

Total war was declared. There would be no holds barred, he decided, no trick that was too vile to use. That night, he wriggled his way out of Miranda's embrace instead of snuggling into her scented warmth. He let her know that he was displeased by turning up his nose at the 'hairball control' cat kibble (which, truth be told, tasted quite acceptable, and had a satisfying crunchy texture) and ostentatiously raking a forepaw beside his dish, indicating that the offering was akin to excrement. He made himself hunker stiffly and uncomfortably on the bathroom commode while she bathed, and refused to look at her when she spoke to him.

"What is it, D.C.? Are you sick?"

He glanced at her and looked away.

"You must be sick, darling! We'll go to the vet as soon as I get home from work..."

It was the chance he needed. By nudging the door of his carrier as it closed, he was able to prevent it locking securely—and when Miranda lifted it out to carry him inside the surgery, it took very little for him to push at the door and leap free, closing his ears determinedly to her distressed cries as he ran. She could not have both Michael and him—therefore he would get out of her life, and live as a free demon, in thrall to no one.

It was soon dark, and he was able to stroll the streets and yards openly, instead of skulking in shadows. That is, until he rounded a corner to a piece of waste ground, and found himself confronting a group of ferals.

To begin with, he was not concerned. He was a demon—all other cats should recognise this and be afraid—or at the least offer him due respect. So why was it that they sat around him in a circle, gazing at him steadily? Their leader, a huge and battle-scarred tabby with torn ears and but one eye, prowled around him, his reek redolent of menace. "Will you fight, stranger?" he snarled.

"I do not need to fight," D.C. said. "I claim right of passage, that is all."

"There is no *right* without *fight*," the tabby hissed, "I say again —*will you fight?*"

"Why should I?" D.C. put his ears back. "I am no ordinary cat! I am a demon!" And he swivelled his ears and slitted his eyes in his most demonic stare.

The tabby laughed, nastily. "You? A demon? *Hah!* Well, I'm the Prince of Darkness! *Fight!*" he yowled, and sprang.

The conflict did not last long, and D.C. fled as soon as he could, pursued by the laughter of the ferals. He ran until his lungs burned, finding refuge at last under a bush. The claw- and teeth-wounds he had suffered throbbed, and he spent a long time laving them with his tongue in the hope of cleaning them. The ground was hard under him, and cold—he curled into a tight ball, tail over nose, and tried to sleep.

The rain woke him, dripping through the foliage. The morning was grey and chill and damp. All his wounds ached, and he could not move without stiffness. Limping, he made his way deeper into the underbrush in the hope of finding a drier lair. He was hungry, but had no strength to hunt. He did manage to lap some rainwater from a puddle, though it tasted bad. Later, it made him retch. Miserable with cold and wet, wretched, he crouched with closed eyes and thought of his warm dry home, of his loving Miranda, of how she would be missing him. The arrogant demon-soul shrank inside him to a thin ineffective whine. D.C. was now wholly cat, wholly mortal—and wished he could die.

He was hardly aware of the woman who found him lying like a dead thing in a drift of damp leaves. He recognised vaguely that her voice was gentle, and that she wished him no harm when she lifted him, murmuring reassurance. But she was not his Miranda, so he did not respond to her stroking.

The woman took him to the veterinarian in a travel-cage, and D.C. was too sick to object when the man handled him, examining his injuries, bathing them with something that smelled sharp, and stung. Needles were stuck in him, but he did not care. Afterwards, there was a pen with a soft fleece to lie on, warm and dark and quiet. A bowl of water was close, and a dish of kibble, and a litterbox. D.C. laid his head on his paws, and sighed, and slept.

The people who cared for him let him rest without disturbing him save for cleaning the litterbox and refreshing his dishes of food and water. He found himself able to eat a little after a while—his wounds felt easier—and then he slept again.

Days passed as he healed and began to take notice again. He was civil to his carers, but showed no interest in them or the people who came to the Shelter looking to adopt a pet. The vet diagnosed him as depressed, and recommended extra attention to stimulate his system. He accepted the grooming and petting as his due, but steadfastly refused to purr.

Then, one morning, he woke from a doze to hear the words "...could be your missing pet, Miss," and he caught the scent of her, the unmistakable scent that was his Miranda! D.C. reared up in his pen, beating his front paws against the bars, and called for her, and she heard him and then he was in her arms, purring so hard that his whole body vibrated. He thrust his face against hers over and over, her tears of joy wetting his head, his paws about her neck. He could not stop purring, even heard himself making the little kitten-cries that he had made to his mother. Oh, he loved her so much! How could he ever have thought he could live without her? Let her have Michael —he did not care so long as he could be with her, she could entertain the whole Host of Heaven...

Even when Michael took him in his arms and ruffled his fur, he could not stop purring. It had been Michael who had co-ordinated the search for him, calling the local vets, posting his description in stores and even appealing on local radio. He had wanted D.C.'s safe return as much as Miranda, and rejoiced with her.

D.C. realised that he had learned a great truth. Although he had truly believed himself to be wholly a demon, he had been deluding himself. He could have been, indeed, but he had Miranda, and he loved her. He had loved her so much that he had been willing to leave her so that she could find happiness—and that was in no way demonic. Love cannot live in a demon-soul.

And so it was that D.C. found a mate for his Miranda, and redemption for himself. From henceforth, he was A.C./D.C. The demon would always be a little part of him, (as it is in all creatures, great and small) though tamed—but stronger by far than that was the part he had from his mother. For after all, his mother *was* an angel...

Prize of a Lifetime

Michael J. McShay

Michael J. McShay lives on the high prairies of Colorado with his wife, dog, and occasional migrating deer. He is an artist and novelist. When not writing he eats Moon Pies, drinks Diet Pepsi, smokes a pipe, and visits with Elvis.

Peedle and Poyfair met at the designated place and time, Jennifer's front door at 4:30 PM. The sleepy suburb of Oakwood seemed the perfect place for heaven and hell to meet. It was close to the mall, in case they needed a snack after tending to business.

Poyfair was coiffured, lip-glossed, and dressed to the hilt like she'd just walked off an exotic fashion shoot. She was twenty-four and well aware that she was a stunner. Her pale violet eyes flashed as she greeted Peedle with a dazzling smile. "So nice of you to come. I see you're still buying your outfits at the geek shop."

Peedle shrugged. His green cardigan sweater rode up his starched white shirt and greeted his polka dot bow tie. "Unlike some people, I'm bound by truth in advertising."

"Oh touchy, I like that," she purred. "Well, are you ready little man?"

Peedle nodded and positioned himself behind her and off to the side. Rules of engagement declared that human beings had to be approached first by their own gender. The rule was iron clad if the subject was a minor.

Poyfair rang the doorbell and glanced back over her shoulder. "You should just give me this one. She's only fourteen, you don't stand a chance."

Peedle stuck a finger in his tight collar and gave it a nervous tug. She might be right, the competition got harder every year. The other side had better PR; more pizzazz, more excitement. If he were human, even he might be swayed.

"The fat lady hasn't sung..." He tried not to sound desperate.

Poyfair smirked. "Fat lady? You goodie, goodies are beyond obtuse." She jabbed at the doorbell again, almost breaking her custom painted fingernail in the process.

They heard a series of rapid thuds then the crash of someone jumping from the third stair from the bottom. Metal jiggled against metal and the door opened two inches. A brown eye peered over the security chain. "Yes?" came the high squeaky voice.

Poyfair licked her lips in amusement. She put on a smile so bright that it could toast a bagel. "Does Jennifer O'Brien live here?"

Seconds ticked in silence as the brown eye darted back and forth between the strangers on the porch. "Yeah, maybe."

Poyfair pulled several pages of official looking documents from her impossibly small purse and scanned them just long enough to build interest. Not a second more.

Peedle had to give her points for showmanship. Lies spiced with drama always sweetened the bait. He wished his side understood the need for style.

Poyfair raise her perfectly plucked eyebrow for effect. "Ah yes, Jennifer O'Brien, also known as Jenny-O on the Internet?"

"Yeah." The voice behind the door piqued with curiosity.

"Excellent! May I speak to her?"

"How do you know my surfing handle? It's secret."

"I'm from the Internet," Poyfair touched the base of her long delicate throat, "that is, I'm here from the website Demons-R-Us. Congratulations, you are the ten millionth surfer to log on!"

"Wow, did I win something?"

Peedle marveled at how Poyfair's shtick hooked them every time. Humans were so gullible they believed TV commercials more than their own mirrors to decide their self-worth.

He coughed softly to urge Poyfair to quit milking the suspense. The sooner one of them won, the sooner they'd finish the paperwork and he could go sit on a cloud and take off his tight shoes.

Poyfair dialed up her most sincere smile. "I'm Ms. Poyfair and this is Mr. Peedle. We're here to give you the prize of a lifetime."

The door shut, the rasp of metal sounded the removal of the security chain, and the door swung open. Jennifer O'Brien aka Jenny-O burst out in all her four-foot eight-inch glory.

Her mousy blond hair fell straight to her narrow shoulders and she wore a Britney Spears t-shirt with faded jeans cut-off at the calf like makeshift pedal-pushers. Her clothes hung on her bone thin frame like a parachute waiting for her feminine form to descend upon her.

One look at the awkward teen and Peedle knew he stood about as much chance with her as winning the lottery. The girl had to be a walking case of teenage insecurity. Poyfair's side fed on that.

Jennifer waved her plastic hairbrush in the doorway like a baton on fire. “What did I win? This is so exciting, Michelle, she’s my best friend, she is going to be so jealous.”

Poyfair opened her hand. “First we must verify that you are the real Jennifer O’Brien. Are your parents home?”

Half a quart of enthusiasm drained from the girl as the prospect of losing her prize loomed.

Peedle knew the ploy. Making the subject work for the prize made it more desirable. Make them want it past the point of good judgment. Poyfair was working the soft spots.

“Then,” Poyfair continued, “we have to check that it was your computer that logged into Demons-R-Us last Wednesday.”

Jennifer lost another half a quart of excitement. She whined, “My parents aren’t home and I don’t have a driver’s license or anything with a picture on it.”

Poyfair stroked her chin. “Well, you have a school yearbook with your picture in it? I think I can talk my boss into accepting that.”

The teenager perked up. “I’ve got one of those in my bedroom upstairs.”

“We could check your computer at the same time.”

Jennifer’s brain thrashed on that a moment and she looked suspiciously at Peedle. “I’m not supposed to let strangers in the house when I’m alone.”

Poyfair cranked herself into full-blown sincerity mode. “Well we aren’t exactly strangers, we come from your favorite new website, and it is the prize of a lifetime. I’m sure your parents wouldn’t want you to miss out on that.”

Peedle’s shoulders tensed. Prize indeed, more like a life sentence. Poyfair had the perfect blend of truth and lies to make her irresistible. And here he was, stuck with the truth. How fair was that?

Jennifer caved in with abandon. She jumped back into the house and scrambled up the long flight of stairs to her room. “Follow me,” she hollered, “we have to hurry though, my mom will be home in a little while.” She took the stairs two at a time.

They walked in and shut the door behind them.

Poyfair smiled and headed up the stairs. “I’ll go first so you can drool at my butt. Don’t want your trip down here to be a total waste of time.”

Peedle started to say something about virtue, but it sounded stupid even to him. He followed the teen and the demon up the long staircase feeling gloomier with each step.

“Come on little man,” Poyfair whispered, “time to win one for the devil.”

Besides her class picture, Jennifer appeared in the yearbook twice, in the back row of both the math and the chess clubs. Peedle allowed himself a split second of hope that somewhere among her flowering hormones that Jennifer had a spark of logical thought. But after all, hope was his business.

While Poyfair fiddled with Jennifer's computer pretending to check it, the hyper teenager swayed and lip-synced into her hairbrush to a Beatles song that blared on the stereo.

Song over, she flopped down on the end of the bed and stared at her hairbrush. "That's a hot group I just discovered."

"Oh?" Peedle hoped a non-committal remark was not lying, in the official sense, about the hot new group being forty-years old.

Jennifer leveled him with a teenage stare, equal parts accusation and curiosity. "You don't talk much, what do you do?"

"You might say I'm in quality control. I make sure things have a chance to go right."

She glared at his bow tie for a moment then became instantly bored. She bolted up and sidled up next to Poyfair. "Well?"

Poyfair turned and with a wide flourish of her hand announced, "We have a winner."

Jennifer bounced up and down clapping.

Poyfair stood and spread her arms wide. "Demons-R-Us, leader in music, pop culture, and what's hot, grants you your fondest wish."

Jennifer went blank. "Yeah, what's that?"

Poyfair put her hands on her hips and struck a glamour pose that screamed see me, the body, the style, the success. You want to be like me, you want men to fawn over you and make lesser women jealous. You want to be me, and you want it bad. She purred, "It's your wish, Jennifer, what do you want?"

Jennifer swept the hair from her eyes. "I want to be a rock star."

"What?" Poyfair's jaw dropped open. For a moment, the edges of her face turned hard.

"A really big rock star that makes Britney and Madonna look like dog food." Jennifer's conviction rose.

"A rock star?" Peedle grinned. Interesting, had Poyfair's vanity play finally screwed up?

"A big one," Jennifer nodded at Poyfair, "and I want it now, not when I'm old like you."

Peedle watched Poyfair struggle to maintain her composure. He knew she'd expected the teenager to ask to be just like her, which would have turned her into a little demon and been a slam-dunk for the other side. She didn't expect to be insulted about her age.

Poyfair took a breath. “Fine, no problem. We can do that.” A wicked smile played across her face. “Actually, that could still work out nicely. Are you ready?”

“Don’t I get a trial run or something? I mean, before I decide for sure?” Jennifer looked innocent.

Peedle picked up the white knight from the chessboard on Jennifer’s desk and made a move. “Seems only fair, don’t you think? I mean before she signs up.”

Poyfair faced him, with eyes that were fiery pits of hate. She hissed, “All right. I have nothing better to do with my time.”

Poyfair turned back to Jennifer and walked around her with an inspector’s eye. “First we need to do something about your image. You’ll never make it looking like a little boy.” She snapped her fingers.

Suddenly Jennifer was standing in a tight fitting blood red costume covered in spangles and gold sequins. The outfit, what little there was of it, barely covered the strategic parts of her lanky frame.

The teen’s face filled with shock, then seeing her reflection in the mirror, her face flushed deep crimson. She shrieked, jumped into bed, and pulled the covers up to her neck. “Jeez lady, you some kind of pervert? I’m almost naked.” Her eyes darted to Peedle, and the blush on her cheeks deepened.

Peedle lifted an eyebrow. “Little extreme don’t you think?”

Poyfair let loose a throaty laugh. “You think your fans are just there for the music, missy? Pleaseeeeee. No way, it’s all about sex appeal. Pure and simple.”

Jennifer lifted the covers and looked down. In a plaintive tone she said, “I don’t have that much to appeal with yet.”

Poyfair brushed it aside. “You’d be surprised. When you strut your stuff on stage you’ll have them howling for more. Trust me.”

The girl eased out of bed, clutching a pillow for cover. She walked over and poked Poyfair tentatively with her finger as if taking a temperature. “So, you’re a real demon huh? Gates of hell, soul sucking and all that stuff?”

“What’d you expect from a website called Demons-R-Us,” Poyfair snorted, “Santa Claus?”

“Aren’t you supposed to have like, horns and a gnarly tail or something?”

Poyfair smiled and a set of two-inch horns pushed their way out through her forehead. The points sparkled. “Happy?”

Jennifer wandered around her room and appeared to be thinking. She came to the chessboard. After a moment’s consideration she glanced at Peedle and moved her queen.

Poyfair drummed her fingers. "Let's get on with it, shall we?"

Jennifer looked up from the board. "First, I want my old clothes back."

Poyfair flicked her hand, and Jennifer's t-shirt and jeans reappeared on her. The demon arched an annoyed eyebrow. "Now?"

"Okay, I want to see what my parallel futures would be like."

Poyfair threw up her hands. "Fine." She glared at her counterpart. "Guess which boring option you're stuck with?"

Peedle shrugged and asked Jennifer, "What do you want to see first? Work, play, end game...?"

"Let's start with the music."

Poyfair walked over, opened a door, and said, "Follow me." Then she disappeared inside.

Jennifer hesitated and turned to Peedle. "Is she nuts? She just went into my closet."

"She's being allegorical. We keep our dreams and aspirations in the closet of the mind." He looked at the girl for a glimmer of understanding and seeing none said, "She's a drama queen and needed to make an exit. Just follow her."

They walked through the closet doorway and reappeared in the front row wings of an open-air amphitheater. Jennifer did two pirouettes with her mouth wide-open taking in the enormity of the facility and the thousands of people it held.

"Yoo-hoo, over here." Poyfair was leaning against a light post, eating a corndog on a stick. They walked over.

"I love these things, we don't have them back at headquarters. Well, we do but they're all burned to a crisp." She burped and giggled. She waved her hand with a flourish. "So, crowd big enough for you?"

"This place is awesome." Jennifer gazed up. There were so many faces in the crowd; they were like grains of sand on a beach.

"They're all your fans, and this is just one stop on a forty location world tour; all dying to see, the great Jenny-O."

Peedle began to worry. How could a fourteen-year old not be swayed by such a gigantic stroke to her ego? Could anyone?

Suddenly music began to wail from the giant loudspeakers throughout the amphitheater and the lights dimmed. A whoop of anticipation rolled through the audience like a tsunami, then everyone gasped as all the lights in the place went dark.

Behind the curtain a kettledrum pounded its way to a deafening crescendo in the blackness. Then in an explosion of eye splitting fire and smoke, Jenny-O flew from the back of the theatre, swooping ten-feet over the audience's heads and wailing like a banshee. As she touched down on stage, her band's music began to rip through the sound barrier. Showtime.

Poyfair elbowed Peedle in the ribs and screamed over the noise. "Pretty nifty, huh? My idea."

Jennifer's eyes were glued to herself up on stage. Jenny-O, the rock star, was a few years older than Jennifer, but it was definitely the teen's alter-ego.

Jenny-O jiggled, wiggled, and heaved everything humanly possible to be provocative as she sang. Her outfits ranged from skimpy to microscopic and the crowd roared its approval with each costume change.

Jennifer's eyes grew wider with every new unveiling.

At intermission the teen's face remained enigmatic. Peedle wasn't sure if it was shock or something else. Maybe she shared his headache from the concert's thundering racket.

Poyfair struck a pose so that the lines of her red silk dress caught the breeze and billowed perfectly to highlight her figure. "So what'ya think about yourself up there?" She gushed, "Pretty cool, huh?"

A blush returned to Jennifer's face. "I can't do any of that racy stuff..."

"Look kid, who do you think that was working the audience." Poyfair jerked her thumb back toward Peedle. "Him?"

"No," she stared at her feet, "but the costumes were really, really small and the way I, err, she moves..."

Poyfair ran her hands down the curves of her body. "Girlfriend, if you got it, you flaunt it. And if you don't got it, there's always liposuction and boob jobs."

Jennifer made a sour-lemon face. "Oh, gross. Nobody's stickin that stuff in my body."

Peedle shook his head. He could always rely on Poyfair to push the point too far and be her own worst enemy. He felt Jennifer start to waver, but the game had just begun.

Poyfair turned and glared at him. "Well that was the work section of our little program, do you have something better to show Jennifer than herself as the fabulous Jenny-O?"

Jennifer piped up, "Yeah, if I decide not to be a rock star, what will my life be like?"

Peedle wished he had something flashy. But, no, his side demanded absolute truth. "Do you study hard for school and help your mother around the house?"

"Yes."

"Go out and have fun with your friends?"

"Yeah."

"Started to notice boys yet?"

Jennifer ignored the question and shifted her eyes to Poyfair who was pretending to stifle a yawn.

Peedle took a deep breath and sighed. Sometimes the truth was just the pits. "Then I guess the next few years will be pretty much more of the same, except there will be more boys."

"But my life is soooooooo boring!" Jennifer wailed. "Everyone has more fun than me."

Poyfair spun Jennifer around. "Fun. You want fun? Jenny-O has tons of fun." She clapped her hands and the three were transported to an exclusive Beverly Hills department store.

They watched Jenny-O ramble through the various departments buying up whatever caught her eye, regardless of price. She had every clerk's undivided attention because there were no other customers.

Poyfair waved her arm. "She rented the entire store for the afternoon just to shop. And, this is her third store today. Now doesn't that sound fun?"

Peedle watched Jennifer's eyes gleam with shopping lust. They followed the Jenny-O entourage out of the store and he counted out twenty pairs of shoes. "Land sakes, she's only got two feet."

Both Jennifer and Poyfair gave him the you-are-a-stupid-man look and in unison said, "You wouldn't understand."

The rock star's group piled into two stretch limos that were waiting at the curb. Jennifer peeked inside. "Wow those things are better equipped than my whole house."

Poyfair's face crackled with smugness. "You'll go everywhere in a limo."

"Your uncle takes you driving in his truck." Peedle offered.

"Or in your own chartered jet."

"Public transportation is less polluting."

"You'll stay in five-star hotel suites."

"Your dad takes you camping."

Poyfair's eyes lit up and she screeched, "Parties..." and clapped her hands again.

The three were suddenly inside an elegant restaurant filled with hundreds of the most beautiful people from the worlds of music and Hollywood. Jennifer stood, star struck, down to her toes.

When she spotted Jenny-O, laughing and holding court in the middle of the excitement, Jennifer's eyes bugged out.

Peedle had to admit, this was a masterstroke. Poyfair was dropping nuclear warheads and all he had in his camp was truth and a peashooter.

Poyfair gave the gourmet food table a quick once over. “Damn, you'd think they could muster up a descent corn dog.” She walked over and nudged Jennifer out of her trance. “Pretty slick, huh? When you're a rock star, there's always a party going on somewhere with an open invitation.”

“Can I get some autographs?”

Poyfair laughed. “Silly girl, this hasn't happened yet. It doesn't become real until you make your wish. You're like the invisible girl here.”

Jennifer nodded her understanding. “Wow, this would be so cool. I mean, look at me with all those stars.”

Peedle stepped up next to her. “There will be parties when you go to college. You'll have a lot of fun there and meet...”

Jennifer pulled him aside. “I have to tell you, Mr. Peedle, all your boring stuff isn't making much of a case.”

Poyfair eased up and put her hand on Jennifer's shoulder. “He can't help being a bore, the halo crowd are all like that.” She led the teen a few feet farther away. “Girl to girl, you like the boys, but they won't pay attention to you, right?”

Jennifer stared at Poyfair's ample bust, her lower lip trembling. “They call me the stick.”

Poyfair nodded, “Men are the pits.”

“But I want them to like me...”

“Who doesn't? Listen, as Jenny-O that isn't going to be a problem. She can have any man she wants.”

Jennifer gazed over to where Jenny-O had every man at her table and even the adjacent ones, fawning over her. They were spellbound by her every move. “She's sure good at it, all ‘cause she has...”

“Charisma?”

“Boobies.”

Poyfair arched a brow. “Well guys are fascinated with them, but that won't keep them interested. For that you need power, money, and cunning.”

“I just want a boyfriend who likes me for me.”

“That's sweet,” Poyfair said turning toward Peedle and rolling her eyes. “You know, Jenny-O has one.”

Jennifer perked up, “Really? What does he look like?”

Poyfair clapped once again and the two of them suddenly stood in a hotel hallway without Peedle.

Jenny-O and a guy were laughing and stumbling up the hall, hip-to-hip in three-legged race fashion. The guy had his arm around the star's neck, clutching a wine bottle. They were both trying to drink from the bottle at the same time while weaving up the hall.

"Ah, the happy couple."

Jennifer turned the other way and covered her face with her hands. "They'll see us."

"Still invisible, remember?"

The girl turned back, "Oh yeah."

"So what do you think?"

"Well, he's handsome. I like dark hair and brown eyes, so I guess her tastes are similar. But, they looked drunk."

"Intoxicated by love."

"Are they really in love?"

"Let's go see." Poyfair took the girl's hand and they walked through the wall into Jenny-O's huge hotel suite. The place looked like a show home.

The couple sat on the bench of a grand piano, mister romance playing a love song and Jenny-O nuzzling his ear.

"They seem pretty happy..." The teen hugged herself and sighed. "I really want a boyfriend..."

"Wait, it gets better."

At the end of his song the guy leapt off the bench, swooped Jenny-O up in his arms, and carried her to the bedroom.

Jennifer's eyes widened and her face paled. "Oh..."

"I told you men want more." Poyfair licked her lips and leaned forward. "Wanta go watch?"

A voice boomed behind them. "I think not."

They spun around. Peedle stood with his arms crossed and an expression on his face like someone had just given him a giant wedgey.

Poyfair tilted her head back and looked down her nose at him. "Oh you're back. We hoped...err...thought we lost you."

"She's a minor, Poyfair, you know the rules; influence, not corrupt. You lose by default."

The demon's eye's narrowed to diamond sharp points. "We didn't go in. She didn't see anything, so technically the ball is still in play."

"Hey," Jennifer punched Poyfair in the shoulder, "I'm not your stupid pawn, lady. And if you haven't noticed I'm still standing here."

Peedle chuckled at Poyfair's shocked expression as she rubbed the sore spot on her shoulder. Then he felt Jennifer's glare upon him. He couldn't read her expression.

"Okay, they're in there having sex, right? I'm only fourteen but I'm not stupid. It's not a big deal, God, adults can be so immature about stuff." She flopped down on the piano bench.

Peedle bit his lip and set down next to her. "You're right," he said quietly. "So you still want to be a big rock star?"

Jennifer swung her feet under the bench, her forehead wrinkled in thought. She looked up and nailed them both with a spiteful glare. "What I want is the truth. She's only showing me the fun parts, and you're telling me I should be happy to be flat-chested and dull. And you both want to suck out my soul or something."

Poyfair hovered over them. "Jenny-O wears a 36-AA and she certainly isn't dull."

He looked up. "You're starting to annoy me."

"Just trying to help." Poyfair brought up her palms in a sign of surrender and took two steps back.

"All right, Jennifer" Peedle cleared his throat. "The Beatle's were a big rock group from way back in the 1960's."

"You're kidding..."

"Actually, the guys that are still around are older than me."

"Oh, gross." Jennifer made a face like she'd swallowed a fly. "Why didn't you tell me before?"

"I didn't want you to feel dumb, but it's time for the truth."

Poyfair rubbed her nails against her silk blouse and then stared at the high gloss. "Fantasy is more fun..."

"Shut up," Peedle snapped.

"And a lot more satisfying," Poyfair quipped, determined to get in the last word.

"You're wrong about that..."

Jennifer stood and shrugged. "Rocking out looks a lot better than my boring life." She swayed side-to-side as if trying to reach her decision.

Peedle could feel her slipping away. How could he explain real life to a fourteen year old and not sound like an old fart? Then it came to him. He pulled a game piece out of his pocket and tossed it at her. "Chess."

Jennifer caught the piece and scrunched her nose in confusion. "What?"

"Life is like a game of chess. You don't just play the people you can beat, do you?"

"No, that's too easy. It's no fun."

"It's the challenge that makes a good game interesting, not just the winning."

She cocked her head to the side. "I guess..."

"The truth is, winning is over and done with pretty quickly, but the challenge of becoming a better player lasts longer and is more interesting."

Poyfair yawned loudly. "God, could you be any more boring?"

Understanding registered on Jennifer's face. "So she's just been showing me winning, not who I'd become?"

Peedle nodded. "Check."

Jennifer turned and stared at the bedroom door. "What about that? I still want a boyfriend."

"Watch the door. I'll show you the next three months at high speed."

The three stared as Jenny-O's bedroom opened and closed in rapid succession with twenty-five different men. The door was still swinging when Jennifer turned back with a horrified look.

"I'm a slut."

"No, she's a slut," Peedle said. "You haven't decided whether to become her or not."

Poyfair patted her hairdo and batted her eyes. "There are worse things in the world. Don't be so judgmental."

"True. Remember the big stage show? Let's take a closer look." He opened a closet door and led Jennifer through, Poyfair followed begrudgingly. They reappeared back stage at the giant amphitheater.

Jenny-O was red faced and screaming obscenities at the road crew. She stomped from one poor soul to the next, waving her arms, barking orders, and throwing equipment around.

Poyfair shrugged it off. "She's a little high-spirited. The poor thing just has a case of stage fright."

"That poor thing throws a fit every night. She's put people in the hospital." Peedle said.

Jennifer bit her lip. "A slut and a royal bitch. Sweet."

Poyfair shrugged. "Genius is often misunderstood..."

"But bad manners are not." Jennifer retorted, "at least according to Momma."

Poyfair's eyes narrowed on Peedle. "Jenny-O is rich and famous, what future do you have to offer, little man?"

"I am kind of a dud by comparison," Jennifer admitted in a meek voice.

Peedle led them away from Jenny-O's tantrum. "Well in the game of life the queen is powerful, but the knight is versatile and jumps over pieces. The bishop is swift, attacking from across the board from nowhere..."

"Yeah, yeah, but the boys call me the stick. Am I always going to be such a loser?"

Poyfair smirked. "You'll study so hard your brain will explode."

Peedle nodded. "Well, you will study hard."

Jennifer groaned.

"But you'll meet new people and have fun too."

"The dull leading the duller..." Poyfair added.

"You'll meet a guy, fall in love, and start a business..." Peedle raced through the words.

"Oh, gag me." Poyfair gestured with her finger down her throat.

"And then what?" Jennifer asked breathless with the possibilities.

"You work yourself to death and die dull. Sounds like a full life to me."

Jennifer threw up her hands and screamed at Poyfair. "Would you please, shut up!"

Peedle nodded his approval. Poyfair crossed her arms and huffed.

"Well?" Jennifer tapped her foot.

Peedle smiled and snapped his fingers.

They stood in a hospital room. An adult version of Jennifer lay in a bed surrounded by family and friends. A brown-haired man in a hospital gown handed her a baby.

"This is her third. Two knights and a queen, if you are interested."

Young Jennifer's eye sparkled. "Is he her husband? He's so handsome. That's her baby?"

"Yep. Eventually they'll have seven grandchildren and three great grand children together. It's not boring at their house at all," Peedle rocked on his heels, "in fact, it's pretty darn interesting."

Poyfair flapped her arms in the air, red-faced trying to redirect Jennifer's attention. "You'd give up clothes, money, and fame for this cornball Kodak moment?"

Jennifer's eyes glistened. "Maybe."

Peedle leaned over. "Did I mention, you...err...she is also President of her own fashion company?"

"Cool."

He led them out of the room and up a hall. "Okay Jennifer, any questions?"

"What happens to Jenny-O?"

"Thought you might ask that."

"Do you have to show her that? Come on, Peedle, is that playing fair?" Poyfair whined.

"Truth in advertising, remember?"

Peedle pointed to the emergency room where a gray-faced Jenny-O lay on a gurney. A team of doctors worked desperately to revive her. Her body was frail and wasted. "Jenny-O does a Janis Joplin at twenty-five."

"What?"

"She OD's on everything you can OD on."

A tear ran down Jennifer's cheek. "She won, she lost."

"The truth isn't always pretty."

He looked at his watch and said, "4:35, time to get back." Then, suddenly the three were back in Jennifer's room at home.

Peedle peeked out the window to Mrs. O'Brien, Jennifer's mother, walking up the sidewalk to her front door. Poyfair followed his gaze to the portly woman and frowned. "You must be kidding, right?"

Poyfair turned, full glamour and smiles, toward the teenager. She waved a transfer of soul form and with a flourish put the form and a pen on Jennifer's desk. "All right, kiddo, are you ready to rock and roll? Fame, fortune, and excitement are just a signature away. First we'll get your wardrobe, and then a band..."

"I've decided," Jennifer closed her eyes, "that I wish to keep my life the way it is...that is, the way it will be."

Peedle smiled.

"Except," Jennifer broke into a mischievous grin, "I want to switch bodies with her." She pointed in Poyfair's direction. "Not the head, the horns, or the attitude, just her body."

Peedle was surprised. "Are you sure that's what you want? It isn't necessary, you will grow into...you know."

"Listen brains are good, but having the total package can't hurt, can it?"

Poyfair stomped around, screaming, "Hey, you can't do that. She can't do that, can she?" Her horns grew longer, and her once elegant facial features twisted into a hideous sneer. "Don't you do that to me, Peedle!"

"Final answer?" he asked.

Jennifer nodded.

"Done."

As Poyfair opened her mouth to protest further, her flashy silk dress deflated and draped upon her now stick like frame. She shrieked and grabbed in desperation where her breasts had been and at the flatness of her rear end. Her eyes filled with horror. "Do you know what the inmates will do to me back at headquarters?"

Jennifer's T-shirt suddenly ballooned to the point of bursting and her makeshift pedal pushers rose above her knees. She appraised herself in the mirror running her hands over her new body. "Wow, I'm a babe."

"Jennifer," Mrs. O'Brien called from downstairs, "I'm hoooommmeeeee." She sang out cheerfully in the key of C.

"Down in a minute, Mom." Jennifer shouted.

Peedle turned to Poyfair. "The fat lady has sung."

Poyfair's head fell. "Man, I hate this part."

Her skinny behorned body became a flickering glob of glowing plasma encased in a ring of fire. Her image blinked on and off, then just before disappearing, altogether, she shook a defiant fist at Peedle and spat out, "I hate geeks."

Then she was gone.

Peedle faced Jennifer. "Checkmate."

"I guess you won, huh."

"No, I just didn't lose. It was more of a stalemate."

"Did I win?"

"You played well, until the end."

"This new body is going to make me pretty popular," came her bright reply, "and I'm going to be a Mom someday..."

"Did you win?" he asked.

"I think I did..." Then an astonished look sprang to her face and she jumped forward. "Hey..." She jumped again.

Jennifer grabbed the back of her pants and jerked her head around trying to see her backside. She ran to the mirror, turned, and pointed her bottom at the glass. A huge bulge was growing on her rear end.

Her face filled with panic from the sudden pressure building in the seat of her pants. The bulge grew at an alarming rate to the size of a football.

Jennifer struggled to catch her breath as her waistband tightened. She tried in vain to release the clasp on her jeans, but the thing building behind her had stretched the fabric too taut. "God," she sobbed, "what's happening? Help me!"

Peedle raised an eyebrow. "Sometimes winning isn't all you thought it would be."

With a jarring rip, the seam in the back of Jennifer's jeans split open and out burst a thick three-foot long green tail. It unfurled and surged with a life of its own behind her.

Jennifer sputtered to catch her breath. Her lip quivered as she beheld the green scaly appendage that stuck out from her rear and swayed with her every move. She flailed her hands in the air. "Oh mygosh, oh mygosh. Look at that gnarly thing," she wailed. "I have a tail."

"It is standard demon equipment."

Tears welled up in Jennifer's eyes. "Well can't you do something? I can't go to school with that thing."

"You made your wish."

"But I didn't know... Isn't there some special dispensation for kids?"

"Well you could learn to control it, like Poyfair did."

"How long will that take?"

"Couple of years if you apply yourself."

"A couple of years..." she blubbered.

"If you apply yourself."

Peedle loosened his tie. His mission was over and he could kick back and relax. He walked over and examined Jennifer's music collection. "We could play for it."

"What?" Guarded hope filled her eyes.

"Chess."

"If I win you'll get rid of the tail?"

"Of course, but you're still not listening. Life isn't all about winning."

"What if I lose?"

He smiled. "I'll still help you get rid of the tail."

She stared at Peedle in curiosity and disbelief, but after several adjustments to her tail, she sat down and moved the chessboard between them. "White or black?"

Peedle eased into a chair on the other side of the board. "White, please."

Jennifer's brow furrowed. "White moves first."

He advanced the white knight. "Mind if we listen to some music?"

She turned on the Beatles, stared at the board, and moved her queen. "Winning doesn't count?"

The forty-year old band played "Ob-la-di, ob-la-da life goes on...," in the background.

"Naw." He moved his bishop across the board.

"Whoa, tricky." She scooted closer to the board. Her eyes narrowed in concentration, unaware that the tail resting upon her shoulder had already begun to shrink away.

Peedle settled back to enjoy himself. Winning was less important than how you played. The enjoyment was in the game.

"So tell me, Jennifer, why is it that women are so fascinated with shoes?"

Perhaps

Michele Hauf

Michele Hauf lives in Minneapolis with her family on a quaint little suburban plot that is frequent host to fairy rings. She's yet to venture inside the toadstool circles, but she's ready to make that leap!

Prologue

"Bring me an angel! Rip one from the heavens for me!"

The master's voice shuddered inside Venedictos' head. The sound was of stone pushed slowly across stone to block the dark orifice of an icy crypt. A deep, evil sound that always made the hairs on his back crinkle beneath the woolen robe he wore.

"Yes, your darkness." Venedictos bowed obediently.

"You can do it?" The dark lord spun around and cast his burning gaze toward the cowering wizard. "Yes?"

"Um...well..."

Damen the Dark strode the castle floor, his polished leather boots crackling across the rotting rushes and brittle leaves underfoot. His gaze captured Venedictos' and the wizard dared not look away. "Are you not the self-proclaimed *greatest* wizard in all the land?" The darkness of his voice took on a sarcastic edge, an edge as sharp as a sword and one Venedictos took pains to appease.

"In the land?" The wizard's voice faltered. "I...I haven't traveled past the Forest of Thorns that surrounds your most humble abode."

"That is what I command of you!" A black and thin shadow, Damen turned on his heels and paced back to the window. Bracing his palms upon the stone ledge, he scanned the gray night sky, illuminated only by a thin dagger of moon. A chill midnight breeze rippled the white silk sleeves against his muscled arms.

"I wish to have an angel," he announced to the skies. "A creature of innocence and pureness, whose wings have been touched by the softness of the heavens. By far that will be my greatest challenge yet." He closed his eyes and whispered his passion. "To seduce an ethereal being and to bring an end to this dreaded curse of light. Aaah...to once again know the comfort of darkness."

A flickering glimmer hovered near the window, a tiny creature whose wings were of transparent black cellophane. Its entire length was no more than a wolf's toe. Damen snapped out and grasped the fluttering insect. The crisp crackle of splintering bones was muffled inside his fist. "Insufferable black fairies." He turned to Venedictos with an inquisitive glare to his onyx eyes. "Why has nothing been done to exterminate these horrendous creatures?"

"Well, your Darkness, you see—"

Damen tossed the broken remains of the fairy out the window and approached his servant in three great strides. "They mill about in great masses. I do not like them! They...they are always buzzing about me. And they get in this intolerable length of hair." He held a twist of his own dark tresses out as if they were alien and bothersome to him.

"It is the m-moon flowers, your darkness." Venedictos shrank from his master's malicious shadow, pressing his back as tight as he could to the stone wall behind him. "They are attracted to the iridescent petals. They do harbor a pleasant scent."

"Flowers? Bah! Why do they not die? Have you not laid poison over the ground? What of the gargoyle? Does he not fly down and stomp upon them?"

A pearl of sweat tickled down Venedictos' back. He strained to control a shiver; he knew his master was acutely aware of his fear. "Th-they seem to be a hardy breed, your darkness. They simply spring up after the gargoyle flies away. I'll try the poison again. Perhaps some boiling oil this time?"

"See that you do. Or I'll lay boiling oil over you and see if you wither and cease to attract the fairies. If that doesn't work..." The moonlight cast an eerie spotlight across Damen's prominent nose and sunken cheeks, highlighting his death's-head smirk. "I'll feed *you* to the gargoyle."

One

Beethoven's Moonlight Sonata was being pureed through the blender top speed. To make matters worse, two cats had been thrown into the foul brew. Notes were strangled and crushed to an erratic cacophony. Surely, poor Beethoven was doing flip-flops in his grave.

Alex Gordon looked up from the monotonous words in his textbook as yet another foul note jarred his thoughts. His best friend sat before the piano, her ankles crossed beneath the bench. Her head rhythmically bobbed up to scan the sheet music then down to locate the proper key. "How many weeks has it been now?"

Her nose to the sheet music and her tongue pressed between her lips, Devon mumbled. "Two this Friday. Sounds pretty good, huh?"

"Um...sure." Alex ground his teeth together and hid his gentle irritation behind his book. *Puree another cat for me.*

He would never tell her it needed a little work. Make that a lot of work. Well, honestly, it flat-out sucked. Devon was too good a friend. Hopefully, this hobby won't last long. Pray the next would be something that did not require sound.

Another tortured note clawed its way across Alex's temples. Devon was intent in her practice. Beside her sat Mister Pusster, her lilac Himalayan. He, too, wore a worried frown, with ears pricked and whiskers alert.

"So, you think this is your true calling?" Alex asked. "Or are you gonna try something else?"

Devon spun on the piano bench, a frustrated twist curling her lips. She pushed long fingers through her wavy hair and blew a stray curl from her nose. "Just because I like to try new things doesn't mean I never stick with it."

"I never said you didn't," Alex suddenly found himself in the defense.

"Unlike you, who doesn't know what to do with his life."

Alex displayed the textbook. "I know exactly what I'm going to do with my life." He drew his finger along the title. "Basic Computers! It's nice and—"

"Safe?" Devon offered.

Alex slunk back into the couch cushions. Yeah, safe. Devon knew him well. Ever since his older brother, Todd, had been shot down while on an overseas mission, Alex had been fearful of life in the real world. No, not exactly fear. Just...cautious.

He'd had plans of joining the service himself. But after hearing his brother had been killed while trying to save the life of another, Alex had torn up his application for the Marines and instead enrolled in college. He was going to be a computer consultant. No guns, no ammo, no secret missions. *Yeah, nice and safe.* Of course, he'd never had an interest in computers, and was finding the homework damn hard. But like Devon said, it was safe.

"I don't want to talk about it," Alex mumbled and immediately changed the subject. "Sometimes I wish I had your freedom. Your inheritance will see you to your death. You'll never have to work. You can be free to explore all your desires—" Alex stopped abruptly.

"It is nice to be financially secure." Devon absently smoothed her fingers over Mister Pusster's back.

I could use a tender loving touch, Alex thought. *Why does the cat always get all the attention?*

"But that won't keep me from writing the great American novel one of these days. You must admit I've stuck with my writing for years."

"Yes, and I commend you on it. How's it going, anyway? Weren't you working on some sort of romance?"

"Of a sort. It's an action adventure, romantic romp sort of thing. But I've hit writer's block." Devon sighed and pushed the cat from her lap. "I need a hero."

"A hero?" *I'm free,* Alex thought.

"Yes. My heroine is stuck up in the villain's castle tower just..." She searched for the word. "She's just—oh—I don't know—bland! I've got her scanning the horizon in search of the hero, but he just hasn't road into my imagination yet. Oh!" Devon sprang from the piano bench and grabbed up a velvet-covered book sitting on the coffee table. "It's almost midnight, Alex. We've got to get outside!"

Accustomed to her abrupt conversation changes, Alex tossed his homework aside and followed Devon and Mister Pusster out the patio doors.

"Off to adventure," he chuckled. "Gotta love the woman." He plucked a burgeoning pink rose bud from the overhead trellis and stepped onto the soft, spongy grass. A pumpkin orange moon cast soft light across the backyard, glinting in the evening dew that frosted the moss covered oak trunks. Thanks to Devon's adventure with topiary, a well-trimmed, silvery-blue yew hedge fenced in one side.

Mister Pusster sprang after a pale-winged moth, his fluffy tail bobbing like a metronome. Devon strolled ahead of Alex, humming and singing absently as she so often did. A path of pea-sized pebbles led to a lacey white gazebo set beneath a massive willow tree that marked the end of the property and the beginning of the forest.

God, he loved her free spirit. Carefree was her middle name. Unrestrained and adventurous in all aspects of her life. Except love. But he was working on that.

Alex zoned in on the words Devon sang.

"*So if you really love me, say yes...but if you don't dear, confess...and please don't tell me, perhaps, perhaps, perhaps.*"

Alex smiled. Yep, Devon was a Doris Day fan. She was also crazy for cats, books, angels, Dove chocolate, sparkly things, (she was constantly dragging him to yet another flea market in search of rhinestone jewelry), and all things gothic, particularly gargoyles.

Devon's voice slipped back into Alex's thoughts. "*Perhaps, perhaps, perhaps.*"

"You know, that's about the sexiest word I've ever heard cross a woman's lips."

"Hmm?" Devon turned around, the book splayed open across her fingers. She took a couple of steps walking backwards. Her smile, a tad crooked, pushing up the tiny brown mole above the corner of her mouth. "What word? Perhaps?"

"Uh huh." Alex couldn't tear his eyes from the wispy strands of burgundy hair that the wind blew across Devon's lips.

"How so?"

"Well..." Alex pushed long fingers through his short crop of haphazard blond hair, striding alongside her. "Say you ask a woman a question. Like, you wanna go out with me? Or even, hey, you want to make out? She pouts her lips and says...mmm, *maybe.* Maybe? How dull. How unforgivably unoriginal. You know?"

Devon shrugged and pulled a finger down the page in her book as Alex continued to explain. "But if she says *perhaps*...well... It's so much more sexy. Perhaps," he savored the word in a hushing breath. "It just whispers off your lips, you know?"

"Sure, Alex." Devon turned back and continued strolling ahead, lost in her book.

If she only knew how he'd love to touch her hair, to run his fingers through the waves of shimmering black-cherry silk. And her perfume, the scent of vanilla and some other spices filled his nostrils and lingered even after she was gone. He had long and passionate dreams of kissing her lips and pulling her body close so he could truly know her soft curves. *Perhaps...*

Devon skipped ahead through the thick summer grass, her flashlight bobbing across the carved yew hedges surrounding her backyard.

He and Devon had been friends since grade school. They'd grown up in the same neighborhood, built sand castles together, went monster hunting, staged elaborate camping trips in their backyards, and since their teenage years had always confided in the other when it came to the opposite sex. They were buddies, soulmates, friends to the end.

Devon would never know just how infatuated Alex really was with her. He'd tried many timesto convince her of his genuine interest. But she'd always pop up with the same answer. *If it didn't work out, I'd hate to lose your friendship.*

"Alex? Come back to earth, Alex."

"Chill, Devon, I'm listening. Sort of." He dove to the grass where she sat, laying next to her, pressing the corner of her book down with the fragrant rosebud. "You know this is the craziest of all your whims. Let's see now...what was it before piano lessons?"

"Home decorating ala Martha Stewart," she replied as she drew a finger down the pages.

"Yeah, and after that it was fencing."

"Hey, you liked fencing."

"I did. But you should have stuck with it longer than two weeks. And what crazy notion did you give it up for? Topiary!"

"You know I like to keep my creativity piqued. By the way, do you still have the topiary tree I made for you?"

Oops. He had planned on never bringing that one up. "Er, well..."

"You *do* still have it, don't you?" She had forgotten her book. "Alex?"

"Well, I um...you see...it was Fred."

"What about Fred?"

"He ah...er...well...he...peed on it."

"What? You let your dog pee on my topiary?"

Alex squint his eyes shut, preparing for admonishment. Not that he and Devon ever fought but he always enjoyed their playful spats. Devon's giggles erupted in the fragrant evening air. Alex looked up into her smiling face. *Damn, he loved that beauty mark.*

"I do have a tendency to get carried away with things, don't I?" Mister Pusster rubbed his body along Devon's leg. She spread her fingers through his fur. "Can you believe that, Pusster? The man actually owns a dog. Such intelligent animals they are that they pee on lovely household decorations. What's with Fred, anyway?"

"Nothing's wrong with Fred." Alex flicked Mister Pusster's tail out of his face. "He just gets a little confused when he sees a tree indoors."

"Yes, well, I suppose, considering the brain size of the stupid beast I have to forgive him. But it's not like you don't have obsessions—mountain climbing, dirt-bike racing, skydiving and kayaking sans kayak. At least, you did have them."

Past tense being the operative phrase. He'd given them all up after Todd's death.

"Yeah, well, at least I don't chase fairies across my backyard. Really, Devon. Fairies? This is never going to work. That book is fable. Fairies are just fantasy, a myth."

His head hit the ground with a thud as Devon pulled her leg away and stood. The book landed spread open beside his ear.

"You've always indulged me, Alex. Come on, just one more time?" She flashed her light across the deep blue-black sky. "The book says that a fairy circle can be found on the seventh night of the seventh moon under a starless sky."

"It does?" Alex rolled to his stomach and pulled the rosebud down the text in the book. Mister Pusster playfully batted at his fingers. "Watch it, cat. Hmm, but it also says that mortals who stumble into the fairy circle are often never again seen. And even if the mortal does possess the magical words that will ensure their return, they don't always work."

The hem of Devon's skirt brushed across Alex's forehead and he restrained himself from dropping his head to the grass and sneaking a peek. Devon never wore underwear; she had confided that juicy little tidbit to him last summer during a playful game of Truth or Dare.

If she only knew how maddening it was for him to play the devoted friend!

"Oh my gosh!"

The flashlight hit the ground near the book with a dull thud. Devon dashed under the willow and sprinted toward the forest surrounding her backyard. Alex looked up just in time to see the tiny wavering light she and Mister Pusster followed.

"Devon! It's just a firefly! Damn, woman." Alex jumped up and his long strides took him around the yew hedges where Devon had disappeared. He came to an abrupt halt. "No way!"

There, at the base of a twisted elm trunk danced a ring of tiny lights no larger than his thumb. Devon stood transfixed, her hands clasped together in glee. Her eyes were wide and bright. Mister Pusster sat at her feet, equally entranced.

"Devon!" His voice did not permeate her astonishment.

Devon lifted her bare foot and placed it inside the circle of light.

"No!"

"Alex!"

A brilliant flash of blue light filled the air, enveloping Alex in a gripping fear. Then all was silent. The circle of light danced on. Devon was gone.

Two

"An angel he wants? Bah! I'll serve his darkness until my very veins are dried to my bones. I'll conjure evil and foul deeds as he commands, but I'll not be privy to the destruction of a sacred creature. It is blasphemy!" Walking through a cobweb that dangled from the rotting beams overhead, he eyed the troll, Gawump. The wretch was supposed to gather the cobwebs and place them along with the other ingredient jars, but the idiot's attention was fixed on the bubbling surface of the cauldron in the center of the tower room.

Venedictos stretched his long, bony fingers above the laboratory table, checking the dust-glazed glass vial that bubbled an oozing, rust-colored concoction. He rubbed a finger beneath his nose, coating the digit with a trail of slime.

He knew he hadn't the power to command an angel to the earth. He hadn't possessed such powers for centuries. Perhaps he had *never* possessed that power. But Venedictos would never reveal his lack of powers to anyone, not even to his assistant.

"But what will you do?" His assistant waddled from the cauldron, his short legs, set beneath a tub of a torso, causing him to wobble to and fro across the rotting rushes. "His Darkness has commanded it. He won't be pleased if you do not produce an angel. And you know what he's like when he is not pleased."

Venedictos shuddered. Images of Predwick his previous assistant, lying screaming upon the ground as the great stone gargoyle stomped on his chest crept across his eyes. "Don't remind me, Gawump." He clenched his fingers into a bony fist near his face. "But I simply refuse to steal from the heavens."

"You can? Steal from the heavens?"

"Of course I can! Am I not the greatest wizard in all the land?"

The troll shrugged. "I've never traveled further than the Forest of Thorns."

"I have and I am! And don't you forget it." He thrust his slime-coated digit into Gawump's face. The troll took a deep breath, inhaling the flavor of the wizard's finger in a most delightful way. "But do you know what would happen if I *did* steal an angel for His Royal Stubbornness? *He* would come down to reclaim it."

They both solemnly averted their eyes toward the tangle of cobwebs that hung from the castle beams like a misplaced funeral shroud. Heaven gave no consideration to this foul castle.

"Oooh. Really?"

"Yes."

"But you said you would get one for his Darkness," the troll persisted. "You said you'd bring an angel for him to seduce. Only then will the curse be broken. What are you going to do, oh Great One?"

"I'll set the spell into motion." Venedictos combed his bony fingers through his long white beard. Behind him tall vials of brown liquid bubbled in a vicious chorus. "He'll have his angel. But it won't be from the heavens. Oh no. We'll find one in the village. Grab the ropes and iron pick. You're going to climb to the rooftop."

"M-me?" Gawump's countenance sluiced from amber to bleached cream. "W-what for?"

"I've business with the gargoyle."

* * * *

Alex stumbled backward and fell into the scratchy yew shrubs. He struggled out and dashed around the corner, plunging to the ground to scan the words in Devon's fairy book.

Once stepped into the fairy circle...never seen again...the magical words...

"Devon, why did you do this! I gotta get you back. How am I gonna do that?"

He glanced over his shoulder. A minute white glow beckoned from around the corner of the shrubs. The circle was still visible. He had no idea for how long. He had to act now.

"I coming for you, Devon. Don't worry." He ripped out the page that listed the magical words, stuffed it in his jean's pocket, and jumped up.

He whizzed around the corner like a junkyard dog chasing a filet mignon on legs, and felt the vicious vibrations as his boot stepped inside the circle of light. "See ya later, Mister Pusster!"

They danced about her head in magical design, tiny creatures with delicate, opalescent wings, fragile and carefree. Two fairies lighted upon her hair, their minuscule toes slipping deep inside the shimmering waves near her ear. They pressed the stem of a crimson ranunculas into her hair, burying it deeply so the crepe-thin petals rested on top.

Their tinkling giggles did not wake Devon from her sleep Or maybe she was unconscious. Or perhaps...it was a bit of fairy glamour.

A jagged silhouette of grayness washed across the perfect blue sky as great stone wings flapped and circled above the meadow. The beast's massive shadow chilled the flowers into submission and sent the fairies fleeing for shelter. A breeze blew across Devon's cheek, lifting the hair about her face in spiraling tendrils. Still dazed, she scarcely noticed.

The shadow drew closer and landed, crushing the emerald grass beneath its stiff stone talons. Great puffs of sulfurous smoke exhaled from its stone nostrils, wilting the delicate petals and suffusing the air with a pungent aroma.

Gawump jumped from the gargoyle's back. Landing in a roll, it took some effort to push himself upright, for his round torso. Leery of the granite beast's sharp teeth, he took a wide circle away from the gargoyle and stepped over to Devon, crushing two fairies beneath the pointed leather toes of his boots.

"A sweet angel," he muttered lecherously as he rubbed his stubby hands together. A thin trail of spittle spiraled over the cracked flesh of his bottom lip and dripped onto Devon's shoulder. "So delicious. A fair maiden in the grass. Dressed in red. Ready for my bed. Perhaps I should have this one for myself and look elsewhere to please His Darkness?"

He reached to touch the rosy pink color of her cheeks, but jumped out of his skin when the warning yowl of the gargoyle stormed through his head. The sound was of nothing mortal or animal; it seemed to birth from the very bowels of hell.

"What?" Devon bolted upright, immediately noticing the vile little man who stood over her. She shuffled backward across the grass. "Who...who are you? Alex?"

"Hurry!" the troll cried. "She'll get away!"

Devon looked to the monstrous beast. Without warning she was captured by its phosphorescent stare. Two great beams of hypnotizing light held her violet gaze. She tried to move, her mind willed her limbs to move, but she could not. Her last waking thought before she passed out was that she was no longer in her backyard. And where was Alex?

Gawump worked quickly to heave the girl's delicate body over the stone mound of the beast's back. He took care not to look into the beast's eyes for he knew the stunning effect would work swiftly on his short, little body. It would only last for an hour on the girl. Enough time.

Securing the faded silk cord Venedictos had given him about the girl's waist, Gawump then slapped the beast's wing. A dull vibration shuddered through his hand as the shock of flesh against hardened stone made his teeth tingle. "Devil's teeth, you are an abominable creature. Flesh of stone and brains to match. We must be going." He bent to retrieve the leather reins he had tied about the beast's neck. "Git!"

The gargoyle lumbered upward, passing over a nearby village. Villagers cried out to see the young maiden's plight, but they were helpless to stop the beast. Nor would they consider rescuing the maiden. For they knew the gargoyle belonged to the devil himself, Damen the Dark.

The sky slit into a narrow gash, then spit out a mess of flailing arms and legs.

"Aagg—" Alex's scream was cut short as he hit the meadow with a dull thud. Soft blades of tender grass and pink flower heads were jammed in his gaping mouth. He spit them out and joggled his head.

From his sprawled position he saw he had landed in the center of a field of tall green grass, dotted generously with tiny pink and crimson flowers. Most definitely not Devon's backyard.

"It really worked!" He jumped to his feet and pumped his fist in elation. "Devon, I'm—"

His elation turned sour as he spun about, only to find that he was alone. "Devon? Where is she?" It had been only a matter of minutes since she had left him. And it had been night, so why was the sky so blue?

"Devon!" he called. "This is not funny, Devon. Come out, come out, wherever you are. Just quit with the jokes, will ya? I believe you. Fairy circles do exist. You can beat on me when we get back home. Devon?"

He spun in a circle, scanning the endless stretch of meadow. Stopping when he saw a swarm of oddly clad people rumbling across the field towards him. His heart sped to a thundering pace. He looked about, wondering what to do. The crowd was almost upon him. They carried long sticks and waved what appeared to be extremely sharp sickles and other weapons. "This is not gonna be good."

Devon wasn't sure what woke her: the pain in her head, like she had been drugged; or the ache in her side, where it felt like she had been clubbed.

Desperately Devon tried to recall how she had come to be here. Then it hit her. "Oh my god. Alex! It really worked! I stepped through the fairy circle." She squeezed her fists in silent elation, but as she looked about, was suddenly taken with a streak of fear. "Where am I? And what...that thing...a...t-troll." She gulped, remembering the leering face of the ugly beast that had stood over her. Suddenly she wasn't sure chasing fairies was such a good idea.

"Alex?" Her whispers echoed softly about her. She had a sinking feeling she should have listened to him for once.

But the book had been right. She stepped through a fairy circle. A real fairy circle! The problem was that she didn't remember the magic words. That created a real problem for getting home.

Devon looked up the ancient stone castle that soared before her. The massive walls stretched all the way to the thick clouds that grayed the sky and shadowed the entire land about her. It looked like something she had seen in the movies. The dwelling of the evil villain—the one who captured the fair maiden...then the hero had to rescue her.

Where is that hero, anyway?

At the very top of the castle sat a gargoyle carved of gray stone. It seemed the size of a racing stallion from Devon's perspective. Its stone wings spanned even farther in length through the chilly air. "A gargoyle."

Devon clutched her knees to her chest as she stared in amazement at the beast. She had only seen gargoyles in books and movies. She was fascinated by them. So grotesque and ugly, yet their purpose was to protect the house or castle from evil spirits. Some were even darn cute, if you didn't mind horns, scales, and long, spiked toenails.

Devon startled. Had the gargoyle moved? Had one of the wings suddenly tucked under?

"No," she whispered ominously. "I've seen too many horror movies. Gargoyles are not real. They're made of stone. Yeah. Right. Next movie night it's going to be a light romantic comedy, Alex, I promise."

Feeling a small breath of courage fill her lungs, Devon stood and steadied herself, wondering where she was. She turned around, her bare feet crunching the scattered stone and debris. Before her and all about the castle circumference, for as far as she could see, was a twisted, dark tangle of wickedly sharp thorns. Big, barbed thorns nearly the size of her fist jutting out of thickly coiled black vines. Coiled about the vines were flowers with sparkling gray petals. Grey was an odd color for a flower. They had a strange luminescence around the edge of their petals, as if they were rimmed with streams of tiny Christmas lights.

Surrounding the castle rose a wall of deadly thorns, twice as high as Devon. The tangled black mass of vines and thorns reminded her of the fairy tale, Sleeping Beauty. The prince had had to battle just such a forest to get to the sleeping princess.

Devon crossed her arms and pensively scanned the castle facade. She tapped the stone finding it good and solid. She nodded as a plan formed in her head. This could be great research for her book. As she really had no place else to go, she decided to go inside.Devon's steps were immediately halted as she spied an iridescent flash out of the corner of her eye. "Oh!"

It fluttered madly before her face. Bigger than a mosquito, yet smaller than a dragonfly. Devon raised her finger and the insect lighted on it. "My gosh, a fairy." Its wings were of shimmery black, while its body was palest white, its tiny limbs void of all color. It didn't look like the fairies she'd seen dancing in the circle. So much...paler. And its tiny face, the dark eyes were drawn back in an elfish slant and the lips were black.

"Ouch!" Devon shook the fairy from her finger. "You nasty little thing. Biting me! Oh, stay away." She shooed the incessant creature from her face, but the fairy tangled into her hair. Devon shook a handful of her burgundy locks and was successful in releasing the awful insect. As she did, she stumbled backward. Her back skidded down the wooden door and she hit the ground with a grunt and a billow of ancient dust.

Behind her, Devon heard the groaning creak as the massive wooden door gave way and opened inside. The fairy buzzed past her face, its wings scratching across Devon's nose as it headed into the darkened caverns of the castle.

Still lying on the ground, Devon peered inside at the two sets of feet that stood not a yard from her face. She craned her neck to the side and looked up into the milky white eyes of a tall man dressed in black wool, then looked four feet below his shoulder into the eyes of a very familiar troll.

"This is the closest thing you could find to an angel?" the tall one muttered as he twisted his tangled beard about his bony fingers.

The troll shrugged and looked over Devon. "I'll keep her if she does not please the master."

Devon whispered to herself. "Now would be a good time for the hero to show up."

Three

Alex was doubly shocked when the entire band of dirty-faced villagers fell to their knees in the meadow before him. The men removed their soft cloth hats, and the women pulled their poorly dressed children down with them. He had expected an attack. But this...it was as if they were worshipping him.

Their clothing resembled something out of the medieval times. Poor medieval times. Ragged wool and cotton covered their haggard frames with patches holding the fabric together in places. Most carried wooden staffs and field tools. The children were barefoot, and obviously baths had yet to make a fashion statement by the crust that blackened their bodies.

"Sent by the gods," he heard a whisper rise amidst the bowed heads.

"Yes." A burly, thick-bearded man stepped forward. He was barefoot, and his thick black hair was tangled about his head and chin with burrs and straw. His cheeks were sunken, but his light-colored eyes glimmered with curious adoration as he looked over Alex. "A warrior sent by the gods to rescue the fair maiden who was pilfered from this very meadow." The man fell to his knees and twisted his soiled cap between his fingers. "We are humbled before you, my lord."

"Warrior?" *Sent by the gods?* These people thought he was sent by the gods?

Well, he did fall out of the sky. He supposed it might look a little suspicious. And if he was in medieval times it was very likely they could think such a thing. *To rescue the fair maiden.*

"The maiden," Alex muttered absently as he pictured Devon's crooked smile.

"Milord?"

"The maiden... Yes! I've...come to rescue the maiden. That's it! Er, did you get a good look at her?" He wanted to make sure they were both talking about the same girl. It wouldn't do to go chasing after the wrong maiden. "Was she wearing a red dress cut down to there? Did she have this long dark hair that falls to her waist?And a little mole." *A very sexy little mole.*

"Aye, red," the villager agreed enthusiastically. "Shamefully bright color for a maiden. Perhaps she was royalty?"

"Royalty?" Alex hitched his thumbs in his belt loops and let loose a hearty chuckle. "Devon?"

"Look!" A woman holding a swaddled baby stood and pointed at Alex's chest. "The sacred sign of the Gods. He is truly a warrior."

Alex followed the woman's gaze down to his t-shirt. He traced his finger over the screen-printed Nike swash. It was the only thing he could find beneath his bed this morning that had smelled reasonably clean. The sacred sign?

"Yeah, right. It's the ah... It means, hmm...just do it! Yeah, just do it. As in, you know, just rescue the maiden." He figured it best to humor these people until he got a better handle on things. If they thought he came from the gods, then so be it.

"And your name, milord?"

"My name, um..." Alex stepped back and looked over the crowd of eager villagers. A small child twirled a twist of blonde hair about her finger, while her mother kept slapping her fingers away. He was a god in their eyes, the mighty warrior Alex sent to rescue the damsel in distress. The mighty warrior Alex? Nope. *Alex* didn't cut it. He needed a warrior's name. Something cool.

"Ah...let's see...it's um..." Alex? No. Alexander? Too prissy. Lex...Lexon...Lexor. "Lexor!" he burst out in his deepest most heroic voice. "I am the mighty Lexor!"

The villagers whispered his name in a stream of random voices, punctuated with awestruck whispers of 'just do it'. Alex felt a surge of mightiness run through his veins as he looked over the humbled people bowing in adoration.

Chill, his conscience whispered. *What are you doing? You're not a warrior! Remember your brother? Only bad things happen to the brave. And where the hell are you anyway? What year is it?*

"Er...um..."

"Milord?" the barefoot man offered.

"I was just wondering...mmm....well, since I'm not from around here..." Alex glanced upward and the villagers did also. There was no sign that the sky had parted to deposit him into this mysterious place and time. "Could someone maybe tell me what year it is?"

The barefoot man stood and proudly replied. "It is the year of our lord, thirteen hundred fifty-six, mighty Lexor."

"1356?" Alex's vision began to spin. The faces before him blurred into a scatter of muted colors and his legs gave out without so much as a warning.

"Oh dear!" cried a village woman.

The man who had spoken bent over Alex's inert figure. "Hmm, the big ones do fall hard. Come! Help me hoist him up. We'll bring him to the village."

* * * *

"She has arrived, Your Darkness. The angel," Venedictos whispered. "She fell to the earth and landed in front of the castle."

Damen sat in front of a silvered looking glass examining his dull reflection. "Yes, I know." He waved the wizard away, the tips of his newly manicured nails glinting beneath the rush light. "See to it she is brought to me immediately. Wait!"

He pursed his lips and narrowed his gaze on his reflection. His hair, black as a bat's wing, was tangled about his head, badly in need of smoothing. Gawump had left to fetch a comb. If such a thing even existed in the castle. Though he was quite pleased with the pale smoothness of his flesh. So different was the texture, almost...nice. And his eyes, though still retaining a wisp of darkness, they could easily play from humble to genuinely concerned. "What is your opinion of this disguise, Venedictos?"

The wizard examined his master from head to toe. "It is quite good, Your Darkness. The gir—er, ah, *angel* will be pleased."

Damen pressed his hands to his chest and looked over his attire. Venedictos had had to make him new clothes to fit this new, slighter frame. Hose and doublet of blackest damask, and suede thigh boots from a freshly butchered calf. "You really think so?"

Venedictos quieted his beating heart with splayed fingers to his chest. "I nearly find myself in a swoon, Your Darkness."

Damen quirked a dark brow. "Not an amusing thought, Venedictos."

"Of course. I only mean that you will be most pleasing to the female eye." Venedictos bowed and backed quickly out of the room.

Damen's reflection smirked back at him. Quite a face. The lips were thin and palest pink, his dark brows jutting down toward a rather strong nose, and a long tangle of dark hair flowing like a river over his shoulders and to his elbows. Not exactly *his* idea of beauty, but a relatively pleasing mortal if ever there was one. Now there could be no chance of his offending this lovely angel who had fallen to the earth.

But he was thankful this mortal form he assumed was only temporary. Besides the hair being a trial to care for, the lack of physical strength caused him no great worry. And his senses had been dulled tremendously. No longer was he able to hear the patter of a mouse in the dungeon four stories below, or sense the inhaled breath of a raven flying overhead in search of prey.

But Damen was satisfied in knowing he shouldn't need to use physical force against an angel.

With a final preening sneer he folded the silvered glass down. Damen paced to the window and looked out at the serrated blackness created by the Forest of Thorns. But he saw none of it. His mind was on the task at hand.

Finally she had come to him! His angel was here. A genuine angel, fallen from the heavens. Innocent and pure and completely untouched by mortal man. A challenge if ever there was one.

"To seduce an angel," he whispered in his sepulchral tone. A delightful shiver overtook his mortal form and Damen released the tremor in a deep, satisfied sigh. "And then the darkness shall reign supreme."

They led the newly named Lexor to a nearby village, explaining there were things to do before he set out to rescue the maiden. The gods did not think to send him in armor or with fighting weapons. Nor had they dressed him properly.

"They were in a hurry," the mighty Lexor explained.

As he was led into a tiny shack made of straw and mud, Alex could not stop thinking, he wished he had paid more attention in history class. He was never the history buff. Though he couldn't be sure he was in an actual historical world. He had traveled through a fairy circle. Didn't fairies live in Middle Earth or something crazy like that?

Poor Devon. She's got to be going mad by now.

On the other hand, she might be having the time of her life. It would be just like Devon to get a kick out of this little adventure. "She's probably taking notes for her novel."

The villagers had said the maiden had been abducted and taken to a castle. Abducted by who? Or what? And what castle? Weren't castles peopled with knights and weapons and...*gulp*...villains?

"I'm in over my head," Alex muttered, leaning against the frame of the door.

"Milord? Is there a problem?"

"Oh nothing." Alex ducked to avoid the low door frame and stepped inside. "Just um...planning. You know, how to rescue the maiden."

In the golden glow of a hearty hearth fire, two young girls hustled to lay out a trestle table, drawing a stained white linen over it. One explained that food would soon be ready for the mighty warrior.

Alex's stomach growled. Food. *Good, I'm starving.* Though he had the feeling the villagers had never heard of Canadian bacon and green olive pizza.

The man who had spoken to him in the field, and who had led him into this little hut, gestured that he sit next to him on a gnarled wooden bench.

"Kind sir, I am Gwilym of Goodwick. Friend to any and all."

"Good to meet you, Gwilym. Did anyone see what happened?" Alex asked, swinging his leg over the bench. "I mean...just how, exactly, was the maiden taken? Was she...harmed?" A sour twinge rippled through Alex's chest. He hated to even think of Devon being hurt. *Please let her be safe.*

A young girl wearing a faded blue chemise and brown leather lace-up bodice laid a trencher of what appeared to be roasted meat before Alex and his table partner. Gwilym immediately dug in, ripping meat from the bone.

"It was the gargoyle," the girl whispered as she filled Alex's pewter tankard with a dark liquid. Her brown eyes were wide with a strange fear and her fingers gripped tight about the beer jug.

"Gargoyles are made of stone, honey. Try again."

"Truly, my lord, it was the gargoyle."

Alex laid a hand across the girl's forehead and pushed gently. "I say yay! You have been healed!"

She cast him a fearful look then scuffled off, holding her fingers to her forehead.

"Now," Alex turned back to Gwilym. "Who else wants to try?"

"My lord," Gwilym said through a mouthful of stringy meat. "It is true what the wench says. 'Twas the gargoyle."

Alex picked at his plate. Well, it wasn't actually a plate. On further examination he found the meat had been laid on top a thick crust of stale bread. Guess the mighty Lexor wasn't good enough for the fancy china. He tried a bite of meat, discovering it was deer.

"A real live gargoyle, huh?"

Gwilym nodded, his mouth bursting with greasy meat.

It could be a possibility. He had after all traveled here via a fairy circle. Stranger things had happened.

Alex pushed the trencher away, finding his appetite scarce. He had more important things to worry about than eating. "Then I'd better get going. Point me in the right direction."

Gwilym sloshed his food down with a hearty gulp of ale. "It is through the Forest of Thorns," Gwilym replied, with a swipe of his dirty sleeve across his mouth. "More!" he called to the servant girl.

"The Forest of Thorns?"

"Aye, my lord. Your armor is being prepared right now."

"Armor? What do I need armor for?"

"The forest," Gwilym said, bits of crusty bread trickling over his lips.

"Armor. All right. Sure." *Play it safe*, his conscience whispered. "Once I get through this forest, what lies ahead?"

"The gargoyle," Gwilym muttered through chomping bites. "Which will not be difficult for a great warrior."

"Sure. Right. A great warrior." Alex felt his toes curl inside his boots.

"And then there is the wizard. Who is not a problem either."

"Wizards and gargoyles." Sounded more like a game of Dungeons and Dragons than real life. But then fairy circles weren't real life either. "No problem, eh?" Alex couldn't control the shake in his voice. "Well then what exactly *is* the problem?"

Gwilym suddenly paused mid-chew. He swallowed with an awkward gulp and met Alex's curious stare with his own color-washed eyes. "The problem, my lord, is Damen the Dark. He's the devil's right hand, he is."

"Oh yeah? Does this dark dude do this often? I mean, steal away young women just for the heck of it?"

"Aye, my lord. At least once a moon we lose another maiden to the hands of the dark lord. He's a great penchant for fairies, too, I'm told."

"And what do these maidens say when they come back?"

Gwilym lowered his head. "They never come back, my lord."

Never come back?

A heavy emptiness lodged in Alex's throat. He couldn't release a single word. And behind the trapped words grew a raging scream.

Four

"His Darkness awaits you."

Devon looked over her two hosts. The one who had spoken was her height. His hair and beard were long and gray. Bony fingers fiddled about the tips of his beard. He wore a long brown woolen robe with bell-sleeves and a shiny gold ball pierced through his upper lip.

Stepping back to the cold wall, Devon averted her gaze to the shorter man. Her second meeting with the little troglodyte, if she remembered correctly. He appeared almost a troll with his warted nose and stubby fingers, and had brilliant red hair that sprouted from every orifice on his face. He couldn't quite be a dwarf for his arms were exceedingly long, so that his knuckles rested on the castle floor. His gaze was lecherous as he observed her fright.

"His...his Darkness?" she managed.

"Yes. Our master."

"M-master?" What sort of sick B-movie had she fallen into? Where's the remote control? She did not like this channel one bit. "Look mister—"

"Venedictos."

"Huh?"

"My name, fair lady, is Venedictos."

"Greatest wizard in all the land," the abhorrent troll chimed in a high, nasal pitch.

"This is Gawump," Venedictos added as an afterthought.

"Gawump?" Devon scanned the troll again, finding the name fit him well. Goosebumps popped across the surface of her flesh. "Hmm, he most certainly is."

"And now, if you'll follow." Venedictos turned and started down the dark passageway.

"Follow?" Devon propped defiant hands on her hips. She'd read enough fantasy novels and seen more than her share of horror movies to know better than to follow the wizard down the dark passageway. Oh no. Never leave crime sight one to go to crime site two. You're just asking for trouble. At least, that's what Oprah always says.

She felt a slippery nudge against her leg. Devon looked down into the crumpled brown eyes of the troll. A stream of clear mucus ran from his nose to the chest of his shirt.

"Maybe I will follow." She skirted the vulgar little man.

"Come." Venedictos reached back and his cold fingers wrapped about hers. "The angel has arrived."

* * * *

"I've volunteered to join you on your mission," Gwilym said. "You'll need someone who knows the land."

"Cool, like a sidekick."

"Sidekick?" Gwilym wondered.

"Yeah, you know, like Laurel and Hardy, Mulder and Scully, Ren and Stimpy, Sonny and Cher—Er, well, nix that last one. You'll be my partner is what I'm saying."

"Most certainly." The servant girl placed another trencher before Gwilym and he wasted no time in digging in.

Alex nudged a thick lump of something that was covered with a dark brown sauce. It didn't look like meat, or a vegetable, for that matter. "What is this?"

"We've been blessed to receive a hearty batch of eels from the village of Fishguard down the way." Gwilym reached for a piece and tore off a hearty strip with his teeth.

"Really?" A repulsive shiver spread across Alex's shoulders. "Um, check please?"

Alex pushed back on the wooden bench, pressed his back to the mud and wattle wall, and crossed his arms over his chest. He observed with a queasy stomach as Gwilym inhaled the food before him. Wouldn't a hamburger with cheese and extra onions be tasty about now? He scratched his fingernail along the edge of the stale chunk of bread his food had been served on, gratefully thankful that McEels had not caught on in the States. "So, when do we leave?"

"In the morn. 'Tis not wise to traipse through the Forest of Thorns come nightfall. Of course, it will take two days to journey through it."

"The Forest of Thorns?"

Gwilym nodded. "Then you've but a day to rescue the maiden and make way back through the forest before the severed thorns start to grow back. A nasty breed they are."

"Doesn't sound like a party to me." Alex rose and stood before the warmth of the hearth fire over which the women had prepared supper. It reminded him of scout camp. His cheeks were toasty, his toes burning hot. But the Boy Scouts had never prepared him for this little excursion.

"Nay, a party it will not be." Gwilym joined Alex at his side, his jaw still working on something. His interest turned to Alex's attire. "You've some fine boots, Mighty Lexor. The gods provide them for you?"

"The gods?" Alex glanced down at his Nike tennis shoes. "Sure."

Gwilym reached over and twisted a slip of Alex's torn t-shirt between his fingers. "Very impressive the way they've painted your heraldry right on your tunic. Fine craftsmanship. Just do it, eh?"

"Yeah, er, you mentioned earlier that someone was preparing armor for me? You think I'll really need it?"

"If you're to journey through the Forest of Thorns, you will. Ah! And here it is now. Lexor, this is Emyr, the village armorer. His work is highly sought after. Emyr, good man, did you find a suit that will fit our mighty warrior?"

The armorer proudly displayed his find. The fire glinted off the shimmering silver disklets riveted to the leather tunic. "Twas my great granda's. He fought the battle of '76."

Alex touched the cold steel. His entire body grew equally as frigid. This was not good. Armor protected from danger. And danger was not foremost on his list. "You're kidding me."

Emyr went about placing the tunic over Alex's arms and fastening up the sides. There was nothing Alex could do but stand with arms in the air.

"Kidding? What is this kidding?" Gwilym asked in all seriousness as he watched Emyr lace Alex up.

"Huh? Oh, kidding, ah...warrior lingo. Don't worry about it." Alex's shoulders slumped under the weight of the armor. Emyr now placed a leather belt about his hips which took some of the weight from his shoulders. A relief, considering the thing had to weigh a good thirty or forty pounds. He looked down over his shiny new ensemble. Movement was not hampered thanks to the scaled style of the metal plates. On the other hand, he looked ridiculous. "No way, man."

"Which way is that?"

"I look like a disco ball!" Alex spun before the two men.

"Dis go?" the armorer wondered.

Alex stopped spinning. "Yeah, you know." He snapped his fingers, assuming the classic John Travolta disco pose, arm pointed in the air. "Ah, ah, ah, ah, stayin' alive, stayin' alive."

"Staying alive." Gwilym nodded agreement. "Aye, mighty Lexor, this will help you to stay alive."

Alex let his arm fall and stood like a mannequin as Emyr measured his arms and legs with a length of scruffy twine. These guys were really serious. He wished he could be as serious about everything. He was still trying to figure out how stepping into a circle of fairies had landed him in this situation in the first place.

Gwilym placed a sword in his left hand.

"A sword?" Alex held it out before him. It was heavy enough that he had to use both hands. A broad sword if he wasn't mistaken. *You were going to play it safe with your life, remember Alex?* Yeah, safe. Like no combat, no secret missions, nothing that requires violence. Especially no swords.

"I don't know about this, man. Maybe I... No. I can't do this." Alex gingerly handed the sword back to Gwilym.

Gwilym's jaw dropped. A chunk of what he'd last been chewing toppled from his tongue.

Alex undid the brass-studded leather belt and lace ties at his sides and pulled the armor from his shoulders. He handed the flashing steel tunic to the armorer. "Sorry, guys. I'm just not the violent type."

"But...but..." Gwilym gulped down his food. "You are a warrior?" The sword caught a blazing flash of firelight as Gwilym moved it. "The gods sent you, did they not?"

Not. He'd come from the twenty-first century. He'd followed his wacky girlfriend into a fairy circle, and now everyone thought he was a great warrior.

With a resolute sigh, Alex nodded. "Sure. But you don't understand."

Gwilym and the armorer both returned questioning stares.

You don't understand. My brother is dead because he was sent to fight for freedom. He had weapons and was on a rescue mission when he was shot down. He died a hero. I don't want to end up like my brother. It was wrong. He should still be alive. I never had a chance to spend time with him. He was always away at military school.

And what of Devon? She needs you.

Yes, Devon. Guilt squeezed the fragile muscles surrounding Alex's heart. She needed him. He would—no, must!—do anything to see her again.

But fight with a sword and head a rescue mission? Only heroes did that kind of stuff.

Devon's sweet voice echoed inside his head. *I need a hero.*

The woman he loved had been taken to a castle. *By a gargoyle.* God only knew what plans this dark dude had for her. Devon needed a hero. Now!

A surge of adrenaline rushed through Alex's system. If Devon needed a hero, well...he'd give it a go.

"Sorry guys, must be a little jet lag. You know, my fall from the sky. The god's have got to find a different method of transportation. Anyway, I don't know what I was talking about." With a renewed sense of purpose, Alex grabbed the sword from Gwilym. He was going to rescue the damsel in distress. "Of course, I can do this. There's a beautiful woman who depends on me and I'm not about to let her down."

Gwilym slapped Alex across the back. "You had me worried for a second there, Lexor."

"He'll need an undercoat," the armorer started, his relief also apparent. "If you'll give me your tunic for size, I'll have it in the morn."

Alex fingered his torn t-shirt. He could use some new threads. He peeled it over his head and handed it to the armorer. But he'd keep his jeans. At least until the women left.

"What is this?" Emyr examined the tag inside the neck of Alex's t-shirt.

"Uh..." Opps, gotta be more careful. "That's the uh..."

"Looks like a sort of ancient writing," Gwilym observed.

"Yes." Alex was relieved. "That's the er, sacred writing. Yeah. The gods sewed it into my clothes so I may never forget it. It's the, er, code of the warriors. Hero kinda stuff."

The armorer seemed impressed.

Alex glanced to Gwilym "Are you buying this stuff?"

Gwilym shrugged and examined the tag over the armorer's shoulder. "I've no need to purchase another tunic. Mine serves me well."

* * *

"My master eagerly awaits your presence," Venedictos said. "You will do your best to see he is pleased."

Devon froze at the bottom of a spiral stairway. Chilling darkness kissed her shoulder where the red rayon had torn. Venedictos walked on. *Please him?* Had she missed something? "Wait a minute. Mister Wizard! What do you mean by pleased?"

Venedictos' sigh echoed inside the icy castle walls. "My child, you will understand when you have met him. Now come, he waits."

Knowing it would have been wiser to turn tail and run straight for the castle doors, Devon faltered on the final step and followed the man.

You're too curious. This is the ultimate in research for your story. What more could you ask for?

Escape!

Yeah, right. Not with the massive tangle of thorns and vines twisting about the castle circumference. She was a literal prisoner in this castle of doom and gloom. But at least she wasn't shackled or chained. That gave her a little hope.

"Your Darkness, she has arrived."

Venedictos stepped aside to allow Devon to walk into the great hall. The room was massive in size. A glassless window set into the far wall cast a hazy patchwork of light across the rotting rushes. There were no furnishings other than one chair, that appeared more a throne for its size and elaborate carvings, and a few candleabras. It was dark and cold and smelled of musty wetness and stale smoke.

The man who had been waiting for her stepped out of the shadows. Devon gasped. *Your Darkness.*

He most certainly was.

Black adorned his lithe figure from head to toe. His pants were of silver studded black leather, his doublet a matching studded leather. His figure was very thin and a bit taller than she. Streams of long black hair flowed over his shoulders and down past his elbows.

Damen the Dark? *Just let him try something. I know karate.* She had taken lessons. Well...two. Enough to know she should kick hard and aim for the family jewels.

"My lady," Venedictos offered. "This is lord Damen."

"Er, um, hi?" she offered shakily.

He stepped up to her with a graceful stride that belied his evil attire. His eyes, of darkest midnight, were set above thin lips that arced into a smug grin. "You have finally arrived."

Whoa. Talk about the voice of the dead. He was a baritone run over the coals and coated with thick, syrupy tar.

"My lovely angel. An ethereal being fallen to the earth."

"Angel? I-I don't understand. Do you think I'm—"

"You are an angel, are you not?"

"An angel? A real, fallen-from-the-heavens angel? Why no. I'm just Dev—"

"My lord!" Venedictos suddenly appeared by the dark lord's side and pulled him to the wall where he whispered so Devon could not hear.

"What is the meaning of this?" Damen hissed. "I demanded an angel. I *need* an angel from the heavens. She says she is not. Where are her wings? She looks to be common village rabble in that awful gown."

"Your Darkness, really." Venedictos patted him on the arm, taking care not to muss his new hair. Combed, even. "I must explain. She *is* an angel. Truly she is. I called her down from the heavens myself. It's just that..." He checked to see that Devon was not listening. "She has no memory of her angelic life," he whispered conspiratorially. "You see, when an angel falls to the earth she must lose memory of her former life. Imagine how you would feel to know you had lived in the heavens and then had no way of returning. It is for her own good, for her very mental stability."

"Mmm..." Damen rubbed the smooth flesh on his chin. "Perhaps you are right. She does bare an exquisite resemblance to a holy creature. Her skin is so lovely and white, and her eyes sparkle with pure innocence."

"As for wings, she has no need for them on earth. It would be rather awkward for her to get about, don't you think?"

Venedictos breathed a sigh of relief as Damen went back to the girl.

"And what name do you answer to, lovely ang—er, my lady?"

"Devon."

"Devon? Odd." His eyes danced down her body. "Is that Nordic? Gaelic?"

"Actually it's—" Devon had no idea what to say. What did it matter the origin of her name? She didn't hear him offering of the origins of 'the Dark'. Though she felt a chill shudder through her body just thinking the name.

When she did not answer, Damen looked back over his shoulder.

Venedictos nodded placatingly. "Memory loss," he mouthed.

Damen nodded and turned back to Devon. "It is no worry, my lady. Devon is a beautiful name for a woman so lovely as you. I trust you've been quite pleased with the accommodations?"

"Accommodations? Oh sure." Devon scanned the walls of the castle. Cold stone and troglodyte trolls. Lovely accommodations. Four stars, most definitely. Now before her stood the king of darkness himself, Damen the Dark. She truly hoped his title wasn't for real.

Yikes, she had no desire to stick around to see what he had in store for her. Research was research, but this was ridiculous. "I really should be going, I—"

Damen's laugh rocketed icy chills down her neck. "Oh, my lady. You've quite the humor. You are my guest! You cannot leave."

"But if I'm your—" Devon stopped suddenly. Damen had wandered over to the window. One of the nasty black fairies had flown in and now the dark lord held it by the wings as it buzzed madly before his eyes. Quick as a panther pouncing its prey, he bit into the tiny creature, then tossed the wings out the window.

"I love the sound of their crunching bones," he added with a sparkle to his dark eyes.

Devon's stomach did a flip-flop. "I think I need an Alka-seltzer."

Damen looked to the wizard.

"Umm, ethereal words, Your Darkness."

"Yes, of course," Damen muttered in his deep, graveside tone. "You've prepared the tower room for our lovely guest?"

The tower room? Devon felt those persistent chills rake up her spine. The tower room is where the damsel in distress was always sealed away by the villain in all the stories, including hers.

Where was that hero anyway?

"Look, mister," Devon pulled her shoulders straight and assumed what she hoped was an I-mean-business stance. Though, at the moment her insides were mushy as a stale banana. "Your castle is really cool and all—I mean the gargoyle was truly incredible—but I'm not staying. I don't know who you are, or who you think I am, but I'm not sticking around for the fireworks. Really. I'm needed somewhere else. So I'll just be leaving—"

An icy hand grasped her by the neck. Devon felt the sweep of Damen's hair as it whisped across her cheek. She closed her eyes tight. *This is just a nightmare. I'm going to wake up at home in my own bed.*

"You're quite the outspoken one, aren't you?" He moved around in front of her, his manner calm, yet dead serious. "You see, my lady. *You* are the fireworks, as you put it. You are here for a specific reason. A reason that I am not at liberty to disclose to you." His lips brushed across her cheek and touched her ear. Devon cringed. "Now," he continued. "I believe *I* shall show you to your room. Just to be sure everything is to your liking."

Devon forgot her host's eerie presence as she stepped inside the tower bedroom. It wasn't what she expected at all, not a dismal, grey room high in a cold tower. Everything was incredibly beautiful and elegant. A four-poster bed of mahogany mastered the room. It was draped with flowing yardage of deep crimson velvet and silver embroidery. On the walls hung tapestries depicting scenes of gardens and unicorns, and all about were glittering gold candelabra with candles lit in sparkling glory.

The looking glass that sat across the room was as tall as she and the edges were bordered with ornate silver and gold spun into cherubs and flowers. She touched the cool metal, then frowned at her reflection. She looked a horrendous mess! Her hair was tangled about her head and her face was smudged with dirt. The skirt of her dress was frayed up to her knees and her left shoulders popped out of the torn material.

"Are you pleased?"

"Hmm?" Devon felt a cold touch on her shoulder and spun around to find Damen right next to her. She hadn't noticed his approach in the mirror.

"The room."

"The room? It's b-beautiful." She backed away from her host's touch, but was stopped by the mirror. *Why hadn't she seen his reflection?*

"As are you, my lady." Damen reached out and pulled a thick clump of Devon's hair from behind her shoulder.

"So!" She slipped away from Damen's attentions and scrambled over to the bed. "Now that I'm here, what are we going to do?"

"That," he slipped his hands behind his back and paced over to her. "Is entirely up to you, my lady. I've some lovely surprises for you later. But first," he gestured to the gown that shrouded an iron dummy opposite the bed. Devon hadn't even noticed it. "You will change and freshen up. Gawump will bring water and some linens. We shall discuss my plans for you later, over food and drink."

"My lady." Damen bowed and left her to examine the gown.

We shall discuss my plans for you. His plans? Like she was an object or piece of furniture that could be pushed about wherever he chose.

Devon went to the dress and ran her hand over the cold iron neck of the dummy. She twisted the black velvet between her fingers playing back and forth over the thick nap. "I don't think so, Mr. Darkness. Don't think for one minute I'm going to let my guard down. The villain is always appealing at the beginning of the story, but I know how it ends."

Devon walked across the room and looked down from her window. The air held a frosty flavor, like frozen dew, yet a dull rot lingered just beyond the fresh scent. Looking down, she ran her gaze across the treacherous cliff of thorns and jutting rocks. It seemed an endless drop, with nothing but solid rock and thorns for a landing. No chance of escape that way.

With a helpless sigh, Devon turned her back to the gloomy scenery.

She couldn't believe the mess she had literally fallen into. Fairies and gargoyles and wizards and trolls. And Damen the Dark. Who the heck was this guy anyway? And why did it seem he had been *waiting* for her? Devon glanced about the room, neatly arranged, obviously waiting a visitor. Like he'd been planning her arrival for some time.

"Don't bother sending the welcome basket," she said. "I'm canceling this reservation."

Five

Alex adjusted his position on the white stallion the villagers had provided. The last time he'd been on a horse was about two year ago. It had been Devon's idea, of course, to go horseback riding. Needless to say, he'd hobbled around for two days after that little adventure. It was no great thrill to be back on the saddle. The family jewels were already threatening mutiny. Gwilym said he would not have need of the horse once they gained the forest. That was a relief.

Alex smiled to recall Emyr's twinkling glee as he displayed the washing label from his t-shirt carefully sown onto the sleeve of his tunic so the sacred words would always be close at hand. He examined the white tag on his wrist. *Wash cold. Rinse well. Tumble dry.* Sacred words if ever there were any.

And there was the heraldry of the gods that had been sown onto his upper sleeves and painted onto his shield. The Nike swash. "Hah!" Alex laughed. "If they only knew."

"My lord, the forest is soon ahead."

Alex looked down over his sidekick, still amazed at two things. The lack of dress he wore being the first. The villagers had virtually ignored Gwilym, save for wishing him well as he left. Gwilym wore his same holey tights and dirty black wool tunic, and was still barefoot. Barefoot? To trek through this damn forest of thorns? Of which, Gwilym had explained, the thorns were razor sharp and deadly. Was the man nuts? Where were his armor and weapons to battle this dark dude?

And if Alex overlooked everything else there was still Gwilym's lack of horse. The man was *walking* beside him!

"I'm sitting here thinking you don't look too prepared for battle. Where's your shoes? And why don't you have a horse?"

Gwilym shrugged. "I cannot wear shoes, my lord. It is forbidden."

"Forbidden?" Alex reined his stead to a slow pace besides Gwilym. His scaled armor chinked in a soft rhythm with each step of the horse.

"Aye, my lord. You see, I've received extreme unction, and the lord sayeth those who survive are to honor and serve his wishes."

"Extreme unction?" Alex flicked a nuisance bug away from his nose. "Isn't that when the priest anoints a dying man?"

A very much alive Gwilym nodded. "Aye, my lord. I'd returned from battle, you see. We took the Carmarthen fortress and brought their army down. But I was carried back on a stretcher for the gaping wound in my side. Damn pike. I lay in bed for two days, sweating and dizzy, seeing all sorts of strange and wicked creatures at my side. I was most certainly a dead man. The priest anointed me and said a prayer. Two days later, I was up and about as if nothing happened. It was very odd. Though I'm thankful to the lord that He spared me."

"So because you lived you're being punished? No shoes?"

"That is correct. It is written...a man who survives after receiving extreme unction must give up life's pleasures. He can wear no shoes, he must fast perpetually—"

"Wait a minute." Alex reined the horse to a halt and looked over his snickering companion. "Fast? You? After the way you stuffed your face last night?"

Gwilym chuckled and spread a dirty hand across his sunken belly. "I was allowed a meal before going off into battle. That is one of the reasons I volunteered to accompany you. I have been starving something fierce. Makes me wish I had died sometimes to watch the wife eat a hearty meal while I have but a stale trencher and water."

Alex couldn't imagine eating bread and water while watching another person stuff themselves.

"I was forced to sell my horse for I had no need of it. That is why I'm walking. And then there is the other thing." Gwilym reflected for a pensive moment. "I can no longer bed my wife.

"Really?" Judging from his cohort's general appearance—looking past the bearded, dirty face—Alex thought Gwilym's wife might be a real good looker.

"Actually..." Gwilym spoke conspiratorially. "That was the one thing I have not so much minded. You see...Helgeth—my wife—she's...er..." His shoulders fell and he seemed to be searching for the perfect words. "Well, my lord, she could stand down a brawny warrior and make him wish for the tonsure. She's a master of the evil eye, she is!"

The two men erupted in a barrage of hearty laughter as their path drew them closer to the Forest of Thorns.

* * * *

Thinking this would be her only chance at some food for the whole day, Devon resolved to follow the spindly wizard to the great hall. Out of curiosity, she had changed into the dress. It was as if it had been made specifically for her; it fit perfectly. There was a silver filigree belt to wear about her hips, and soft-soled, black velvet shoes.

Venedictos led her into the great hall where Damen sat like a king on his throne behind a vast table laden with sparkling ware.

"Oh, how lovely." Devon left the wizard by the doorway. The table was covered with white cloth, and not a spot was empty. Massive silver candlesticks, bowls, plates, and tureens of shimmering liquid were placed everywhere. The silver sparkled like water-sprinkled diamonds. And the food, Devon observed, was all white!

Martha Stewart would be envious.

"My lady."

Devon spun around to find Damen waiting by her chair. He wore the usual villainous black, though a fragile flower had been pinned to his ruffled shirt. One of the gray-petaled flowers she had seen growing about the thorns. He seemed quite casually dressed, no doublet or sword. Just a billowing shirt and hose and knee-length black riding boots. He cut a very dashing figure actually.

Halt! *What are you thinking?* Devon's spine stiffened at the presence of her inner voice. *Did you just think him dashing? Open your eyes, girl. He's the villain, remember?*

"So where's the hero?" she muttered.

"My lady?"

"Thank you." She sat in the high-backed chair that sparkled of inlaid silver. *There is no hero. It's all up to you. You're all alone and no one is going to help you, so keep on your toes.*

Turning her lips into a feeble smile, Devon scanned the table again as Damen took his place across from her. Yes, by all means, play along with his game.

"The wine is an exquisite Bordeaux," he offered.

Devon looked over the silver dishes and spied the wine goblet sparkling seductively before her. She lifted the huge, shimmering goblet with both hands, but paused when the cold silver touched her lips. Damen's dark gaze fixed to hers as she contemplated drinking. *What's he waiting for?* She sniffed. Pungent grapes, slightly vinegary, a hint of, hmm...earth? Smelled like wine to her. Not that she knew what poison smelled like. But things weren't always as they seemed. Especially in the fairy tales.

"If I were to poison the wine," Damen offered. "Would that not spoil my merriment?"

"All the same..." Devon set the chalice down with a splash. "I think I'll pass." Her host did the same. "And what *merriment* is it you plan to have?"

Damen shrugged. "You shall see, my lady. You shall see."

Oh yeah? Devon crossed her arms and assumed a pout. She had played this game with her parents when she was a child. She was a master at holding out until she got what she wanted. And she wasn't about to let 'his darkness' intimidate her. She held strong under Damen's observant gaze. So preying, so sly.

She raised her chin and Damen conceded.

"Forgive my manners, my lady. It seems my admiration of your beauty causes you more than a small amount of disquiet. But you must appease me, it is only because I have never lain eyes on one so lovely. You are like a fine jewel. An exquisite piece that should be well guarded."

A fine jewel? Devon raised a finely tweezed brow. The pout slipped from her lips. He did have a way with words.

Since when has flattery ever won you over?

Summoning up her pride, Devon spread her hands across the white damask table cloth. "Yes, but it is the valuable jewels that are the most troublesome, my lord. They can never truly be possessed, for they belong to all. And if hidden away, all will try to claim rights to the jewel."

"Ah, but once placed in a marvelous setting the jewel is often content to shine and be possessed," Damen growled sweetly.

This is getting really thick.

"Are you not hungry, my lady?"

His eyes so quickly changed from defeat to genuine concern. There hung a certain sadness about him. Devon had always been the one to fall for the villains in the movies and stories. Were they not just misunderstood little boys that sought love and companionship like all the rest?

Oh, and I suppose Hannibal Lector was misunderstood too?

Devon shook away her thoughts. "Hmm? Hungry? Oh..." She sighed. All right, she was really hungry. A full stomach would help her to think better. Stay on her toes. Plan her escape. "Very well."

She scanned the dishes before her. Nothing looked familiar. The contents of a heavily embellished silver tureen appeared almost of liquid platinum. Couldn't be very good for the digestive system. Wrinkling her nose, Devon checked to her right. A plate of round cakes glistened with sparkling dust. There were white rolls and an oblong bowl of white creamy stuff, silver coated fish with red jewel eyes and—

"Oh!"Devon jumped up, her chair scraping across the stone floor. "What is that? It-it moved!"

Damen leaned over the table, a great wavy-bladed kris dagger glinting maliciously in his hand. One quick stab and the pulsating white thing ceased to squirm. It looked like an albino eel, bleeding brilliant red blood into the silver serving tray.

Devon pressed herself into her chair. A spot of blood dripped onto the floor near her shoe. "Gross."

"Forgive me, my lady." Damen wiped his blade across his hose and replaced it in the scabbard at his waist. "Apparently the cook had not finished with that one. Venedictos!"

The wizard magically appeared and, seeming to know exactly what his master had wanted of him, whisked the officious sight away.

Devon firmly crossed her arms over her chest, the bloody mess painfully in her peripheral vision. "Don't you have any pizza?"

"Pizza?" Damen peered over the rim of his wine glass. "Mm, must be more ethereal words."

"Ethereal words?" What was it with this guy and the ethereal angel stuff? "All right, that's enough. What do you want of me!" Devon slammed her fists on the table, sending the serving knife flying through the air. "I don't even know you! I don't belong here! This is ridiculous." The knife landed on the stones behind her with a tinny clatter.

Damen pressed his lips with a white linen and settled back into his chair. His forefinger tapped a slow pulse on the arm of the chair, his diamond ring dancing flashes across the ash-coated walls. "You wish to know why I have brought you here?"

"Yes! Didn't you hear me?"

Death's wicked grin curled Damen's lips. His dark eyes glittered madly. Gestures so barely there, motions so minute; yet the results of these small actions so overwhelming. "Why to seduce you, of course."

"Really?" Devon sat back with a huff. She wasn't in the least surprised at this announcement. What else did the villain do with the damsel? Besides rape her if she did not cooperate.

The muscle in the back of Devon's neck tensed. Rape? "Er, what was wrong with the rest of the women out there? W-why me?"

"Because you are an—"

"A what?" Devon saw that her dark host was not going to enlighten her further. Instead he sat calmly observing her, his dark eyes first washing over her face. An ugly rash of goosebumps overtook her flesh as his eyes slithered over her breasts. She felt a mist of heat pink her cheeks. This damned velvet dress was cut so low! No man had ever looked at her with such intent distraction. Well, except maybe Alex. But he was always doing that.

This was an outrage! How dare he keep her prisoner with the sole intention of seducing her. Really! She was not one to be seduced. She would have a man when she was good and ready, and when *she* wanted him, not because he wanted her.

Her anger growing, Devon stormed over to Damen's side and leaned before him. "You're the villain! Why don't you just rape me and get if over with?"

He gave her another calm shrug. "You must give of yourself freely."

"Freely? Ha!" She spun about and stalked over to the window where she noticed the sky was still the same dull gray as when she had arrived. Did the sun never rise in this hell forgotten land? She turned back to Damen, her fists clenched tight to her sides, her jaw firm. "I will not!"

"You will!"

Devon almost laughed to see Mr. Cool and Calm standing with tight fists, his eyes so demanding. So, she had gotten under his skin. Perhaps she could use this.

Go for it, her conscience whispered. *Show him your spirit.*

Lifting her skirts at her hips, she strolled past him. An awakening surge of control ran through her. It seemed he wanted her badly, but not bad enough to rape her. He wanted her to make the first move. "I don't think so, Mr. Dark. Seduction will get you no where."

He caught her by the arm and pulled her to his side. "You think so?"

She could not look him in the eye. The scent of power, of a musky warmth hung over him. No man had ever been so forceful with her.

"I-I do!" She pulled away from him and dashed out of the room.

"We shall see about that, my lady. We shall see!"

* * * *

"This is not good."

Alex fingered the tip of a thorn with his leather glove, producing a shrill scratching noise. Much like fingernails down the blackboard.

"You weren't kidding about this stuff, were you? These thorns are like armor." He turned to find Gwilym pulling a pair of thigh-length leather boots from his bag. "You sneaky bastard. I knew you couldn't be that stupid."

"Aye, I've a brain up here." Gwilym tapped his forehead. "Couldn't keep me from being forced to married the village sow, but it can keep me toes from bleeding."

"How the hell could anyone *force* you to marry?"

"Well, if you accidentally shoot an arrow through her father's best steer I imagine you'd do anything to avoid the punishment of having your hand severed from your body. Even lay with a sow," Gwilym muttered.

Alex sat next to Gwilym, his armor clinking madly with every movement he made. "So tell me, I mean...she can't be that bad."

"Oh ho." Gwilym pulled on his boots and dug about in his leather sack, producing a double-bladed battle ax. "Let me tell you. I nearly smothered on our wedding night. The woman's breasts are as big as a small goat. Had I not convinced her I'd the wheezes and should spend the night on the floor, I think I'd have needed the extreme unction then."

"Ha!" Alex slapped his hand across his knee in a clatter of armor.

Gwilym swung his ax in two great whooshing arcs before him. "I snuck this along, too. No sense in letting you do all the work. We'd best get started. It will require two days to journey through the thorns. And as I've told you, two days after they've been cut down they begin to grow again. So that'll give you little, if any time to rescue the maiden and flee back through the forest before you must battle with them again."

"You sure this is the only way in?"

"Aye, I wish it were not." With a grim set to his jaw, Gwilym scanned the dark, prickly facade of the forest. "I cannot remember a time when there grew anything else. Legend has it Damen the Dark has lived many centuries. They say he is the devil in disguise. A demon who can take on the shape of a man to serve his purposes. He feeds this great forest with the blood of the maidens he kidnaps from nearby villages."

Alex swallowed a gulp. He didn't want to hear any more about the blood of maidens. Especially not *his* maiden.

Gwilym stood aside and gestured toward the treacherous thorns. "We'd best be going, my lord. The maiden awaits."

Six

"This isn't as bad as I thought it would be." Alex swung the heavy broadsword across the severed netting of thick vines. He had developed a system. Swing. Step back to avoid the flying thorns. Swing the other way. Step back. Repeat. Though his arms were getting sore. And the clatter of his armor was giving him a supreme headache. He figured he had been at it for about five hours.

He looked behind him. A narrow path was cleared. He had only gone about fifty feet. That was ten feet per hour. God, he hated math.

Alex gave his head a good jerk, which was all he could do to clear away the sweat. He had already once tried to swipe it away with his hand, stupidly forgetting he wore the heavy gauntlets. He was sure he had a bruise above his right eye. A glance over his shoulder found Gwilym pushing the severed vines aside with his ax. The man had no gloves and his hands were bloody, as were his arms and upper thighs where his boots did not cover.

"You don't have to do that, man." Alex placed a hand over Gwilym's ax. "You're my guide. You're not outfitted to be doing this kind of work. I don't want you bleeding to death before we get there."

"It is a sacrifice I do willingly, mighty Lexor" Gwilym offered. "I only wish I could be of more service."

Alex turned back to the thick netting of thorns. *Yeah, so do I,* he thought. Gwilym was a good man, but what he really needed was a big Caterpillar to plow down this snarl of vines. He had gotten himself into this crazy mess; he had to get himself out.

He wasn't leaving without Devon.

He swung again. The vines made a dry crackling noise, like static electricity, then a shrill *whoosh* as Gwilym flipped them away with his ax.

Swing and crack and *whoosh*. Swing and crack and *whoosh*.

"Ahhgg!" Alex dropped his sword like a hot iron. Pulsing red pain sizzled through his palm. He jumped about, clutching his right hand to his chest.

"What is it?" Gwilym wrangled him around and saw the thick thorn that had pierced the leather of Alex's glove. "Hold firm," he grunted as he twisted the hard thorn out of Alex's flesh. The entire process took less than three seconds.

"Oh yes! This it not what I had planned to do today!" Alex pressed his thumb into the bleeding hole in his palm.

Gwilym calmly ripped a thin strip from the bottom of his tunic and pulled the heavy gauntlet from Alex's hand. He pulled the strip tight, tied a knot, and replaced Alex's gauntlet. Alex held his heavily armored hand to his stomach. He bit his lip to redirect the pain. Gwilym wasn't even wearing armor. He had scratches and blood all over him. And he was giving *him* first aid!

"I'm sorry, Gwilym. That was a selfish thing for me to say. It's just, well...let's just say this is my first mission from the gods. I've never done anything like this before. You know? Gigantic thorns and swords and stuff. Well, it's pretty new to me."

Gwilym cracked a bloody grin. "A training mission, eh?"

"Exactly."

Alex closed his eyes and for the moment tried to imagine home. He could smell the summer breeze and feel the softness of the grass as he lay down. *Perhaps, perhaps, perhaps,* Devon's voice whispered in his ear and her delightful giggle warmed his heart. God he loved that word.

And her.

Remember the girl. You would *die for her.*

Alex looked at his hand. The wound was a mere nick compared to death. He was acting stupid. Devon needed a hero. And he was going to be that hero for her.

He drew in a deep breath and felt courage spill into his veins like cool water over his tired bones. *You can do it. Just do it!*

Alex snapped to attention. He lifted his sword over his head in a classic barbarian pose and commanded in a firm voice. "Let's do it!"

* * * *

Devon slipped carefully out of the tower room and scanned the hallway. Everything was so dark! She wasn't sure how long she had slept after dinner because the sky was still the same color as when she dozed off. Would morning never come? Maybe it was morning? It was impossible to know unless she saw the sun. A vision Devon wasn't too sure she would ever see again.

Good enough reason to look for an escape.

"Right," Devon muttered. "I've had enough hands-on research." She now knew what an actual castle looked like, how it smelled (like rotten grass and dust and some other foul substance she couldn't quite place) and that it was never a comfortable temperature. She also knew what the clothing of the times were like. A bit too risqué for her comfort. And she'd met an actual wizard, a disgusting troll and a real live villain.

That was enough.

She listened intently at the door, then slipped out down the spiraling stairs. Fortunately her host trusted her enough not to bar her door from the outside. The air was icy and dark. At the bottom of the stairs lay the great chamber she had first stumbled into after being attacked by the vicious, biting black fairy.

Devon quickly tiptoed across the ill-cared-for rushes and tried the iron-banded door. It would not budge. It wasn't barred from the inside, though she felt sure it was from the outside. How was that possible? Was there a back door somewhere?

"Damn!" Devon slunk down against the door. She knew if she gave into her fears and worries the tears would come. She was determined to be a survivor. If she gave up, she'd end up becoming Mrs. Darkness.

What would Doris Day do in a situation like this?

Devon knew exactly what the blonde movie goddess would do. She'd call for Rock Hudson and he'd come to the rescue. And if that didn't work, she'd make toast.

Devon pulled her knees up to her chest and rested her chin in her hands. She had never felt so utterly alone as now. The pulse in her wrist beat mercilessly against her flesh. This was fear. Something she'd never been privy to in her life of easy answers and living as she wished.

"Will you come for me, Alex?" She scanned the great gothic arches above her. They resembled the ribs of a bloated skeleton. "Or are you sitting in a classroom right now studying computers and pretending to be interested?"

No, her conscience whispered, *he's looking for you right now. He would never let you down.*

Yes. He would come for her. They'd been friends far too long for him to just forget her now. Like the time when he'd talked her into white water rafting. What a thrill! But that last big rock had sent the rubber raft flying and Devon had almost fallen out had Alex not had a firm grip on her legs. He'd saved her that day. Devon remembered cuddling close in his arms and shivering as he'd calmed her. He wiped her hair from her eyes and pressed a soft a kiss on her forehead. He was always so caring and gentle.

"You'll make someone a great husband someday, Alex."

Devon sat upright suddenly. Who had said that? *You, silly girl.* No. She had never before thought of Alex that way. As a husband? "He would though, wouldn't he?"

She could picture the tall blond rocking a tiny baby in his arms as he sang a silly little love song. Then later, after the baby was asleep, he'd wrap his strong arms about his wife and make passionate love to her...

"Whoa!" Devon jumped to her feet. "You're going mad, girl. Shake it off. Come back to reality." Drawing in a deep cleansing breath, Devon released all lascivious thoughts of Alex Gordon from her mind.

* * * *

Venedictos laid the small rosewood chest before Damen. His master gestured with a flip of his fingers to open the gold inlaid lid. If you could call the black leathery appendages fingers. More like claws or talons, Venedictos thought. Not that he was offended by his master's demonic state. He rather liked it as compared to the hideous mortal form he took to please the wench.

Make that *angel*.

Yes, his plan had gone very well. Damen was not in the least suspicious of his blatant lies. Though he would begin to think something wrong after he took the wench's maidenhead and saw that the curse would not lift. But Venedictos had plans to be long gone before that happened.

Oh yes, one could only serve the dark side for so long before getting dully tired of it. Maybe a nice vacation at sea. He would reel up a mermaid from the depths and she could show him Atlantis.

Stashing his dreams safely away for a time soon to come, Venedictos lifted the lid of the elaborate chest to display the wares that Gawump and the gargoyle had scavenged from the abandoned, war-ravaged castle down by the sea.

Narrow black lids closed over Damen's fiery eyes and he gave a satisfactory nod. In his demonic state his voice was even more deep and steeped with the fires of hell. "Very good, my ingenious wizard. Your magic will please the angel, I am sure. Leave it with me. I'll bring it to her myself."

Seven

Devon startled at the knock on her door. She hid away the extra bed linens she had requested of Gawump between the feather mattress and the ropes that supported it.

"May I enter, my lady?"

Mr. Personality himself. "Do I have a choice?"

"Er…No!" His very long pause had given her a moment of hope.

"Well, then, come in."

He wore black again. Not that she expected him to surprise her by wearing red or plaid. He carried a small chest under one arm, which he laid on the bed.

"I've a gift for you. Come. I wish for you to open it."

Never one to walk away from a gift, and feeling quite bored and perplexed, she saw no danger in humoring the guy.

Devon walked over to the bed and sat next to the sparkling gold chest. She ran her fingers over the smooth wood, marveling at the fine craftsmanship. The entire chest was inlaid with a mass of carved gold roses. "This is lovely."

The touch of cool flesh to her cheek startled her.

"I only wish to touch, my lady," Damen cooed in his deep, seductive voice. "Grant me that, please. It is only that I've never seen such lovely, pure white skin. I can not, in all my years, recall touching something so soft."

Strangely taken with his confession, Devon sat rigid and allowed him to pull his finger along her cheek. It was all she could do to not move when he closed his eyes and let out a little moan of delight. All right. That was enough.

"Well!" She knocked the dark lord out of his reverie and he jerked away. "Thank you very much for this exquisite gift."

"Open it," he persuaded gently.

"Open— Oh, of course. Silly me." She had wished this was it and he could leave. Oh well, might as well check this thing out.

Brilliant flashes of light danced across Devon's face as she lifted the heavy diamond necklace before her. She couldn't speak. She'd never seen anything so beautiful in all her life. So many diamonds! There had to be thousands of them all brought together in an elaborate design of silver filigree. "Oh, Damen."

Her hands shook. Devon had always heard that diamonds were a girl's best friend, but had never thought it could truly be. What were they but cold rocks? But oh, these were so lovely. And so large.

"Allow me, my lady." Damen took the necklace and gestured that she turn about on the bed. As the heavy webbing of jewels fell across her breasts, Devon grew aware that her accelerated breathes made the jewels rise and fall against her pushed-up cleavage. "Lift your hair."

Devon did. Caught up by the enticing allure of the jewels, Devon touched the hard diamonds, ran her fingertips over their slippery smoothness, played with the reflections against her palm. A lingering heat hushed across her neck.

"These baubles are no match for your divine beauty," Damen whispered in her ear. His deep throated whispers were like fine chocolate.

He kissed her neck and spread his arms around her waist to draw her close to his body. The feel of a man's arms about her made Devon's heart race. She closed her eyes and let her head fall back against Damen's shoulder. His lips were hot against her flesh as he trailed them down her neck and across her shoulder. Losing herself in the luxurious sensation, Devon didn't even notice Damen's hand stray upward to cup her breast.

Suddenly aware she was becoming aroused, by this man! The villain! She pulled away from Damen's caresses and, faster than a whip cracked, darted to the window. "You jerk!"

"My lady?" He offered a confused splay of his hands.

"How could I have been so stupid? Stay away from me!" She backed from Damen's approach. "Get it straight, Mister Dark, I am not interested in you. And I never will be!" She struggled with the clasp behind her neck. The diamonds fell heavily in her hands. "And don't think this will do the trick either!" She threw the diamonds at Damen's booted feet.

The dark lord clutched the air with tense fingers. "You!" He rushed for her, his hands curled into choking claws. He pinned her to the wall, but by the time the claws reached her throat they had mellowed to gentle fingers.

"Oh, go ahead and kill me," she snarled. "Who will you play with then? Hmm? You like this game, Damen, and you know it."

He pulled away and paced to the door. "You try my patience, my lady. You will not win this one!" He drew in a voluminous breath and commanded, "There will be a formal ball this evening. And you will attend!"

The door shuddered in its frame as Damen's hasty footsteps echoed down the spiral staircase.

"This evening?" Devon glanced out the window. "And what is it now? Morning? Afternoon?"

Brave words aside, Devon's knees finally gave way to terror and she collapsed onto the floor in a heap of velvet and tears.

Her laughter quickly turned to tears, a then sniffling slumber. She didn't sleep long. When she woke, the first thing she remembered was her date with "his darkness." Reluctantly, she decided a little freedom, ever under the watchful eye of her captor was better than a night spent alone in the tower room.

Leaving the diamond necklace in the exact spot it had landed, Devon followed the repulsive little troll down to the great hall. A sweltering blaze of rush lights illuminated the room in dancing golds and elusive shadows.

Damen waited for her across the room. His head held regal as a prince, his black clothes sparkled with hints of diamonds about the wrist and neck. It seemed he had forgotten their earlier.

"My lady." He bowed and offered his hooked arm.

Devon examined the silk that covered his arm. Black as usual. Didn't seem like there was much muscle beneath the fabric. Hmm. *Could I take this guy? Don't be stupid, even if you could, then you'd have the wizard and the troll to deal with.*

"I guess."

"Pardon?"

She walked past Damen ignoring his proffered arm. "So this is the big shindig?" She and Damen were the only two present. Not that she had expected guests. "Looks like everyone who's anyone is here. But if it's all the same, I'll just sit this first dance out."

She was spun about abruptly. Damen pulled her to him and locked both hands in hers. "It is not all the same. And you *will* dance." He began to move to an unheard rhythm. It was all Devon could do to follow his odd little steps.

"There's no music," she complained.

"Dance to the rhythm of your heart, my lady."

Oh brother. She rolled her eyes. Where did he get this stuff? "Be careful, I wouldn't want to bump into any of the other dancers. The dance floor is quite crowded, don't you think?"

"Sarcasm, my lady, does not suit you."

She looked to the side, rudely mimicking his words under her breath.

"Venedictos!"

The wizard, always seeming to have some supernatural knowledge of what his master needed of him, swiftly filed in, followed by Gawump. The tall wizard bent to the troll and the two began to spin about the dance floor in a silly little jig.

"Ah, so much better," Devon said. If she was going to be forced into this silly charade then she had plans to milk it for all it was worth. She had, after all, spent a hundred and twenty dollars on ballroom dancing lessons.

"Here goes nothing," she muttered.

"What was that, my lady?"

"Fall into step, Damen, I don't know what you're doing, darling, but I'm dancing the waltz. Come on now, one, two, three, one, two, three. There, that's it."

The dark lord granted her a silly little, I-did-it smile as his steps began to match hers.

Yeah, whatever.

She took the lead and spun her demented partner across the rushes. His confusion gave way to elation as his eyes never left hers. "All right now. Everybody! Change partners!" Devon commanded.

Executing an elegant pirouette, Devon left Damen empty-handed and barged in between Venedictos and Gawump. She slipped her hands into the wizard's bony grasp and proceeded to lead him toward the opposite end of the hall. Standing quite alone and confused, Damen accepted the troll's hands when the little beast sauntered over to him.

I'm going crazy, Alex, Devon thought. *I sure hope you are looking for me. I can't keep this up forever.* She granted Venedictos a gracious smile. "You're very light on your feet, wizard."

"And you are very light in the head, my lady. What is this foolishness? Do you risk your life so easily with His Darkness?"

Devon observed Damen's frustrated efforts to get Gawump to follow his lead. The troll was helplessly in possession of two left feet. "He seems to be having fun."

"You'd best give in to His Darkness' demands."

"Never."

"Let it not be said you were never warned."

"Change partners!" Devon announced and spun Venedictos right into Damen's embrace.

Thoroughly peeved, Damen pushed the wizard away. "That is quite enough! Out with the two of you!"

Venedictos and Gawump bowed their heads and rushed away.

Devon came up behind her infuriated host. "Really, Damen, asking our guests to leave. And after only one dance? I should think we'll never be able to entertain again once word gets out."

He turned with the most quizzical glare, his eyebrows knit tightly above his glittering orbs. "You, my lady, are simply mad!"

He stormed off in a huff, leaving Devon clutching her stomach. When she was sure he was far enough off not to hear her, she released a barrage of uproarious laughter.

Eight

Stark hunger had taken over and, after Alex discovered that Gwilym had neglected to bring along a stash of food, he turned to the next best thing.

His sword hilt secured between his feet, blade in the air, Alex carefully pulled a section of vine down the sharpened steel, peeling away the black thorns to reveal the stringy white pulp beneath.

"Tastes like a banana," he muttered, as he tried to convince himself. A bit of the dry pulp caught in his throat. Banana, schamana. This junk was disgusting. But he was too hungry to care right now.

Gwilym choked down a portion of vine. His voracious appetite had not returned. "Aye, and I thought I was in such misery before. Makes me thankful for bread and water." He swiped his arm across his forehead, leaving behind a smear of his own blood.

Alex winced. He looked down at his armor, wishing he could give the man part of it, but it was all one piece. He'd offered his leather tunic earlier but Gwilym was a proud man.

Damn these vines. How much more did they have to hack through before they were upon the castle? He craned his neck toward the vicious netting above him. The vines formed a thick ceiling above their heads.

Now matter how much remained, Alex knew they should get cracking. Time was dwindling, and if Gwilym's story of the vines growing back was true, they hadn't more than a day left.

But it felt too good to sit and relax right now. Just a few more minutes, Alex thought. That will allow my spirit the rest it needs.

Everything on tonight's menu was completely dead. Devon made sure before she sat down to the luscious spread of white and silver glittering food. She was more hungry than self-conscious of the dark man pouting at her from behind the sparkle of a dozen candles.

Probably still mad about the ballroom fiasco, she thought. Served him right. He should be thanking her for teaching him the basic steps to the waltz. He's lucky she didn't expose him to her tango. It was really hot.

"So..." Devon said between bites on what tasted much like lobster. "You're just content to sit and wait? A wait that might be forever?"

"Nothing is forever, my lady."

His baritone voice was beginning to grow on her. At first she had found it horrifying and bone chilling. Now it was almost...seductive.

Devon sucked the juice from a piece of white-fleshed fruit. She had no idea what it was. But it was delicious and so fragrant. Like a cross between a strawberry and a nectarine. She wiped her fingers on a white linen napkin and sat back in her chair to scrutinize her opponent.

Two could play at this game. She narrowed her gaze on Damen. *Give him a taste of his own medicine.* Yeah, that would jar him. The two locked in a heated stare-down. It seemed to Devon the dark lord rather enjoyed her attention. A satisfied smirk slipped across Damen's lips and his eyes subtly changed from sharp anger to smirking desire.

This is not working! Why can't you just leave well enough alone? Now he probably thinks you're flirting with him. Damn!

Devon stabbed her knife deep into the creamy flesh of some sort of bird. A hearty gulp of white wine and she was looking for desert, thinking sweets should calm her irritation. Or at least she'd get such a sugar high she wouldn't care how he looked at her.

She pulled a creamy concoction in the shallow silver dish closer. One bite of the sweet smelling custard-like stuff and Devon had to have more. This was heaven.

Wood scraped across stone in an irritating interruption The fingers of Devon's left hand tensed upon her lap, her other hand studiously spooned custard past her lips. She observed out of her peripheral view that Damen had come around to her side. Having no desire to hold a conversation, she ignored him, paying utmost attention to the creamy treat before her. *Let him stare.* Staring would get him no where.

He touched her hair, so gently, yet she felt a few strands pull as he slipped his hands across her skin. The flesh on her neck tingled. *Ignore him. Yeah, but why isn't he at least warm? So icy, like death.*

"So lovely, your hair," he whispered in a hush dripping with restrained passion. "Of blood dried upon a great black stone."

Devon choked on a spoonful of custard. "Blood on a stone? You really should try some less colorful descriptions, my lord."

Damen's hand pressed over hers before she could scoop up another mouthful of dessert. "I have tried to gift you with the finest things. Jewels, clothing, music... These obviously were not enough."

"Material things are not the way to a lady's heart, Damen. All the jewels in the world could never buy the prize you seek."

"I have come to realize that. What is it, my fair lady, that you desire most?"

"Desire?" Supper had come to an abrupt end. She wrestled her hand out from under his. He did not move away.

"From a man," he continued. "What sort of *man* could capture the fair Devon's heart?"

"A man, eh?" Devon gulped. *Humor him.* At least until he loses the dagger at his hip. "Well, let's see."

What *did* she want in a man? She'd never really thought much about it. Though she instinctively knew...yes, there were certain qualities she desired in a man—qualities she witnessed every day.

"Well...I would like the man to be my friend first and foremost. For if you cannot call him your friend things will never work. And let's see, what else... Sincerity, kindness, oh and playfulness." She pictured Alex following her about as her whims took her from ceramics classes, to fencing, to the summer renaissance festival. "And tolerance of my whims," she added. "That's very important."

"What of his appearance?" Damen's breath was hot upon her exposed shoulder.

"Looks are not so important. Although I shouldn't care to date an ugly man. I like good, clean healthy looking men, men with a twinkle to their eye and the same twinkle in their hearts."

"Dark hair?" he whispered, with a vain toss of his own midnight veil.

She had always liked the dark-haired villains. There was just something about them... Devon felt his breath hush across her cheek. "No! Not-not anymore, at least."

Damen clenched the white tablecloth into his fist. "You try my patience, lady Devon." His other hand reached around her and clamped her by the neck, holding her firmly in check, yet not threatening to choke. Malevolence spilled over the sparkling centers deep in his eyes. "I should ask that you give me the respect I deserve when you are under my roof."

Devon eyed the table. One false move and he could snap her neck. She pawed the table, not particularly reaching for anything, but something hard and cold brushed under her fingertips. She was able to curl her fingers about it as her struggles to breathe waned. "And you are trying mine!" Devon jabbed the knife deep into the back of Damen's hand. A spurt of bright red blood spattered her cream dessert.

Suddenly free, Devon dashed for the door while Damen wrestled to pull the knife from his hand. "Lock her in her room!" the dark lord growled.

Venedictos appeared to wrestle Devon into his grasp. He pushed her toward the spiraling tower stairs. "You are not doing well, my lady. Perhaps you should practice your manners."

"Manners! Look who's talking!" She struggled out of Venedictos' grip and raced up the stairs. When she reached the tower room she slammed the door behind her and cringed when she heard the thick bolt being pushed across on the other side.

Nine

Devon scanned the jagged tops of the Forest of Thorns from her window. *Maybe that hero will come riding up soon.*

When cats tap dance and puppy dogs fly.

She looked up towards the crenellated castle battlements that held reign over the entrance and recalled her flight to the castle. "Well, gargoyles really fly, so I wouldn't be surprised to see a puppy soar past me right now."

She sighed and slumped against the window frame. "I can't believe I'm actually living in one of my stories," she muttered. "It was only a fantasy! I'm sorry. Whomever I've offended in storyland, I'm really, really sorry! Now, will someone please just let me go back home to my nice normal home where my nice normal boyfriend—Wait!"

Devon jumped at the use of the word. It had slipped out unawares. "Boyfriend? Alex?" She cupped her chin in her fingers and let a thoughtful sigh echo across the stone walls of her room. "Perhaps."

She had never thought of Alex in any way other than as a platonic friend. Never once looked at him objectively as a real live, boyfriend potential...man. He was like a brother to her!

Come on. Tell the truth.

Well, maybe there was that one time, when they'd went to the beach and he played the he-man rescuer and carried her out of the water in his arms. She had mocked unconsciousness, her wrist thrown dramatically over her forehead. But that day she had noticed more than his laughing smile and sea-salt tipped brows. Oh yes. Alex was well-built and muscular, tall and handsome. His eyes were kind and he had this habit of always looking her directly in the eye whenever they spoke. He gave you his utmost attention, as if your words were the most important thing in the world at that moment. Oh, and she could read his mind if she looked long enough into those vibrant mirrors of blue.

"All right, so maybe I have noticed," Devon said to the little voice in her head. "But he's never noticed me."

Oh yeah, so how come he's always saying the two of you should become more than just friends?

"All right, all right! So he is interested in me." Devon jumped to the floor and wandered over to the bed. Candlelight flickered on the walls in long shadows and a gentle hiss of sulfur curled about her nose. She plopped down on the bed. "I've been a fool, Alex. I've been blindly in search of a hero when I was too stupid to see he was right there all along."

Ten

"Your Darkness."

Damen wrapped a white linen about his hand to stifle the bleeding. Wretched wench. How could she possibly be an angel? With her manners? Such violence for a heavenly being. He had thought to change into his natural state where he would heal instantly. But he couldn't risk it with the angel about. "What is it, Venedictos? And please, it had better be good."

"Of course, my lord. It's just, well, the gargoyle has alerted me that a great warrior has been sent to rescue the maiden."

"Maiden?" Damen spun around and paced up to Venedictos. The wizard immediately looked to the floor. He tried to discern his body language—to see if he lied—but the wizard was always staring at his feet and twisting his beard. Nothing new. "I thought she was an angel?"

"Oh, of course, Your Darkness. She truly is. I called her from the heavens m-myself."

Damen scrutinized the wizard's face before turning and pacing to the window. Venedictos fidgeted with the cuff of his wide sleeve.

"He's entered the Forest of Thorns?" Damen prompted from his windowside perch.

"Yes, Your Darkness. He will be here in a little less than a day, if all goes well."He chuckled "Of course, no one has ever made it through the forest. I'm sure there's nothing to worry about."

Damen gave a sneering grunt and Venedictos took that as his cue to leave.

"Amazing." Alex held his forefinger carefully before his eyes. An iridescent creature lighted on it and fluttered her wings. "I never believed in fairies, until—She's like a little Tinkerbell," he whispered.

Gwilym came up behind him and tossed his ax to the ground near a pile of severed vines.

"Chill, man, you'll scare her away."

"That is what you'll be wishin' if you don't spook that nasty insect right now."

"What?" Alex looked to his sidekick. Streaks of blood ran down his arms and neck. He was sweating and looked near collapse. "Ouch!"

The fairy flew off through the tangle of black thorns then zoomed back to hover above their heads. Alex sucked his bleeding fingertip. "What the hell?"

"They're a blood-thirsty breed, those black fairies." Gwilym took up his ax. "We'd best be back to work. We've but a day to finish and get back through."

"Oh, man." Alex sucked on the inside of his cheeks. It had been over twenty-four hours since the meal in the village. A meal that he had not indulged in too greatly. Now he wished he had, no thanks to the lump of vines that sat festering in his stomach. "I could really use some water. Pop, juice, Gatorade, anything. Yeah, Gatorade, for that deep down body thirst."

"What is this Gater ayde?"

Alex picked up his gauntlet. "Water, man. Anything. I'm parched."

"Aye, I could use a bit of refreshment myself." Gwilym eyed the hovering fairy. "This way. Black fairies are good for one thing. Follow her. She'll lead us to a fairy pool."

Alex grabbed up his sword. "As long as her friends aren't waiting there for us. I just gave blood last week."

The two followed the flashing light of the fairy to a dark mirror-like pool. Alex rushed into the circle clearing and knelt before the sparkling pond. The fairy pool was motionless and dark. A terrible foreboding overtook him. A cold tickle spread across his scalp.

"Um...I don't think so." He sat back on his haunches and eyed the pool from various angles. "Nope. Something's in there."

"What? The devil take you, there's nothing in there."

"Oh yes there is. You know, like Freddy Krueger or something. Devon and I have seen enough movies to know better. Something's in there just waiting, ready to leap out and grab me."

"You're a crazy case for a warrior." With a dismissive wave of his blood-smeared hand, Gwilym propped his ax against a tangle of vines and knelt next to Alex. "There's not a thing in there but good cold water. I'll show you." He bent over the sparkling pool and lapped up the water. He drank for a good minute before sitting back up and swiping an arm across his lips. "You see. God's grace, mere water has never tasted sweeter than now."

"No kidding? Hmm." Maybe it was safe. Alex muddled it over for a moment. It was sure they didn't have special effects in this age. There were no Freddy Krueger claws or mechanical monsters lurking in the dark shadows ready to spring at him.

Relieved of his worries, Alex bent to drink in the cool liquid. But he didn't get more than two swallows when a long, scaled tentacle sprang up and wrapped itself around his neck.

Eleven

Thank goodness her mother had forced her to join the Girl Scouts. Personally she'd never liked the stupid green socks and sashes she had to wear, but Devon was more than grateful now. She finished off the last square knot, pulling the white linens into a firm knot.

She was not about to sit around and wait for his royal darkness to come sauntering up with wine and roses in an attempt to seduce her. She'd been collecting sheets since she arrived, complaining to Gawump of the extreme cold. The brain-dead troll hadn't been the wiser.

Devon tied one end of the sheets around the bedpost then went to the window to scan the ground. It was a long climb. She figured the sheets would run out a good ten or fifteen feet from the ground.

Hell, if she made it that far, the jump would be worth it.

"If you're not going to come for me, Alex Gordon," she said as pushed the sheets out the window, watching them tumble down the wall, "I'll just have to rescue myself."

The air was cool and smelled of dull mildew as she stepped up onto the window ledge. Devon looked down. A tumbling vertigo spun her head. "Oh no." She clutched the stones. "Don't do that, girl. You'll fall for sure. Just concentrate on not letting go of the sheets. And don't look down, all right?"

Yeah right. They do this in the novels all the time. Do you think the writers actually try it themselves? No! They're not stupid.

"I'm not stupid either," Devon answered the little voice in her head. "I'm just...adventurous. Like Alex always says. He likes that about me."

Why all of a sudden does it matter what Alex thinks?

"Oh, would you just shut up!" Devon slammed the door on her mental voice and turned to the business at hand.

She hiked her skirts up around her thighs and lowered herself over the ledge to begin her descent. The sheets pulled taunt about her hands. "Won't this make a great chapter in my book? Yeah, we'll call it Chapter Eleven, the chapter in which the heroine risks her neck to save herself because the hero is most likely at home channel surfing with the remote control."

* * * *

The scales cut into his neck with each squeeze from the great beast. Alex kicked across the ground in an attempt to free himself. Thorns from the surrounding vines tore through his flesh. His own blood made his grip slippery. The beast squeezed tighter. Alex gagged. He was lifted from the ground and whipped back down in a bone jarring crash.

Gwilym grabbed Alex's sword and stabbed the scaly creature. A gurgling spurt of orange blood sprayed Alex's bluing face, but the beast did not falter.

With a great battle cry, Gwilym raised the sword over his head and brought it down through the scales and black flesh of the beast. Amber globs of blood oozed out and its tentacle slipped from Alex's neck. A great splash pulled the beast back into the darkened hollows of the pool.

Alex inhaled many deep, gasping breaths.

Gwilym dropped the sword by his feet and fell back in dazed amazement. "God's teeth, that was an ugly one."

Unable to find his voice, Alex pushed the slithering remnants of the scaled beast from his lap and cast Gwilym a look of pure shock.

Gwilym seemed to know exactly what he was thinking. "Opps."

Alex's eyes widened. "Opps?" He stood and kicked the tentacle away. He swiped his palm across his lacerated neck. The scales had not cut too deep. He looked over Gwilym, his hands on his hips. The man had actually said *opps*!

"No problem, eh? Nothing but cold, clean water!" He gathered up his sword and stamped past Gwilym in a clatter of steel.

He wondered how long it would take to get back to the village. All he had to do was find the chick he'd left the 'sacred writing' aka—the magic words he'd ripped from Devon's—

Devon.

Damn it, Alex, you can't do this to her. She's all alone in a nasty situation. You've got to save her. What ever happened to walking the worlds for her? And lying and dying for her? You love her. Prove it to her!

He turned and looked back at Gwilym. Blood rained like tears from the poor man's body. He was unselfish and brave, coming along on what was proving to be a death mission. And he didn't even know Devon. He had no idea what a fabulous chick she was. Furthermore, he thought himself to be the sidekick to some great warrior.

Alex's shoulders slumped. Here he was, ready to walk away from it all just because of some stupid pond monster. He pulled his hand over his face and pushed it back through his sweat-soaked hair.

"I would die for her," he muttered. Alex felt his heart swell and begin to pulse rapidly with a new surge of adrenaline. "Let's go. We've got a maiden to rescue."

Alex prepared to swing his sword through the thick vines but stopped and turned back to Gwilym. The man was a hero in his own rights. "You saved my life, man. Thanks. I owe you one."

Gwilym bowed. "You owe me no more than to see the maiden safely from the clutches of the dark lord who lives just beyond." He gestured ahead and for the first time Alex could see the castle. The saw-toothed battlements jutted above the tangle of thorns in wicked sharpness, set against a dreary black sky.

What was going on behind those cold walls, Alex didn't want to know. He had to hurry. "A few more hours?"

"If we begin now, my lord."

With a resolute sigh, Alex pulled on his gauntlets and took up his sword. He closed his eyes and drew on the inner strength that he had always read about. Was it in there somewhere? Did he have inner strength?

Devon's sweet smile flashed across his mind. Her tinkling laughter and that flirty little mole...

The sky was dismal and flat as she looked out across the jagged tops of the thorns. Devon closed her eyes and summoned her inner core, her very being, the only thing left that could save her and possibly reach out farther than the vicious tangle of the Forest.

"Alex," she whispered. "Alex...Alex..."

"Did you hear that?"

Gwilym shrugged. "Hear what?"

Alex closed his eyes and tilted his head. He had heard her voice. It drifted like dandelion tufts on the wind, gently and so softly. He knew it. He wasn't going crazy. "There it is again! She's calling me. She needs me!"

Gwilym cast his cohort a worried glance and shook his head. But Alex didn't notice his worry. Instead he thrust his sword in the air above his head. "Let's do it!"

* * * *

"What is it that can tempt an angel?"

Damen strode the floor of the upper hall, his fingers to his lip as he tried to figure it out. "Heaven can not offer the temptations I do."

He had plied her with tables of delicious, extravagant food. That had done nothing but sicken her. Perhaps angels don't eat? He had gifted her with the finest clothes and lovely furnishings for her room. And diamonds. Well, they hadn't gone over so well. Might have been too much too soon. But the music, he had given her divine music from his heart. What was a *waltz* anyway?

Damen rubbed the wound on top of his hand. An oblong gauge had formed a scab in his palm. Vicious little widget.

"Soon I shall not have to endure this silly charade." He paced to the middle of the room. There was a strange thrashing sound in the distance, but he was too caught up in his worries. "Surely I am not offensive to her in this form?"

He dashed to the looking glass and preened over his face. He pulled his hair back and looked over his smooth, scarless skin and stretched his lips over his oddly white teeth. They were cut straight, much unlike the sharpened fangs he normally sported. "Certainly not," he resolved. She had said so herself. "Perhaps it is that she is frightened of discovering the carnal delights?" Grim satisfaction settled across Damen's human mask. "Ah yes, I must guide her slowly and gently in this process. I have been too forward."

He resumed pacing, going through plans in his head. *Woo her gently. Do not be so powerful.*

Suddenly Damen could not ignore the thrashing. "Hell fire, what is that infernal noise?"

He stepped over to the window. The thrashing had grown stronger. It was accompanied by the stony yowl of the gargoyle and the frantic screams of a woman.

Looking outside, he saw Devon clinging to the side of the castle just outside his window. The gargoyle held her at bay. Its wings thrashed through the air, and its harsh cry echoed through the night.

"What is this?" Damen stepped up on the window ledge and tried to grab hold of Devon. "Do you wish death upon yourself?"

"Help me!" Devon cried, as she clung to the white sheet.

Amazement overtook his shock. She had escaped out of her window. Ingenious little wench. But there, just below the window ledge, the bed linens, they were ripping! "Grab hold quickly!"

Devon stretched, but her fingers barely touched Damen's. "I can't!" She kicked and strained to keep hold of the linen rope. "Get that beast away from me!"

Damen knew the gargoyle would not leave until the girl had either fallen or was safely inside. He had no control over it, only Venedictos could command the stony beast. He glanced up to the tower window. The sheets were almost torn apart. "Swing toward me!"

With a most unangelic grunt, Devon pushed from the castle with her feet and threw her weight to the side. The sheet broke free. The gargoyle let out a triumphant yowl. And Damen was able to grip Devon's wrist. Her weight pulled him over the edge, but he held firm to the ledge with his other hand.

"Don't...let go." He struggled to keep a grip on her wrist while his other hand slipped across the stone ledge. This mortal shell he wore was weak and lacking in muscle. A brief idea flashed through his thoughts. *If she truly is an angel, would she not fly if I released her*? Damen's eyes met the frightened, teared orbs on Devon's face. Her mouth pulled into a fearsome line. *No. She has no memory of that. She would not know.* He pulled her up until she was able to hook her elbows over the ledge and stumble forward into his arms.

"Thank you," she shuddered in his grasp.

She shivered and streams of tears ran down the rosy circles of her cheeks. Damen held her tight. Ah, so precious. A lost child in his arms. So grateful of her rescue.

Grateful? A death's head grin crept across the pale flesh of Damen's disguise. Oh yes. Things could not have worked better if he had planned them himself. She would be *so* grateful.

Now to play it for the prize.

He pushed his fingers through her hair, so soft and smooth, like mink's fur. She still clung to him and shivered madly. Her need caused him to feel an odd flutter inside his chest. Much like his heart was squeezing or perhaps *feeling* a new sensation.

Feelings? Bah! He pushed all foolish emotion aside.

"That was an idiot thing to try. If you had not fallen, the gargoyle would have surely crushed you against the side of the castle."

Devon merely whimpered.

"Oh, my precious angel. It is over now." He kissed her forehead. Her skin was hot and as smooth as her hair. So divine. His heart pulsed heavily. The wait would truly be worth it. Ah, yes...and then he could return to the netherworld. He nuzzled his face into the silken folds of her hair. "You are safe in my arms. So safe—"

Suddenly Devon pushed out of his grasp and scrambled away. Her hair was tousled about her shoulders in a nasty mess and her dress was torn to expose her leg to the thigh. Oh, to touch that glimmering white skin. Damen reached out.

"No!" she screamed and pulled away. Her violet eyes were wide and manic. "Don't touch me you-you creep!" She paced past him, flinging her arms out as she raved. "This is just too much! I gotta get out of here." She swung around on him. "This," she pushed her hand through her hair. "Is what you call a bad hair day. Okay? So that's reason number one to be at sorts. But this!" She held out her hands. They trembled as if from the cold, but Damen had just touched her flesh, she was hot, almost as if with fever. "This is what you call stress!"

She turned and began to pace. As she did she mumbled, as if a chant, "I need chocolate. Not dark chocolate either. *Milk* chocolate. Scads of luscious Lindt and Whitmans and Godiva and chocolate covered cherries and—and pizza! And yeah, give me a big bottle of Alka-seltzer to go with it..."

Damen shuffled toward the door as the frazzled angel went on and on. Venedictos had appeared to stare in amazement at the girl.

"What did I tell you?" Damen muttered. "Do you not see that madness has taken her mind? What is this strange nonsense she goes on about? Chocolate and pizza and this Alka-seltzer?"

Venedictos cleared his throat and cast an observant glance over Devon. "It is not madness, Your Darkness, she is chanting. More ethereal words. Perhaps it is a spell of sorts. I do not know. Whatever it is, it seems to pull her into a great and lovely rage."

"Mm, yes," Damen agreed. "She is lovely as she rages about."

She was a wild creature, pure of heart, and chaste of body, enraged before him in the most delicious design. The blood-black hair was a wicked tangle about her raving eyes, and those lips, so tender and soft as they spouted some secret madness. "Very delightful," he whispered.

Twelve

Alex climbed forward on his knees. Finally there were no more of the wretched blood-thirsty thorns. His face fell upon cold, hard ground. But it was thornless and that was all that mattered.

He laid there a moment, taking deep breaths, feeling his heart beat heavily against his chest. His armored scales, which had been bruised and bent, chinked softly with each subtle movement. A cool breeze tickled through his hair and began to dry the sweat and the blood droplets to his chilled skin.

"You see," he huffed, his cheek still glued to the earth. "That wasn't so bad. We made it. And by my figuring we've got about half a day to spare before that damned forest starts to grow on us again. Gwilym. Gwilym?"

Shrill squawks of unnatural origin began to echo about Alex's head. He lifted his head just in time to see a great stone beast swoop down upon his partner and knock him to the ground.

"What the hell is that?" Alex pulled himself up and looked about for his sword.

"Run!" Gwilym yelled.

"Run? Are you nuts? Where's my sword?"

Alex dove for the glimmering needle of steel just as the gargoyle came rushing down again.

Gwilym held his arms up to block the beast's wrath, but its great stone talons dug through his flesh in red streaks and cracked the bone. His screams were drowned out by the shrill cry of the gargoyle.

Alex touched his sword but quickly dodged to avoid the return swoop from one of the wings.

So there really was a gargoyle! Impossible. But who had time to worry about possibilities? Gwilym struggled for his life.

Alex swung his sword through the air. It chinked against the beast's wing. Shock waves reverberated through his hands and arms in an electrifying jolt. "Yikes. This thing is solid rock."

"The heart," Gwilym cried as the talons gripped his throat and lifted him from the ground.

"The heart? Where the hell—"

Confused and angered that his struggles were futile against the shrieking beast, Alex fought for control. He felt the blood come in a hot gusher as a talon tore through his armor and the leather undertunic and ripped a gash in his arm. He ducked beneath the great beast. Gwilym's feet left the ground. The gargoyle was going to fly off with him.

Pressing both hands about the heavy broadsword, Alex whispered a quick prayer and plunged the sword upward into the belly of the gargoyle. He did not feel resistance. Steel cut through stone and slid straight into the heart. Gushers of black ooze poured over the blade and Alex's hands and head.

The gargoyle dropped Gwilym in a heap and faltered into a backward roll. Its wings crashed against the side of the castle, sending it into a hurtling spin. The beast cracked and crumbled and scattered across the ground in a massive hail of tiny rocks.

Alex stood petrified as the black ooze slithered down his cheek. It slipped between his fingers that still clutched the sword above his head.

It was a long time before all was silent. The shattered gargoyle had settled to fine dust. Alex's arms were coated with the beast's dark blood. A drop fell from his eyelash. He blinked, bringing himself back to reality.

"Shit," was all he could say.

He dropped his sword in a clatter and pushed his hands over his head to squeeze away the ooze. "This stuff is like tar!" Then he remembered Gwilym.

Alex spun around and fell to his knees beside the man's inert body. He lay bent backwards at the waist, an impossible angle. The beast had broken his back. There wasn't much left of the man's neck either. Alex threw his gauntlets to the ground and touched the man's bloody forehead. He was hot and sweaty and slippery with his own blood. There were spots of the gargoyle's thick black blood splattered all over him.

"Lex...or," Gwilym managed though his eyelids did not lift.

"Oh man, you're still alive. I gotta get you some help. Call 911!" he instinctively yelled.

"Your...magical numbers can...not save...me now... I am honored to have guided...your way...oh great...and mighty...Lexor."

"Damn!" Alex felt the man slump beneath his touch. The anger at Todd's death came flooding full force and overtook his body in a vicious shudder. "You can't die. Please! Come on, we never had a chance to spend time together. I was just getting to know you. You were always the older one spending all your time with your friends! I was always too little to tag along. Todd, Please!"

"Fight...your demons," Gwilym whispered. His head fell heavy in Alex's hand.

"Oh god." This wasn't his brother. But he wished it was. If only he'd had the chance to say good-bye, or maybe a simple, I love you. *Todd, I love you.* "Come on, Gwilym, please you gotta live." He shook his shoulder and the man let out a gasp. He was barely alive.

Alex stood and thrust angry fists into the sky. He yelled to the darkened heavens. "What am I going to do now? I'm just plain and simple Alex Gordon from the twenty-first century. I'm not a warrior! I'm just some—guy—from the future trying to save the girl of my dreams!" He turned back to Gwilym. "Then you got all tangled up in it—an innocent and good-hearted man—and now you're lying here...dying."

Gwilym's eyelids fluttered and he spit up a stream of blood. "It does not matter what is on the outside." The man reached and was able to tap the bent scales of Alex's armor. "It only matters what is beneath the armor. Find her...Alex...and when you do..."

Alex lifted Gwilym's head. "Yes?"

"Kiss the maiden for me, will you?"

"You better believe it. I'll tell her about the brave man who helped me find her."

Gwilym's head fell heavy in Alex's hands. A gasp escaped his lips and his final breath was released to the air.

Alex pressed his forehead to Gwilym's chest. "This is wrong. This is so wrong." He hugged Gwilym for the longest time. His heart burst and poured out a stream of tears for the dead knight and for Todd. "I love you, brother."

Kiss her for me...

Alex sat back. He wiped the back of his hand across his face, smearing sticky gargoyle blood away from his eyes. *Yes, kiss her for Gwilym.* He had to do this! He had come this far. Devon was but a mere mortal in this crazy land of gargoyles and fairies and pond monsters.

He scanned the facade of the castle. It stretched high above him, its great towers disappearing into the low-misting gray clouds that shrouded the building in a cloak of wicked evil.

"I will get to her, Gwilym" Alex stood and replaced his sword in the scabbard at his waist. "I'll save her from Damen the Dark and give her that kiss for you before the day is over."

"Chocolate, pizza, Alka Seltzer. Chocolate, pizza, Alka Seltzer. Chocolate, pizza—"

"Ahem."

Damen spun around at the sound of Venedictos' voice. The wizard granted him a quizzical lift of his brows. "Er, I was just trying them. The ethereal words the angel speaks. Thought they might have some power."

"Your Darkness," The wizard gestured to the window. "If you will."

Damen looked out across the Forest of Thorns to see the pathway that had been cleared all the way up to the castle.

"The warrior has arrived," Venedictos pointed out. "He will be upon us within the hour."

"Alert the gargoyle," Damen commanded sternly. "I'll see to the angel."

The door was open. Odd in a castle, but with a gargoyle to defend it, maybe they weren't too worried. Alex walked across the threshold.

As far as castles went, it was darker than midnight and cold as ice. "Musta missed the party." He stabbed his sword through a thick spider web. "So this is Damen the Dark's place, eh?"

Not much for decorating. Or heating. The silver platelets of Alex's armor chinked as the cold took to his bones, but the cool air could not keep the sweat from beading. He swiped his hand across his forehead and wiped the mixture of sweat, gargoyle blood, and his own blood off on his leather pants.

With a name like Damen the Dark, Alex figured he probably didn't buy cookies when the Girl Scouts came knocking. In fact, the Girl Scouts were probably never seen again.

Alex had a terrible thought. "Devon used to be a Girl Scout."

Slowly, slow enough so his armor would not chink, he made way down the hall until he came upon a large empty room. A slash of moonlight simmering through a window high above his head provided enough light to make out his surroundings. There stood an empty hearth across the great room and a few overturned wooden tables. Everything was coated in a thick powder of dust.

He sheathed his sword and turned, only to knock his knee on something hard.

"Oww!" Alex reached for his knee and came face to face with something peculiar. "What the heck?"

Two beady orange eyes stared up at him from beneath a great frazzle of red hair and wrinkles. With a gleeful grunt, the troll swung his ax in a great *swoosh*. Alex jumped the low sweep with ease.

"Cripes, it's a troll! What next?" He pulled his sword out and prepared to stab the ugly little critter, when a pang of guilt fell over him. His arm froze mid-air. He had never killed a living being. Stone gargoyles did not count. He couldn't do this.

The troll grunted and swung his ax over his head. This time his swing found its mark, tearing through Alex's leather pants and ripping flesh.

It was obvious the troll hadn't the same reservations.

"That's it!" Alex kicked the little man. He was so light he went flying against the wall. "I may not be able to kill you, but I can certainly take you out, you ugly little bugger."

He hobbled over to the troll and bent to examine his odd size. His arms were as long as his body. The creature shook his head and stared up in fear. Seeing he had the advantage, Alex pulled his lips into an intimidating sneer and muttered, "Do you wanna get rocked?"

"Huh?"

Bam! Alex's fist connected with the troll's nose and knocked him out cold.

Now she was nothing but upset. This time she'd been woken from a dream. A really great dream. In fact, she was just about ready to kiss the dashing hero—a hero who bore an incredible resemblance to Alex Gordon—when that deep dark ugly voice whispered in her ear.

"I need you, my lady."

Damen said her presence was urgently needed below.

Reluctantly she had left her hero behind. *Oh god, Alex, where are you?*

"So what is it now?" she wondered as Damen took his place on his throne.

"There are some things that can wait no longer, my lady. Circumstances have gone beyond my control."

"Circumstances? Like what?" Devon surprised herself by shouting.

"Silence!" Damen hissed.

Devon shrunk back against the wall. Venedictos was no where about. For once he was not guarding the door. She could turn and run, but that would be futile. Escape was not possible with the great stone beast guarding the castle.

But give in to this vile man?

"Ahah!"

A sweetly familiar voice echoed through the chamber. Devon spun around and felt her heart jump to her throat.

Thirteen

"Alex!"

He bowed grandly, his bent and scratched armor glinting in the rush light. His hair was matted down with blood and tar-like black stuff, but his bright blue eyes shone.

Devon couldn't believe it. He was here! He had actually come for her. He must have stepped in to the fairy circle right after her. But—It had been days. "What took you so long?"

Alex righted slowly from his bow. "What took me so long?" He stared at her incredulously. "What took me so long? Well, let's see..." He tucked his sword under his arm and began to count off on his fingers. "First I had to thrash through the Forest of Thorns. I got the flesh torn from my body and nearly died of dehydration..."

Devon crossed her arms and started to tap her foot. She noticed out of the corner of her eye that Damen sat forward on his throne, quite interested in Alex, though not worried enough to make a move.

"And speaking of dehydration I ran into this ugly white snake-thing—"

"Ah," Damen stepped down from his throne and Devon clenched her fists in infuriation. "Did you like the scawaga?"

"The scawaga?" Alex shook his head, seemingly unaware that the villain was inches from Devon. "So that's what you call it. No sir, I did not like it one bit." He rubbed a blood-crusted hand across his neck where the scales had cut thin lines into his flesh. "Now, where was I? Oh yes, I had to fight this gargoyle from hell—a damn stone gargoyle!" Alex looked to Devon. "You know that saying, you can't get blood from a stone?"

She shrugged, unbelieving that he was going on when Damen hovered just over her shoulder. They had much better things to be doing right now than relaying his journey here.

"Not true," Alex continued. "Stone does bleed. It's thick and black and disgusting. Like tar. I'll probably never get it out of my hair without spending a fortune on conditioners...and then there was the troll..."

"Oh, you met Gawump," Devon added, finding Alex's ranting quite humorous now.

"Gawump? Hmm, it most certainly was. But anyway, after all that, all you can say is what took me so long?" Alex threw up his arms in a great clatter of scaled steel.

"It seems your hero is a trifle peeved."

Devon stared into Damen's laughing eyes. She saw nothing but the horror of what would happen to her if Alex left her behind. "Wait!" She screamed as Damen wrangled her into his grasp. "Alex!"

"Alex!" Devon repeated in a more urgent tone as she spied Venedictos coming up behind him.

"All right, all right," Alex sauntered forward. "I was just kidding."

"Alex, watch out for the—"

Kachung!

"Wizard." Devon sank in Damen's arms as she watched Alex stagger to the floor.

Venedictos set Gawump's ax down by his foot and proudly looked over his handiwork. He had clunked Alex a good one with the side of the blade.

"Mercy," Alex was able to mutter as his face hit the cold stone floor.

"Oh, Alex." Devon was surprised when Damen let her struggle loose and slip to the floor by Alex's head. "Alex, can you hear me?"

Venedictos picked up Alex's feet.

"Do what you...can," Alex whispered weakly. "Buy me some time. Anything. Tap dance, teach him topiary." Suddenly he grabbed her wrist and pulled her down to his face. "I love you," he whispered. His eyes rolled upward as the wizard toted him out of the chamber.

Devon stood up. "He loves me?" Her heart gulped. Hot surges of electricity raced through her body, setting her senses on alert.

He had actually said *I love you.*

"Oh dear, what would Doris Day do in a situation like this?" She twisted her hands together as the scent of Damen's foul breath drew closer. Suddenly she knew. "Make toast!"

"What?" Damen eyed her curiously.

Her host already thought her a lunatic. Why change now? "Uh, you wouldn't happen to have a toaster, would you?"

"A toaster?"

"Nah, I didn't think so." Devon hiked up her skirts and sprinted for the door, but Damen was too quick. He slammed the door and caught her body in his arms. Devon tried to squiggle away but Damen held her firm.

"So, your hero has been vanquished." A wicked glee danced beneath his midnight brows. "Do you not think it time to relinquish your negative words and give to me the one thing I wish?"

Devon drew in a deep breath and examined her options. She only knew the one tap dance routine. It was two minutes long. Most likely not enough time for Alex to get his butt back here and rescue her. She searched her mind in hopes of finding something she could use as a distraction. But she didn't think Damen was in the mood for another ballroom dancing lesson right now. Nor would he understand the finer points of topiary.

"Lady Devon?"

His harsh voice reverberated behind her ears. He repeated her name but it was the firm squeeze on her upper arms that brought Devon back to reality.

"Will you relinquish?" he prompted.

Here goes nothing. Or...all.

Devon tossed her hair to the side and fluttered her lashes as she whispered seductively. "Perhaps."

Fourteen

The world was spinning round and round and round and round...

A sudden jerk of consciousness pulled Alex out of his daze. He shook away the confusion and tried to rub his head, but found his hands were manacled to the wall.

"Oh man, I need some Tylenol." His body was cold, his hands even colder. "Where am I, anyway?"

He sat on the floor of a small room. One thin slit arrow-hole window was carved out near the ceiling. His legs were spread wide, and his arms hung above his head. Alex looked up at his lifeless hands hanging inside the big iron manacles. He tried to wiggle his fingers but the blood had run out of them. "Damn. I was right there! I could have grabbed her and run."

But no, his conscience jibbed. *You had to be your casual wise-ass self and joke around. And now look where you are! And she's in the hands of that creep!*

"Damn, damn, damn!" Alex gazed up at the manacles, not believing he had been so stupid. The longer he sat around on his butt, the less time he had to beat the damned forest before it sprouted again.

Then he noticed something. The manacles. They were in fact...very large.

He twisted his arm in an attempt to bring some blood back to his hand. Eventually the feeling returned and he was able to press his fingers close together and pull his hand free. No problem, thanks to the generous greasing of gargoyle blood that still coated his skin.

Alex slipped his other hand free and stood up. "Geez, are these guys stupid or whooaa!"

His jaw kissed the cement on a cloud of ancient dust. Too stunned to move, Alex wiggled his foot. Just as he'd suspected. His right leg had been manacled. And on the end of the chain was a huge iron ball. "Maybe they're aren't so stupid."

"If we're going to do this," Devon slipped one knee alongside Damen's leg, then the other, so she was straddling him on his throne. She hadn't taken too much time to think over her plan.

Which was just as well, because if she started analyzing what she was about to do she'd throw up for sure. "We might as well do it right."

Damen's smile drew up into his cheeks. He smoothed a hand along the side of Devon's face.

Though her seductive smile remained as his fingers touched upon her lips, inside Devon cringed. *Flatter him,* her conscience whispered. *That's how you seduce a man. Flattery and gentleness. Appeal to his own vanities.*

Damen was not privy to her inner torment as Devon took a deep breath and began her debut as an actress.

"Oh, Your Darkness," she cooed. "You're so...so..." She scanned his expectant face in search of the answer. So what? Dark? So disgusting? "Your hair!" She pushed her fingers through the dark tresses. "It's so long and rich and...and dark!" Devon pulled a veil of his silken hair across her face and closed her eyes. Hell, if the heroines in her stories could do it, so could she.

But she made a mental note: this was the last time she was going to do any physical research on villains.

Damen slipped his hand down her back, sending arresting shivers through her body. Tiny goosebumps spread up her arms. This was not good.

Don't get involved, that little voice whispered.

For once she was thankful that the little voice was still there. Devon slipped from Damen's embrace and skipped toward the door. "Venedictos!"

Damen watched curiously as the wizard brought in a tray of wine and glasses.

She had yet to figure out how the wizard always knew when and why he was needed, but was just thankful it worked for her.

"Thanks, er, I tried for the black tie look but he just wouldn't cooperate." She took the wine and glasses and Venedictos backed out of the room. "So!" She handed a glass to Damen. "What shall we drink to?"

Damen's eyes never left hers as she began to pour the wine. "How about to dead heroes?"

The wine spilled over Devon's fingers onto the dark lord's leg. "Dead?"

Damen's look chilled over her face.

No, Devon thought. Just be cool. He's not dead. Play along with him. Alex will be here any minute now. And you won't have to take this evil bastard to bed. She pulled up a measure of her dress and wiped the red liquid from Damen's knee.

"Dead," she said as she poured herself a generous helping of wine. The better to loosen her inhibitions. "Of course. To death!" She held her glass high and Damen rose to meet it in a sparkling crash.

"Oh!" The wine splattered over her dress and neck in a spray of crimson droplets.

"Forgive me, my lady." Damen took the broken stem from her hand and tossed it over his shoulder. He brushed his fingers across her neck and chest, wiping away a few spots of the spilled wine. His eyes observed her fright as he licked them clean. "It is only because I grow impatient. We shall have wine and conversation later. But now—how shall I say this—let the debauchery begin."

He dove against her neck with quick bruising kisses, intent on devouring the remaining alcohol. Devon tried to push him away but found his strength remarkable. This wasn't working. She needed more time! "W-what about the seduction?"

"It is over," he growled, all patience gone. He kissed her mouth in a strong, demanding press. "Now I must have my angel."

Angel? Did the man really believe she was an angel?

Devon pulled back from his lecherous attentions. "I think there is something you should know. I'm not an angel," Devon said with a sheepish shrug.

Damen allowed a smile to curl his lips. "Poor child. Madness does not suit you. You are an angel, dear one. My wizard pulled you from the heavens. But you are unaware of it because your memory of that time has left you with your arrival here on earth. As your wings have also left you."

"My wings?" He really believed her to be an angel! Was he that stupid? "Oh, Damen," she said with an amused chuckle. "Dear, sweet, demented Damen." She waved her finger before his face. "Who has been filling your dark little mind with such silly ideas? Surely you must realize that an angel would never come to this earth in human form? Angels are unearthly, heavenly bodies. They are protected by the greatest power of all. I am just a plain, simple woman. Ask the wizard."

Damen's eyes blazed furiously. So furious, Devon stumbled back until she hit the wall. She covered her ears as he yowled.

"Venedictos!"

Fifteen

"All right now, this is gonna work."

With a great heave Alex hoisted the iron ball from the floor. He grunted as he strained to position it just over the chain. He nearly toppled over while trying to maintain a firm grip on the heavy ball.

Finally, when he could hold it no longer, the ball slipped from his sweating fingers and crashed down on the chain in a great crunch of iron and dust.

"Yes!"

The ancient links cracked under the pressure. He twisted and pried at the rusting metal until he released one link and was able to pull his leg free. The manacle remained firmly attached to his ankle, but at least he was free.

He stood and checked his sword belt. Remarkably, the sword was still there. What luck. "Guess these guys really are as stupid as I thought."

Devon shrank up against the wall, searching for a way out. She hadn't meant to anger her captor so much.

"You said she was an angel!" Damen's voice echoed inside the chamber.

The wizard fumbled with his length of white beard, as well as his words. "Wh-why would you think otherwise, Your Darkness?"

"Because angels do not come to this earth in human form!"

"R-really?"

"Yes!"

"H-how w-would you know?"

"She told me!"

Devon winced at Damen's accusing finger.

Venedictos stuttered. "I-I told you that angels lose their memory when they fall to the earth. How could she possibly—"

"Be done with your lies, wizard. She is no more an angel than I am. How could I have been such a fool? You've seen the way she acts and the things she says." The demon held up his hand to display the knife wound. "At times she is an unsavory and wild beast. She is mad! Deranged!"

"I resent that!" Devon jumped in, but slunk back when she received matched stares from the wizard and Damen.

"Tell me where you found her?" Damen commanded.

Venedictos fumbled with the frayed gold trim around his sleeves. Damen walked him up against the wall and finally the old man broke down. "Very well. The troll found her in the meadow. By the village."

"The village? I demanded an angel and you bring me common village rabble?"

"I am not rabble!"

Damen blasted her with a cold stare. "Silence!"

"You s-see my lord. I, well..." Damen met Venedictos nose to nose. From where she stood Devon could see beads of sweat form on the wizard's brow. "I'm just not that proficient when it c-comes to the h-heavens. I could not perform the spell. I am old, Your Darkness. And so very weak." In proof, Venedictos slumped, in hopes his master would go easy on him.

Damen spun sharply and paced away, his hands behind his back. His boots cracked across the rushes as he passed Devon. He groaned miserably. "I should have known better than to ask an aging old man to help me. Your duties to me are finished. Be gone with you, wasted wizard."

Venedictos bowed out of the room.

"At least he tried!" Devon pointed out.

Damen glanced up from his pouting. His lips curled into a questioning sneer.

"You are a cruel and vicious man, Damen the Dark. If that's what you are? It serves you right to be left alone in this castle with no friends at all. He was your friend. How can you treat him so?" Devon had no idea why she was sticking up for the cowardly wizard.

"He lied to me! I wanted an angel. I *need* an angel if I am ever to return to my dark throne. An innocent and pure creature that I can seduce and bring over to the dark side. And I get...you!"

"Innocence and purity comes in many forms," Devon found herself taking her own defense. She was just as pure as the next one. Well, more so in twenty-first century standards.

"Ah," Damen dismissed her with a wave of his hand. "I've had hundreds of village maidens. Unless they are pure it is not worth my time."

"And what makes you think I'm not pure?" Devon proudly thrust her shoulders back and stuck her jaw in the air.

"Hmm." Suddenly interested, Damen looked her over, his eyes falling from her breasts down to where her legs met her body in a sensuous curve. "You say so?"

"Yes!" Devon answered proudly.

"Well, then I certainly wouldn't want to waste a pleasure." Damen stepped to the door and called down the hallway. "Venedictos?"

"My lord?" The wizard had been standing just outside the door.

"Perhaps you could do me one last favor."

"Um, certainly, Your Darkness."

"Secure her!"

With an evil glee dancing in his eyes, the wizard headed for Devon. He wrangled her hands and pulled her across the room. Devon tripped as he pulled her up a stone dais and pushed her against the wall. This was not what she had expected. Maybe she had been too hasty in proclaiming her innocence. The wizard clamped one manacle around her wrist. Oh my, it was really going to happen! And it was all because she'd boasted so proudly of her innocence.

"I'm baaack!"

"Alex!" Relief showered over her body. Devon tried to move but the wizard had already manacled both her hands to the wall above her head.

Alex stood with shoulders squared and feet spread. His armor took on a sparkling brilliance in the rush light, and even his eyes glittered with great strength. He looked the hero. *Most definitely the hero.*

"I am the mighty warrior Lexor, and I've come for the maiden," he demanded in a strong voice that impressed even Devon.

"You can have her." Damen dismissed his gallantry with a wry jerk of his head toward where she hung from the wall.

"Really?" Alex's shoulders dropped. He seemed shocked that Damen had given in so easily. "Cool. Let's go then, Devon. Hey you, mister wizard, could you toss me a key? We've really gotta rush. I think there's only about an hour left before that damn forest grows up. And I don't want to have to deal with those thorns again."

Damen stepped onto the platform where Devon squirmed. She was quite sure by the look in his eye he was not giving her up so easily. "Certainly, you may have her, great warrior."

"Um, that's the *mighty* warrior Lexor, if you don't mind."

"Lexor?" Devon wondered.

"Yeah, pretty cool, huh? I'll explain later."

"All right, Lexor." Damen nodded to the wizard and he in turn seemed to take his silent orders as usual. "But first there is one thing I must have before you take her."

Alex eyed the villain coolly.

Damen's lips curled into a deliciously evil grin. "I'll have her maidenhead."

"Her what? Maidenhead?" Alex scratched his head with greasy fingers.

Devon couldn't believe Alex was actually holding this inane conversation with a man who was at this very moment loosening the ties around his waist. "Alex! He means my virginity, you clod!"

"Virginity? You?" Alex gripped his stomach and rolled out a hearty chuckle.

Damen tossed his hair over his shoulders and curiously eyed the laughing knight.

"What's so funny?" Devon yelled.

"You're not a virgin." Another roll of laughter echoed through the great hall. Then he sheepishly asked. "Are you?"

She stomped her foot. “I’ve never ever had sex with a man, Alex. You would be the first I would tell, and you know it.”

“So you’re really a virgin, huh?” Alex rubbed his beard-stubbled jaw and nodded. “I’ve always had great respect for you. More so now. I really love you, Devon.”

“Oh, Alex, I love you, too.”

“How precious. But please, spare me.” Damen hooked his foot beneath the hem of Devon’s dress and kicked it up into his hand. He pulled the black material high to reveal her thighs.

“Alex! Help me!”

“Hang on, Devon. I’ll save you!”

But the wizard blocked Alex’s path. Alex raised his sword, prepared to fight for the woman he loved. In a surprising display of magic, the wizard raised his hand and sent the sword flying from Alex’s hand.

Venedictos examined his hands. “It really worked.”

“No fair, man. No magic allowed. Hey! What the hell is that?” Alex pointed over the wizard’s shoulder and the old man took the bait.

Alex smashed his fist into the wizard’s jaw, knocking him to the floor.

Damen’s hands moved up Devon’s waist, pressing roughly over her breasts. He leered and breathed heavily. She turned her head away and caught the action below. Venedictos staggered backward and Alex had retrieved his sword. Damen’s slobbery kiss delved lower into her cleavage. A repulsive quiver shuddered through her body. How could this be happening when Alex was so close?

She tried to kick out but in one quick move, but Damen had her legs pinned to the wall with his own. He reached down and pulled open the ties at his waist.

“Whip it out, buddy.” Alex suddenly appeared near Devon’s shoulder. “But I promise” —he pressed the tip of his sword to Damen’s crotch— “you’ll lose it!”

Damen drew in a hissing breath as the sword cut through the black material of his hose. The two men held a clash of wills, Alex’s grip firm on his sword, Damen’s eyes gauging his opponent’s bluff.

The dark lord relinquished. “It seems you have the advantage, *mighty* warrior.”

“It seems I do.” Alex tightened his grip. “Now, unlock her.”

Damen hesitated. Alex pressed the sword deeper into the folds of Damen’s pants. With a reluctant nod of his head, he quickly produced the keys and freed Devon’s wrists.

The first thing she did was wrap her arms around Alex and hold tight. She wanted never to lose touch of her savior. His arms were strong and possessive. His relief apparent in the great sigh he pressed to her ear. “Oh, Alex, I’m so sorry. I’ll never step into a fairy circle again.”

“We can discuss that later. For now, we’ve got this demon to deal with.”

But Damen was no where in sight.

Sixteen

“Where is he?” Devon stepped from the platform.

“Guess the mighty Lexor scared him off?”

Devon turned and looked her friend up and down. He looked atrocious. But a cute sort of atrocious. “The mighty Lexor, eh? Looks like you’re ready to do a little disco dancing, if you ask me.”

Alex let out a disgusted sigh

“Alex!”

“What!” he spun around and caught her mouth over his lips.

Devon pressed her body tight to Alex’s. The hard steel scales dug into her ribs.”Mmm,” he groaned into her mouth. “What was that for?”

“I love you,” she whispered.

He gently broke contact. “Really? You mean it?”

She nodded. “Something wrong with that?”

“Not at all. I just—Well…” A healthy blush pinked his cheeks. “I mean, you always said before—”

“I’ve changed my mind.”

“Right. Well, I think we should discuss this later. Damen could be anywhere.”

“You’re right. And that damn Forest of Thorns is probably sprouting at this very moment. We’ve got to get out of here. Come on.”

He tossed his gauntlets to the floor by Venedictos’ body and pulled Devon out of the room. They ran down the main hall.

“Which way to the front door?” Alex wondered.

“Just around the corner.” Devon gestured onward.

They reached the door and Alex pulled up the great wooden beam that blocked their way and slid it to the floor.

“Leaving so soon?”

Both spun around at the sound of the deep voice. Devon stifled a scream.

Damen held a crossbow up near his face. A face that had changed. His entire body was of nothing the two of them had ever before seen. It was part beast, part human, all bound together in a tight sheath of muscled black flesh.

"You gotta stay out of the sun, dude," Alex tried a nervous joke. "The crispy look is out this year."

"He really is a demon," Devon whispered.

Damen placed a long black talon on the crossbow trigger. His hooves stepped silent and stealthily as he approached the two. "Won't you be staying a bit longer, lovely one? We've a debt to settle."

"Yeah, well um, we've got a date, you see," Alex said nervously. He pulled Devon close and shielded her with his body.

"Ah, the brave hero." Damen's chuckle was hollow and hoarse and coated with the shadows of foul demons dancing in flames. His claw-like talon preyed repeatedly over the trigger. "Too bad he left his sword in the upper chamber."

Alex patted his hip. "Oh, shit, I did."

Devon pushed Alex aside and stepped between him and the villain. "No, you can't do this! You can have me. Do what ever you want, but please, just let him go."

"Devon!"

"Shut up, Alex."

"Again with the disrespect." Alex crossed his arms over his chest and leaned against the door, now quite heedless of the crossbow aimed at him.

Devon turned on Alex. "Oh, and do you think he's going to let either of us live if I don't? All he wants is to spoink me, Alex, then he'll be satisfied."

"Spoink?" Alex and Damen both wondered simultaneously.

Devon flung her hands to her sides in a huff. She turned back to Damen. "Are you going to let him go, or what?"

Damen's sigh was a growling release of air. "It's a wonder I don't push you both out the door right now. My lady, you've tried my patience to great lengths. And you," he gestured dismissively to Alex. "What a hero you are, allowing your lady to offer her body in return for your safety."

"Oh yeah?" Alex slipped in front of Devon. His action caused Damen to pull the trigger. Alex let out a painful yelp and fell to the castle floor at Devon's feet.

"Alex!" She dove to his side and touched the arrow. It had lodged in his thigh. Alex's hands were too greasy with gunk to allow a firm grip on the arrow. "I'll be cool," he managed weakly. "Just...run."

"No, I'm not leaving you."

"Run!"

The demon's hooves crunched over the stone floor. Devon looked up into the dark lord's eyes. They glowed red, unreal and demonic.

"No," she whispered. Her protests were futile. Damen lifted her with ease and carried her away from the fallen hero. He dropped her in a corner and stood proudly over her.

"Mortal woman, do not make me crush your pretty little throat before I've had my fun."

"That's what you're going to have to do!" she yelled. "Because I'll never let you have me!" She sank to the floor and veed her arms before her in feeble defense. She could see Alex crawling along the floor. Damen's laughter caught her attention and she looked up to see the beast's burning red eyes.

"You gotta be nuts if you think I'm going to let you touch her," Alex yelled. "She's the greatest woman you'll ever come across in your lifetime, and there's not a man alive that deserves her love."

Damen sneered. "Including you."

"That may be," Alex hitched his forefinger over the trigger. "But at least I'll have the satisfaction in knowing I saved her from your slimy hide."

Damen stood tall, flexing his arms in great bulging black muscles. He growled viciously and lashed his talons through the air like a savage beast caged. "So eloquent you are, my hero. The mighty Lexor, was it?"

"You got it, man. Now, say bye-bye."

The demon began to laugh, a great, monstrous laughter that hurt Devon's ears. Damen raised his hands above his massive ebony horns and touched his talons together. A laser of red light beamed from them and struck the crossbow out of Alex's hands. He tried to grab for it but another beam struck him on the ankle. It burned right through the iron manacle.

Alex shook off the fried iron and scrambled backward on hands and feet. The demon followed, shooting lasers at every part of his body. One hit his knee. Alex let out a tormented scream and rolled to his side, clutching the burning flesh.

The two men paid little attention to Devon. She scrambled across the dried rushes and picked up the crossbow. It was still ready to shoot. She lifted it with a bit of difficulty and yelled, "Take this, you bastard!" The arrow struck the demon's heart and pinned him to the castle wall.

The demonic black beast fought and growled against the thin weapon, but it worked as a stake would to a vampire. Great hisses of steam rose from his chest and he began to disintegrate before them.

Alex jumped up, limped over to Devon, and turned her away from the sight. "Let's get out of here."

They stepped outside the castle. The sky was still gray and cold. The Forest of Thorns was tall and black and thick—

"It's grown back!" Alex approached the forest. "We were in there too long."

"Oh," Devon knelt next to Gwilym. The man was covered in caked blood, red and black. She pulled her fingers over his eyelids to close them. "Who is this?"

Alex knelt on his good knee behind her and wrapped his arms about her waist. "He was my guide," he whispered in her ear. "Gwilym of Goodwick. A very brave man."

She gingerly touched the burn on Alex's knee. "You are a very brave man, Alex. My hero."

"There's something Gwilym wanted me to give you."

Alex stood and pulled Devon up into his embrace. He spread his hands up through her mass of cool tresses and gently kissed her cool lips.

"That was from him?" she said incredulously.

"Yes. And this is from me."

Their lips seared together in passionate heat. She had to gasp for breath when Alex suddenly pulled away.

"How are we going to get back home?"

"I don't know," he said. "I lost the words from the book. They're back at the village with my clothes. The only way to get home is to go back to the village. And we can't get there now because of the damn forest. I'm sorry, Devon. I've failed you."

"Failed me? Alex, how can you say that?" She lifted his chin and smoothed away a smear of blood from his temple. "You're my hero," she gently reminded. "Remember the heroine who was sitting up in the castle tower?"

He shrugged. "Yeah?"

"That's me and you're him. You're my hero. You have been all along, except I was too stupid to notice. Anyway, it doesn't matter what happens now. As long as I'm with you..."

They kissed again. Above their heads fluttered a great fairy light.

"Oh no, not another one of those vampire fairies."

The light began to pulsate and glow and formed into a woman.

"You have killed the demon, mighty warrior," the fairy declared. "For that my sisters and I shall be eternally grateful. The villagers as well shall never again have to live in fear. In thanks, I can grant you one request."

Devon looked to Alex. He ruffed his hands down over his arms and gave a shrug. "Could you see to it that Gwilym is returned to the village?"

"Of course." The fairy fluttered to her original size and zoomed away.

"Oh great, " Devon said. "Why didn't you ask her to bring us home?"

"I'm sorry. I just, well, he deserves a proper burial. Without him I—"

A mass of fairy lights appeared in a cloud above them. They hovered over Gwilym's body and lighted on the ground around his figure. In a graceful motion, his body was supported by the fairies and lifted into the air.

Alex watched as Gwilym was ushered over the tops of the Forest of Thorns. "Cool."

"Can you do that for us?" Devon asked a single remaining fairy.

"Come to the meadow," she said in her tiny voice. "We shall dance a great and magical dance so you may return to your home."

"The meadow?" Alex wondered. "So you're gonna fly us there like you did for Gwilym?"

The fairy took to flight again, whooshing over their heads and to the castle top.

"I don't think she heard you," Devon muttered, her heart sinking to know they had been abandoned.

"Oh shit, it's another one!" Alex blocked Devon with his body as a stone gargoyle whooshed over their heads and slowly stepped over the rubble pile that was once its match.

Devon peered over Alex's shoulder at the great beast. "Don't look into its eyes," she whispered.

"I could really use that sword now."

They stood like statues, watching, as the beast sniffed about the rubble of its former mate. It looked up to them, and they quickly averted their eyes to its stone feet. The beast bowed elegantly, its wings spanning out behind it. A welcome of sorts...Devon knew.

"No, Devon, wait!"

"It's all right!"

She stepped over to the gargoyle and carefully reached for her head. The beast was strangely warm, though it was hard and firm as stone. It nudged its head up into her palm as she pulled her hand over its scalp and down its wide pug nose.

"She's going to help us, Alex. Come on."

Alex stepped carefully to her side, his armor chinking in dull clicks. "I don't know about this, Devon. I've already had one run-in with these things."

"Trust me."

He helped her to the gargoyle's back and, after much struggle with his armor, slid behind her. "Guess this is okay. Hmm..."

"What?"

"I wonder if the sun is setting on the meadow?"

"Why?"

"Well, it seems like we've come to the end of our little adventure. I just thought it would be cool for the hero and heroine to go riding off into the sunset."

"Oh, Alex, somehow I have a feeling it is."

"All right. Let's get this thing moving! Giddiup! Mush! Onward!" Alex gave a gentle kick to the beast's side and suddenly they were airborne. "Yes!"

As they soared over the massive tangle of black thorns, Alex hugged Devon to his chest and buried his nose in her sweet smelling hair. Far off on the horizon, the sun really was setting in a brilliant orb of hot orange and reds.

Devon tilted her head back until she felt her cheek touch Alex's. "What'd I tell ya?"

"So you did. Now," he whispered. "Now in these romances, at the end don't the hero and heroine get married and live happily ever after?"

"Sometimes. Depends on the romance."

"Is this something we could discuss? Maybe later?"

Devon reached back and spread her fingers up through her hero's hair, pulling him close to her. Her lips curled into a teasing smile. "Perhaps."

If you liked this book, consider one of our other titles!

Gates of Hell by Susan Sizemore

ISBN: 0-9671979-2-9

A plague is sweeping the galaxy. There is no cure, only a drug that offers immunity in return for a lifetime of addiction. A renegade pirate may have a better answer, but he is dying of a slow poison. A woman, a member of an elder race, could save him, but she has her own plans for finding the cure for the plague and she doesn't need a pirate's help!

"science fiction at its best." Four 1/2 Stars. **Romantic Times**

To Kill an Eidolon by Winifred Halsey

ISBN: 0-9671979-1-0

Susan has powers she doesn't know about; a being she can't see is stalking her and several of her professors want to kill her because they know what she doesn't: she could be the mother of a new plague. She could also be the best weapon mankind has ever had against disease.

"An intriguing medical thriller...a unique, very enjoyable tale." **Midwest Book Review**

Project Resurrection by Karen Duvall

ISBN: 0-9671979-5-3

In Alaska's frozen north, a group of scientists are reanimating cryo-preserved humans, not knowing they are stealing the souls of the living. LaNaya Seville, a descendent of a tribe of Inuit sorcerers, knows the danger of the spirit world, but even she isn't prepared for the catastrophe the project is wreaking, tearing apart the barrier between the living and the dead. It will take more than LaNaya's mystic skills to save mankind. In the world beyond the physical, she finds the one person she needs to help her: a man who is already dead.

"Mixes science fiction, horror and reincarnation romance in an intriguing New Age witch's brew of an adventure." **Catherine Montrose**

Tribute Trail by Terri Beckett and Chris Power

ISBN: 0-9671979-0-2

Kherin is the Goddess' Chosen. Rythian is a skilled hunter and scout, destined for greater glory. On the Tribute Trail, they meet--one a ruler, the other a slave. Together they forge a new destiny for both their people and find a love destined by the gods!

"more than enough twists and turns to keep even a jaded reader reading faster and faster." **Fantasy Reviews**

Blind Vision by Marguerite Krause

ISBN: 0-9671979-4-5

A seer can see every future but his own! Phillipe must win the Lady Zuli's trust to save the Duchy from the coming destruction, but the Duke's sister doesn't believe a word he says, and she has her own plans for saving her people.

"a shining new talent on the story-telling horizon." **Midwest Book Review**

Of Honor and Treason by C. J. Merle

ISBN: 0-9671979-3-7

Is it honorable to serve a brutal, half-insane Emperor? Is it treason to defect when the alternative is interstellar war? Two beings, one human, one not, one fabulously wealthy, the other a genetically-engineered warrior messiah, work together to stop a war before it begins. Space opera at its best!

"takes the best of Star Wars and Star Trek and blends them into an exciting space opera...going to be a best-seller." **Midwest Book Review**

Raven's Heart by Jennifer Dunne

ISBN: 0-9671979-6-1

In a future where Earth is torn apart by prejudice and religious strife, the Auric League fights for its survival against those who fear their genetic gifts. Val Tarrant is a ruthless Inter-Continental Police agent who has been betrayed by both sides. Raven Amistead is a devoted Auric League member, framed for murder. Reluctant allies, they become fugitives in a world where they must make their own laws.

"a classic tale of love beyone boundaries." **Romantic Times**

Visit our website at: www.speculationpress.com and read the first 25 pages of our books, author interviews and more!

Speculation Press books are available from our website, Barnes & Noble bookstores, Amazon.com, Borders.com, or ask your local bookstore to order our books from Ingrams or Baker & Taylor!